3 1312 00062 6905

W9-BUH-400

4-85

Date Due

CHICAGO GIRLS

a novel by
EDITH FREUND

POSEIDON PRESS
New York

Library of Congress Cataloging in Publication Data
Freund, Edith.
Chicago girls.

I. Title
PS3556.R447C5   1985   813'.54   84-17784
ISBN 0-671-50291-3

In appreciation
for the collection of the Chicago Historical Society,
the collection of the Historical Society at Madison,
Wisconsin, and Kenan Heise, Chicago writer and
historian, who read this work in manuscript form.

To Robert, who is generous and steadfast

INTRODUCTION

The band played, trumpets sounded, a quarter of a million people cheered, steam whistles blew, forty Indian braves danced into the midst of the throng and President Grover Cleveland, in the flesh, put his finger on the golden pulse of an electrical key which rested on a blue and crimson velvet cushion, which in turn rested on the folds of an American flag used to drape a table that rested on the vanguard of American progress. It was May 1, 1893, at 12:09 A.M.

By this act, the World's Columbian Exposition was opened. Water was released into the Frederick MacMonnies fountain, a thousand flags surged to the top of their masts to embrace a snappish wind, the band played another song because no speeches could be heard through the din in that unamplified time, and Daniel French's sixty-foot statue of the Republic, female, well-draped, stared back from the lakefront, gazing steadily westward, toward MacMonnies' earnestly rowing stone maidens who would never, in all the months of the fair, come any closer no matter how much water was allowed to them.

Within the grounds of the World's Columbian Exposition, a citadel had risen. There was the intramural railway, the moving sidewalk; soon there would be George Washington Ferris' marvelous magical wheel. It was like no other city in the world, and when the population grew to be overwhelming there was always the comforting thought that they would go elsewhere at night and the city could be reclaimed by its makers.

Out on the Midway, the jugglers and fakirs and pitchmen juggled and shouted and roared. Was "Little Egypt" there? Of course, she was. No matter what hour of the day or night, no matter what day of the week or month of the year a customer might enter the Egyptian show, Little Egypt was always there; tall or short or fat or thin, she was the girl of the hour, doing her belly dance, the *danse du ventre*. Dressed more modestly than a grandmother on today's beach, she gyrated and spun and teased and brought forth such salacious fantasy that there were those who swore they saw her naked and that every muscle moved. Little Egypt's reputation amortized the $10 million loaned by the proper Chicago businessmen who began the fair and both they and twenty-two-year-old Sol Bloom, the fair's concession manager, knew it.

There was everything anyone might have wished for in a world tour: Beaux Arts buildings reinterpreted as large as any American would want them, replicas of Columbus' caravels, a wooded isle where Frank Lloyd Wright saw his first Japanese hoo-den—which later evolved within his fertile mind into the prairie style; there were Austrian and Irish and German villages, oriental tea ceremonies, Africans, laces, gondolas, ducks, royalty, knickknacks to take home— some with Mrs. Potter Palmer's picture on them—steamboats, thousands of fish in a fisheries building on the reasonable assumption that Columbus would have liked that, a hundred thousand earnest endeavors, Krupp cannon, fireworks, Seltzer water, band music, restaurants, washrooms, free drinking water, places to sit and dream, rolling wicker chairs, strange animals, great noise, quiet serenity, *vistas*—

Like world travelers, fair visitors went home confused, enchanted, newly religious, never to sort out in their minds what it was all about; perhaps they were meant only to gain a sense that something had happened—that everything they had seen was to be remembered as larger than it was, that the future was coming at last, coming faster than before, that it would be as wildly divergent as the country's past, that it would hold surprises, that the surprises could be trusted, that the future would be all right.

In those moments of the fair, wrapped as it was in the overwhelming sentimentality of its time, the swamps of Jackson Park had become the White City, an electric city, conceived in a dream, built in what appeared to be the wink of an eye, to live for a day and then disappear, a true summer folly by the lake.

GERTRUDE

CHAPTER I

1

Gertrude Jahn was born in Chicago's Maxwell Street area in 1877. Her father was a German Catholic and her mother a beautiful orphaned Jewess from Vienna. How they had come so far together, how they had met in the first place, how they had arranged to marry across the obstacles of their religious prejudices, they never shared with their children. They loved each other passionately and produced a child nearly every year to prove their love. Gertrude was the fifth, the third girl, of their eleven children.

Gertrude went at first to the Catholic school where the nuns spoke German and she did well there, learning to read quickly, although she did not like reading much. She continued at that school until she was about eight. One afternoon a Sister kept her after school and made her kneel down beside the teacher's big desk to pray, pray for her heathen mother who was one of the tribe that had crucified Jesus. The nun's voice ranged higher and higher and she leaned over Gertrude in her black habit, waving her sleeves like wings. Gertrude became hysterical and ran home crying, leaving behind her dinner pail. When her mother scolded her about the loss of the pail, she began to cry again and confessed her sin of running away from the nun and from the prayers that somehow made her mother seem to be so wrong. Her mother listened to the story and a strange look came over her face.

13

When Gertrude's father came home, her mother told him the story and from then on Gertrude and all her brothers and sisters were sent to the big public school. There she was lost in many ways, but the teachers also spoke German for part of the day and Gertrude was again able to excel in her schoolwork, not because she was meant for learning, but because she was determined that there be no more trouble in her name. She learned to sense what others wanted and to try to please.

For several years her father had worked where he could, by the day or the week, but finally he found steady work at the McCormick manufactory near Black Road. Gertrude was too young to understand what steady work meant to the family, but she knew every penny must be guarded, every advance kept within the family, lest "the Evil Eye," a mysterious power that prowled the streets among the poor, steal the bread from their mouths. The Evil Eye found them anyway.

All Gertrude knew about her father's work was that he was one of the "molders and joiners" at McCormick's. He went away every morning with a dinner pail and didn't come back until suppertime. Her father didn't talk much. Sometimes at night he sat in the lamp-light and carved small boxes out of ashwood. The boxes were made so that the lids, a separate piece of wood, slid in and out in grooves along the sides. The boxes were perfect for hiding things away, but Gertrude had nothing to put in one. Her father sold them for pennies to merchants in Maxwell Street.

One Saturday night when Gertrude was about nine, her father came home looking like death. There was trouble at the plant. Wages of joiners had been cut without warning. At this time the family lived in three rooms. There were nine of them, and three rooms for only nine people of the same family was considered luxurious by Maxwell Street standards. Other people—greenhorns—lived sometimes with as many as twelve or fifteen in one room, only a few of them related to one another.

Gertrude and her brothers and sisters knew things were bad at home. Some of their friends' fathers worked for McCormick's, too. Too many greenhorns were coming in, everyone said, coming from every country in the world, crowding into the gates of the plants, even willing to pay a few coins under the table to foremen who would get them on a payroll and keep them there. Conditions like that drove down wages, let the owners do as they wanted with the poor and helpless who'd been working for them for years. What kind of trick was that for the owners to use to repay loyalty and hard work?

Gertrude's father, Otto Jahn, joined a union, and with the union, there came a lock-out. There was no money anywhere. And there were no jobs at all. The owners were angry, her father said. He said they would not allow the union and had hired spies and bullies to break the hold the union had on the workers. The union said each man should work less—eight hours only—and that way more men could be hired. But when the plant reopened there were spying workers—scabs, "dirtyscabs," her father would say in one word—hired among the regular workers. Otto went out to union meetings at night, secretly, and came home in the morning exhausted and dirty and smelling like beer.

During the day he sat in his underwear and trousers at the kitchen table. There was no use going to look for work, he said, because every place he went, they asked where he had been working last. If he said McCormick's, they said he would bring the unions and they wouldn't take him on. There was no money put by, her mother said. Her mother tried not to cry when Otto was at home. She'd not told her husband she was pregnant again. She feared he would run away like Mrs. Schultz's husband, who'd left in the night, abandoning his family. Mrs. Schultz had gone mad and run down the street in her nightclothes, her hair flying out behind her, her nails tearing at the flesh of her face. The older Schultz children had been taking care of their mad mother and feeding the babies every since. Gertrude watched her mother weeping every day over the stove, the table, the laundry and the cooking. Gertrude hated the look of her mother weeping silently into the bread dough.

During the weeks of the plant closing, messengers came and sat with Otto when he was at home, telling him this and that about the plant. There had been confirmed news: Scabs were actually going to do the work of union men. The dirtyscabs were spies and would try to wreck the union. The men pounded the table and her father, who had never had much to say before, now shouted and pounded the table with them. The visitors and her father seemed to be shouting the same words, but they acted as if they were fighting with one another.

All of them swore they would never work for McCormick's again.

But when the plant reopened, with concessions to the workers, every man who could do so crowded inside the plant gates and went to work. There were hundreds of men left standing outside, her father said. Some of those men were "agitators." But some of them, Otto told his family, were Pinkerton men in disguise. Gertrude liked the sound of it. There was mystery and trouble in these words, and there was power in the terrible game—owners-against-the-workers, unions-against-the-owners—in the *Zeitung*, which her father read, and in the *Verein*. Her father, who'd once been so quiet, talked all the time now. He never stopped going on about "the struggle," and the eight-hour day. He reported all sides. The family was pulled one way or another by what the various factions were reported to have said. Wasn't that power? Young as she was, Gertrude could feel the energy of it moving through their lives, could sense the fear in her mother, and she wondered if the baby inside her mother also could sense that fear and know that it would not be welcome in this family.

Her father paced and swore and the nights seemed darker than Gertrude ever remembered.

The reduction in wages meant they had to move to two rooms and she and her mother spent days finding someplace that wasn't too bad. Tessa took her up and down back stairways, through littered streets past wood-frame houses, past shops and small workrooms. Finally, they found something, but it was even older than the rooms they'd had before and there were words written on the walls. They had no money for paint. They were lucky to be able to buy food. Her mother said she would cover them with dresses hung from nails. In the new place, the two parents sat often in the kitchen looking like woe.

What happened next was terrifying.

Papa came home again in the middle of the day, cut and bleeding on his mouth. New workers had tried—had been allowed—to crowd in in front of the old workers one morning when the opening bell rang. There'd been fighting at the gates of the works. Pinkerton men had come through with clubs and some other men had tried to go downriver by boat to board the relocked plant through its loading dock. Her father said the troublemakers were foreigners. They wanted to force the eight-hour day so more men could work there. But the workers had fought both one another and the Pinkertons and then, when police came through with horses and billy clubs, everyone who could still walk had run off. Shots had been fired. Men were dead.

The next day one of the union workers came to Otto with a copy of a circular that read in German:

REVENGE!...
Workingmen to Arms!!!

Your masters sent out their bloodhounds—the police; they killed six of your brothers at McCormick's this afternoon. They killed the poor wretches, because they, like you, had the courage to disobey the supreme will of your bosses. They killed them, because they dared ask for the shortening of the hours of toil. They killed them to show you "Free American Citizens" that you must be satisfied and contented with whatever your bosses condescend to allow you, or you will get killed!

If you are men...then you will rise in your might, Hercules, and destroy the hideous monster that seeks to destroy you. To arms we call you, to arms!

Your Brothers

Otto pounded the table. *"Dummheit!"* The messenger pleaded with him to come out with him into the streets. But Otto wouldn't budge.

"They are using us," Otto said. "Everyone. The unions and the bosses both. I'll lie about where I worked before. I'll go no more to the *Verein*. I'll find some kind of work where there is not so much *sturm und drang*. I have this great family to feed and soon another one—"

He gestured at the room around him and then sat with his hands covering his eyes. He told the union man to go away. The unions were trouble for a man, he said. Whoever was right, Otto told the man, he didn't know, but he had to feed his family and he could not take such chances.

The next day there was more trouble, more bloodshed. The other men who still stayed with the union committees went into hiding. Gertrude didn't understand it all, but there was some sort of riot, north of them, near Halsted in the old Haymarket. The unions and the anarchists were broken up. Some said for good. The foreigners who couldn't speak any English were to blame. Everyone said so. Her father came in from the street, breathing very hard and fast. He gathered up everything in the house written in German. Then he took down the Great Bible, the one from his family long ago, the one with everyone's names in German script at the back. He sat at the table reading from it while he burned the other papers in the stove. Last of all, he stood, and with a terrible moan, he threw it in the fire.

Tessa cried out and tried to clutch his arm, but he pushed her away. "It's bad luck," she screamed at him. "You are burning Torah—"

"What luck has it brought us, woman, that we should be lost because of it? What has it done for you and me? And they are going to search the houses. You'll see. Just like everywhere—"

But nobody ever came. Yet from that time on, everyone in Gertrude's family always spoke English.

Her father went to the stockyards, to a man he knew there. He promised the man money each week, if he could just get a paying job that wouldn't have trouble connected with it. He was put on right away and from then on Gertrude could always tell when her father was home. His clothes smelled sour like old blood and grease and no amount of boiling could ever remove the smell. The times remained hard and her father never again regained the confidence he'd had before the strike.

2

About the time of Gertrude's twelfth birthday, her friends began going to activities in the old Hull mansion on Halsted Street, where two wealthy young women had begun holding open house for the neighborhood. Gertrude's father forbid her to go there. He said the women were like the nun at school and also that they had taken the wages of workers from their husbands and fathers, who were owners and operators of businesses and manufactories for which men like Mr. Jahn worked.

"They take bread from our mouths and then give it back to us in bits and pieces for which we must bow and toady and be grateful," Otto ranted. "And then they want to steal our daughters and our sons."

He said the women at Hull House would ask her to renounce her mother and father and become Protestant. He said her sisters had never wanted to go to such a place as that. But Gertrude's friends told her the women at Hull House were all right. And there was a girls' club there that a girl could join for a penny. She could learn to sew on a machine and to do certain dances that the schools didn't teach. Her father still said no. Her mother said she could go, but they couldn't afford the penny. Gertrude had her own mind, and she went anyway. No one asked her for the penny.

The women at Hull House were not at all like the nun. They treated the girls who came, including Gertrude, with love and acceptance, offered as if these girls had never had love and acceptance before. They said the poor and the rich depended on each other and they should know each other and be tolerant and respectful of each other.

When Gertrude told her father what the women had said, he told her that there must be more to it, that someday something would show the true colors of the rich women who lived in the house and then the poor would be the ones who would pay.

"You lie down with dogs, you get up with fleas," Otto shouted and then said to Tessa, "tell your daughter not to go there. Haven't I any say in this house—just because I am a poor man, my daughter doesn't listen to me?"

Gertrude hadn't told her father everything about her excursions a few blocks north to Hull House. Several of the women were nice, but there were others who made her feel—well, strange. Strange and foreign. She and her friends were first-generation Americans of foreign parents. She could speak German and Yiddish and Polish and some Russian and she was only twelve years old. Her friend, Estrella, spoke Italian and even knew some Latin. But all used English almost exclusively in day-to-day speech, so they could all understand one another. They were not greenhorns.

"I'm no greenhorn," Gertrude had complained to Estrella after her first day at Hull House. "I don't like the way they talk baby talk to me, as if I'm too dumb to understand. I'm never going back there—"

But Estrella said the days of the dances were better. On those days, someone would play the piano. "Think of it, a real piano," Estrella said and in this way coaxed Gertrude back to Hull House.

Estrella also wanted to learn to use the sewing machine. She'd never seen one or used one, but she'd heard this was a good job to have and there were lofts opening up where girls as young as thirteen could make good wages if they could run machines.

"You don't even have to be very skilled at it. You just have to know a little so they don't have to train you about everything," Estrella said.

Gertie didn't want to work on a machine. She wanted to be a teacher or an office girl and in this she was encouraged by her teachers and her mother. But Gertrude also loved music and dancing. Her mother knew the polka and some other country dances and Gertie and her sisters had danced at night in their crowded kitchen, learning the steps from one another. But there was hardly room there for them to sit, let alone dance.

They lived now in the two rooms. The kitchen was roughly divided in half each night and all children, regardless of age, slept there divided by sexes, the room itself separated by a blanket curtain. The youngest child, now almost two, slept in their parents' bedroom with an old quilt for a bed. While the rooms were dark and always smelled of smoke and of cooking, they were clean and on almost any day Tessa had some washing boiling away on the back of the stove. She would hang out the wash from the bit of back porch that overlooked the dirt alleyway. When she took the clothes in at night, they were flecked with soot and almost as soiled as before she'd washed them.

So there was no place at home for Gertie to dance. She went back to Hull House. She wanted to hear a piano close up.

At Hull House, Gertie learned her father could be wrong about the world. Her father thought the women there were Protestants, but one of them, Miss Ellen Starr, was more Catholic than he. He thought the women would coax them to stay away from their families and their home, but instead Gertie and the other guests were encouraged in their home lives.

But on Girls' Club Day, Gertrude noticed other women who came to Hull House to help Miss Starr and Miss Jane Addams. These other women *were* the women her father had warned her about, the daughters and wives of *owners* who lived on the wages her father said belonged to the poor. While at the Girls' Club, Gertie and her friends learned to design and sew their own clothing. But they also learned things from the high-toned women that were not part of the regular lesson.

Gertrude looked at the women who came visiting from the world of the rich and saw they did not wear so many ruffles and flounces. She noticed the way they wore their gloves and the plainness of their collars and cuffs against their dark dresses. Gertrude heard the muted tones of their accents and the way they spoke softly to each other and the differences when they spoke to the girls. Truly her father's daughter, she noticed that sometimes the women spoke to one another as if they thought the girls would not understand the English. Gertie thought it strange that they would speak privately to one another, as if in secret code, as if their pupils were stupid, when the women were supposed to be helping Miss Starr.

In watching such visitors, who had come to spend time in the slums because it was a new style among the idle rich—which Gertrude couldn't know—she learned how to stand very straight in her newfound height and how to turn her dark, wild hair into a neat row of curls pinned to the top of her head. She looked even taller than she was, but looked also much, much older than thirteen.

"And who is this?" the women would say, grasping her by the chin, turning her head to look at her face. "Such lovely amber eyes—"and they would walk away smiling, having said a nice thing to the poor girl from Maxwell Street.

Gertrude's older sisters, Agnes and Lillian, had beaus and they said they would not go to Hull House. They teased her when she pinned up her hair.

"Do look at her, giving herself airs," Agnes said.

Lillian stood up in imitation of Gertrude. She made a small mouth and walked funny. "That's how she'll look when she's an old maid," Lilly said. "Just like the old maids at Hull House."

In less than a year both Agnes and Lilly were married. Otto had forbidden it, but they each had a sturdy young man who was employed in the shipyards and they went on with the marriages anyway. Lilly stayed close by in the neighborhood, but Agnes moved up to the north, nearer to Greektown. Otto refused to have them come to the house, but Tessa wheedled and coaxed and soon enough the girls and their new husbands were allowed to come visiting again. Gertrude would come home from school and one or another of her sisters would be there, sitting with her mother. The family had moved again, this time to three rooms. Tessa had found a place to take piecework—fine embroidery and handwork for bridal trousseaus. She and Agnes or Lilly would sit at the kitchen table in poor light and pick away at some bit of white cloth, endlessly talking. Soon enough, Agnes announced she was expecting. Gertrude almost got sick thinking about it. Children, children, everywhere.

3

In spring, 1890, after graduation from the grammar school, Gertrude made plans to go on to the high school. Tessa had talked of this over and over during the past few years, as if it were a settled thing. Gertrude had come to expect it. She would be the first child of the family to go on to higher learning. She could be a teacher.

But now Otto declared, "I need your wages. The younger boys need things for their schooling. Everything costs more today. I don't know where the money goes. If you go to work, your little brothers can go on and make something of themselves. It's better so—look at Agnes. Schooling is wasted on women—"

Tessa tried to smooth it over and coax him into letting Gertrude enter school, just a year. She'd get much better work if they could only allow that.

"No, no, she learned how to work one of them machines. She can go to the shirt factory and give her wages to you," Otto said, trying to bribe Tessa.

Gertie thought her father was taking advantage of her. She could see why Agnes and Lilly had both been so anxious to leave home. And her father—like as not he would come home every night from the tavern in sad condition because her new earnings would make this even more possible.

Her older brothers, Emil and Frank, were never in sight. They came home near dawn on weekends, if at all. Only she was going to be asked to sacrifice, because she was the one they could depend on.

Gertie thought it very unfair, and ignoring her father's instructions, she bypassed the shirt factory, where the dust of the cloth hung in the air and the noise of the machines ate into one's mind. She found a job with two friends at a nearby cigar factory. The smell of cigars was foreign and exciting; it smelled like men and business and importance and the pay was good if Gertrude worked quickly. She soon learned how to roll a cigar with just the right degree of tightness and was the quickest of the women. She was never sick and went to work every day for two years, dressed, her fellow workers often said, like a duchess. Once there, she put on gloves and a smock to keep stains from her clothing, and even with the impediment of gloves, could work the fastest.

Each week she saved most of her earnings, except the amount she gave to her mother and the small amount she allowed herself for clothes. Each day seemed just like the one before and the earnings, once she'd reached her maximum speed, did not increase. This routine went on and on, until Gertrude had begun on her third year.

One morning in spring Gertie caught her mother retching and knew at once that her mother was pregnant again. Love, thought Gertrude, does not conquer everything. She thought her mother— and her father, whom she blamed the most—foolish to burden the family with more children, more mouths to feed, and no end to it. No matter how many daughters married out or went to work, there would never be enough money for the boys and the household. Gertrude didn't see why she should have to pay all the time for these new children her mother and father seemed determined to bring into the world. Gertrude knew about sex. She'd seen enough of its results and the streets were full of ribald stories that even young children could repeat and partially understand. No one who lived in a family of eight or ten in a three-room flat needed to be told about sex or giving birth. They lived close to it every minute.

She resolved then and there that morning to put some distance between herself and her mother's folly. Otherwise, she, Gertrude, was going to have to pay for it.

CHAPTER II

1

She tucked her savings, over $150, into her drawstring bag and went off to work as usual. She really didn't know what she was going to do, but she was going to do it that day. She loved her mother, but she didn't see how she could help her much by sacrificing a second life to a bad lot.

That morning at work, Gertrude rolled her usual number of cigars, thinking all the time. The work loft was divided into two parts, one for men and one for women. Between them, on a raised platform, sat the foreman and a reader who was paid by the workers themselves to read aloud newspapers and other journals during the workday. Nobody noticed when Gertrude said nothing during the entire morning. She rarely talked much and besides, everyone wanted to hear the reader.

For the past three years Gertrude had been listening to stories about the World's Columbian Exposition, among other things. Gertrude didn't believe the World's Columbian Exposition would ever happen. There was too much fighting about it.

First, the world had fought about whether to have it, then they fought about what country to have it in and then they fought about which city would get it, with many cities calling Chicago names—"the Windy City," they said. Then there'd been a fight about where to put the fair in Chicago. Gertie had never seen Jackson Park—

23

she'd only been east of the Chicago River once—but she'd heard there would be fantastic things to see there if they ever got it done: elephants and ships and monkeys and kings. She supposed she could walk eight miles and back again to see a king and a monkey all on the same day.

Today's articles said the southern senators were filibustering in the Congress to prevent Sunday openings for the Exposition. The southerners said it was ungodly. The Chicago men who put up the money for the fair—millions and millions of dollars—said it would be good business.

Gertrude thought all this fighting was terrible. If the fair wasn't to open on Sunday, nobody she knew or had ever known would be able to go to it.

I'd like to see something, she thought. Something marvelous.

Her hands went on at their usual rhythm. There seemed never to be anything new or different in her life. Just her mother's new pregnancies, one after the other, and the same old hard times at home. The closest she got to the world was through the voice of the reader and sometimes the things of the world did not sound so pleasing: crime, accidents, people who wandered away and were never found again. The world could be dangerous.

The pile of rolled cigars in her tray grew higher. There was danger here, too. The cigars were a definite measure of it. She could be caught here forever, doing what others told her to do, not deciding for herself. Unfortunately, she could think of nothing for herself beyond the act of leaving. She finally decided she'd just have to do it to discover what came next.

Off in one corner of the loft was a small office and there the owner of the cigar factory sat, writing in ledgers, smoking a cigar, eating greasy sandwiches from a dinner pail, meeting with buyers. On this particular day, at the noon hour, Gertrude took off her smock and her stained gloves.

"Going shopping, Gertie?" someone asked.

She nodded and shrugged and went off toward the owner's office. She told him she was quitting and would like her wages to date.

The owner was a nice man. He knew her father. He looked at Gertrude and said, "Getting married? I ain't heard nothing."

"No," said Gertrude.

"What then?"

Gertrude looked at him. She probably owed him an explanation but she couldn't think of one. She still didn't know what she was going to do next. She shook her head and smiled, as if confused by his question.

"You're my best girl worker, you know that? I kin use you any time." He eyed her suspiciously. "You in trouble? Some feller here bothering you? Got you in the family way?"

"No," snapped Gertie. She tightened the drawstring on her purse unnecessarily. "I just want my wages and I want to leave now."

"You could work till the end of the day—" he grumbled turning out the drawers on one side of the desk. He pushed two back in and reached into the third, extracting the work chits that showed how many cigars she'd done each day. He counted out her money, handed it to her, staring at her, trying to get some response for his effort.

"And to think I know your pa and you up and leave me like this. A nice girl like you, you should know better—" Then he appeared to have another thought. "Nothing happened to your pa has it?"

She shook her head. The owner was kind, but she wasn't going to tell him anything. She didn't know anything except that she couldn't spend another winter with diapers drying on the stove. She turned, found her way to the stairwell and went down to the street.

She felt free and yet oppressed. What to do next?

She straightened and began to walk along briskly as she'd seen the rich women at Hull House walk along the street, looking neither right nor left, her head held high, not pausing to look in shop windows. She walked like this for a long time, toward the main business part of the city. She had never traveled this way. Walking might help her think and in spite of the fact that she'd been born in Chicago, she'd rarely gone far from her accustomed routes of home to school or work. Now she was well past fifteen and dressed as a young lady should be dressed. She looked adult. She could go anywhere along the city streets with no one by her side and she began to feel the excitement. There were horsecars and cabs moving up and down. Private carriages whisked by and men and women of every sort moved by her in what appeared to be well-planned rivers of humanity, each half of the river taking, as if by common agreement or law, one-half the sidewalk.

Gertrude came to a large hotel and on the corner there was a coffee shop. She'd never been inside a restaurant and she didn't know what to do, but her wages were in her purse and she'd not had her dinner. The air was damp and heavy and she could smell coffee. The thought of it made her blush with hunger. She turned into the shop. If she was going to eat in a restaurant, it might as well be this one, paneled in wood on its walls, intricate gas lamps above small tables along the sides, the floor white and black tile in large squares. She'd never seen anything like this.

A man came toward her. She knew he was some sort of waiter and would seat her. She had learned that at Hull House. But he leaned forward around two men and looked directly at Gertrude. She involuntarily looked behind her, but it was she who had attracted his attention. He disappeared with his male charges and then returned and stepped around another party of men and spoke confidentially to Gertrude.

"We don't seat unescorted women here," he said.

She stepped back from his confidence. Beyond him she could see some women in the restaurant, but they were, she noticed, each with a man. She reached up with a gloved hand to touch her hat nervously. "I'm—I—sorry. I was just hoping to have coffee."

He looked her up and down. For some reason she felt herself bristling. She stretched tall under his gaze, pulling again at the drawstring of her purse.

"Are you staying at the hotel?" he asked.

"Yes," she lied.

He looked back over his shoulder, ignoring the party of men who had become interested in the conversation.

"Well, you look refined." He picked up a large menu, almost as large as the table ahead. "Come this way. We'll serve you just this once—"

Gertrude felt her cheeks flush and she moved forward with as much dignity as she could manage. He held out her chair and as she moved to sit in it, she said curtly, "Thank you."

A duchess could have done no better.

The coffee, priced at a nickel, was delicious. With it she had a schnecke, another nickel. At this rate her money wouldn't last long. She knew she would have to leave something on the table for the waiter. A feeling of panic arose, conditioned by the years and years of money-struggle in her parents' marriage. Money. Always money. Anything you wanted to do could be cut off in a mment by the need for money. But she fought down her panic by looking around her at the restaurant and its patrons. She had some money in her purse today and she was going to do this nice thing for herself.

She'd been seated off to one side at a table in a corner. A large exotic plant screened her from the street entrance of the restaurant. At the far end of the room she could see another open doorway, evidently leading into the lobby of the hotel. Lights were turned on the entire length of the room, even though it was daylight. The paneled walls gleamed in the artificial light. The hard clatter of dishes and tableware was muffled against fine table linens. The waiters wore white coats.

Gertrude Jahn felt like a woman of the world.

Along one side of the room were windows, heavily curtained in dull green velvet, held back by brass catches into a thick swath. At each of the tables along the window were male diners. The women with escorts were seated along the inside wall or in quiet corners away from traffic in the aisles. There were only about six women in the entire room, including Gertrude, but there were many, many men. Gertrude's protective waiter had gone off somewhere and she was free to munch at the sweet roll and sip her coffee. At the next table, near a window, was a young man, facing her but reading a morning paper. As she glanced at him, he looked up and smiled. She lowered her eyes.

From then on she found she must keep her head lowered or she would be looking directly into his blue gaze. Whenever her glance stole upward, he was waiting, and bowed with a small nod of his head and a smile. Gertrude was furious. She had every right to her privacy. If he should cause any disturbance, the waiter would—

Humph, she told herself. Why do you care what that waiter thinks? Have you ever seen anything like this man with his vest and his chain and his mustaches? Her father never looked so fine. She knew her father had never eaten a meal in this restaurant. She stared at her plate and fingered her napkin. Where could she go to get away from this? She began to search through her purse, as if looking for something, her gloves, her money—

A hand reached for her check. A nice hand, well-manicured, a small gold ring on the last finger.

"Allow me," a man's voice said. The young man was standing beside her. Gertrude looked everywhere but at the man. Where was the waiter? He was not in sight. Another man was standing behind the elaborate cash register and still another waiter was seating customers. In her mind something turned with a decided snap.

Ah, well, her mind said, why not?

She rose quickly, bowed slightly and murmured, "Thank you so much."

As they left the restaurant, the man tipped his hat, pulled on his gloves and offered his arm to Gertrude.

"I don't want to be a bore, but I am walking east—"

"Why—so am I," said Gertrude, with some surprise in her voice. She had at last discovered her direction.

"My name," the young man said, "is Myron Davis. I'm here to do some work on the great fair that's going to take place next year. I'll be in town for several weeks."

Gertrude inhaled sharply. "My name is—" she hesitated. "My name is Trudy Jones," she said. "Miss Trudy Jones."

CHAPTER III

Gertrude thought the young man looked *marvelous.*

His profile was handsome. He didn't appear to be thinking of anything except the fine weather and clearing the way for her along the street. She knew, instinctively, that her mother would not like him and so she gave her name as Trudy Jones. Her mother need never know. This adventure would be perfectly safe because she, Gertrude, was not at risk. After all, there were many other people present, if but for the moment of their passing. Was it that implied safety which made Trudy so happy in his attentions?

Or did she step forward without thought, through the most important streets of the city, carefree in her newly created life, daring herself to go on—to say, *Why not?*

She didn't realize that by taking his arm she was committing an act so irretrievable, she might never restore her reputation in his eyes. Ninety years later, women would engage in casual sex outside wedlock with less stigma.

He took no risk. His position in society was not lost. But he knew immediately, when she accepted his arm, that she was not what she seemed; she had shown herself to be either simple-minded or a whore. No respectable young woman of the city or its surrounds would have taken the arm of a young man to whom she'd not been formally introduced. That she accepted his arm on a city street in the businesslike atmosphere of a weekday morning made no difference. In fact, if anything, it made matters worse. She had declared herself.

And who was he? What did he expect as he walked eastward into the morning sun on a busy Chicago street with a young woman, a stranger who knew no better than to smile up at him and take his arm? Only the smile in his eyes as he looked down at the girl gave clue to that. It was early in the morning for assignations. His clothes were natty, but of the best construction. His air was confident, his accent, in the few words he had spoken, eastern and upper crust. He looked much too well-put-together to be an advance man for a white slave ring. Still, strange things happened in Chicago to young innocent girls like Gertrude Jahn.

2

They were on Washington Street amid the bustle of the major business district. The streets around them lay in shadow because the tall, massive buildings allowed no light except a narrow shaft from the east. This light caught her in the eye, annoying her, making her tip her head. She couldn't know he thought the light brought out the hidden glory of her hair, that it emphasized the trust and sparkle of her glance. He was frankly looking her over. Her clothes were plain and in good taste. She walked well. Her shoes, however, were of poor quality leather and worn, her gloves, though clean, were slightly frayed. On such items could one's life be judged.

They came to Garland Place.

"Come," he said, "let's walk in the park." In this way, he presented her with another subtle challenge. Would she take it? Or would she now plead a previous engagement, the greatest adventure of her life thrust aside, the episode lost—mysterious to both, but lost?

But she, the newly created Trudy Jones, with no mother to warn her, knew no better than to say, "I think that would be fine." After all, she'd often heard her mother tell stories of princes who scooped up serving maids and took them away to live in castles. How could that happen, unless the serving maid was open to chance?

As they moved into the park, he spotted a bench and guided her to it, as if by mutual agreement.

The park they had entered was, at that time, the last vestige of the Fort Dearborn preserve. The little park was at Washington and Michigan and was dedicated, sometime around the time of the Great Fire, to public use in honor of the Grand Army of the Republic. Soon after the day on which Trudy Jones and Myron Davis sat there it would become the site of a library building; on that April morning it looked neglected.

Trudy had never seen such a fine park.

They settled on the bench, facing each other. Trudy Jones put her gloved hands in her lap, folded with the drawstring of her purse around them so that no passerby could snatch her money and run away. After all, that was a kind of wrongdoing she knew about and her life savings were in that purse. Having met that minor danger, she sat up straight and let the greater danger chat with her about the city in which she had been born.

"Are you familiar with this park?" he asked. "But, of course, you must be, since you've lived here for some time—"

"No. I've never been here before. In this park, I mean." There was a pause, as if she were uncertain what to say next.

Her answer was not enough to satisfy Myron Davis. He planned to give her a small quiz, to see if she was intelligent and careless, or if she just might be someone's idiot female relative who had wandered away from home unattended. If the latter, then he must prove himself to be the gentleman he appeared.

He tried again. "Have you lived in Chicago long?"

"All my life," she answered.

"Dearborn Park is an interesting place—" He was seated so that he faced a small plaque and he cleared his throat to begin to read the plaque to her as if it were his own personal knowledge. He didn't notice she'd been distracted by the scene around her. She had caught a glimpse, over his shoulder, of the lake itself, which she had never before seen because she was too poor and too provincial and too young to have done so and today it sparkled in the sunlight with an emphatic twinkling blue, so like this gentleman's eyes.

Close at hand was the busy thoroughfare with industrious pedestrians marching by. Along the length of the avenue there were fine carriages, better it seemed than those on any other street. Between the pedestrians and the avenue and the lake in the far distance ran a train—no, several trains—unaware of the seeming threat of that great large stretch of water at its side. All these powerful things came together in that one moment, startling Trudy Jones into a cry of "Oh—"

Altogether the distraction of it was in the young man's favor. She thought he was lord of it all.

In that moment, Trudy thought the fairy tales had definitely come true. Just by taking a chance, she'd come to a magic land where the men were handsome princes who lived on the shore of a beautiful sea. Never one to talk much, after her first exclamation she lapsed into silence.

Myron, encouraged by her obvious awe, continued, "The park is dedicated to Civil War—"

There was sudden reaction. Tension cut through her. She stiffened and turned away from him. Myron looked around, but all he could see was an old veteran, a shoeshine boy.

As if on cue, this walking bit of paraphernalia from that ancient war limped past them. Trudy released the sharp breath she'd taken. She knew him. He was no veteran, but only masqueraded as a poor old soldier to gain sympathy for his shoeshine business. He lived down on Maxwell Street, near one of the flats her family had occupied over the years. His name was Shoeshine Joe and once he tried to pull her into an alley when she was about ten. She ran home and told her father and her brother Frank beat up Joe the next time he saw him.

Shoeshine Joe hated her. She knew that. He always shook his fist at her on the street after that. Shoeshine Joe was the old life reaching out to spoil the new—

But he limped by without so much as a wave. Yet he *had* seen her. She was certain of it.

Myron Davis, noticing her distraction, thought she wanted to repair the condition of her shoes.

"Here, boy," he called, not noticing that the man was not a boy. "Shine. Do the lady first—"

The man walked back a few steps, holding his shoeshine kit in such a way that he appeared to limp.

He knelt before Trudy as if making a proposal of marriage and busied himself with rags and potions from his wooden box.

Trudy's consternation made her tremble. Myron noticed it and believed she was trembling because she was pleased to receive such attention. An older, more mature Lothario would have known no lady liked to have her appearance repaired in public and would have assigned her trembling to that.

Throughout the elaborate ritual, Trudy kept her head down and looked only at her purse. She didn't want to risk some sign of recognition form the old ruin kneeling before her, especially some sign that Myron Davis—Mr. Myron Davis—might catch. What would this fine gentleman at her side think if the ragpicker at her feet should rise and call her *Gertrude?*

Trudy clutched at the drawstrings of her purse and held her arms rigid in fear.

Davis began to chat as if the man were not there.

"Do you live nearby?"

She glanced at him and then looked down again. "No," she said. She noticed that her knee was shaking and pressed her gloved hand against it.

Damn, thought Myron, *will she say nothing else?*

The kneeling man switched to the gentleman, but in the process of moving his goods he managed a swift glance at the young lady from the corner of his eye. Their eyes met briefly, but she turned her body again so that she faced northward, away from the two men. She attempted to keep her attitude cheerful and unalarmed, but inside she knew—knew—he had recognized her. Only they knew the truth of the scene, in spite of the sophisticate beside her who believed he was in charge of the moment.

"Do you live outside the city?'"

"Yes," she answered, although she knew no area outside the city she could name if he should press her for a location.

"Do you have an early engagement in the city today?" Even he realized this sounded asinine, but he must hear her speak more fully.

"I—I—" she stammered. What could she say? She didn't want to tell him about the cigar factory or her decision to leave home this very day. She was not stupid. So she said, "Yes, I had an early engagement, but it's—it's too late—"

"Where were you going—perhaps I can take you there?"

"No—no. There's no need. It was—" she cast about in her mind "—voluntary. At Hull House. I had a voluntary engagement at Hull House—"

His smile widened. "At Hull House. I've heard of that place. It has a reputation—" He appeared to look her over again from head to foot, perhaps making a new judgment.

What could he have been thinking? That her clothes were not of the best materials, but that they were stylish, not the kind that maids or serving girls would wear. Her diction seemed clear enough. Not foreign. A clergyman's daughter? Intelligent, well-bred, but a bit too trusting that the rest of the world was as well-intentioned and kind as she? Inexperienced, but impoverished? His eyes narrowed slightly.

He tried again. "Is that why you were in the restaurant?"

"Oh, no—" she hesitated again, not looking directly at him in order to avoid Shoeshine Joe. "I—I—was lost. I never found—where I was going—and I was hungry, so I—" she stopped again. She couldn't lie successfully with Shoeshine Joe not three feet from her.

She risked an irritated glance at the shoeshine man. Myron read her look and glanced down. The shoeshine was finished but the man was dallying, reassembling his kit.

"Here," Davis said, tossing him a handful of three-penny bits. The man took the coins, but waited. "That's enough," Davis said brusquely.

As Shoeshine Joe skulked off, a wave of release rushed through Trudy. He'd not given her away. She sighed, her head dropping momentarily forward with relief. Myron Davis, seeing this, could only think that she was annoyed at being questioned. In respect for her reaction to his probing, he said nothing more.

Now she looked up at him freely, her body giving evidence of her relief. She smiled—a beautiful smile—and then began to laugh.

He didn't know why she'd done that, but he felt like laughing, too. Nothing stretched ahead of them but open air and sky and some train tracks running along at the edge of the lake. They both laughed without restraint. They stood up as if they were one. He took her hand and without a word they left the park and began to walk south, matching their strides to each other, going south along the great avenue in perfect harmony, she walking to his right, looking up at him. In this way he was framed against a backdrop of the lake beyond and ever afterward she would think of him this way—his eyes blue against the light sky, his presence mutable yet sure as the lake itself, almost as if he were the agent of this mysterious body of water that reached out from the horizon to touch a young woman walking with her first beau along a Chicago street.

Myron Davis had been sent to help Gertrude Jahn escape into a new life. The forces that had sent him seemed to be powerful and all around her.

Later, she thought, I will tell him about the way I used to be—

CHAPTER IV

Otto came in from the corner tavern. It was late. He hung his cap on a nail and went to his place at the table, although he had eaten hours before. He took this chair no matter what time he came home in order to remove his boots and oversee his world. He had his head down, puffing at the stubborn footwear, and didn't say anything to Tessa. Such was his way—silence unless he had something important to say.

Tessa went to stand before him. He caught a glimpse of her swaying skirts and looking up saw that her apron was wrapped around her hands. Trouble.

"We can't find Gertie," Tessa said. It was perhaps ten or eleven at night.

"Send one of your sons by Agnes or Lilly. She's gone there and you forgot what she told you—"

"No." Tessa's face was red from weeping and this had brought out the darkness of her eyes, emphasized her long lashes, returned some vestige of the beauty she'd been in her youth. "We went already to Lilly and Agnes. They haven't seen her. She never goes without saying. But one of the girls where she works, she said Gertie left by noon—"

Otto looked out into the dark room. The corners were invisible. There was only the oil lamp on the table, turned down to save fuel.

Most of their light came from the kitchen stove, their only source of heat. The room was so quiet, he could hear the wood inside the stove burning.

Then Otto spoke. "Did the girl say Gertie left with someone?" Tessa said no.

"There. You see. Trouble for nothing. Ain't we got enough without you invent—"

"No. That's not all of it. Besides, the stores are closed now. And her money. She thought I didn't know. She had money. Lots of it. She'd been saving all this time, you see. Hid it away. I looked and it's gone. All gone. Something has happened. I know it. I know—"

And she began to keen, her hands as high as her chest now, clutched with the apron against her bosom.

He knew too. It came to him in one instant. Daughters ruined. Daughters of the poor. Sometimes by choice, sometimes by chance. Going to backstreet abortionists who ruined them still further; going to backstreet brothels to live out the mistakes of their short lives.

He couldn't say these things to her, his Jewess, his beloved. She'd been all to him and he remembered now. The strange forbiddenness of her, her dark hair framing her pale face. The red of her lips, their taste on his own like some exotic fruit. But he'd had her. And he'd married her. And in the Old Country there'd been stories that he could never tell her—then or now—of old men in faraway countries who would pay for a beautiful Jewess, old men in backward countries and in modern countries who would have paid gold for her.

She knew, too. Thoughts she couldn't say to him, this goy she'd married, if she'd wanted to. Of stories in the Old Country. True stories of old men who would pay for a Jewess, a young virgin. Stories of girls lured away, stolen by Gypsies, snared in the barns at night by Christian soldiers, bundled up and tied like rugs, thrown over the pommels of saddles, carried away over mountains to Spain and to Turkey. And to other places like New York. Tied and untied. Displayed, naked and cringing, held hand and foot by evil eunuchs while some old man, some heathen, some goy, came to her with—

Tessa screamed and dropped her apron. Her bare hands flew to her mouth to shut in what she might say. But Otto knew her, knew her vision. Silently, his heart screamed also. He stood up. To erase her terror and his own, he shouted at her, blamed her for everything.

"You *women*. Always fighting amongst yourselves. She wouldn't go without no word. You must have quarreled. She's gone for that. I know you had a quarrel with her. Don't think I don't know how you are—"

Did he know her no better than that? She never fought with her daughters. Never. He fought with them. Or they fought among themselves. She was the peacemaker. She ruled all with love.

She cried out, but he insisted.

"There must have been something that happened—"

"No." Yet as she said it, she remembered. Gertie had seen her that morning at the slop bucket. This thought came and she pushed it away, but not before Otto caught a glimpse of it reflected in her eye—

"You see! I knew it. Something has happened—"

"No. Nothing. I swear it."

He didn't know yet she was pregnant. They thought she was beyond her bearing years. She couldn't tell him at this moment. She held her hands over her face and the anger grew in her. Why was it always her fault, when he, he was the one who did everything— quarreling with the children, coming to her at night with his need, tearing into her with his hurry and now blaming her for it. Again—

She looked up at him, made her heart cold to him. For the first time she shook her fist at him and whispered, "Not me. Never. It was you. You burned the book. What do you know, you goy? So stupid as to burn your own holy book? With the names of your children in it? You brought down on us all the evil in the world in this place—"

The force of it, the truth of it, hit him with full power and in his own defense, for the first time, he balled his fist and hit her in the face.

2

She and Myron had gone on calling each other "Mr. Davis" and "Miss Jones" and been very proper that way for the entire afternoon. Myron had gone to some offices and Trudy had sat in the waiting rooms of those places, her hands folded in her lap, her gloves and hat on as she knew was proper for a young lady, as she'd been told at Hull House. In each instance, Myron returned from his business and they went on again, finally to another restaurant, an even grander restaurant, and Myron finally asked Trudy what she'd planned for her life. She admitted she must look up a room or some sort of new quarters somewhere, that she had the money to pay her own way, but she was determined to have a new and finer life than her life had been to that moment.

He asked her what sort of accommodations she had in mind and she said *modest* and told him she was planning to think about her entire future just as soon as she was well settled. She didn't add that her money would last only a short time at the prices she'd noticed he'd been charged. Myron didn't appear too interested in the amount or location of her funds and this factor set her mind at ease. At least he wasn't after her money.

He really was a handsome, pleasant person and when he smiled, as he did just then, he had teeth like baby's teeth, all in a delicate line that somehow thrilled her. His shoes, she'd noticed that afternoon in the park, were beyond her previous experience: blood-red leather, shiny as copper once Shoeshine Joe—she shuddered at that close call—had done with them; if she brought her hand near them, her glove was reflected in the leather.

What a magnificent being was Myron C. Davis.

Following a dessert served by bowing waiters and coffee stronger than any Trudy had ever tasted, Myron, without any discussion, took her to the Palmer House, and acquired for her a suite of rooms— a suite—by saying she was his sister, come to do *something* at the fair.

Myron, himself, had something to do with insurance for the fair and he went out to Jackson Park every day and once or twice he took her with him. But she didn't like it much out there because it was very dirty and she had so many new clothes. She'd been very busy shopping with the money he gave her to buy things. He'd told the hotel clerk that night that her trunks had been lost by the railroad and he asked where they might find good shops for replacement items until the trunks could be relocated. The hotel had been very nice and sent out for some items for immediate use and the next day she'd gone, with Myron and Myron's money, and shopped for other cloth s.

Myron hinted at other purchases to come later. Trudy wasn't stupid. She wondered if Myron were waiting to see what would happen and decided that he was and she thought it over in her mind and looked around at one thing and another and finally thought once again—well, *why not?* and eventually, after several days, she was just as nice to him as he'd been to her.

She could not see why there was such fuss about it. It had been as pleasant as he was, really, after that first dreadful time—and her mouth quivered now with the memory of other times and how his arms felt and the warmth and movement and the overdressed bed and the joy they found when they decided they could even be naked before each other. What a night that had been. He was glorious and she was amazed at the way it all worked and she loved the kissing and his physical demonstrations of need, which she could almost watch come over him, and his delight when he took her and after one or two of those times, she was able to bring herself into it, which delighted him even more and it was even better for both of them after that. They often wondered about the other guests at the hotel, if others could hear the sounds of it, and they would spend some time laughing and once he'd even thrown a cup from their dinner service against the wall in his haste to get to her.

Well, now she, Trudy Jones, had clothes enough for two trunks, because Myron had not waited long to shower her with things.

And every morning she stood for a moment before the glass to examine her face for signs of change, to look at her dressing gown in disbelief and at the room reflected in the mirror and at the brightness of the light in the room—which was another thing she'd never experienced in any place she'd lived—and as she stood there, even though she wished it wouldn't happen, she would think of home and wonder what they might be thinking about her absence.

3

Myron C. Davis left his hotel each morning wishing he could stay, wishing the girl in the rooms upstairs had dressed and come with him, almost afraid she might be gone when he returned. Throughout the entire affair—these past nineteen days—he'd had only one regret. He had no one he could tell about her.

What a first-rate piece of luck—he'd picked up a filly on the street and she'd turned out to be a virgin. He had never been the kind to kiss and tell before, but something like this almost demanded an appreciative brother or chum. He wished he were back in college where a girl like this one could be talked about freely. She wasn't anybody, so it didn't matter.

He'd never had a virgin before. One couldn't exactly practice seduction on the girls of one's own set, the kind of girls who would probably be chaste. The only girls he'd experienced were the ones in those first-class brothels, the places with the gold spittoons and gilt pianos. In those places, there were girls who could act the virgin, but once a man got right down to it and got in, he found he was no more than a tugboat in a very large harbor—competent to do the job, but the place was meant for larger ships.

So Myron reasoned to himself: Wasn't this girl perfectly willing to live at his expense in a first-rate hotel under an assumed name?

Wasn't she perfectly willing to accept his gifts, to take actual cash from his own hand to buy goods for herself? Didn't she return to those rooms each evening and sit with him, alone and unchaperoned? She must be aware. He knew she was. He'd touched her once when they were alone in the elevator and she'd moved away like a shot. Later, in her suite, he'd put his arm around her in the same way and she hadn't objected a bit. So she knew proper behavior, but evidently had decided to cast her lot with him, to let him do the job. Better a gentleman like him than some brute.

On the opposite side, he'd been concerned it was a scheme, some plan to get *him* into a compromising set-up and then an irate papa or brother or wronged husband would appear. He'd been mighty cautious at the outset, thinking at any moment someone would round the corner and put a firm male hand on his shoulder. But after two or three days nothing had happened. He was relieved.

Dining with her, taking her about, he couldn't understand how such a ripe plum had been left unplucked, but he decided that she was younger than she'd first appeared. Maybe eighteen instead of the twenty-two or twenty-three he'd first thought her. And perhaps she'd recently been orphaned and had nowhere to go. She was reluctant to talk about her past. Her entire conversation contained admiration for him, acclaim for the scene around her, gratefulness for the things he bought her. Of course, he couldn't exactly blame her. He probably was a step above what she was used to meeting. She'd probably met no one like him before. No wonder the girl was full of admiration for him.

He loved the look she gave him from under her lashes, the unabashed worship of his person that he saw in her eyes. He could hardly contain himself. Even a monk would have been affected.

And in that vein, he'd come to the second night of their relationship having hardly touched her. But he was determined to pace this out just to prove to himself that he was a man of the world. On the second night he looked frankly down her décolletage and let her catch him doing it. One of his fraternity brothers had told him years before that frankness was the key. Never explain, but don't pretend you're not doing it either. That way, the girl can't say she didn't know. And if she does not object, she is giving permission for the next step.

On the third night, in a prolonged romantic evening in her suite, he kissed her in every way he could think of, until, if he hadn't been so overwrought himself, he would have died of boredom. The trouble with all that kissing was there was no natural end to it. The full scene had its own energy and moved to a recognized—dare he say it?—climax. As it was, after kissing her for some time, he had to excuse himself hurriedly and return to his own room to ease the tension.

He lay on his bed and thought of her. He imagined her breasts, her thighs, her long legs wrapped around him in outright enjoyment of their coupling. He supposed that would be too much to hope for outside a brothel—that she would ever enjoy it as much as he. Binding his distressed organ in a towel, he let his imagination flow into it until finally, moaning, he gasped out her name to the ceiling.

Would the day never come? After that he slept, exhausted, dreaming of her still.

The next day he bought her a bracelet of garnets and pearls, not too expensive, which he presented at a candlelight dinner served in her rooms. He said a lot of silly and inconsequential things to her, and promised her nothing. That night they kissed and caressed for some time on the settee.

He went nearly mad that night with the touch and scent of her and he had to admit she seemed equally shaken. His hands seemed to startle her and when he finally opened her bodice and touched her breasts, he could feel her trembling in his arms, just as if this were all new to her. He touched a nipple with his tongue and it hardened under his mouth. But at last, on the fifth night, some change came over her—or perhaps he couldn't have accomplished his goal. He could sense her new attitude the minute he came into the room. She seemed—not more willing and relaxed, but somehow more determined and tense. After a few preliminaries, he called her to him and she came right away to sit on his knee. He noticed she wasn't wearing stays. He'd had a feeling she enjoyed his explorations of her breasts and so he began to nuzzle her there. A sharp intake of breath. He moved the cloth away and put his mouth frankly on a nipple and let his lower hand begin to caress her about the hips and belly. He'd had enough of games.

She objected to nothing. Her breasts, exposed to the dim light of the room, were round and white, jutting between them like an accusation. She didn't move to cover them or to stop his searching mouth. Her eyes were closed, her mouth slightly open. Her breath came quicker and quicker as he worked on her. She turned her lips to his, kissed his throat and ear, nibbled at his mustache.

"You sweet thing," he murmured, "you dear, little girl. You are my sweet girl, aren't you?" She seemed to breathe some reply. It wasn't "no." "You know what we're about, don't you—you little tease, you—you know about it" —he was almost singing as he crooned his message to her, holding her— "let me touch you, let me take you in the other room for just a while, just the two of us, we can be so warm, so close, we can lie down awhile—"

His hand was working for him, moving beneath her skirts; she was trembling, no doubt of it, but he'd heard often enough that these girls could want it just as much as a fellow could. Maybe she was one of those—who had to have it all the time. "I don't want to hurt you," he said. "I'm afraid I'm going to hurt you if you're not quite ready for me—let me get you really ready—I wouldn't want to do anything to hurt you—you're so sweet to me—let's get really close together—"

There was no denial in her. His hands seemed to disturb her mightily and this fueled his own desire so that he was able to stagger up with her in his arms—difficult because she was a tall, healthy girl, but he'd managed it somehow—and they'd gone like that, easing through the door to the dark waiting bed where, without either undressing, he'd got her arranged and settled and gone down to her, bringing her quickly into a state of intense excitement, his lips at her breasts, her hair, her mouth and eyes; and finally, his hands fully occupied, his mouth full of her, he let his penis—engorged with a week's frustration—find its own way to the place he was probing at last and—

She'd been a virgin after all!

What a time of it he'd had that night, but he'd managed, forcing her just a bit because he'd heard that was all a man could do with virgins sometimes—and there wasn't any doubt she'd been so, because she'd been, and still was, tight as a drum everywhere—and that first night she'd appeared to endure the whole thing in determined silence. For her sake as well as his, he'd just gone ahead with it, because after all there wasn't anything a poor fellow could do under the circumstances.

He was very pleased she had not cried.

4

"He is darling to you, really," said Mrs. Asunda in her mysterious accent and Trudy could not argue that.

She'd met Mrs. Asunda one morning at the elevator. On days when Trudy went down to breakfast alone, she usually avoided the elevator and took the marble stairs, but on one fine day she'd stopped and gone back because she saw a woman standing there. Trudy didn't like to admit to Myron that she was afraid to enter the elevator when there was no one in it but men, for fear it would break down between floors and trap her with a car full of them. That morning, Mrs. Asunda, whom she'd noticed over the last eight or ten days in and out of the hotel, was wearing a smart traveling suit and looked so self-assured, Trudy thought the elevator wouldn't dare malfunction with such a person aboard.

They went down in the elevator together, breakfasted together, discussed the various stores that were near the hotel and, finally, made a date to attend a matinee, which Mrs. Asunda said would be very enjoyable. Throughout their early meeting, Trudy maintained the fiction that Myron was her brother and she was *Miss Davis*, come on from New York while Myron worked at the fair.

But as the days passed, it became clear to Trudy that Mrs. Asunda probably suspected everything anyway and would not be offended by the full information and so, one day, Trudy told her all about Myron and herself. What could be told, that is. She and Mrs. Asunda had been redressing their hair in the privacy of Mrs. Asunda's boudoir at the hotel and Mrs. Asunda suggested that Trudy remove her street dress in order to keep hair strands from it. Trudy sat on a chair in her new underclothes and Mrs. Asunda brought her a Persian-print wrapping gown. In putting it on, she noticed a bruise on Trudy's shoulders.

"Did he do that?" asked Mrs. Asunda, her eyebrows rising.

Trudy looked back over her shoulder and saw the bruise for the first time and realized how it had been earned. She could feel herself blushing and she had looked down and away and Mrs. Asunda had laughed in a tolerant way and said, What happened? and Trudy had confessed how she adored the bath, not ever having known a private bathroom before nor one that had all those "things" in it and she could hardly be persuaded to leave the warm soapy water and he had become impatient and come to her in the bath with some suggestions and in his eagerness he had slipped and she'd fallen harder than they both intended against the tub.

She described it so plainly that she and Mrs. Asunda had finished up laughing, almost as much as she and Myron had done at the time, and then Mrs. Asunda had laughed so hard she'd dropped the hairbrush.

A woman of the world, was Mrs. Asunda.

But more important, Mrs. Asunda knew things. Oh, what she knew. She asked Trudy if she were being protected by Myron and Trudy said, yes, that Myron said he was protecting her in the continental manner, in the French way. Mrs. Asunda suggested other ways, ways a woman could make certain, because men, you know dear, sometimes, inadvertently, in their rush, forget such things when they are sure of us.

And what ways. Mrs Asunda seemed a veritable encyclopedia of such things. She spoke of Mrs. Sanger, who was lecturing in the city and elsewhere, and she gave Trudy a pamphlet. For the first time, Trudy learned that she was not alone in her opinion of the lives women like her mother led. But Mrs. Asunda, while very serious about the subject, was also full of naughty fun.

Best of all was a business with a silk scarf, a superfine silk scarf, of which Mrs. Asunda just happened to have a goodly supply, and she showed a few things to Trudy—"And after all," whispered Mrs. Asunda, "there is the delight of it against the skin, the delicacy of the fabric so nothing is lost except what is wished to be lost and he can use his continental method as well and you needn't ever let him know that this is also a way. Tell him only that it is for further delight"—and she put her finger beside her nose—"but we know that the woman must have her wits about her or *she* will be lost—"

Trudy was determined not to be lost. She followed Mrs. Sanger's advice and Mrs. Asunda's rules and felt she would prosper. But sometimes she studied herself in the cheval glass in her rooms and was surprised that nothing more than a slight flush on her cheeks revealed her as the fallen woman she was. She considered the warnings against her present life as just another example of poor advice received in her youth. Now she'd become a woman grown through her own decisions and devices, she could see there was no comparison between the deplorable state of matrimony and her present condition of living with Myron C. Davis. She was pleased she'd decided, that day in the cigar factory, to get up on her own two feet and walk out. She was not at all surprised she'd walked straight into Myron.

All her life she'd known she was meant for something better than her sisters and her mother had found, something better than babies and the stale air of tobacco crumbling from the leaf. Could anything be finer than this hotel? All gilt and gold and plush and promise?

But there were also magical aspects of their meeting; that they, of all the people in the world on that very day, should have met in that restaurant on that street, was something the two of them often reviewed together just before falling asleep at night.

5

Trudy learned several matters of fashion from Mrs. Asunda that were quite necessary. She learned three ways to arrange her hair, some new ways to dress, what to do during the day when alone in the city and what sort of attitudes were correct in her new life. Added to one thing and another that Trudy had learned at Hull House, Mrs. Asunda's advice could help a girl get along anywhere. Trudy tried to be very adaptable that way in order to achieve a firmer footing in this wonderful world.

She thought Mrs. Asunda very agreeable as well, but then she noticed Beverly had a habit of asking forward-seeming questions that annoyed. One day at luncheon—Mrs. Asunda asserted that this meal in the middle of the day was always called *luncheon* in smart circles— at luncheon she asked, "Dear Trudy, what's ahead for you—what comes next?"

"What do you mean?"

"You do know what I mean. I'm sure that in spite of your pleasure in your first affair, you've given some thought to how a young woman should make her way through life. I won't pry into your former living arrangements, but I assume you have some family somewhere. Can you return to them now, in your new clothes and with your new style? I think not."

Trudy felt a lurching in the region of her heart. She didn't like to think about the easy way she'd left home, without a backward glance. It was a kind of unfinished business she meant every day to do something about. But every day provided some new adventure, some pleasant event or avenue to be explored, and so she'd put it off. Nor could she think of just sending off a note to say she was now living in the Palmer House and would be home by and by. There'd be questions aroused by such information, questions she didn't want to answer.

She thought of her sisters—of her mother. Of the look of her father when he was displeased. She took so long to rejoin her conversation that Mrs. Asunda reached out to touch her hand.

"Trudy?"

"Yes?"

"Has he made any provision for you, given you some assurance that you'll not be abandoned in Chicago when he goes back to—to wherever he comes from—"

"New York."

"Yes. New York. Well? Has he said anything about that time?"

"Yes. He told me not to worry. He said we could always have—fun—together—"

"Fun?" Mrs. Asunda said this so sharply a man dining at the next table turned around to stare. Perhaps he wanted an excuse to turn around to see such handsome women lunching together. She spoke more softly. "He has a responsibility to you. You have altered your life for him. He should settle some funds in an account in your name. That's how these things are done. Do you want me to tell him? You've made a great sacrifice and he has made none—"

Trudy noticed Mrs. Asunda's face could take on a very hard look sometimes and lines would show slightly around her eyes. She was embarrassed that Mrs. Asunda would think this was a matter of money exchanged for goods received. "Myron gives me money all the time. Everything I want. More than I want. I can't ask him for anything else. He's not so rich, you know. And we're—" she couldn't say lovers right here in this restaurant "—we're *friends*." She leaned forward and lowered her voice. "I can't make it seem like—" she could feel herself blushing "—a payment. What would he think of me—"

"He would realize you are trying to regulate your situation." Mrs. Asunda's eyes glittered. "Has he indicated how long he will stay here? How long do you think this will last?"

Trudy sat as tall as her height would allow. "I'm not worried. He isn't going back to New York yet. He's very fond of me. He said so. This will last just as long as I want it to last—"

But Mrs. Asunda and she both knew she lied.

6

Right away, which she thought of as that night he had lolled back on the bed cushions and told her he was very sorry, but he would never be able to marry her; it was one of those things having to do with what was expected of a man of his set, since his mother was awfully rich and prominent and his father was the head of a large family firm for which Myron was representative. Myron was not independently wealthy and while he made some money through his representing, which pleased his father very much, he wouldn't really be rich in his own right until he inherited at some future date and that could probably take place only if his father—his mother really, because she controlled his grandfather's estate—was pleased with him when he turned thirty, and that would be six years from now.

He said straight out that he hoped this would not be a shock to her, since he'd never meant to give her the wrong idea at any time, but he felt there would be no problem in their relationship continuing—for as long as she might wish, he said—since he certainly enjoyed it and had a lot of respect for her.

Trudy thought this was about as reasonable an arrangement as she might expect, what with one thing and another. "That's all right," she said. "I hadn't planned to marry—for a long time, if ever—"

Myron had smiled and called her to "Come here," and she'd gone, of course, and the next day he gave her a necklace of some sapphires and some brilliants.

The next time Mrs. Asunda suggested she ask Myron to "regulate" their relationship, Trudy showed her the jewels and Mrs. Asunda looked at them through a jeweler's glass and said, "Darling, really," in her high-toned foreign voice.

But then she said, "And if this affair were truly under your control, he would settle some money on you, an amount you would be asked to name. Since he holds the purse strings very carefully in his hands, you must get something more definite for the longer term. Your father couldn't give you better advice than this and in his absence, I'm duty-bound to say this to you: Tell Myron you want your own bankbook. Tell him you want some substantial jewels. Otherwise, it may all be for nothing, just like a marriage—"

Trudy could no more make those demands on Myron than she could go home.

7

Myron, for his part, had had to wire his father for money on the private company wire, newly installed, and when his father had wired back, Why? Myron had quickly replied, Lost it on a filly, and his father, an inveterate horseman, had promptly wired more than enough.

Myron's only worry was that he'd found Trudy to be even more than he'd hoped for, even more than he'd sensed when he raised his eyes in that restaurant and had seen this doe-eyed vision in front of him. She'd come with him like a lost pet, trailing along, willing to please, her false gentility charming to him. And now—

Now he was beginning to worry. He hated the time he spent away from her, he dreamed of her at night. She was such an innocent beauty, such a sweet love. There was something about the way her ears stuck out through her hair. That was the only fault he could find with her and even that wasn't apparent when her hair was dressed and she was wearing her hat. Only when her hair was loose and tumbling down—oh, god—he sighed. He could not imagine never again seeing her ears peek through her tumultuous hair.

Myron decided he was going to have to get away, leave this girl and take a breather. He was exhausted from the sexual demands he was making on himself. He wanted her all the time and he wasn't getting much sleep. Besides, he wanted to think. He had to take a look at the larger picture. He needed to be among men, to show that he could remove himself from the scene at any time. He wanted to establish that he was a *man*, free to come and go as he liked.

"I'm going away for a few days," he told Trudy. "I might be back next week—or the week after. I have to take care of some business—"

In truth he was going hunting with some men he'd known for a while. They went all the time, loading wagons and horses and guides into train cars they commandeered from their own railroad lines, traveling up into Wisconsin to hunt and fish and play cards and drink and live without women for a while.

"When will you be back for certain?" She tried to keep the sound of panic from her voice.

His voice also sounded strained. "It doesn't matter to you, really, now does it? Just amuse yourself. There are matters to be adjusted, matters to be looked into, matters that I certainly can't discuss with just—anyone. I'll leave some funds for you. I'll take care of the rooms."

They had been maintaining two sets of quarters in the Palmer House for the look of the thing, but since he was going away, he thought he'd save money by releasing his. He had his trunks put down into hotel storage.

Trudy, in going down the stairway, happened to see his cases removed from his room. She sensed something was happening and began to wonder if Mrs. Asunda were right. And she began to wonder about home, three weeks behind, an unsettled issue. Now this man appeared to be tiring of her already. She returned to her suite. The sight of Myron's trunks being removed had given her an awful headache—no, more than that. She thought she might be sick. Only last night he'd seemed to love her, had been in a frenzy over her, had said he wanted to eat her and had touched every part of her with his tongue, tickling her with his mustache, doing unimaginable things to her. Maybe he could do those things to anyone, and thought nothing about her when he did them, only of himself and the act—

Oh, what was she going to do?

When he came to say goodbye, she was torn between being cool or embracing him, telling him to stay because she couldn't let him go. She settled for a confused demeanor somewhere between. He went away and they were both miserable.

8

She was certain Mrs. Asunda had been the person who'd tapped, ever so lightly, on the door about two o'clock in the afternoon, but Trudy let the knock go unanswered. Why should she let Mrs. Asunda make her feel worse than she already felt?

Myron had been gone since Friday night and here it was Sunday and raining. The rain falling outside the Palmer House seemed much worse than any she'd ever seen on Maxwell Street.

She decided she would try on some of her new clothes. But as she began to lay garments out on the bed and to set shoes and slippers here and there, she came across the shirtwaist she'd been wearing that first day she'd met Myron in the restaurant. She could already look at it with a different eye. Against the other garments, new and of superior cloth, it looked tired and old. She smoothed it out and in a fit of homesickness, tried it on with one of her new skirts. Rummaging around in her goods, she found the shoes she'd worn that day, slipped out of her bedroom slippers and put the old shoes on. My, they felt friendly.

Trudy sat down in a chair dressed in her former style. She reached up to touch her hair and the bracelet of garnets and pearls he'd given her not long after they met slipped back on her arm. Absently, she removed it and looked at it and then set it on a table beside her. She sat there for some time as if she were thinking, but she wasn't thinking at all. She felt as if everything inside her were turned off, flat and cold as the outside rain.

There was no way for her to go. She could not go back and she could not go forward. She could only sit here and wait and it didn't suit her. She'd never been the kind to sit and wait.

Whether she sat there long enough for night to come on, or whether so severe a storm was brewing that it had encroached on the remaining hours of daylight, she finally noticed she was sitting in dusk.

Trudy stood up and smoothed her hair to put on her old hat. She took up a new shawl and started for the door. On second thought, she came back and put on a long walking coat that would be better in the rain. She checked her purse to see that she had some loose change and some bills. Her savings were hidden in the false bottom of the trunk. Myron had shown her that. But she didn't want to go out without money. Once again, she didn't know what she was doing, but she wanted to be ready.

She opened the door cautiously, half expecting Mrs. Asunda to be standing there, but the hallway was empty and she went quickly down to the stairway and found her way to the lobby. There, she picked the most unimportant-looking bellman for her question: "Pardon me, can you tell me if Halsted Street is very far—?"

He looked at her. He'd seen this young woman come in and out over the past month, sometimes with a handsome blond woman from the fourth floor and sometimes with a blond young man from the second. She was the kind of girl you didn't miss. She somehow had the startled look of a lamb every time he saw her.

He motioned toward the doorway of the hotel. "It's not so nice out for a visit to the—" he almost said slums, but caught himself in time "—to the west side. Are you looking to meet some train?"

"Um. yes."

"What station are you looking for? Can someone go with you? That part of town out there isn't so good for a young person such as yourself—"

Trudy didn't know what to say, so she said nothing and looked out at the rain.

He tried to help her. "Where are your folks coming from? The ones that'd be coming in on the train? From east or west or north or south? Do you know what line it is—?"

Myron had gone on a train from the Wells Street Station. "They're coming from—New York. Would that be the Wells Street Station?"

"No, ma'am. That could be Polk Street for the Erie or the Grand Trunk or the Wabash. Or the Van Buren for the Michigan Southern or the Nickel Plate. Or Union for the Pennsy or Grand Central for the Baltimore and Ohio—fastest train from New York is the New York to Chicago Limited on the Michigan Line at Van Buren—"

From the loft of the cigar factory she had seen the tower of the Grand Central after it had been built two years before. "Grand Central," she said.

She and her sisters and friends knew no one who took trains. Immigrants came in on the trains and then went no more to the stations; Chicago was their destination, not a place from which to travel.

"Grand Central," repeated the bellman. "Then that'd most likely be the Baltimore and Ohio—I'll get the doorman to call you a cab, miss. There's a bad storm out. Can't you find someone to go with you?"

"No," Trudy said. "I'm going alone. Where exactly is the Grand Central Station?"

"Far west of here. But not as far as Halsted. It's at Harrison and Wells. You'll have to watch out at the station, miss. Don't take up with anyone—man or woman. The stations are dangerous for young ladies such as yerself. Get in and meet yer folks and then get out quick. Take a cab in and a cab out. The Grand Central's better than most—safer. But around about there, outside, it's not so safe—"

Trudy cut his warnings short. "All right," she said, "I'll have to take a cab then."

She'd never taken a cab alone, but both Myron and Mrs. Asunda always did. She'd seen how they handled it, so she went outside and stepped into the conveyance. The doorman gave the address of the station.

She knew very well where Harrison Street was, and Wells Street she'd heard of. Halsted was just on the other side of the river.

After they'd been traveling along for some time, Trudy tapped on the window separating her from the driver. She'd seen Myron do that when he wanted to give directions. When the driver looked in she said, "Do you know the Maxwell Street area?"

"Yes."

"Then take me there instead," she said.

"Are you sure, miss? It's a bad night out and all. I don't go down there much. Are you looking for some settlement house, miss? Or a church? Is there some church I can take you to—?"

"Yes," she said. "Take me to Hull House."

The man seemed satisfied by this respectable address and he turned to his driving and pulled the little curtain. Trudy was left to think in peace.

She knew her way now. She was going home. She dreaded the scenes that were sure to follow. More than that, she didn't know that she could tell her family much of anything except that she'd found another place to live for the time being. They must have guessed that much by now; and more. It never occurred to her that they might think her dead or injured. She'd thought only of her decision to leave, of how she'd lived since then, and assumed her entire change of condition could be read in her clothes and her hairstyle. Tenuous as her present situation might be, she feared it was written across her forehead for her mother to see.

She put thoughts of punishment and recrimination out of her mind.

What could they do to her, really, now that she was a grown woman? They couldn't stop her from living her own life. But for her own peace of mind she had to see them again, say goodbye to them, if nothing else. She didn't think Myron would want her traipsing down into the crowded slums if he were to return to her. And if she lived elsewhere, alone, what then? Wouldn't they always be trying to coax her home so that she might help out with her wages?

Yet some part of her would not let it be so. She missed them, the noise of the place, the smells. She didn't want to miss that, but she did. And her mother, her mother's eyes looking at her with approval, the touch—

There was a vague notion that some sort of bridge to the past might be kept open if not crossed every day. If the thought came to her that maybe Myron would not return, that she would need some way out in case that happened, she put it hastily away and sat in the cab, thinking.

She'd left home so easily, so unconsciously, she hadn't realized it would take this long to go back. She'd gone that day first to the cigar factory and then northward and somewhat east from there, until she'd found the restaurant where she'd met Myron. After she'd taken his arm they had walked eastward, conscious of each other and not the distance. Could it have been this far that she'd come? Of course it was, and much farther in other ways. She was a different person now.

This thought brought a tear and another and after a small bit of weeping into one of her new handkerchiefs, she settled down with some anticipation for her return to the arms of her family.

The cab rattled over a bridge and Trudy knew then they were crossing the river. She looked out. Still raining. She knew that to be a good thing. In Maxwell Street, as in slums all over the world, warm sunny days and fine nights brought the population out into the streets. Trudy wanted to go home without an audience, without catcalls from the denizens of the stoops and stairways. She wanted to slip in, make her peace and go.

Not the least of her thought was that on Sunday nights Otto was always out on one bit of business or another—usually at his tavern, which he entered on the Lord's day by the private entrance. She would prefer that her father not be at home on this first visit of his lost daughter.

When the cab had deposited her at Hull House and she'd paid the driver, Trudy, in her excitement, carelessly went on south without waiting to see that the driver turned the corner for his return trip.

She was almost running as she went, counting the streets ahead of her. Not far. Two blocks and around the corner.

As she came up to the place, she was shocked at how it seemed to have shrunk, how dark and uninhabited it looked in spite of the numbers of people she knew always to be within. Her family lived to the rear on the second floor. A high wooden stairway led from an alley up the side of the building; it was usually decorated with residents out to take the air but now she was pleased to see there was no one. The rain was bone-chilling and had driven everyone inside.

As she looked upward she remembered her mother coming down this stair each morning and again at evening with the slop buckets. She thought of her mother scrubbing the back porch to make it clean enough for her brothers and sisters to play on, of the way her mother looked at night when she thought no one could see her in the dim light of the kitchen, when she was tired and there was no money.

And now that she, Gertie, was gone there would be much less money. And much more worry.

She sobbed and her hand went to her mouth the way her mother's flew to her own when she was dismayed. "Oh, " Trudy cried out and as she said it, one of the shadows against the building separated itself from the rest and came forward. It moved toward her with a limp.

He came closer and she started to move off quickly in the opposite direction, to escape this dark menacing place. But his arm swung out in a swift, forceful move and he had her, pulling her toward him, dropping his bundle as he did so.

It was Shoeshine Joe.

Trudy twisted in his grasp. "Let me go," she snarled at him. "Let go of me. I'll get Frank—" She thought she could bluff him with this.

But he knew. "Hee, hee, I seen you, miss." He had a tight hold on her. The words came in sour bursts from his mouth. "And I told Frank myself a thing or two. He didn't believe me till I told him what you was wearing and that the swell and you went off down Mitchigan arm in arm. Give herself airs, does she? Damn little cunt like all the rest. Got her a *price*. Jest a higher one—"

Trudy gave a swift kick rearward, but it did no good. All she succeeded in doing was moving herself further into the tramp's arms. He had such a good hold on her he could afford to laugh.

He pulled her back and forced her up against the building, coming around in front of her, his knee shoved between her own, tearing upward at her skirts. With everything she had, she bit down on his hand and he swore and inadvertently stepped backward. She gave him an instinctive shove and started to run.

She tore down Maxwell and around the corner onto Halsted, glad she was wearing her old shoes. Oh, why did this street have to be deserted? She now cursed the rain that drove everyone inside.

As she ran, her hair tumbling down, her hat finally lost, her gloves torn, she did not care how she looked, what a problem this could be for her. What respectable citizen would help her? She could think only one thing—if I can get to Hull House they will know me and they will take me in....

As she came up to Taylor Street, parallel to Maxwell, she saw an apparition—a horsecab, her horsecab—waiting there. The driver had doubted her safety and had gone around the block and waited, curious about what errand could lead such a fine-looking girl off into the rancid streets of the slums. Besides, if he played his cards right, she could pay for his trip back to the hotel.

He flung open the door and she threw herself in, panting and huffing. He took off, slamming the door as the cab began to move. During the drive back to the hotel, she repaired as much of the damage to her person as she could manage and thought, *How could I ever have lived in such a terrible place? I can never go back there again—*

Home was no longer the place where she'd spent over fifteen years. It was the luxurious quarters she'd occupied for the last six weeks. Her life was not behind her, but ahead, wherever her new life might take her.

At the hotel, she felt in her bag for her money, gave the driver a generous tip, and avoided his glance as she stepped out, moving like a duchess.

No one said anything to her as she went up the staircase to her rooms. When she entered her suite she found Myron waiting.

"I tried," he said, "but I couldn't stay away."

CHAPTER V

Myron's trunks had been brought out of storage at the hotel and installed in Trudy's rooms. They were standing open and at home in the bedroom. Trudy adored looking through them, one especially. It was fitted with all kinds of silver-backed items: hairbrushes, shoehorns, flasks, combs, clothes brushes, shaving gear and the like, and the luster of its silk-lined interior, reflected in the built-in mirrors, reminded Trudy of nothing so much as her mother's well-polished kitchen stoves.

For the past three days they'd hardly left the suite. Myron had done no work for his father's firm. They'd lain about and talked and made love and in one exuberantly wicked moment, they'd shaved off Myron's mustaches, revealing his face to the world. Trudy thought the result very fine, but Myron wasn't so sure.

The waking hours had been dreamlike and mysterious for them both, but during the night Trudy had twice cried out in her sleep and once woke sobbing. Pressed for some reason, comforted and held by Myron, she would admit only that "some man chased me." She could not tell him that her family was removed from her for all time. All she could do was try not to dream of her mother, of the look on her mother's face that morning when the new pregnancy had been discovered, or think of the way things must have been after the wages she'd earned at the cigar factory had stopped.

To distract herself, she would talk to Myron about anything and during these past few days she'd spoken to him more than she had during their previous weeks together.

She rearranged all the items in his trunks to her own satisfaction and made him explain his life to her. "Tell me about your work at the Exposition," she said. "It looks so dirty and wild and flat out there. I don't see any fair in it at all. And what does it have to do with insurance?"

To Trudy, insurance had something to do with a man who came once a week through the tenements, knocking on doors, collecting nickels here and there for something called insurance that her father had said couldn't be eaten or worn or smoked.

Myron was very pleased to explain. He was happy she was bright and interested in his work. He told her how the various individuals and companies that were going to exhibit at the fairgrounds could be insured against loss through fire or theft or other disaster—and how some exhibitors wanted to be insured against failure of the fair to open. That anyone—a company or a man who owned an invention or a work of art—could apply to several listed companies, of which his father's was one, to have their goods or display insured against such unplanned "acts of God."

He stood up and paced back and forth as he explained this and Trudy thought he looked very fine and she was sorry she had so disliked the muddy expanse of the fairgrounds that she hadn't looked at anything but the hem of her new dress the whole while she was there. But there was one thing that confused her. Myron said if things went wrong, there was a pool of money from which some people were paid.

"Do you mean it's like betting?" she asked. "Do you mean you bet that things will go wrong?"

"Oh, no," he answered, taking her onto his knee. She was wearing her kimono with her hair trailing all around and she looked very appealing. "No, I don't bet that they will go wrong. I bet that they will go right. I don't want to have to pay out any money—"

"Ummm." She didn't say anything for a while but later said, "No wonder your father must be very rich—he gets to keep all that money."

"Not really. Sometimes we don't judge right. And our company is very small. But we're trying to grow. That's why I'm here. To make certain things go right for the fair and to make certain my father's company isn't securing buildings or goods that don't exist or are in such poor condition they're not worth what their owners say. Of course, there are other matters. Big companies will have displays of things such as jewels and watches. Some of the paintings we insure in private collections will be on loan here. I have to see to security."

All this made it seem as if the success or failure of the fair itself was something that rested on Myron Davis' shoulders alone. Trudy sighed. He was such an important man.

"Tell me about you," he said.

She told him about the cigar factory and the girls there. She thought it was safe to do so now. He'd come back to her. He didn't care what she'd been or who she was. She could tell him anything—well, not everything. She didn't tell him her real name or where they'd lived.

Now that she chattered to him at length, rather than responding to his questions in short answers, he noticed her speech was somewhat accented. She spoke in soft rushes of words grouped in ways that were slightly different than he was accustomed to hearing. She had a sibilant sound on many words and her *g*'s in some words like *sing* and *finger* were either too hard or too soft for native speech.

He asked her if she were foreign-born.

She turned sharply to look at him. "I'm an American," she said. "I'm no greenhorn—"

But he persisted and she finally admitted she could speak some German and that satisfied him. Besides, he didn't really care how she sounded. It was the way she was that thrilled him.

And for his part, Myron had a lot he wanted to say.

He told her she reminded him of Lily Langtry and he said they could be like darling Lily and the Prince of Wales in England and have friends and go about together and whatever happened otherwise would be just a small interruption in their lives. Whatever wonderful thing this was could continue as long as they liked because even when he came into his inheritance or if he had to marry some stick of an ugly girl his parents chose for him, he would always want to come to her.

Trudy thought about the marriages she had known and could see they didn't guarantee any of the delight she was experiencing and she thought Myron very wise and she wondered what the hotel management thought of their new arrangement—Miss and Mr. Davis, supposedly brother and sister—sharing a suite.

What old prudes the world is composed of, thought Trudy, as she touched her finger to her new three-strand necklace of respectable fresh-water pearls fastened with an ivory clasp.

Myron came out of the bathroom, shaved and smelling glorious. Shaving was altogether a new experience for Trudy. Her father and brothers did not shave their faces, but trimmed their beards. The scents and rituals of clean-shaved chins were an amazement.

"I think," Myron said to her, "we should go to New York."

When Trudy told Mrs. Asunda the news, Mrs. Asunda said, "I think you ought to have your ears pierced. You must be ready for anything. And do have *fun*, my dear."

Mrs. Asunda was very wise.

2

Ah, well, thought Trudy once again as they took the imposing train for New York. The Lake Shore & Michigan Southern, Myron said, was the Commodore's train.

"Commodore who?" asked Trudy.

"Vanderbilt," said Myron, smiling down at her.

"It's very clean," Trudy said. "I didn't think it would be so clean. I didn't need to wear this long traveling cloak over my suit."

"You look fine," Myron said and gave her the kind of admiring look from head to foot that made her shiver.

Trudy thought Myron the handsomest man on the train. His hair, if he did not part it just right, or after they'd been tussling, often fell in his eyes, but in public he wore his hat. His eyes were very, very blue and his whiskers, now that they were not on the face proper but extended from the sides in a glorious way, gave his face a look of maturity and strength.

Myron had engaged a compartment for them, but Trudy could not stay in it. The train ride itself was exciting: The fast movement, the noise, the passing scene outside the window, the passing scene within, were part of the adventure she didn't want to miss. She went up the aisle of the train one way and then back the other, looking about her at the hats of the women and the silver handles on the men's canes, and the men looked at her and the women looked at her hat and the train swayed on its way to New York.

And to top everything off, she was going with Myron.

Myron, for his part, stayed in the compartment and reviewed his past month and his spur-of-the-moment decision to leave Chicago and its business behind, let the fair wait, and come to New York with Trudy. He wasn't sure there was a sensible muscle left in his body, only this mad desire for a girl of no parentage or background he could wring from her. She had curious gaps in her experience of the world, almost as if she'd been shut away somewhere during her growing up. But her hours with him at night showed a quick mind, a fine sensibility.

He had taken this compartment for many reasons, not the least of which was that he did not want to be recognized. He didn't think his mother's friends would be on the Chicago to New York run; after all, they thought the West was Ohio. But his father's friends might travel this way. And once in New York he was going to have to scare up decent, equally private arrangements. He knew people he could go to, people who had this sort of thing nailed down.

Myron leaned back, tasting a cigar she'd tipped for him. She knew everything of that sort. She said she'd once made cigars, that she could make cigars for him and he wouldn't have to buy them ready-made—but she complained that the work stained her fingers and he said he would never want that and kissed her palm and then they'd not done anything more about cigars except once in a while she clipped one prettily and left him alone while he smoked it.

He smoked and listened to the rhythm of the wheels and he thought as the smoke rose above his head what the rhythm would be good for and he dreamed and let Trudy exercise in the corridors of the train.

There was a light tap at the door and she entered, closing the door and standing back against it. She was wearing her best hat, tilted forward slightly over one eye. Her cheeks were flushed from the wonders she had seen and a bit of hair was curling out around one ear. She was holding something in her hand, wrapped in her handkerchief. Some sort of small box.

"Oh," she said, looking toward the windows. "You've drawn the shades."

He was lying diagonally across one of the seats, his blond head on a snow-white pillow. A small glow of sun edged under the blinds, hardly there at all. She came to him and knelt down, putting the little package on the edge of the seat between them. At this moment, she was sixteen and he, twenty-four.

She smiled up at him. "Do you know what they have on this train?"

He took his hands from beneath his head and reached for her, but she evaded him and unwrapped her handkerchief. She moistened her lips.

"A man," she breathed in excitement. "A man who sells choco-lates."

MARGARET

CHAPTER VI

If a train leaves Chicago and travels east and a train leaves New York and travels west, both traveling at their maximum rate of approximately seventy-six miles per hour, at what point will they pass each other in the night, exchanging glimpses of each other's passengers, of the lighted coaches and earnest tenders, like a nod on the avenue between passing friends?

As the fast train from Chicago passed the fast train from New York, Miss Margaret W. Marsh paused a moment in her trek down the aisle of the westbound New York and Chicago Limited to look at the lights and the passengers of the train of the same line going the opposite direction.

There was the nervous cry of the whistles as the two trains moved briefly parallel and then roared on. She could see passengers in the dining cars, white-coated waiters in the aisles; passengers at window seats of the day coaches, reading or talking; and finally those in overnight compartments—one with the dark-drawn shade underlit by a bright yellow line hinting at meetings and partings within.

Shaken by the brutal swiftness in that moment of passage, the train on which she rode was itself unsteady and Margaret put out her hand to touch the back of a plush seat, holding fast as she stood waiting for the ride to smooth out again.

Isn't it odd, she thought, *that we humans must rush about so from one end of the earth to another? Too bad we can't just arrange to do one another's errands and live one another's lives and then we might remain in one place and enjoy it more—as people used to do in the old days—*

For a seasoned traveler who had gone from place to place throughout the world in her twenty-four years—and who had been as far east as Turkey—this was an odd thought, but some people thought of Margaret Marsh as an odd girl.

Although the train car was quite warm, heated by a small stove at the head end of the car and by some recently installed pipes that brought steam from the area of the engine as well, the other women passengers wore long traveling cloaks over their clothing and every woman except Miss Marsh was wearing a hat, sometimes with a veil so commodious it was guaranteed to put the wearer into walking oblivion.

Miss Margaret wore nothing above her ears except her auburn hair, neatly tucked into a row of curls around the top of her head—and, of course, wherever she went her brains went with her. Many young men considered this to be unfortunate.

She carried with her a small book into which she'd tucked a small lace handkerchief to mark her place. She stepped down the length of the train corridor in her forthright way, found her place and took her seat, arranging her annoying semi-bustle with modesty and resignation. Her spine hardly touched the seat back, so straight did Miss Marsh sit on the mohair.

Margaret and her mother, Mrs. W. W. Marsh, had left Boston three days earlier. They had taken the White Train because her mother enjoyed the idea of that silly conveyance with its attendants all done in white and gold and its whitewashed coal. They had arrived subsequently in New York, where her mother had done some necessary shopping and made some brief calls, since they planned to be some time in the West. They had then entrained for Chicago on the New York and Chicago Limited of the Lake Shore & Michigan Southern—the Commodore's train. They expected to be in Chicago in twenty-four hours. The Vanderbilts ran a very good set of trains.

Margaret and her mother always took Vanderbilt trains when they could, because the late Mr. Marsh had been such a good friend of William K., the Commodore's grandson.

The two Marsh women had traveled extensively, all over the world, while W.W. had busied himself with railroads such as these and with other money-making ventures that tied him to Chicago and the United States. Whatever wonders of the world the Marsh females had discovered, they also had discovered soon enough that if they were *not* going to travel by private coach as Mr. Marsh wished them to do, then they must take other accommodations in addition to their small compartment on trains and ships in order that one or the other might have a place of escape when the imposed compactness of sensible travel became too much.

Margaret had come out to her reserved seat in the day coach in order to think. The sight of Margaret, silent and thinking, sometimes annoyed her mother to such a degree that Mrs. Marsh, never given to verbosity on other occasions, might begin to tell lengthy anecdotes about the opera, which never had interested Margaret.

She removed the handkerchief marking her place in the book and lowered her head to begin to read. From this angle her hair appeared to be a bouquet of auburn curls. From this angle no one could see her remarkable green eyes.

She had been trying to read this silly book of poems, sent by an admirer, for some time. She had used that as an excuse to escape the sleeping compartment. It had a ridiculous theme of love and women who are ill with love and dying because of love—which Margaret could not believe for a minute—but she would see her admirer soon and she knew she didn't tell social lies particularly well, so she would have to read the book in order to say she had.

But almost immediately she sighed and turned to the window. The window of a Vanderbilt train was as clean as the window of any train could be, so she was able to look through it and beyond at the swiftly moving dark shapes of the landscape and these seemed to her, without conscious recognition of it, to represent the dark thoughts that were running through her mind about this train journey and about Chicago and any extended stay in that city.

Margaret had never forgiven the city for its weather two years before, in February, when she had needed comfort and sustenance and had found only bitterness and cold. Except for Russia, she could think of no more unsuitable place for a funeral than Chicago in winter. It had been gray, too cold for the grave to be dug; the equipment—carriages, horses, even the people—had been strained to their utmost by the weather. And the entire tone of the terrible season had been further marred by a hard business edge not set aside even during the period of grief and mourning. Her father had loved his city. In the moment of his death, Chicago had failed him. It had seemed to Margaret an impenetrable wall of unfeeling citizenry whose only concern was economics—their own. Her mother had not spoken to her father's partner since that time. Margaret had been attending school in the East and after the funeral they had quickly returned, shutting the entire Chicago scene away from their lives. But in doing so, in Margaret's opinion, she'd lost even more of her father—his personality had been imbued with the best of Chicago. She still missed him. And she knew the city would not restore him, once she returned.

Last year, in answer to a grief she did not have time to recognize, Margaret, who had no middle name, had adopted the middle initial W to honor her father. At that time she'd inherited all his fortune—because her mother had her own she was not included in the will—and it was because of this inheritance that they must return to their empty Prairie Avenue house and to the business dropped so precipitously two years ago. Waiting for Margaret in Chicago were securities and stock, horses and carriages, maids and helpers, cash and jewels, bankers and lawyers, lands and properties. No one, least of all the trust department of her father's bank, doubted that Miss Margaret would be able to handle this shower of riches well. Except Margaret.

She sighed once again. She often felt as if her life moved energetically ahead without her. As if she, herself, was chosen by it and had no inner direction of her own. She knew she was competent. She'd just graduated from the Massachusetts Institute of Technology with a degree in biology, a difficult and thought-consuming challenge, but she'd done it. Now there was the question of her life. Everything she had set aside must be confronted. And whatever emotions were brought to the fore by the process must be dealt with in private moments such as these. Mrs. Marsh, a perfectly wonderful mother in most respects, did not like emotional displays. Her own grief on her husband's passing she had faced and contained in private. She expected her daughter to do the same. They mentioned W. W. Marsh only in the most pleasant and casual of ways in any conversations that required that he be mentioned.

Margaret looked down at her book. The print swam before her eyes. She was not exactly crying—she would never do that in public and she considered this train car a public place—but her eyes refused to focus. She turned again to the window. They were passing through a town, the train moving at a brisk but sedate speed. Bells were ringing as they passed. There were dark houses in the distance.

Somewhere in her muted grief she'd known the same sensation that this landscape gave her. Within the emotions of her father's death there was an element that was elusive and remote. It seemed to run along, just outside her understanding, much like the unnamed town outside the window. Mrs. Marsh was not the sort of wife and

mother who could be pumped for such information. But Margaret
had sensed within her mother some irritability with the daughter's
hero-worship of the late husband and father. Had there been some
unknown fallibility, some business matter that wasn't what it should
have been? Why had they fled Chicago so quickly after the funeral?
Why had their Chicago acquaintances been so strained? What ill
feeling between partners had there been, so terrible as to involve
even nonactors in its drama? But perhaps Mrs. Marsh herself didn't
know, didn't fully understand some complicated business dealing
and wished to leave such matters behind, and to never speak ill of
the dead.

But now it was imperative they return. Margaret dreaded what
lay ahead.

2

In their private car on the same train, Arthur Baxter said to his brother,
"Do you know who I saw just now in the day coach?"

Steven put down his book with complete patience, as if humoring
a child, which is the way he thought of his older brother. "No, I
don't know," Steven said, *"whom* did you see?"

Arthur, the heavier, more athletic of the two, moved about the car
with impatience. Steven, tired at last of reading, rubbed his eyes and
waited for whatever bit of news this was that Artie had drug in from
the outside world.

"Miss Marsh," Artie said. "You know Miss Marsh? That little
strawberry blond of W.W.'s?"

Steven set his book on a table. Their car was furnished with their
own family furnishings. "In the day coach? I don't know the daughter, but I knew her father by reputation and his daughter would have
her own car—or at least a compartment. And she surely is not traveling alone?"

Arthur shrugged very casually, but his eyes were bright over his
mustaches. "Well, she's a free-thinker or something. Suffragette.
Runs around with educated types. With Alva Vanderbilt, and you
know how *she* is. Marsh went to some men's school or other and
took up some subject like mathematics—"

"Well, no wonder you are certain she's wicked," Steven drawled.
But Arthur completely missed his brother's wry tone.

Arthur was terrible in mathematics. He said he would always have
other people to add things up for him and he wasn't ever going to
have to do logarithms, so Steven had done the mathematics and Art

had taken art and rowing and some easy courses during his time at Princeton. They'd not yet graduated, either of them, but were coming home one full year in advance of the World's Columbian Exposition to prepare their mother for the influx of eastern classmates who would want to attend the great fair, and stay at the Baxter's North Side mansion in Chicago while they did so.

Steven yawned in his brother's face without much concern. "Did you speak to this dreadful person or did you cut her dead?"

"No. She was dozing. Or had her eyes closed. I didn't want to disturb her, especially as it would never do to ask her back here with us."

"Well, you said she's a free-thinker."

"Oh, I meant it would never do for us. You never know what a girl like that might do next. At least, I have heard they are not ladylike and you know Harriet and her mother—"

Arthur had just become engaged to a hatchet-faced girl named Harriet whose father was the richest—or was it the second-richest?—man in America. Arthur wasn't marrying her for her money, but because he had so much of his own. Neither Harriet nor he trusted any other romances since one never knew what was behind the attentions of those with less. But ever since Arthur's engagement, he'd been acting like a very old, prim man, a cautious religious prelate, though Steven, as the younger, knew this was out of character.

Arthur had begun to pace. "Do you think we should ask her to visit with us? It's rather late in the evening, but we could leave the door open. Just think of it. W.W.'s daughter in the day coach. She must be dreadfully uncomfortable—"

Steven sighed. "No, probably not. She probably doesn't want to smoke." He watched Arthur, who turned in his pacing and stared, half-believing that Steven was serious.

"You don't think—do they do that? I mean those suffragettes?"

"No, don't be silly. I don't even remember who she is. I know nothing about her. Nothing." He made his face bland. "Of course, this isn't any insurance that she *doesn't* want to smoke. Just because I don't know about it."

Arthur swallowed the suggestion whole. He threw himself into an overstuffed chair. "Gad, these women. Her father's a nice fellow, but he and Papa never got along. He's a Republican."

"Was. I think he died. Some time ago."

"Oh, I guess you're right. But he was a Republican and wanted a high tariff and you know how Papa and Mama felt about that—"

"No. I don't remember that at all. I don't remember Papa at all, even though Mama says I do. I only remember he liked corn mush for breakfast and he had a gouty foot and that's the sum of it. His politics and his whims remain as Mama interprets them and certainly you can't call Mama a free-thinker like Miss Marsh. Whom do we know that knows Miss Marsh? I can't seem to place her at all—"

"Oh, you're always off talking to the help at parties. You never know who anyone is, man or boy, woman or child. You never remember which girl is which. You're a—you're a—" Arthur's vocabulary failed.

"A misogynist?"

"Well, you would know," grumbled Arthur, who didn't like to feel stupid. "Anyway, she lives down there on Prairie and she knows the Fields. Mr. Field, anyway, knew her father, and she knows the Glessners, I'm sure. I think she might even know Fanny, because Fanny used to go to Mrs. Glessner's Tuesdays."

Steven was tired of this. "There are no southern families down on Prairie. At least, I don't remember any. They're all sort of New York-ish." That was indeed all Steven wanted to know about Prairie Avenue. He and Arthur and their mother, Mrs. Ulysses Baxter, when in Chicago, lived in a North Side enclave of southern relatives, other southern expatriates, went to churches led by southern ministers, went to tea dances with visiting southern belles, went abroad at the same time as their neighbors to the same hotels, met one another there, were extremely loquacious with one another but talked to no one else and were careful about forming new friendships. Since the Haymarket riot, Chicago rich had learned to be very careful.

For the early part of Steven's life, he, his brother, their sister, Fanny, and their mother had spent their time going about the world, living in hotels. At Princeton they had learned it was nouveau riche to live in hotels no matter how large or old one's bank account. If one did not take a private house on one's travels or at least find a compatible club, then one had come too close to living as a drummer might. The fact that the Baxters had moved from place to place just as they traveled on trains, with mountains of luggage, with their own linens and maids and nannies, with small pieces of furniture and pictures and paintings and china, meant nothing to the overall déclassé picture formed by the easterners when it was learned that one had lived until the age of more than twenty in *hotels*.

Arthur and Steven were on their way home right now to prepare for an adjustment in this view of Chicago. Arthur, especially, had great plans. He was going to open the eyes of the Princeton crowd. Let the fellows think it was a city of the Wild West, where cowboys roamed the streets with guns and the saloons and bawdy houses stayed open all night. He would show his friends that Chicago was nothing like that at all.

"Do you think we can convince Mama she should buy four good horses?" he asked Steven.

Steven picked up his book again. His dark eyes darkened still further as he thought of his mother. "I doubt it," he said, because he didn't want to waste time trying to change his mother's mind about unimportant matters.

"She'd do it for you, old man," Arthur said, poking his brother's foot with his own. "If you would just ask her—she'd do it for you."

"The horses we have are sufficient. We're not in the Chicago house with her that much. As it is, we'll have our hands full with the house—"

"Maybe if I could get her to invite Harriet's family, then she'd have to have some better horses, just to make a good impression."

"Harriet's father wouldn't notice a bit. You know he wouldn't. He still has his first nickel."

"No, he doesn't. You've seen their place. All their estates are very well equipped. They have several carriages at all three places, the very finest. It's in other ways he doesn't spend foolishly and I agree with that—"

"As in wages. He doesn't splurge on wages."

Arthur refused to answer. He took out a cigar from a nearby humidor and lit it. It was a very fine Havana.

Steven laughed. "How are you going to get on with her father, I wonder? There you are with your expensive cigars and your silk shirts and your handmade shoes and your—oh, what a model of cautious junior partner you look. I can't picture you as a man with an iron will and his first penny attached to his watch-fob. You like to live too well—"

"Oh, leave off my sins, will you," snapped Arthur, who did like to live well and liked parties and enjoyed beauty wherever he found it, even if his mother had to pay for it.

He rose and went to the doorway to push back the curtain.

Steven watched him, his brother who seemed so strong and yet who depended on him for everything, every arrangement in life except its luxuries. "Poor Miss Marsh," said Steven, "she'll never know what she's missed tonight."

"Oh, she's not poor," Arthur said. "But she might be lonely and we could cheer her up."

He straightened his brocade vest, opened the door and went out, but when he came to Miss Marsh's place in the open coach, she was not there, and although he waited for some time, she did not return.

3

When the train stopped in the Van Buren Street Station, Arthur Baxter was the first to disembark, and because private cars were closest to the concourse, he was the only person on the platform for a few minutes. He had hoped to exit the entire station before the rest of the passengers struggled up the ramp in his direction. It could be done if one moved briskly. Their luggage would be transferred to their residence, a home remarkably similar to this station in its exterior and only slightly smaller. When he and Steven or any member of their family traveled, they had all the service that visiting royalty could expect. But Steven was never brisk. He was inside the train car, talking to their porter, who had served the family for many years. Steven always had to thank the help and ask about their families.

Well, here was some good luck. The Marshes had also made a quick exit from their car and were the first to come toward him. Arthur went right over and, lifting his hat, introduced himself.

As Steven emerged onto the platform of their car, he saw Arthur directly below, talking to two women. Arthur looked up with a hail, and without waiting for Steven to come all the way down to the platform, introduced his brother to Mrs. W. W. Marsh "—and Miss Margaret Marsh—Steven Baxter."

Steven, still on the last step of the train, nodded and acknowledged the women's presence, but he hoped they would move along. He didn't want to get into a tiresome social chat after that long trip. Besides, he was not gregarious like Arthur. He couldn't just begin to talk to any female he met about almost anything at all.

Arthur was saying that everyone would soon be home to make ready for the Exposition, that there would have to be a big event for Chicago-born college students, that he would have to organize something and it would have to be organized soon in order to get a place on everyone's busy calendar.

Mrs. Marsh replied that they only intended to be in town for a short while. They didn't plan to stay more than a few months—

While this was going on the young woman—Steven couldn't see if she was actually a strawberry blond or not since most of her hair was covered with a hat—was looking around and she happened to look up at Steven, standing on the steps of the train.

And he burst out, "Why—your eyes are green!"

Her mother turned to Steven and smiled. Miss Marsh looked to the right and left in some confusion, blushed, and looked downward. Then she made a very honest reply. "Why, thank you, but I know."

CHAPTER VII

1

The cook's son, fourteen years old and for the first time wearing the dark-green gabardine of the Marsh livery, was waiting at the entrance to the station. He waved his cap and shouted at Margaret in spite of his new dignity.

"You look handsome in that uniform, Henry," Margaret said remembering him when he'd been just a child playing near the kitchen door. He led them to their carriage and held the door for them.

The carriage, which had been Mr. Marsh's gift to his wife several years ago, had been used by the two women in his funeral procession. The sight of it brought Margaret's emotions to the fore, but she kept her face as unruffled as possible as she and her mother settled themselves on the woolen seats within its pearl-gray interior. At their feet were carpets of mouton lamb. Margaret knew that under the seat, in a storage bin, was a laprobe of blue fox fur for colder weather. Mrs. Marsh had never liked Chicago's winters. Her husband had tried to please her.

The conveyance moved out into the bustle of Van Buren. Mrs. Marsh drew the small damask curtains at the window. Margaret would have preferred to have them open, but her mother disliked being on view to passersby in the streets.

To pass the brief time of the ride, Margaret said, "I have one or two things I want to do right away. I want to get some sort of work to do at the Woman's Building at the fairgrounds. Something quiet and simple, off in a corner somewhere, so I can look around and see how things are here—with one thing and another."

Margaret knew her mother didn't like talk of suffragist matters and for a short time neither woman spoke, each thinking about what was ahead for them in the next few weeks.

When Alva Vanderbilt had learned that her friends, the Marshes, were returning to Chicago, she'd contacted Margaret. "You're just the one to go there and keep an eye on things. Do nothing controversial. Just let us know what's happening. You're the perfect one. It's your home and you do know Sophia."

Sophia was Sophia Hayden, a fellow graduate of MIT, the woman architect who'd designed the Woman's Building. A man—a *man*—had volunteered to design it for nothing, but that Mrs. Palmer, Potter Palmer's wife, had taken over the Board of Lady Managers, and sweeping all such considerations aside, she set up a competition for a woman architect, of which there were only a few, and Sophia had won. The building was under construction now. But there were difficulties. The various factions of genteel Chicago womanhood were quarreling over the building and what should be in it until the uproar could be heard in the East. She'd not welcomed the call from Alva Vanderbilt. Margaret found eastern women, especially eastern society, knew nothing about Chicago at all.

Yet Margaret could imagine what the women of Chicago were doing with that building. In fact, she cringed inwardly at what must be happening, as Chicago's females turned an international event into a provincial fight over lace and antimacassars. In Margaret's opinion, the problem was that Chicago was a masculine city, a difficult, severe place to put something called a Woman's Building and from what she knew of the ladies in Chicago—and Illinois—they were mostly women of assumed gentility, wearing it on their sleeves, their parlors full of brass and fringes, their clothing dark and overpleated, their minds the same, tuned to some ill-defined concept of "doing good" as long as the object of their charity was far away.

Bitter thoughts about Chicago, the actuality of riding in this carriage, made her miss her father even more. She had been able to talk to him about anything, although they didn't always agree. He would listen and then let her see how things were, taking her with him now and then through his days in business. In this way, she'd seen when she was no more than eleven or twelve that men are not so very different from women; some are adequate to the tasks they have before them and some are not. Even at that age, Margaret had been able to reason that men who dealt in trains had learned their business, that it had not been born in them.

But her father's business acquaintances, on seeing his daughter at his side, had chided her father: *Women can't be made to understand business. Especially a pretty girl like this little thing—*

I wish he were going to be there, waiting for us on the stairs, as he used to be, Margaret thought.

"Mother?"

"Yes, dear?"

"You do know Mrs. Palmer, don't you? We have met her?"

"Of course. You've met her also. I've known her for years."

"Is she too—too formidable?" Margaret cast about in her mind for an image of Mrs. Palmer and found none. "I don't suppose she'll want to clasp a suffragist to her bosom," she said laconically. "Why don't you tell me frankly, Mother, why you don't like her?"

"I didn't say that. She's an interesting lady. I hear she's collecting the modern artists—those Impressionists we saw in France. But she's not a dilettante. I've been told she's working toward better conditions for working women. In that way, she's modern. But I think she's a bit like Chicago, itself. There's a puritanical streak in Chicago, my dear. They're known for it—"

Here Mrs. Marsh gave a great sigh, which was so unlike her, Margaret turned in her seat to look at her mother. Her eyes were downcast and she appeared to be unfastening and refastening her purse.

Margaret decided to move the conversation on to her second Chicago project. "You don't mean Mrs. Palmer is something like Uncle Findley?"

Mrs. Marsh made a sound similar to a snort, except she would never snort. "I wouldn't compare my worst enemy to your great uncle Findley—"

"Just the same, when I think of Chicago people, he's the first person who comes to mind."

"To your mind, perhaps, but to no other. You'd never find Uncle Findley among Mrs. Palmer's circle. No matter how great your uncle's fortune, he'd never suit—"

"Then they're concerned only with social standing—"

"No. But he's so—so—graceless. Besides, the Palmer claque is civic-minded, which your uncle is not. Uncle Findley is too old-fashioned and backward-looking for the current social set in the city—and I don't care to speak of him either. He just goes through life sampling here and there—"

"Mother, I hesitate to speak of money, but do you think Uncle Findley is well off? That is, does he have enough? He was older than my grandfather, so that must mean he's past seventy. I especially worry that he might not have enough to live on—that he stays at the Tremont because he can't afford something better. He seems well off, but it could be a sham for our benefit, you know. We see him so seldom, he could be marshaling his resources for our visits—"

"We see him often enough—"

"Just the same, I mean to have him come to us, Mother, as soon as we're settled." A feeling of stubbornness filled her. She meant to have her way in this.

"I mean this in the kindest way, Margaret, when I say you must realize the properties here are yours to do as you like. If you want to feed and house Uncle Findley, have revels with him, if you like, then I can't stop you. I want to know as little as possible about him. He's your relative, not mine. Your father—" a short pause here, which both Marsh women recognized as emotion "—your father insisted that I let you be friends with Findley even though I thought it unsuitable—"

"Well, we must change that. I'm adult now. There's no reason you can't have him around now and then—"

"He won't come. His dislike of me is greater than mine of him. He won't write notes and he won't come to the house and he won't even answer a telephone—he's impossible."

There was a puritanical streak in her mother as well as in Chicago and Mrs. Palmer, Margaret thought. Now she said, "He's just—well, his opinion of the telephone is reasonable in his own mind. He believes it destroys privacy and orders people about. He—um— believes that others can listen through the receiver even though the instrument is disengaged."

"You see. A madman. More than eccentric. You'll have to send Henry with a note. I really don't like having you go to the Tremont by yourself."

"I'll use the ladies' entrance."

"You haven't used a ladies' entrance for two years, Margaret Marsh—"

Silence being her best defense in this, Margaret let the point lie idle and the carriage traveled on.

2

Although she was an intelligent girl, Margaret had never questioned why her father's Chicago mansion had been built on Prairie Avenue only ten years before, after her mother had inherited lands and properties in the East. Her father's business was in Chicago; he was an important man. It seemed only natural to Margaret that her father had to stay there and could not relinquish his life work to join her mother and herself on frequent trips to Boston or on journeys to Mrs. Marsh's summer home in Vermont. Nor did it seem unnatural that the two Marsh women should spend time abroad without husband and father. It was often done. Her father, handsome, imposing, was as pleasant as a visiting uncle during the days and weeks Margaret was in residence in Chicago. But when her mother traveled, as she often did, Margaret was expected to go with her to see something of the great world outside the midland city that was nominally her home. Margaret went without complaint because she saw nothing to complain about. Her mother, as pleasant and unruffled as anyone could be, taught her daughter that complaints were wasted on things that could not be changed, and her father, as reasonable as anyone could be, taught his daughter that complaints should be saved for causes greater than personal discomfort.

So Margaret learned early how to go easily from place to place, how to ship her luggage ahead to the final destination, how to leave home and come back again without expending needless emotion and how to make any place into the home of the moment. But with all the lessons she received, she still felt a stirring of some emotion— unease or excitement—on coming back to her father's house.

The Marsh mansion was on a corner of one of Prairie Avenue's stylish blocks, its double lot dwarfed by the great size of the house and its garden wall, which together filled the lot nearly to its boundaries.

The house faced east and was like an upsidedown L, if viewed from the top. The garden wall, almost twelve feet high and made of the same granite as the house, presented an impenetrable facade to the street and neighbors. Viewed from outside, the front seemed to allow no way in except a green-painted carriage door, slightly offset. Actually there were five entrances to the building, but only this one for the use of visitors. The main entry for family and guests, once the green door had been breached, was within the garden, away from the view of prying eyes.

The carriage paused at the garden door and Henry jumped down to manipulate a device within the wall and the green door disappeared upward. The carriage went through and Henry followed on foot.

In the base of the L, where the kitchen and sink room and butler's pantry lay, there was a sign of movement behind leaded-glass windows, although the Marsh women would not have noticed. The house had been designed with care, even to the leaded-glass windows for kitchen and pantries so no curtains, easily soiled by cooking fumes, would be necessary. This particular design, which brought servants up from the basement and put them on the level of the first floor, was one reason servants in the Marsh employ had always been content. The effect of the plan, conceived to allow the cook to see arriving guests and work accordingly, had the added benefit to the kitchen maids of allowing them to see the ladies' finery and bonnets and to flirt with visiting carriage drivers without leaving their posts.

"There they are, bless them," said the cook, Mrs. Riley, who'd worked for Mr. Marsh for over twenty years with only a few months off here and there to give birth to Henry and to another child who had died in infancy. "The dear girl and her mother are home again at last—" She was speaking to two maids, one her own helper and another who would serve the main floor as waitress.

"I kin hardly wait to hear what's in that luggage that come yesterday," said one girl. "Oh, look, she has red hair. I can see it under her bonnet. Oh, look, what a plain hat. Don't she look plain, though? Like a schoolteacher—"

"Miss Margaret ain't plain," said Mrs. Riley. "She's as pretty as can be with them green eyes and that complexion."

"She walks funny," said the other. "Stiff as a poker. Her mother looks nice. Not as cross."

Margaret did look cross. She was on the stairs and the sun had at last come out full force and struck her in the eyes. Her back was stiff and her thin frame appeared tense and uneasy.

"I hope the rest of her clothes ain't like that," said the kitchen-girl. "I thought you said she was smart," she said accusingly to the cook.

Cook snapped, "It's what's in her head not on it that I meant and if you had as much in yours—"

"If I had as much in me pocket as she has, then I'd be smart—"

"No, you wooden't," said her fellow-worker. "You'd be married to that William what works at the mills. And that wooden't be smart at all—"

"Hush, the two of you," said the cook. "We don't talk of money in a house like this. Besides. Money ain't everything. She's had sorrow, that little girl—"

"Little girl? Must be six feet tall. Thin as anything—"

"Hush. She's not six feet. And she's slim and stylish as any lady'd like to be. Wait till you see close up. And she's good-hearted when she's not being absent-minded or reading a book—"

"What kind of sorrow?" asked the kitchen-girl, picking up the intriguing hint.

"Not for the likes of you—of us—to know. But she's lost her

father, which you ain't, and he was a great, good man—"

Mrs. Riley choked on this last because Mr. Marsh had been very kind to her, not only at her own loss, but in finding her husband a good job at a fine club for gentlemen. Mr. Marsh had been and still was idolized by the cook and so she told her helpers, "Think of it; he died without any of his own around him and his little girl far away at school."

Mrs. Riley shut her mouth tightly against her own inclination to say more. She would never get over the way of Mr. Marsh's death, and it wasn't for such as these to know about. She'd done what she could after what she'd found that dark winter morning. She'd made things smooth and calm and sent word to Mr. Findley Marsh, the uncle, and to the lawyers in that big building in the city. Henry, little Henry, only twelve then, had helped her and he wouldn't tell what he'd seen. But what information was in her own family about the Marshes would never escape to the world at large.

And today was a new day. Miss Margaret had come home.

"Hurry on now," she told the girls. "They'll be wanting their luncheon and whether in their rooms or in the dining room or the solarium, we must find out. I wonder—" she paused.

"What?" asked the waitress, who felt the entire conversation had been unsatisfactory, with much implied and nothing much said. "What do you wonder?"

"I wonder who'll be in charge," said Mrs. Riley. "The daughter or the mother. The daughter owns it all now."

3

In the front hall the butler, Knox, who'd been sent on from Boston to make certain everything was ready, was waiting with the second man and two chambermaids. Henry followed the Marsh women up the front stairs just to the door to deposit the two small pieces of hand luggage with which they'd traveled. Then he retreated, since, far down on the list of servants, he was not allowed at any time to enter by the front door. The two bags were gathered up by the second man on a signal from Knox. There was a slight pause.

Margaret, sensitive to this, turned to her mother gracefully. "Mother—" she said. That was all, but the servants knew then that Miss Margaret wanted her mother to go on as before as mistress of the household.

Mrs. Marsh spoke quietly to Knox, giving orders about which bedrooms would be occupied—the usual ones—and when they would want lunch. The chambermaids were introduced by their last names. They were new. Mrs. Marsh asked if the fires had been laid in the bedrooms. Knox said they'd been lighted to freshen the rooms. Mrs. Marsh said they would not unpack until later and would take a slight rest before luncheon.

Margaret, distracted by memories, nodded absently and the two women went upstairs. The servants disappeared to a back stairway, since they were never never allowed on the front stairs; the butler forbade it.

4

On the North Side of town, the homecoming was different.

In true southern style, the Baxters did not use the front door of their Chicago mansion. All their family entrances and exits were made at the side, under the porte cochere. Steven and Arthur Baxter were met in this auxiliary entrance by the Scandinavian housekeeper. By this their suspicions, which led them to advance their planning for the great Exposition one full year, were confirmed.

"Where is Mama?" Steven asked the housekeeper. "She is here, isn't she?"

"Ah, yas," the woman said. "She don't go out."

As she spoke, Arthur moved into the hall toward the receiving rooms and parlors, motioning for Steven to follow. "You see," Arthur said. "I told you so—"

Steven let the housekeeper return to the kitchen before he said, "It doesn't mean what you think. I'm certain there's an explanation."

"I think she should have a companion."

"She'd never allow it. Never. Much too expensive."

"Well, look at this place. You'd think it was to let." The house had been built for the Baxters nineteen years ago and at that time, every stick of furniture, every leatherbound book chosen by an eminent New York decorating firm, had been in place when the family took up their initial residence. But now the rooms in which the brothers stood were nearly empty. What small amount of furniture remained was swathed in dust-covers. Ceiling lights that in festive times provided either gas or electric were draped in dark cloths. Books had been removed from the wall shelves in the library. There were no carpets anywhere on the floors. The draperies were down and only scrim curtains, brocaded shades and outside awnings kept the curious from being able to look with shocked intimacy on the elegant emptiness of the Baxter mansion.

The brocaded shades were at half-mast.

Steven turned back toward the elevator. "Let's just ask her—"

"That thing is too slow. Let's take the stairs."

The stairway was of satinwood, inlaid at intervals with chased steel. The newel post was simple, but each of the rungs below the curved railing was of a different turning. As children, the two young men now ascending had loved to inch down the stairs, sitting on each step in turn, taking as much as half an hour to make their descent as they ran their fingers over each of the different spirals. Returning from abroad during his twelfth year, Steven had said to Arthur, "Did you ever think—someone did this? Some man, I mean, spent a long time making each one of these different from the other, just so we would have amusement as we walked up and down the stairs?" His question seemed to be "Who are we to have such luck?" When he was just a few years older, he noticed for the first time that the railings did repeat, that there were roughly three sets, each alike, but spread so far apart in the construction that the similarity was difficult to detect. The day he discovered this, Steven felt he had lost his childhood forever.

Their mother was not in her suite; not in the dressing room, the bedchamber, the sitting room or bath.

"Where do you suppose—?" muttered Arthur. He went to a steam radiator and felt it. It was cold. The entire house felt clammy, appropriate in Chicago in May weather.

Steven pointed to the next flight of stairs. "She's probably in the schoolroom. Unless the silver vault. Did you look there?"

"She's not there."

There were no servants anywhere, no bustling maids, no dustmen taking out the cinders. There were no cinders. That there were no servants in this house, only slightly smaller than the Van Buren Station, meant things were very bad indeed.

Steven took the next flight of stairs two by two with Arthur following more slowly. Though they had rarely lived here, this had been their only real home and still was. Years ago, after they had just settled in, their father had died. He was an old man, very ill, much older than their mother. But her entire existence faded without him. She'd put her life then into steamer trunks, gathered up her children and left for other scenes. How could she be expected to cope—with children, with household help, with decisions about schooling and community life—when her only solace had left her for the sweet evasion of death? She felt abandoned and cheated. But she was an heiress.

Mrs. Ulysses Baxter—Delight to her friends—had inherited $20 million in her own right from her husband. Her three children were to divide among them another $20 million as soon as they reached an age determined by her husband in his will. Until each child reached the age of thirty—or until they married—their estates were to be managed by their mother. Somewhere in the will, the word *conserve* had been used. Mrs. Baxter took that word very seriously.

She was a motherly woman, slightly plump, and her sons couldn't remember when she'd not had white hair. Her cheeks were meant to be rosy, but her inclination toward melancholia turned her complexion most times white as paper. Her hair was fine and escaped every kind of restraint, falling in wispy curls around her ears or fuzzing at her forehead. Between her eyes there was a deep line of concern, a line that her children, when young, had tried to remove by rubbing. In her youth she'd worn glasses, but as she aged, her eyesight improved, until she could now read without them, although she went about with such a preoccupied air that she sometimes cut friends and family on the street because she didn't recognize them as they walked within feet of her.

"Mama!" shouted Steven. He turned the corner at the top landing and went down the hall toward the schoolroom. Arthur trailed, running his finger along the beaded-board wainscotting as if he were a reluctant child headed for the tutor who used to hold sway in the room ahead.

In the schoolroom—which Fanny now liked to refer to as a ballroom, because Mrs. Vanderbilt had a ballroom—they found Mama. She lifted her head like a bird peering out of its nest. She was rummaging in some trunk or other and she had a bit of paper tucked between her teeth. Trunks were all over the room, some with lids raised.

"Stevie—" The bit of paper fluttered down. "Steven. My dear, my dear." She looked at them, almost sheepishly. Then at last: "Arthur? You're here, also?" She shut the lid somewhat hastily and stood among the containers.

"I'm so sorry, my dearies. I didn't expect you. I'm so sorry." She smoothed at her white smock. It was soiled and rumpled, its large pockets apparently full of stuffing.

"We wired—" Arthur said, the fact coming down like a delicate accusation.

"So you did. Of course, you did. I was just—" She smoothed her hair now. "I was just cataloguing—"

Mama Baxter's life was in these trunks. She'd taken it all with her when they left on their hegira, and she'd brought it all back—plus receipts and mementoes, plus changes in size and style, plus sales tickets, hotel stationery, baskets of fine lace, everything a distraught woman of the late Victorian era might collect. In addition to her natural instinct for squirreling things away, she had a dreadful fear of being called someday to an accounting of their inheritances and being unable to show that she had *conserved*. That she had only spent the interest from her own portion seemed not enough to ease her mind. She felt she must have receipts and bills and the very goods where possible, to show that she had indeed bought Fanny the right dress in Paris, that Arthur had had a terrible ear infection and been treated—unsuccessfully—by a doctor in Zurich; that Steven had been given a pony trap for the time of their stay in St. John's Wood. Her stewardship would shortly end for Arthur, when he married Harriet, the richest—or second-richest—girl in the world. But it would continue for Steven for another six years, if he did not marry first. And when the date of accounting came, Mama Delight was going to be ready.

"The carpets are up," began Arthur.

"You didn't have time—" interceded Steven.

"I'm dreadfully sorry to be so late," finished Mama.

The three of them stood looking at one another, the currents of the implied dispute circling over their heads. Suddenly, Mama and Steven broke ranks and embraced each other as if he were a child still and she the one who had just returned.

Arthur stood by, and their subsequent embrace was more restrained.

"Where are the carpets, Mama?" Arthur asked again.

He was a stubborn youth, never to be put off. Arthur liked perfection, good appearances and the grand gesture; the empty rooms below dismayed him. What if Harriet's family should someday travel through and decide to stop off on the way to Monterey? How could he face them with nothing in the reception rooms, with no table on which to dine?

"The carpets," Mama said primly, "are put away. To save them from the heat—"

"But during the winter—" Steven and Arthur said together.

"The steam heat. It's so drying. The carpets are in cold storage with moth preventative. We'd just have a terrible expense replacing them. And the servants drop hot coals willy-nilly—"

Arthur said, "I didn't see a sign of a fire in a fireplace anywhere. And where *are* the servants?" Arthur liked plenty of service. He was thinking of getting a valet before his wedding. Might as well start his own household in the style to which he knew he was entitled. Why in England, even the sons of clergymen had valets, Arthur had heard. He also knew to the penny the total in his trust account. There wasn't any secret about it. His mother had their funds in only two forms—company shares of his father's old firm and savings accounts at very old banks. There was no chance that money was going to disappear.

His mother stood facing her handsome, dapper college boys. A little old for college they were at twenty-six and twenty-four, but she'd been so hard-pressed to part with them while Fanny was away at Agnes Scott. Once Fanny returned, she'd married and that still left Mama all alone. But she'd promised the boys their time at university. That is, she'd promised Steven and insisted for Arthur. Arthur would just as soon become a gentleman of leisure right away. But Mama had felt it unseemly that a young man as sensitive as Steven should go so far from home alone. Arthur, who was certainly no student, could hold his own in the world at large, so she'd installed them in college together, as if they must prop each other up— the scholar to aid the bon vivant and the bon vivant to coax the scholar out of the corner. Mama, sent back to Chicago by herself, hoped she'd done the right thing, the *conservative* thing. She hoped she would not be too lonely.

Oh, but she was. She tore her household apart, put the pieces in storage, sent things that had never been used to be repaired and cleaned, locked up the silver and linens in Spauldings, released her servants and lived as if she were a mouse forced to survive on hard cheese.

She would not entertain in Chicago while they were gone because "there was no one she wished to see." She stayed in her room, reading religious literature, meeting with her doctor and her minister, both of whom were willing to make frequent house calls on this unfortunate fortune-laden lady. And these two worthies didn't care whether she had furniture and Turkish carpets in her parlors or not. They were men of the mind, she wrote to Fanny, who—being *enceinte*—was a prisoner of her own domicile in New York.

Steven said it was because of Chicago's wretched winter weather.

But in summer, when her family made an effort to be with her, Mama was just the same. "It's cooler with the carpets up," she would say. "Oh, let's not be bothered with dining at home. Let's go to the Boston Oyster House or the Grand Pacific Hotel that we so enjoyed when Fanny was here last—"

In the meantime, she still mended her own petticoats and talked of conspicuous waste when she had to buy a second pair of gloves for the harsh Chicago winter.

5

The three of them, Mama and sons, stood in the dusty ex-schoolroom amid the boxed contents of Mama Baxter's life and knew the fray for the coming months had begun. Mrs. Baxter felt pressured and alarmed. Something was being planned. She could see it in Arthur's eyes.

"Where are we to dine tonight?" grumbled Arthur, who was hungry.

"I can have a tray brought up to my sitting room," Mama said.

"A tray," Steven laughed. "You know you couldn't put enough for Artie on one tray. He'd eat the tray itself, albeit elegantly."

"Well, we'll have three trays then—" Mama said gaily. "We'll have a tea party—just like old times."

"I don't want a tea party." Arthur was sour. "I want a substantial meal."

"Mama, there is no butler to carry trays," reminded Steven. "We'll have to eat in the kitchen." The thought pleased him and he smiled. He liked to sit in the blue and white kitchen near the warm stove.

"Not in the kitchen," Arthur said, properly horrified. "We can go to a restaurant. The Auditorium. Or the Grand Hotel. Or that Boston place you like." Arthur was accustomed to getting around women. "Why don't we arrange a reservation for that seafood place you like?"

Mama knew she was losing control of her life again. They were planning for her, turning her around. She made one last mild protest. "I can't go," she said. "I—I haven't a thing to wear."

CHAPTER VIII

Margaret Marsh sent young Henry into town with a note for Uncle Findley and told Henry to wait for a reply. On the boy's return, Margaret asked, "How is he? How does he look?"

"Tall as ever," answered Henry.

Margaret understood. Uncle Findley was not yet bent or bowed by age. In spite of her suggestion that they eat in the ladies' dining room at the Tremont, his scrawled reply suggested luncheon at the German Room at Kinsley's over on Adams, some distance from the hotel. But in deference to what she considered to be Great Uncle Findley's age, she ordered the closed carriage.

Margaret could not imagine Uncle Findley living anywhere other than the Tremont at Dearborn and Randolph, once the stopping place of famous actors and actresses, because it was so near the Randolph Street Station of the Illinois Central Railroad. The hotel was in its fourth or fifth metamorphosis, she didn't know exactly which. The tide of theater crowd had moved to other places—the Sherman House and elsewhere—but some of the lesser lights still booked their residence in the Tremont when they were in town. Uncle Findley liked the fast life, betting, flamboyant friends, the political atmosphere of the old hotel, which he'd made his home. Margaret had never seen his quarters, but he referred to *rooms*, so she assumed he had a suite. Her mother insisted that she and Uncle Findley always meet in the lobby. Mrs. Marsh believed the clientele in the halls of the Tremont were not for her young daughter's eyes.

As she entered—not through the ladies' entrance, but through the main door—Margaret found the Tremont was grown seedy now in some of its aspects, but in its very seediness, it had hardly changed. Its black walnut staircase still gleamed dully in the light of oil lamps. The stairs were marble and worn into shallow dishes by many feet. The Brussels carpets still filled the lobby with flowers underfoot.

And there was Uncle Findley, sitting on a settee near a pillar, now standing because he'd seen her, looking as Henry had said, tall as ever, dressed in natty clothes, leaning on his old gold-headed cane, his white hair a gentle shock to the dark surroundings.

The Tremont may be seedy, but Uncle Findley is not, thought Margaret, and went up to him in delight and kissed his cheek. He took her hand and gave it a squeeze.

"I'm so glad to see you, Uncle. We came only yesterday and I've come here first—"

He looked down on her. His eyes, a faded version of her own, seemed to water for a moment, but he smiled. "I appreciate that. I really do, m'girl. Let's get out of here and see the day—"

Margaret indicated the carriage, but Uncle Findley, putting on his top hat, said he'd prefer to walk if she thought five or six blocks wasn't too much for her. They sent the driver on with an order to call for them after lunch.

"We'll need to be carried away from a lunch at Kinsley's," Margaret said, laughing. But at the same time, she was glad to see he was still walking everywhere. Uncle Findley set a rapid pace.

Margaret noted, "There seem to be more people than ever. And so much building going on. New buildings everywhere—or great holes in the ground where new buildings will soon be. I've never seen so much traffic, here or in New York—"

Uncle Findley gripped her elbow to guide her along. "I remember this town when there wasn't a dress suit among 'em," he said. "And although there was always more horses than people, now they's at least two horses for every man, boy, woman and child who comes to the city and that's too many people and too many horses. Watch yer skirts, Maggie. Not good for the health—"

2

Uncle Findley had come to Chicago—run away from his mama, he liked to say—when he was fourteen or sixteen. He told the story both ways. He liked to tell how there were "Injuns in the streets and this was the Wild West." He'd taken up with a man named "Injun Joe" who may or may not have been part Indian. After making his fortune, an amount of about forty dollars, Findley had sent word home to Vermont that Chicago was the "best place ever," and told his younger brother, Tommy, a boy of only thirteen who was Margaret's grandfather-to-be, to "come along." Since there were three boys and a girl still left at home, their mother was glad to send another son out to a place where fortune could be found and she even advanced money for a steamer fare across Lake Michigan. But Tommy had saved the money, gone through Indiana with many adventures, and come to Chicago with a little money in his boot. He and Uncle Findley had invested that bit in wood to make a cabin on land that wasn't theirs. After it was finished, a man came along who insisted in a rough way that he wanted to buy the cabin. They didn't want to sell, yet they didn't want to admit they were squatters either. The man threw the money at them and evicted them.

"We took that money and lit out," Uncle Findley had told Margaret when she was small. "We went upriver and lived with Father Jesse Walker on the Des Plaines. He was a Methodist circuit rider and a lot o' Indians used to go to his camp. I went there because Injun Joe told me about the place. After winter was over, Tommy and me went back to town and they wasn't anybody lookin' for us and we had the money for the cabin yet and the man had left. We found out he'd made money on the place, sold it for four times what he paid us."

So the two brothers repeated their act, this time building three rickety houses and selling them to the first greenhorn off the boat who was willing to take all three. This time they went north to Ouilmette's claim and came into town only when they heard there was going to be a great Indian powwow—that the Indians were going to treat with men from Washington.

Margaret liked to get Uncle Findley going on these stories and her favorite was the one about the Indian treaties. Chicago as she'd known it in her childhood had been very prim and proper and no one else would talk to her about Indians or "Old Times," as she called it. Most of Chicago's society didn't want such talk in their drawing rooms; such talk didn't fit with plans of architects and grand hotels and opera houses and symphony orchestras and art imported from as far east as possible.

But Uncle Findley would sit with her and spin out his reminiscences. He would begin: "We came into town and there were Indians everywhere in turbans and sashes, made up in the white or red paint to show which son they were. The white men got them drunk and let them race around in the sunshine and then at night they would treat with them under an open tent on the prairie by the river. We used the old shell game on 'em. It was a terrible sight. For medals and whiskey and fancy goods and turbans—and horses that wasn't ever delivered—they signed away their marks in land *they* didn't own neither. Nobody owned this place. Maybe the lake itself owned it. Then the Indians was rounded up some time later and went west to Iowa. Things was never the same after that. Now the land had deeds to it, and squared-off marks somewhere in a book of record. Yer granddaddy, Tommy Marsh, and me made a few dollars on it, I'll tell you. And then we bought a horse—"

And he would be off to the races. He would name his horses, each one, and tell about how he'd won time after time. About the cards he played—"I wasn't a gambler. Those that played with me was the gamblers. What they called me was 'card-reader.' For that's what I did then. I'd remember where every card went and all of a sudden— whoosh. The game was mine."

That money, Margaret knew, want into real estate in Chicago, carefully selected by her grandfather, who had an eye for such things, and into grain and goods and tar and pitch and wood for axe handles and plows and reapers. But when the Civil War came and Uncle Findley wanted to sell to the highest bidder, Thomas Marsh had separated his business from his brother's. Uncle Findley was "speculating." Thomas Marsh went into the new field of *commodities* in a dignified way. Findley did not and for this he was still considered disreputable by the business community of the 1890s. From that time on, after the Civil War, although he'd remained friends with his brother's family, he'd lived his own life, staying at the Tremont, keeping his business in his hat—literally the tall hat he was wearing today, not quite a stovepipe, higher than a derby, a little Irish-looking, made-to-order for Findley Marsh, Esquire.

Margaret's father had loved Uncle Findley dearly and one time, when the uncle and Margaret's mother had some falling out and Margaret was forbidden by her mother to see him, Mr. Marsh intervened for his daughter. Margaret, from that time on, visited Great Uncle Findley in luncheons at Chicago restaurants, giving her a sense of grown-up formality and respect important to a young girl.

Although she didn't quite realize it, Margaret had gained much instruction on life from Uncle Findley over the years. He was her first "unauthorized friend" and every time she went to meet him, there was the thrill of the forbidden, of knowing that her mother disapproved. With Uncle Findley's stories went cautions and homilies of every sort.

"Never trust a gov'ment, Maggie. I'll never forget watching the Indians. Glad I learned that lesson early, girl. A democracy is like a mirror. It gives back what it sees. If it sees a great populace, strong and thinking folk, it turns up a Jefferson or an Adams or a Washington. But if the population is full of weasely little men or pompous overbloated ones, then there's a weasely little gov'ment or a big overblown one, reflecting it. From them kind, git outta the way and make your own place to suit yourself. No matter who criticizes you for it. Don't pay any mind to gov'ment rules in those cases—"

The idea of designing one's own life was exciting to Margaret. Rules could be examined, the sources of rules could be assayed, and if there was some factor of truth wanting, a person could set the rules aside and live life on a personal standard. Her father, who'd often stepped out for elusive causes, who was known for being a sensitive, honest man, must have learned those same lessons at Uncle Findley's knee.

Margaret had proposed marriage to Uncle Findley when she was four. But he explained to her that by the time she would be old enough, he'd be too old and she'd have to find "some edicatted feller" that knew the right knife and fork.

"Society gets stronger ever' day," he told Margaret then. "And by the time yer a big girl, you'll have to go about in it all the time—"

From this Margaret had formed an idea of Society as something like fog or rain or smoke and when, shortly afterward, the city off in the distance had burned and she'd been taken to the roof of her Michigan Avenue home to watch the flames, and the smoke had turned and come back over them, she'd somehow thought this terrible condition was Society.

3

After the waiter left them, Margaret busied herself with her tea and, keeping her face down, asked, "Well, how are you, Uncle?"

"Didn't you just have a devil of a time keeping up with me on our trek over here?"

"That's not what I mean. I know you. You can marshal up a smile and a good front any time. You know, Uncle, I've never asked you—do you lack for anything? Is there anything I can do for you? You know, I have papa's money now, and I'd be glad to give you some—"

A great shout went up from Uncle Findley and other diners turned to look.

"My dear girlie," he said at last, "I've just made a new will. I've left half my money to the horses—you don't need it, do you?"

"No, of course not. But to horses, Uncle?" Her own father had made generous settlements on local orphanages.

"Well, a good part of my money came from the horses. The rest, don't worry, is properly set out on people. But the streets are full of horses and about ever' third one is mishandled. They aren't long fer this world. I may outlive 'em. They've put in that damned—beg pardon—loop of streetcars and now they've gone to the overhead trams. Mark me, Maggie, they're goin' to do away with the horse. An' then what about those that are fillin' our streets? So I've left some money set up for a place where horses can be humanely put away."

"I like to walk about, as you know," he said. "I still like to keep on the go. I walk straight up Dearborn to the old cemetery—Lincoln Park, they call it now—and then I go a ways along the lake and then double back to the ridge on up to Ouilmette's old place. Start early, home late. Passes another day—"

She caught an echo in there of loneliness. "Do you still play cards?"

"Twice a week. Still win, but not quite as often. If you win too much, it puts people off, y'know. Sometimes natural talent has to take a back seat—"

Again a wistful note that was unlike him. "We're going to be in town awhile," she said.

"I'm very glad to have you back, Maggie."

"You might come out to stay at the house, if you like."

"Mother know about this?"

"It's my house, or it will be once the papers—"

"Lawyers," he said. Disdainfully.

She didn't want him to start on lawyers, so she asked, "Have you been out to the Exposition, Uncle? What do you know about that?"

"Walked out there one or two times. What a mess. Although," he drew the word out, "you know Chicago. They're likely to bring it off. Money being poured into that place. Merchant princes wanted it. And the architects. Thought it would be good fer their business. Well, then they went to federal gov'ment and they got it in the neck. Wanted money and so the federal men said it had to be federal control and a national event and a national commission running it and the locals almost lost out. Then to make it palatable to the whole country, they had to spread out the architectural commissions and the majority went to the East. Only one or two—Sullivan and one or two others, Boyington, I think—made the list."

Margaret could tell Uncle Findley was starved for talk. He'd hardly touched his lunch, so engrossed was he in spreading himself over the contemporary Chicago scene.

Findley said, "Do you know they began it here?"

"Here?"

"Yes, in Kinsley's. Meetings over dinner. I heard some of them talking here and there. They were looking to make it a nice little exposition, a step up from a country fair. But then the big boys and the women got hold of it and now it's way out of hand and running wild. Potter Palmer's wife ran rings around them in Washington, all on her own. The society folks are all in a lather. They're going to show off to everyone. New York said it'd be a cattle show and in my own opinion, that was what was going to happen—with a bit of department store fol-de-rol and some soap manufacturers and dress goods thrown in. But the East has called 'em and now they're going to make a big show of callin' for the pot—educational and all, with Theodore Thomas and his orchestry and even electric light."

"But what did they think they'd get from it, with all that—?"

"Trade. Stimulate trade and give the world a look at the center of the country, at the train sheds and the cattle pens and the banks and the buildings—have you seen the Monadnock Building? That's new since you were here last. Or the Manhattan? Give the world the idea we're at the center of the universe. And so we are. Anybody does business in Chicago really does business. But Bertha Palmer thinks it oughta be artistic—and ladylike."

"What does the Woman's Building look like?"

"It's smaller than the rest. But I've seen what's done there and the architect's renderings—girl your age, Maggie, put that up—"

"Yes. I know her, Uncle. She was at my school. She graduated two years before I did, but I knew her slightly—"

He was drinking his brandied chocolate and didn't say anything, so Margaret gathered he didn't like the building.

"You don't like it."

"I didn't say that. But they're all some'hat the same. Bit of a world tour. Little sample of this and that. Saw the projection. Every building's going to be held up by angels on the roof and the Woman's is no different—all going to have statues on the roof, y'see—"

"I'm disappointed. I'd hoped to get a job out there. Some sort of volunteer position—"

"What do you want to get mixed up in that for, a smart girl like you?"

"I'm interested in women's suffrage, Uncle. The franchise. Activities of women everywhere. I'd like to be part of what's happening at the fairgrounds for the time I'm in Chicago. Just to say I've had some hand in it—"

"The franchise." He began to laugh again.

"Don't laugh. It's only right. Women should have the vote. There are things that should be changed."

"Maggie, Maggie. I don't doubt what you say. But women will never do it. Think of it. Women voting. I have one way I test all such new ideas, I think about your mother. If I can't picture your mother doing it, then I know it's poppycock—"

"My mother is an intelligent woman."

"Of course she is, of course she is. But she'd never vote. She's above all that. She'd think it a dreadful business and put on her hat and go to a matinee instead. Nothing would be accomplished and you'd open a fine chance for another sort to vote and vote and vote again. The Chicago way—"

Margaret put her head down in annoyance and he wheedled.

"Now don't get yer back up, Maggie. What kind of job do you want at the fair? I can help you there. I've got a few dollars in it myself on invitation from some of the boys—I'll just put out the word that my niece wants employment and you'll get just what you want."

"Not employment, Uncle. I could never take money—"

"Why ever not? If you work, you should be paid."

"But there are others who need the money. I don't. I would rather have some secretarial function, something quiet, in the Woman's Building—"

"Nonsense. I know everyone in Administration—"

"How is that? I thought you didn't like the idea of it."

"Well, I try to hedge my bets. Besides, everyone in Chicago who can get up the money is in on it. And City Hall has their men over there—permits and suchlike."

"No. Just something that I can enjoy doing—"

"All right." He waved for the check. "I'll take you out there Friday. I'll walk out in the morning and we'll trot down there and see what can be seen—"

"Come for breakfast and we'll take the carriage."

"Maggie, I eat breakfast at 5:00 A.M. and this meal you call luncheon, I call dinner. None of that fancy eastern talk for me. Why don't I come out to your place around nine and we'll go on out south to the grounds, if that's your aim. Then I'll stay for my dinner with you at the house—"

"Fine. But I insist on the carriage. It's at least five miles out to Jackson Park. I wouldn't be able to walk there and back. Unless you will allow me to wear bloomers and ride my wheel—"

Uncle Findley's pink cheeks were instantly suffused with dull red. Then he laughed. "I've seen you dressed many a way since your infancy, but if you want to be taken to the heart of the society grande dames, I wouldn't go in bloomers to seek employment. But I'd rather forgo the carriage. Makes me feel like a duke—or Andrew Carnegie—perhaps that's the same thing."

"Oh, I'll take the trap and drive it myself."

"Done!"

4

On Friday, Margaret and Uncle Findley drove down Prairie Avenue then went west to Michigan for the balance of the distance south to Fifty-ninth Street.

At the Midway Plaisance they turned east again to head for Jackson Park. Immediately there was much small construction in view. The buildings were larger than Margaret had anticipated. But by the time they reached Jackson Park, she'd lapsed into total, nonplussed silence. She'd seen artist's renderings of the proposed Exposition buildings. She'd read something called the *World's Columbian Gazetteer*, which came to her through her attorneys because she'd learned her father, two years before, had purchased some of the first shares in the Chicago Company, the financial organization backing the fair. Now, with the actual scene before her, none of what she'd read in print seemed to be true.

She stopped the horse. She couldn't see a way to enter the grounds. Everything ahead appeared to be in a state of desolation. There was, somehow, the look of an abandoned Venice. Yet at the same time, there were men and horses and the sounds of hammering everywhere.

She turned to Uncle Findley. "Why nothing is complete. Not even the lagoons. I'm certain I saw some pictures or drawings that represented completed lagoons."

"You've been reading that *Gazette* on the fair. They show pictures of the gardens in Mexico, of the boulevards of Paris, of the gardens in Lincoln Park up north, of the new paths in Washington Park—

and nary a true picture of Jackson Park graces their pages. Burnham's men brought this land up to grade last year. The rest is still going on. Don't believe they'll finish in time."

Uncle Findley took over the reins and turned the horse toward a small bridge that went over the lagoon alongside what was evidently to be the central basin, much pictured in its complete form in various periodicals. To look at it today was similar to looking at a human form in skeleton. On the far side, Uncle Findley handed the reins to Margaret once again and he stepped down to lead the horse across the uneven ground. Like a pioneer crossing the plains, Uncle Findley pointed ahead to their destination.

"That very large structure over there is the Manufacturer's Hall. They say it's thirty-two acres in its interior. That little building, the only one without a scaffold, which lies between us and the Manufacturer's, that's the Woman's Building, m'girl."

Margaret reined in the horse and stepped out of the carriage to join Uncle Findley in walking beside the horse. It was too hard for the horse to pull the wagon with her in it over this rough terrain, and she was much agitated by what she saw before her.

Margaret was silent with dismay.

How will I ever reach the building if I do find work here? she thought, but she kept her doubts to herself.

5

Margaret was not the only person to regard the Woman's Building with dismay. Newspapers jibed at it continually, men decried it, and a substantial portion of the female population also thought it demeaning. It separated women into a special category, as if to be born female was to be born handicapped.

When talk had begun of an international Exposition to honor Columbus' discovery of the New World four hundred years before, groups of suffragist women, headed by Susan B. Anthony, had lobbied for the inclusion of women for the first time as equals on whatever national commission should oversee displays and exhibits. At the same time, these women suggested a Woman's Pavilion on the fairgrounds, in honor of Queen Isabella, who had financed Columbus' journeys with her jewels. In this pavilion, should it have been built, would have been a statue to the queen and a place for women to rest and meet and discuss—in a world congress of women—matters pertaining to their progress. The women behind this project were known as the *Isabellas*.

Unfortunately, there were many other ladies who found the Isabellas strident and their symbol of Isabella unfortunate—for though she'd been the inspiration for Columbus, Isabella had also inspired the Inquisition. In Chicago these other women called themselves the *Women's Auxiliary* and wished to have a Woman's Building on the fairgrounds for the administration of female endeavors.

The Isabellas lobbied in Washington. The Auxiliary members, most of them married to influential men, lobbied in their parlors with much greater success. When the federal government passed the bill establishing the commission for the Exposition, the bill did not allow for women as part of the governing board. Instead Congressman William Springer of Illinois introduced an amendment to the bill setting up a Board of Lady Managers, an unfortunate title that the press was delighted to see, with no exact number of members specified. This board was to judge women's exhibits and to serve as an "auxiliary."

Somehow, through much backstage manipulation and unladylike maneuvering, the thrust of the women's board was removed from the feminist camp and handed, still undefined, to a governing board of women, two from each state and territory, plus nine women from Chicago and another eight members at large. The total count on this feminine list came to 117 women who still had not been given a charge nor any money for it should they get one. As president, they unanimously elected the beautiful, rich socialite Bertha Honoré Palmer.

And when Congress appropriated only forty-two thousand dollars for the entire administration of the national Exposition, Bertha Palmer went to Washington and spoke to the Congress in her charming way and they more than doubled the appropriation, earmarking thirty-six thousand dollars as the women's share for administration.

Bertha seized on a suggestion by one of her board that a Woman's Building should be built on the Exposition grounds to house the administrative functions of the Board of Lady Managers. But this building, once approved, evolved into a building that would be finished inside—as other Exposition buildings were not—to display the endeavors and workstyles of women from every country of the world and every state of the Union that could be coaxed into sending an exhibit to the fair.

In order to acquire these exhibits, the lady president found it necessary to travel extensively at her own expense in Europe. She wrote diplomatic letters—which had to be rewritten by even more diplomatic *men* not quite so obsequious to royalty—and did everything she possibly could to insure publicity for the grand endeavor. In the process, she annihilated the suffragists, alienated women artists, offended anyone who appeared to stand in her way—and if she had been uglier, poorer, or a bit less *charming,* she might have been displaced herself. But in an age when chivalry toward the grande dame was opening to full flower, Bertha Honoré Palmer, the innkeeper's wife, was a flowering success.

Margaret had every right to be worried about the Woman's Building, and about Bertha Palmer.

6

Two men came toward Margaret and her uncle, carrying a very long board, and they made it clear by their calls that the Marsh buggy was to be moved out of the way. They scurried to one side and waited until the men passed, then made their way to the loggia of the small building just ahead, where they hitched the horse.

She and Uncle Findley went inside and picked their way through the debris and pillars, trying to find an office or someone to talk to who might have some authority. There were few women on hand. Chancing the uncertain look of the upper stories they came upon a woman, dressed in traveling duster and bonnet, directing several workmen who were carrying heavy bundles into what possibly was a storage room; Margaret couldn't be certain.

The woman came to meet them and looked them over. Her manner was not welcoming. "You shouldn't be up here. There's no one here and you might be injured. Work is going on everywhere. You'll have to watch out and find your way out immediately. No one is allowed—"

Margaret stammered, "I'm here about a—I'd like to offer my help—"

"Unless you can carry boxes, I don't know what you can do. These things keep arriving, although it's much too soon. They shouldn't have sent exhibits until next spring. But every day more and more goods are sent—" Her voice was exasperated and Margaret decided that might be the woman's natural tone.

"Is it possible to speak to Mrs. Palmer?"

Now the woman really looked Margaret up and down, with a side glance toward Uncle Findley, who was looking, in Margaret's opinion, very sporty. The woman said, "Mrs. Palmer? Who suggested you might find Mrs. Palmer here?"

Margaret stammered again, "I just thought—"

"Mrs. Palmer is in Europe." The statement was lofty. Europe was heaven. "On the business of the Exposition."

Uncle Findley brought a gloved hand to his mouth and coughed politely. Margaret caught a twinkle in his eye and she took his cue.

"Perhaps you would be so kind, madam, as to leave word that her cousins from Kentucky dropped by to see her. This is Colonel Beauregard Honoré, from Lexington—"

"Yes, m'dear lady," said Uncle Findley in his best imitation drawl. "Tell Bertie we just stopped by to see her new palace—" He offered his arm to Margaret and the two of them swung about and started to walk away toward the stairs.

The woman called after them, "Did you say *Honoré?*"

"Yes, I did," Uncle Findley said over his shoulder, "Colonel Honoré, her cousin, twice removed—"

The woman was running after them now. "Oh, Colonel Honoré, I should have known. You're very like Mrs. Palmer. Of course you are."

Uncle Findley turned to confront the biddy. "We're so sorry. We didn't catch your name—Miss—?"

"Mrs. Dale. I'm from Toledo, myself. I'm not aware of Mrs. Palmer's return from Europe. Can I help in any way?"

"Miss Margaret Marsh, one of Mrs. Palmer's Kentucky connections, is looking for some work to do at the fairgrounds—as a type of public service, you understand—for the next few months while she's in residence here—"

This seemed to upset the lady even more. "Oh, Colonel," she said. "I don't know if you're aware or not, that every job or position we have for this building must be approved by committee and we must have had at least ten thousand applicants for everyone. Every girl in the Republic wants to be on hand for the fair—"

7

Margaret found her mother dressed to go out. She surmised that Knox, the butler, had told Mrs. Marsh that Uncle Findley was expected and Mrs. Marsh had planned accordingly. But when they caught her in the hall, she was cordial if a bit cool toward her late husband's uncle.

Mrs. Marsh bowed primly without lowering her head one iota and without extending her gloved hand. "Findley..." she said, letting the name trail off into the air.

Margaret had seen this performance before and it annoyed her. "Why don't you join us and have a cup of tea, at least," she encouraged her mother.

Knox came in just then and said the table was not yet ready and asked if they could wait in the drawing room. Her mother and uncle continued to be stiff and unbending. She had to carry the entire conversation, chattering about their trip to the fairgrounds and its unhappy results.

"You don't mean you went down there to get yourself named to their committees?" asked Mrs. Marsh with a malicious glance toward Uncle Findley.

He sat silent and Margaret was forced to answer "yes" to her mother's prejudiced question.

They chatted on about other topics and then Knox appeared again to say the table was ready and the meal was served. Mrs. Marsh said she really must be excused now and she went out as Margaret led the way to the dining room.

"Is Mrs. Riley still your cook?" asked Uncle Findley as they walked through the hallway.

"Yes, I didn't know you knew Mrs. Riley."

"Oh, I used to come out here and dine with your father. Just the two of us. Mrs. Riley and a houseman who came in twice a week were all the help your father kept inside. Cleaning people came in from time to time, but Riley was the only one on scene every day. And her little son. She's a good friend to this family, Margaret. I was afraid your mother might have discharged her."

"Mother? Why would she do that?"

"Oh," he said vaguely, "not fancy enough for your mother. Mrs. Riley is a plain cook and housekeeper—"

"You mean she was more my father's style than my mother's?"

"Something like that. Your father was a strong man, a good man, and he didn't like much fol-de-rol."

They were seated by this time and Knox moved around the table, filling the two wine glasses. Uncle Findley let his sit in front of him for a time and he watched the butler as if the man were made of some foreign matter. After Knox left the room, Findley smiled at Margaret and said, "We seem destined to meet across a dinner table, Margaret—" and lifted his glass in toast "—to the Honoré family of Lexington, Kentucky."

As he did so, Mrs. Marsh came into the dining room, stood at the edge of the Aubusson carpet and said crisply, "I made a call or two, Margaret. You may start work with the women's committees any time you choose. My friends said they'd be delighted to sponsor someone with your education and social standing." She turned then and left for her afternoon, her perfume floating backward in the rush of moving draperies.

In the silence that filled her wake, Uncle Findley began to laugh. He laughed and laughed and wiped his eyes and then, catching Margaret's, began again. When at last he could speak, he said in falsetto voice, "And that, m'dear, is how it's done by the upper clawses."

The waitress returned with their food, a light meal, on Uncle Findley's request; a roasted bird dressed with mushrooms instead of sauce, fruit salad, new potatoes accompanied by asparagus, although the season was a bit past for asparagus.

"Fine food," Uncle Findley said. "Riley has a light touch. You know, my brother Tommy was a florid man and heavy sauces killed him. He died young and I put it down to going into society, eating that rich food, drinking those well-aged, heavy spirits he favored and not walking anywhere. Terrible hard for him and the strain of it and his eating habits did him in."

A thought came to Margaret. She hesitated to bring it up, but it had bothered her for two years and she had no one else to ask.

"Was it that—rich living—that killed my father, Uncle? The doctors at the time were so vague about it. No one would explain why he died so suddenly and at such a young age. He was only forty-eight. Much younger than Grandfather. Grandfather lived till he was sixty-five—"

Uncle Findley's head was down. He was carving at his roasted fowl and didn't look up. He appeared not to have heard her.

"Uncle—"

He lifted his head and she saw tears in his eyes. "I wish you wouldn't ask me that, Maggie. It upsets me so. There's no good answer as to why God lets such things happen—"

That was not the question she'd asked him, but her own eyes were full of tears and her throat had closed so she couldn't speak. She let him eat his dinner in peace and questioned him no more.

8

In Chicago in the 1890s, it was still the custom, even in prosperous neighborhoods, for houses to have great porches or stoops that faced the street, offering a place where the occupants, sometimes accompanied by servants, could spend the warm-weather nights.

Only the Marsh household with its mysterious green carriage-door presented an unfriendly facade to the street. But on its north side, set within the line of the house proper and opening to the street, was a two-story porch facing the coolest and shadiest aspect of the weather and this had been built, not for the family itself, but for any live-in servants who might wish to sit there after their day's duties were complete or to come and go after hours without disturbing the household.

At 2:00 A.M. the figure of a woman emerged from this entrance and walked eastward along the side of the house toward Prairie Avenue, turning south on the street itself, walking along at a rapid pace.

The air was heavy with the solemn promise of May rain and as the woman walked along the entire sky lit dully with a general kind of lightning, followed by a grumbling thunder. This offstage illumination revealed the woman to be Margaret Marsh, dressed in casual costume, looking much shorter than usual because she wore no hat. She'd taken up a shawl and thrown it around her shoulders, intending to put it over her head if she needed it, but the air was so sullen, she let it fall loosely around her. Her skirts were full and free and she wore sturdy, high-topped walking boots. She often walked at night, but usually she went out much earlier in the evening.

In a steady, even pace she put one foot in front of the other, trying to walk away the malaise she felt. She gave no thought to safety. To her mind the world was safe, just unfathomable.

She'd gone to bed at her usual hour, fully expecting to sleep. And then she'd lain there, unable to find any rest at all because feelings of irritation and mistrust filled her. If she'd had any focus for these feelings, she might have been washed into sleep on a wave of ill-will toward one particular person. But instead, she had the same muddle-headed feelings she'd had other times in her life, as if the major scenes of a dream were being played out elsewhere and she was left to piece together the minor bits, sometimes building a wrong conclusion from scattered remarks of those around her—much as a child learns about the world, sometimes wrongly, by what it sees and hears, but what is not explained.

Her thoughts had oppressed her. She had stood and paced her bedroom. It was large as rooms went, but too small for her unhappiness. She did miss her father. Uncle Findley had been upset by her questions and had answered vaguely. No one was available to answer her questions, to make the way plain. She'd dressed hurriedly and gone out to smooth her mind by walking.

Margaret found a street she remembered and went left. This short street dead-ended near where the Illinois Central tracks went north and south behind the easternmost Prairie Avenue homes. She looked across the expanse of tracks. At this hour of the night there were no trains. The rich merchants of Prairie Avenue would not allow trains to disrupt their slumber. There was no way across the tracks here; no one was supposed to cross.

But Margaret was not afraid. Night and rainstorms, wherever she found them, were fascinating to her. Her feet remembered an old path that had been made in the way children often make paths—against the advice and wishes of adults. She'd not begun it, nor would she be the last person to cross over it. She walked down to the rails and found the place and went across, stepping high and finding her way by the light that is always there once eyes are accustomed to darkness.

On the other side she walked but a short distance across a grassy knoll to find what she was looking for—a small sandbar reaching out into the lake, somewhat larger than she'd remembered. She walked out to the end of it and stood looking at the shore. Anyone who believed Chicago was an inland city had never stood next to the lake like this, close enough to feel the power of it, close enough to sense that the lake was older than anything here and would remain dominant over man's inventions on its shore. Across the water, a flash of backlight showed on the horizon. There were whitecaps on the low line of waves now and the lightning occasionally organized itself into a jagged line. Suddenly the lightning struck the water just beyond her with a sharp crack, startling her. Her skirts billowed around her knees. She walked back and forth, hemmed in by the shortness of the finger of sand, but taking some comfort from the growing storm.

She should go back. Electrical storms near water are dangerous and any vertical on the flat shore of Lake Michigan could attract lightning. But still she kept pacing, taking on the displaced energy of the storm. Her body felt taut and angry; her heart pounded, not with fear, but overexcitement. Why she felt that way, she didn't know, but sometimes in her life she'd felt as if her body were not large enough to contain the feelings that moved within it, as if there had only to be one spark, one flash of lightning like this and she would catch fire, burst into flame as she'd heard eastern mystics could do.

The rain came in earnest, drenching her. With terrible reluctance, she put the shawl over her head, turned back toward her father's house, her house now, somewhat—but only a little—eased by the vastness of what she'd seen.

CHAPTER IX

The solarium of the Marsh mansion was on the second floor over-looking an enclosed garden below. The round ceiling of the room was shaped like the segments of an orange and these were glazed in glass obscura, which let in light without the nuisance of shades. The windows of the room itself were bowed outward, forming half a great circle. They hung like a prow out over the garden, as if reaching to meet the sun. The upper third of each of these windows, for there were three that formed the giant curve of the southern aspect, were a continuous design of leaded glass by William Morris, executed by a Chicago studio. This design provided flowers and vines and ruby-throated hummingbirds for the Chicago winters.

But in summer—it was now the end of July—the windows were partially opened and had to compete with the actual vine that had been prettily trained by a succession of gardeners to grow over and about them from some source far down along the battlements of the massive stone structure.

As a further conceit, the architect, a famous admiral of the Beaux Arts fleet, had cleverly planned that the ceiling windows would open like a flower into a star-shaped vision of sky and form an efficient updraft from windows opened below, thereby bringing in cool air in the hottest of Chicago summers. Because this air came from the garden, the room during warm weather was always filled with the scent of flowers and earth.

Visitors to the Marsh household might be amazed at the hidden closets in the bedrooms that opened to wall-sized cabinets at the touch of a secret spring. They might admire the spareness of the dining room, which seemed to hold nothing but two modest round tables, because its functions and necessities were also concealed in hidden silver and china vaults; they might enjoy the mosaics of the fireplace in what had been Mr. Marsh's study, or the brass and copper trim of the schoolroom fireplace. But it was the solarium that they always liked the best.

In this room on a late afternoon sat Margaret Marsh, staring out at the last sunlight illuminating the lovely windows, seeing nothing, dreaming, curled on a green damask divan. She faced the windows and did not see her mother enter, carrying a lap desk.

Mrs. Marsh stopped in the doorway, arrested by the sight of her daughter against the green of the furniture. What a beautiful picture for a mother to see! Margaret was dressed in a soft shade of peach— or was it actually a white dress glowing with the natural auburn coloring of Margaret, the light from the window diffused through the stained glass? Mrs. Marsh, whose hair had been dark and was now turning gray in wings of white against her temples and brow, knew she'd not been the source of her daughter's beauty, but she took pleasure in it and was often ashamed of this unexpressed thought: that Margaret would have been beseiged by more eligible beaus in her debut season five years ago if only she'd had the good sense to hide her intelligence and wit. That Margaret had then further educated herself beyond the "finishing school" polish had additionally narrowed the field of young men to whom she would prove alluring. This was just a fleeting notion, nothing that Mrs. Marsh allowed to cloud her enjoyment of her daughter from day to day. She felt guilty for having the thought.

The fond mother stepped into the room and sat down on a chair facing the window, but still Margaret did not turn, did not take up her usual straight-backed posture.

"Dear," said Mrs. Marsh, "is something wrong?"

Margaret started and turned, holding her hands cupped in her lap in an odd way. "No. I didn't know you'd come home. I was just— thinking."

"Are you—" Mrs. Marsh looked around to see if there were servants anywhere about "—are you unwell?"

Margaret blushed. "I've asked you not to do that. Just because a woman is—thinking—doesn't mean she is menstruating."

"Hush," said her mother. "You needn't be so technical." For the first time she noticed that Margaret was holding something in her lap. She leaned forward. "What is it? What do you have there?"

Margaret opened her hands briefly to show a bird, eyes closed, head to one side in her lap. It lay on its back with feet in the air.

Mrs. Marsh shuddered and pulled back. "It's dead," she told her daughter. "Don't hold on to that dead thing. Where did you get it?"

"It's not dead. There's a faint heartbeat. It was confused by the vine and the window. I heard a thud and went to look and there it was on the sill. I'm warming it so it won't go into a state of shock. Nothing seems to be broken. It's just unconscious—"

Mrs. Marsh shuddered again in distaste. "You shouldn't hold it like that. In your bare hands. Those things have lice and fleas. You'll revive it and it will be in pain and then what will we do with it?"

Margaret petted the wing of the bird with the tip of a finger. Her face was soft and thoughtful. "It's not in pain. I looked over its wings and its legs. They aren't limp or disfigured, so unless it dies of fright or a cat gets it, it will probably live and be able to fly away."

"Let me ring for the butler. I can't bear to see you handle that dreadful thing."

"I'm not handling it. I'll just let it lie here to warm it. I'm waiting."

The bird began to twitch slightly and Margaret brought her hand down to make a loose cage. "You see," she said and bent forward to look at it. But there wasn't a further sound; it continued to lie in her lap. "Its heart is beating ever so fast," she whispered to her mother.

They sat in silence for some moments and finally, to break the silence, Mrs. Marsh asked quietly if Margaret's day at the fairgrounds had been pleasant. A quick shadow of some emotion fell across Margaret's face and then passed. "Fine," she said in a voice that was crisp and unrevealing.

As if looking for a more comfortable position in which to hold the bird, she moved her body on the divan. Her feet tapped once or twice on the floor and then were stilled as if she had willed herself not to move. She began to count the stitches in the hem of the handkerchief that lay beneath the bird on her lap.

"Now I know there's something wrong," her mother said. "You haven't the least interest in needlework. I'm willing to listen—" She left the last part of the sentence open.

"Oh, it's just that—they do it *all* the time—" Margaret paused.

Mrs. Marsh had opened her lap desk and was sorting through letters to be answered. *"What* do they do? And *who* are *they?"*

Margaret appeared to hesitate, to hold back against her own inclination to confide.

"Well?" asked Mrs. Marsh. She looked up at Margaret. Margaret was blushing again, whether in anger or dismay, her mother couldn't tell.

Finally Margaret burst out: "I believe the theme of the fair was chosen on purpose to define the battleground. Imagine. A classical fair—and you couldn't invent the Greek intrigues that are being carried out there every day. Women! And *ladies* at that. They put such *emphasis* on being *ladylike*. And when they embrace, imaginary knives are almost visible in the backs of the objects of their affections. They criticize everything about one another while they smile and smile. And then—and then—" She gasped as if all this had been waiting on the tip of her tongue and had been held back by a great amount of force "—and then—"

"Well?" asked her mother again, interested. She'd suspected this might be the case. Hundreds of women, allowed for the first time to run a major portion of a major event—much frustrated energy would be released in those circumstances, she knew. She had a sense about those things and avoided large gatherings of ladies where men had no influence. In such circumstances, Mrs. Marsh believed, women were likely to reveal their silly side.

"Well," Margaret finished limply, "well, I just get so angry. The men predict these fiascoes. They say women can't get along, that they're not businesslike. And then the women go and prove them right. And it makes me so angry."

"Men argue, too, dear—" said Mrs. Marsh, still rustling through her papers. She looked up at Margaret. Margaret risked a hand away from the bird to wave this away. But Mrs. Marsh went on. "Men gossip and politic and scheme. It's just that they don't have men—or women—pointing at them while they do it. And men have every day to do it in—they are always at business every day, even in church, I believe. You've seen that yourself; the best pew, the best silk hat; the best carriage. A form of masculine display. It's not their wives they are pleasing. They do those things to please themselves. So there is no cure for it. It seems to be very human."

Margaret said, "At least in church, there's a referee—"

"That's why there is such pressure in the ministerial field, my dear," said her mother. "I think you might have noticed the number of society ministers who at some time suddenly find their call to go to the aborigines or the Chinese? Probably not long after dealing with the Women's Christian Betterment League—or handling a dispute over pew assignments—"

"Oh, Mother, be serious."

As if in agreement, there was a noise from the bird. It began to peep, weakly at first and then with a steadiness not unlike a tiny bell persistently rung. Margaret opened her hands again and said, "How it does complain. It isn't moving at all, but listen to that racket—"

Her mother again gave her involuntary shudder. "I don't like wild things in the house." Her hand went to her handsome coiffure. "They're not meant to be and they're—disturbing."

"It's only a tiny bird—" Margaret said, bending down now in a fluidity of motion Mrs. Marsh envied. "Look at it. It's so little. And it might be lost without us—"

"Or not suffer because its agony has been extended," Mrs. Marsh said. "You are prolonging its anguish and when it wakes—if it does—then it will get loose and fly about and we'll have to watch it suffer or kill it to rid ourselves of it." She thought she might make a lesson out of this to good effect.

She continued. "Something like these worthy causes you seem attracted to elsewhere. If you wouldn't give your time and strength and, may I say, generous contributions, these things would die peaceful deaths of themselves and they wouldn't founder, half alive and half dead. Can't you find an interest in some inanimate object?" She refrained from mentioning "a young man." That would never do, to say *that* to Margaret, but Mrs. Marsh thought it.

"Oh, Mother, be serious."

"I'm dreadfully serious about this—stay out of these semipublic endeavors. Arrange life for serenity. That's the way *I* like to have things arranged—"

Everywhere they'd gone in the world, Margaret had always watched her mother's arrangements toward serenity with pleasure. Mrs. Marsh did arrange life; not the other way around. She'd been that way long before her husband's death, and remained so after. She seemed to have a central plumb line that established her equilibrium and nothing, not earthquake or flood or lost luggage, could make her tilt to one side or the other. While Margaret enjoyed the pleasant atmosphere that always surrounded her mother wherever they went, she sometimes suspected—felt inwardly—that questions of importance were left behind, unmet, unaddressed.

Her mother had spoken out once at Margaret's first involvement with the suffragists' cause and then had been silent. That, too, was her mother's way. She didn't nag or harangue. She spoke her objection and if it went unheeded, she dressed and went out to the opera and enjoyed herself. In this way, her mother was freer than

Margaret could ever hope to become. Her mother answered to no one and refused to engage in quarrels that required someone to answer to her. Her mother, Margaret knew, *was* the lady whom the women in the Woman's Building hoped they were.

But did that mean that to be a woman and a lady, one had to be removed from reality and day-to-day concerns, living in a falsely smooth world of one's own creation?

Margaret hoped that was not so.

She didn't look directly at her mother, but kept her head down, watching the bird. It was a small songbird, brown and white. Now that it had begun to move slightly under her hands, twisting into her skirts, skittering to right itself, and she could feel its tiny claws through the cloth, she was beginning to share some of her mother's apprehension. What if it should get loose in the room?

"Please," her mother said, "let me call someone." Mrs. Marsh rose and went to the bell-pull and rang.

"It's coming around, Mother. Listen. Hear how much stronger it sounds. Hear it squeak?"

Near the fireplace was a small table display of various objects, among them a basket with a lid that held fresh handkerchiefs. Still holding the bird, Margaret gathered up her skirts and went to the table and said, "If you'll take those handkerchiefs from the basket, I can put the bird in there."

Mrs. Marsh was not hard-hearted. She put down her letter papers and between them they managed to get the bird into the basket, which at Margaret's suggestion, had been lined with one of the handkerchiefs. When the butler arrived he was sent away for some warm water and a face towel so that Margaret might freshen herself. Margaret watched the bird carefully and within minutes it was so lively within the loosely woven basket she was afraid it would injure a foot by getting one caught. She took the basket to the window and with a tender admonition to the bird that it "be careful" she set the container on the windowsill and lifted the lid. "Goodbye, little thing," she told it, and then shut the window.

Margaret turned back to Mrs. Marsh with a rueful smile, communicating her sense of having proved something to anyone who wished to learn.

"It can fly again," she said and came to sit once more on the green divan. The butler brought in the water and she cleaned her hands and brushed off her skirt because her mother was watching. After the man had withdrawn, they sat on in the growing twilight.

Finally Mrs. Marsh said, "Some people are coming through town and are not to be avoided. I will have to ask them to dine. They're from the club—you remember where I stayed last spring? The island that your father never had time to go to. The place with the white deer."

"Yes," Margaret said, "I remember. You said it was dull."

Mr. Marsh had been one of the organizers of the club, but had never sampled its pleasures. The club itself had been established when several men involved in shipping and the railroads had been precluded by the Interstate Railway Law of 1887 from getting rebates from the railroad line on their extensive shipping. Mr. Marsh had advised his clients against opposing the implementation of this law. Various groups of men had gathered in Chicago, Cincinnati, New York, and Rochester—men of substance who shipped that substance by rail. They wanted a way to keep their cake and eat it in a railroad car. Someone—some said it was Jay B. Darling—had come up with the idea of shipping their private cars at no expense to a place far enough away to make it worthwhile, a place where the common everyday sorts who lived in the area could be controlled. Someone suggested an island and the Sporting Isle was born. All they had to do was acquire an offshore island and there could be a number of interesting pursuits enjoyed there. The cost of the whole thing could be shunted through the railroads' books without anyone the wiser.

Mrs. Marsh had visited Sporting Isle for two winters. She found the season, Christmas through May 1, dull, but after her seasons in New York and Boston, she often needed a slight rest. Unfortunately, island society is small and in a weak moment she'd gone to dinner at the Chestertons'. Now she must return that courtesy in her own city.

"We'll need some young men. Some of your friends might come to dinner. To meet Mrs. Stanley Chesterton and her three daughters."

"What are the Misses Chesterton like? Are they very silly?"

"Well, yes, I do believe they are. And their mother as well. She is the southern lady, you know, even though she comes from the North. She has taken on the worst of the style and her girls giggle and have thin, high-pitched voices. They are very charming in that way," she finished wryly.

Margaret knew any number of young men, but they were intelligent and would be terribly annoyed with women who couldn't make conversation.

"I suppose I could ask those Baxter boys," Margaret said. "That younger one was so funny. I didn't know what to say to him when he told me my eyes are green. Did he think I'd never noticed?" What Margaret really meant in her own heart was that she never knew what to say to compliments, especially those by handsome young men. But she went on in a brittle way that she'd learned from her mother, "I don't think the two of them add up to one good mind between them. And they're southern types, too. Don't you remember the story Father told, about how their father went around promoting the South all through the war and was about to be arrested? And then Father went out into the streets with his friends on that march to save old Mr. Baxter's skin in the name of free speech and the Constitution and then Lincoln himself called off the arrest?"

Her mother laughed. "How could you and I remember? Your father and I weren't even married until three years later. You only remember the anecdote. What I do know is that from that time on, Mr. Baxter cut your father dead every time he saw him—" Privately, Mrs. Marsh believed her husband had made that march because he thought his Uncle Findley, who was selling supplies anywhere he could, might be next to be arrested.

"Well, I'm going to have specially happy thoughts when inviting the sons of that old martyr for dinner. Shall I?" Margaret went to telephone.

And while she was at it, to liven up the evening, she sent Henry around to the Tremont with an invitation for Uncle Findley.

2

Arthur Baxter was surprised when his brother did not resist an invitation to dine at the Marsh household. When Arthur, who'd taken the call, asked if Steven would be willing to attend a dinner for some out-of-town friends of the Marshes, Steven looked up from his book and said he would go. Amazed by this, Arthur returned to the telephone and asked Miss Marsh if evening clothes were required. He knew Steven would resist that in summertime. But it was to be an informal party, beginning in late afternoon.

The Marshes had invited two other young men to round out the young people's party and only Uncle Findley to represent great age. That was somewhat of a surprise to Mrs. Marsh, because Margaret had somehow forgotten to mention Uncle Findley until they were arranging the table seating. And to further annoy Mrs. Marsh, on the afternoon of the event, Uncle Findley was late.

Because the Marshes' home was famous, the guests, after being

introduced to one another and told there was a delay, asked to tour
the house. Because he held back at this suggestion, Steven was left
with one of the Misses Chesterton by default. The Misses Chesterton,
he felt, came all of a group, with three heads and appropriate ap-
pendages. He could not remember their individual names and when
one spoke, the others chimed in, as if they were a chorus. He had
taken note of the earrings of this young lady as, at first, offering
some clue as to which Miss Chesterton she might be. But, during
the course of early conversation, first one and then the other of the
remaining two took identical earrings from their purses and put them
on. Steven was dismayed and he noticed the other guests watching
this adornment with what appeared to be equal discomfort.

Whichever Miss Chesterton graced his arm, they went about the
house, a house not as large as Steven's own home, with the proper
air of respect for the architect who had died during the construction
of the little masterpiece. In the library, Steven asked Miss Chesterton
if she liked to read.

"I rather like to play croquet, although I do have a library. Each
of us do—"

"Do you mean that in your household each of you has a room of
one's own for a library?" Steven considered a house with three libraries to be a wonderment. That would be the sort of a house he
would like. A large kitchen and a library for everyone, so each might
study without interruption from another.

"What a pleasant idea," he said.

"Oh, no," said Miss Chesterton. "You mistake my meaning. Although I do believe I have a book or two in my room. Yes, I do
believe a book was given to me last year. But the *library* is a collection
of leatherbound volumes my father had made up for each of us by
a firm in New York—" Miss Chesterton said *New York* as other New
Yorkers do; as if there could be no doubt as to the supremacy of the
selected books. "They are boxed up in storage. The books, I mean.
My father had the company of decorators make a selection for each
one of us in proper-colored bindings and on our marriage each will
have her library complete. And then we won't have to bother with
books when there will be so much else to do—" she finished in a
rush. And then blushed when she noticed Steven looking at her
oddly.

"Of course, I'm not even engaged," she said wistfully. "Not yet."

Uncle Findley arrived just then, rescuing Steven and the others.
The old man, looking very dapper in his summer best, was introduced all around. Mrs. Marsh was quite annoyed to learn he'd walked
from downtown while they'd been waiting, but she said nothing

since Margaret was pleasantly chatting with Mrs. Chesterton and Mrs. Marsh understood that sacrifice.

At dinner, the talk was of tennis and the Sporting Isle, where the Chestertons and Mrs. Marsh had met. The Chestertons were actually from Great Neck, New York, but wintered on the island.

"There is another island club being constituted nearby," said Mrs. Chesterton. "Others have taken up the idea and are going through with their organization. I understand—" she lowered her voice and leaned forward, although the entire table could hear her "—I understand they're planning a gambling casino on *their* island. On *our* island, we're fresh air fiends—!"

She laughed and Mrs. Marsh had an immediate and accurate recall of the ladies of the hotel verandah, languishing through the afternoons, their parasols in full flower, rousing only to play an hour's worth of croquet before a late dinner. And if they played tennis, they played tennis indoors at Jay B. Darling's Playhouse.

Uncle Findley, who knew a thing or two about Sporting Isle and the men who went there, asked, "Does Mr. Chesterton enjoy the island life, ma'am?"

"Oh, yes, he certainly does. At least, it gives me the opportunity to encourage Mr. Chesterton to let business go for a time and seek enjoyment in the out-of-doors."

"Yes, no doubt," said Uncle Findley drily, although no one else at the table, except possibly Mrs. Marsh, could have had a hint of his meaning.

But Mrs. Chesterton wasn't done with islands. She and the "girls" were on their way north to visit a new hotel on Mackinac.

"Another island," murmured Mrs. Marsh.

"I do like islands," said Mrs. Chesterton. "The society can be controlled on an island. One doesn't have to see anyone one doesn't wish to see at an exclusive island club."

Mrs. Marsh doubted that. After all, she had met the Chestertons there. But she was demure.

Someone at the table changed the topic to the work Miss Margaret Marsh was doing at the fairgrounds. What had she seen? What was her contribution to the work there?

Margaret described her first view of the fairgrounds itself, leaving out the mischievous prank she and Uncle Findley had played. She explained that she'd first been sent to a building downtown—the Rand McNally building—where the Board of Lady Managers had their offices. There she'd been trained to fill out forms on exhibits and to log in items for display.

"They were quite disappointed that I wasn't a typewriter," she said. "They didn't know quite what to do, at the beginning, with a biologist—but now that I'm at work on the actual materials out at the fairgrounds—"

Something fluttered in the direction of Mrs. Chesterton and she exclaimed, "A biologist? Oh, my dear." She quickly looked round the table—which was in itself round—as if she wanted to stop the conversation right now and take her daughters away. There was no telling what turn biology would lend to the conversation. But Miss Marsh was not dwelling on biology, thank heaven.

Miss Marsh said she'd been assigned to unpack boxes. There were items coming in from all over the United States and its territories and from all over the world, exhibits of women's handiwork, of their technical and mechanical skills, and of their charitable projects. All needed to be handled carefully and put in some order to await interior decoration of the building when much of the materials would be incorporated into some finer whole. Mrs. Palmer had had her way in the matter of a New York firm, selected by herself, to do the decoration. Mrs. Palmer had said, Margaret reported, that there must be harmony in the whole as the diverse exhibits were interwoven in a grand design. Mrs. Palmer believed, Margaret said sharply, that some persons had a talent for interior design and some did not.

Mrs. Chesterton, feeling she was one of the former, said, "I can certainly agree with that. Tell me, what is Mrs. Potter Palmer like? Is she very formidable? I've heard she is so terribly soignée. Is she pleasant to know?"

Uncle Findley cleared his throat and said, "The Chicago newspapers know how to treat Mrs. Palmer. The *Daily Inter-Ocean* has been putting her regularly on page three and yesterday it was right next to an article about a thirteen-year-old immigrant girl who was forced to marry a fifty-year-old man—"

Steven Baxter coughed and Mrs. Marsh cast a look at Margaret, who found an immediate interest in what was on her plate.

Arthur Baxter, graceful in company, said, "Mrs. Palmer is a friend of my—our—mother. She's very public-spirited. At least, they are always having meetings at various homes to discuss better working conditions for the sort of woman who must be employed in shops and mills. They do things for women who—well, who are down on their luck or are sent to madhouses and run into the law—that sort of thing. I think she's very earnest about it all—women's matters, I mean."

Margaret forgot she was hostess and snapped, "I don't think the bulk of the women's question can be solved by visiting madhouses and jails. The majority of women do not reside there—yet."

"Margaret—" began her mother, belatedly.

But Mrs. Chesterton was there before her. "Do you think there might be some chance for me to be presented to her while we are here?"

"Margaret knows her Kentucky cousins, once removed," said Uncle Findley.

"Twice-removed," said Margaret, managing not to smile. "But they've gone out of town, I believe."

"The world," Uncle Findley continued, "seems to be divided into parts, like Gaul: those Mrs. Potter Palmer knows, those who want to know her, those she will let know her and those she wants to know—such as royalty and New York's four hundred. It's difficult for those of us here, country folk as we are, to know just which part we—or you, madam—belong to." Here he gave such a gracious nod to the New York matron she was confused, uncertain whether she should take offense or not, so she claimed none of the divisions for herself and her daughters and the moment passed.

This time Margaret turned to look at her mother, who looked back and offered no help whatsoever, but smiled and nodded to Knox about something the second man was about to serve.

Steven Baxter took up the banner of conversation. "I beg your pardon, Miss Marsh, but I understand Mrs. Palmer believes every woman should have a fine home life, but if she can't, if she can find no good man to provide it—or through other circumstances—and a lady is forced to work in the marketplace, then the woman who goes to business should find there a fair and equitable wage and good working conditions. Women do need special working conditions. That, I think, is a fair summary of her position according to my mother."

There was a slight pause in the conversation while some portion of the dinner was passed and then the conversation resumed.

Margaret, blushing, said to Steven, "I think you're generous and understanding about Mrs. Palmer. I believe you are quite correct that she has been very active in such causes and for that she's to be complimented. But she could solve some of those problems just mentioned by asking her husband and her husband's friends, and the husbands of her lady friends, to establish better conditions for their women employees. Taken altogether, the members of her social circle probably are the major employers of women in the city. But no, she works through the tedious meetings of women's clubs and the newspaper publicity attendant thereto—the long way round, I think—"

"Oh, my," said one of the Misses Chesterton, "I do love melon. I don't believe I've had such a sweet bit of melon this year—"

"The newspapers seem to have given Mrs. Palmer a terrible drubbing lately. All that headline stuff about the Board of Lady Managers. They've made the ladies into a laughingstock. You're not part of that?" asked Arthur.

"No. I just work there. That is, I volunteer my time. And I must say, Mrs. Palmer is truly a lady and a manager. In managing, I might say, she has no peer. She even went to Washington and spoke eloquently before Congress to obtain funds for her building—"

"Her building?" This was Steven.

"It's definitely her building and I can safely say I think she regards it so, no matter what she might say otherwise out of modesty and politeness."

Margaret was quite surprised that the Baxter boys knew so much about their community and was sorry she'd inflicted the Chestertons on them. She'd thought they were brainless, but Steven, especially, seemed very bright. She steered the conversation into more calm waters. She explained how she'd also been assigned to a committee that was working for a Children's Building to be erected on the grounds near the Woman's Building. She did not mention that in this she felt inadequate. She'd been around very few children and no infants in her life. The idea of teeming youth—from babes to fourteen-year-olds—climbing the apron of the Children's Workshop to reach the lap of Margaret Marsh terrified her. But her inner doubts lent a softness to her features that had not been apparent when she'd spoken of Mrs. Palmer. Her cheeks looked pink in the candlelight. From that night on, that was how Steven thought of her, with her green eyes looking thoughtful, talking of children as if—he thought—she could nurture all. She was the great, beautiful, auburn-haired mother of the world that night and Steven saved the vision in his heart.

3

Steven and Arthur Baxter escorted the various traveling members of the party to their homes, including Uncle Findley, who wanted to walk because of the pleasant weather, but Steven insisted he come along in the victoria.

Several days later, when he and Margaret had another outing, Uncle Findley said, "Those Baxter boys look like great specimens to me, Maggie. You ought to set your cap for one of them. I can't believe old Baxter fostered those two. He must have been in his sixties when that youngest one was born. By the way, the young one asked me all sorts of questions after we'd dropped off the visiting royalty—most of his questions were about you—"

Margaret blushed. She wanted to ask what Steven had asked, but was afraid of being teased more by Uncle Findley. But he only said, "You'd do a lot worse than that young man, Maggie. I take it his mother is still living—"

"Yes, she was much younger than the father. Almost thirty years younger, I believe."

"Potter Palmer did that, too. Married a much younger woman. Yet Mrs. Baxter and she are different, don't you think—"

"From what I've heard," Margaret said, "Mrs. Baxter seems to be a quiet, homebound sort. Very fond of her children and interested in religion and spiritualism."

"Well, her son is interested in you. I don't doubt you'll hear more of him this summer."

CHAPTER X

1

That his mother's love for him was special had been brought home to Steven Baxter many times, but he put down her excessive devotion to the loss of his father while he and Arthur and Fanny were still small. Steven believed that as the youngest, he had become a replacement for the father as object of his mother's full heart.

But Fanny and Arthur saw their mother's devotion to Steven as unhealthy; domineering in such a subtle way, it undermined Steven's sociability, approving as Mama Delight Baxter was about his lone forays into the library rather than the ballroom. Steven was the arm on which she leaned, the mind with which she consulted, and consequently, he acted the part of a person much older than his twenty-four years. His interests were solitary and in them he had his mother's tacit approval, since there was no danger in having to share her knight if no other human—besides Arthur—became his friend. To reward his faithfulness, Mama lavished all her affection and concern on "her boy." And if called down on a particularly overbearing act of selfish kindness—which Fanny and Arthur had become adept at detecting—Mama would sputter and weep and say she was only trying to do what was best. Steven, who'd had a "delicate constitution" as a youth, had once attracted such attentions in the matter of his health. But he was grown now and strong, although pale from indoor study and too much introspection.

From his father he'd inherited a sharp, inquiring mind and from his mother, a soft and encompassing nature. He loved his fellow man and wherever he found himself in the world, he went about quietly trying to do something to improve the lot of those less fortunate than himself.

He kept such endeavors quiet, not even telling Arthur, for even in these activities—donations to settlement houses, funds for lending libraries, gifts of money and goods to orphanages and cradle organizations—even of these his mother could become jealous. He understood better than anyone the oppressiveness of his mother's love. He just didn't know how to return her gently to her proper role.

No one did.

2

Arthur Baxter had admired the butler at Mrs. Marsh's. That butler seemed to know how to run an establishment and didn't appear to have to be directed by Mrs. Marsh constantly. Arthur believed that Mama Delight should have a butler like that, but Mama, on learning of Artie's plan, vetoed it. She was not going to hire a butler. They were so domineering. She preferred a housekeeper. She reckoned without her daughter, Fanny. Fanny and Fanny's husband were going to bring friends to the fair when it opened next year and they wanted Chicago to appear a cosmopolitan place. And arrangements should be made soon so that all would have time to become customary before the onslaught of visitors began to arrive in May of 1893. That gave them ten months in which to accomplish perfection.

"In no case," wrote Fanny from New York, "should the servants appear to be under new employ—"

Arthur understood perfectly and concurred. He well knew how easterners thought of his city. Floating in limbo on a column of hot air—somewhere between a swamp and a sluggish river on the banks of a lake.

"If it was in Egypt, they would love it no matter what," grumbled Steven, who didn't care what the easterners thought.

But now the World's Columbian Exposition was becoming a reality and the houses of Chicagoans would for the first time be under scrutiny of their eastern friends.

Fanny told Arthur to find a butler no matter what Mama said and Fanny said that if Mama objected, she, Fanny, would pay for all the staff with her own money. Fanny also said the house was to be put back together and there were to be flowers in every room, even the bedrooms, every day. She wanted the household to come to life. She said she wanted to see the coal bills. And if they didn't use enough in her opinion, she would order some shipped in. She said she didn't want to hear any more reports of Mama languishing in her suite, rummaging in trunks in the ballroom. She wanted her mother to be happy, to dress in something other than black or dark blue or gray. Their father had been dead for nearly twenty years.

"The World's Columbian Exposition looks like the perfect time," wrote Fanny to Arthur, "to sweep aside all Mama's objections and make the house a home—"

Once Mama understood that Fanny was firm about paying the bills, Mama said she would do it herself and she even allowed Arthur to select the butler.

The butler, Arthur told his mother, could "help the fellows with their clothes." Mama thought the butler should do more than that.

Steven decided the drive under the porte cochere should be paved with macadam and the stables should be cleaned and restaffed with competent help that knew how to handle more than one horse at a time.

"I think," said Arthur, "we should buy another carriage. Preferably a swift trap."

Things could be carried too far, thought Mama. She bought a new victoria. And she had other ideas. Now that the carpets had been put back into place and the window hangings renewed, the furniture reinstalled and the books treated for leather-rot and tucked away on the shelves, now that Fanny's generous bouquets were in every room, Mama thought she might write away to the southern Baxter connection. There were young ladies who would be glad to visit Mama Baxter and her two handsome sons. She would have musicians in and have a dansant. They would be very gay for the fair.

Mama wrote to every auntie and maiden child she could remember. She wrote to Agnes Scott College, the school she'd chosen for Fanny, to invite entire classes of young college women to luncheons and teas during their visits to Chicago. She would have an Agnes Scott Day for Fanny. There would be special guides hired by Mama to accompany her visitors to the fair. Mama, when she put her mind to a thing, had a tendency to overdo.

Among the plans she made was one in which Steven was to escort her through her excursions to and from the fair. In order to please her, it would be necessary that the boys not attend school again for some time, postponing their reentry into Princeton until the winter term of 1894. That meant that they would be out of school for almost two and a half years.

Steven was shocked to learn of this. But Mama had written to his college and given notice of the change in plans.

"But I have so much to do," he said. "I wanted to finish next year."

"You'll have plenty of time. And you'll have time after Arthur's wedding to handle any subjects you may have missed."

He knew Arthur's wedding was planned for November of 1894. Steven could feel his life escaping from him in the busyness of an imposed social scene. He hated society. He preferred to spend time alone, to study in a corner of the house, unreached by servants or relatives or telephone. He did not like a small lunch brought to him on a tray or the curtains adjusted behind his head. He wanted to be alone.

To escape, Steven would take the victoria out by himself and drive until he found a place along the lake where he could sit and read. The weather was warm. The best breezes were off the lake and they blew most freshly when not around Mama.

"Where have you been?" Mama would ask anxiously. This was her darling son. Where did he go on these melancholy rambles? She didn't treat Arthur this way, she knew, but Steven seemed so young, so refined and tender.

Steven, for his part, felt pressured. Somehow, in his mind, he always felt as if the time to be allowed him was too short for what he hoped to accomplish in life. He had no vocation, but he loved learning and he didn't want to be denied access to the academic world for two and a half years while he was put through his social paces like a tame pony. Arthur, his best friend and brother, was no substitute for the give and take of debate, the thrill of discovery. Whether Steven was discovering an ancient Greek already well-discovered, or the precision of mathematics, learning had a comfortable predictability and he liked that.

He went off one day and no one could find him, but that wasn't unusual. This time he'd left the victoria and taken a cab. He went southward through the city, without conscious destination and yet, when they were within blocks of the new University of Chicago, he'd directed the driver to take him there. If he could not have Princeton, he'd pick up the thread of something and if it could not be finished here, he would work it back into his Princeton degree at some later date. Or he would simply study alone in Chicago at the college for the sake of study. He must have some way to occupy his mind while his feet were expected to dance.

After a private consultation with Dr. Harper, Steven went out to walk around on the Midway Plaisance where portions of the fair, were being installed just to the south of the college. Everything was under construction, but visitors were allowed. Steven walked along, looking at the odd buildings that were going up in great variety, at the beginning of a great mechanical construction called a Ferris wheel that was taking shape near the stub end of the concourse. What intriguing patterns these earnest endeavors made against the sky. He walked on and eventually he could see the bulk of the main grounds looming ahead of him; large buildings covered with fret-works of scaffoldings, the whole edging up to the waters of the lake beyond.

On impulse, he went into the grounds and, after several false attempts, found Margaret Marsh at work among her boxes. She looked up and smiled at him. Again he was struck by the motherliness of her. Her face was smudged with something and there was a delicate white dust in her hair. As staff was applied to the buildings, the entire fairgrounds had now turned to this dull white in its progress. Steven thought Margaret looked charming and there was, again, the shock of her green, green eyes.

"Hello," he said. He felt doltish and stupid, but it served.

"Have you come to help?"

"Is it allowed?"

"Oh, I should think so," she said, laughing at his look. He had just noticed that there were few men in the place and those that were there appeared to be workmen of the building trades. "I think we can trust you," Margaret said. "You won't damage the goods."

Margaret led Steven on a tour and she was pleased that he knew so much about the world and the work of women in it. He even knew about laces, since his mother had a fine collection, and when he saw the African materials, he was able to explain some of their uses to Margaret. He stayed with her for the balance of the afternoon. She, who had never cared what others thought, noticed the women around her looking at Steven and smiling gently. He *is* such a gentle man, she thought, he seems to call forth those gracious benedictions.

They went home together. He stopped at her door and they went up the front steps so that he might pay his respects to her mother. But Mrs. Marsh was out. She was dining in the city, the butler told Margaret. On impulse, defying all convention, Margaret invited Steven to dine with her and they spent several hours talking and laughing. They discovered they shared some of the same ideas about Society with a capital *S*.

For the first time, Margaret noticed she'd somewhere taken up the habit of touching another's hand as she spoke. She did not remember ever doing this before, but surely it must be a habit picked up from some friend or other. Or could she only want to touch the hand of this man, who seemed to her to be the most understanding man she'd ever met? His ideas, his interests, were so close to hers, as if they were one person who spoke and yearned as one. Margaret, who knew many young men, had always felt separated from them finally by the ruggedness of their interests. She didn't care for any sport but tennis. She hated parlor games. She could barely stand croquet, which she played only when it became a way to escape what she thought of as "silly chatter" on a verandah. Her interests in life were serious and she'd always had a devil of a time in not letting her seriousness show. With Steven it didn't matter. Or rather, it did matter very much. He was pleased with her seriousness and she with his. Yesterday she would not have cared if any young man had approved of her or not. And now here she was with one of those Baxter boys, touching his hand, talking to him as if they had always known each other.

He left and she thought of him. She felt panic when she could not remember the color of his eyes. He was constantly telling her of the surprise he felt at the color of her own. She remembered his nose. He had a wonderful nose; not coarse or broad like some. Straight and slightly flared at the nostril. His ears, she'd noticed, were perfect.

What are perfect ears, asked the mind of the biologist. Be still, said the girl's mind. I don't want to talk to you tonight. I'm going to dream a little—

In the ride north along the lakefront, Steven had his own thoughts. Margaret, Maggie, a beautiful tall suffragist. Her hands were long and slim and elegant; her shoes were handmade because of her long slim foot. Yet in Steven's mind she was petite. He was at least four inches taller than she, but he forgot *he* was five foot eleven. He saw her among her boxes, waiting for him with green eyes, her mind full of wonderful things he could talk to her about forever.

At his right, the lake and the sky seemed to be one tonight, as if there were no division at the horizon. Steven saw this as an omen, although such conditions are common to lakes. In the cool evening, the warm lake evaporated into the arms of the air; the air had accepted the rising vapor of the lake into itself. There was no end to either. They would be like this till well past dawn.

3

Steven Baxter was in love and all his friends except his mother—and Steven himself—knew it. He, who had chatted with various servants in hostesses' orangeries, who had sat up front with numerous coachmen on large outings, suddenly began to make social arrangements, was willing to settle down on the most prominent settee. Shameless as a matchmaker, he maneuvered and plotted in his own behalf. But he did it half-unconsciously, as if keeping from himself the obvious conclusion of these earnest activities.

He looked at the world around him in search of opportunities— which he presented to his brother and his friends as opportunities for cultural advancement. If others noticed that cultural advancement always included Miss Margaret Marsh with Steven by her side, Steven was unaware of the change in his behavior. In his own mind, he was "settling in" in his old home of Chicago, the place where he'd so seldom been in residence.

Margaret, for her part, may have been equally unaware, but she had also become even more beautiful. Her eyes had become larger, and if possible, greener and more luminous in her slim oval face. The gowns of the 1890s were perfect for her figure and wherever and whenever she appeared in public in evening dress, her laces, satins, scallops and fans were profusely described in the press with additional attention to her work for the Children's Building and the suffragist cause.

Far from being "put off" by this notoriety, Steven was pleased. He fully expected any female he might have an interest in to be involved in such things until she married. Perhaps even after. Until, he thought, she had her first child.

During early summer, Margaret's speeches and talks were given, not for the cause of women's suffrage, but to earn funds for the children's arcade for the fair.

When Margaret had first come home from Boston, she'd been assigned, in addition to her duties of unpacking some of the exhibits, to the committee on children's programing. At first, she'd felt out of her element and longed for the packing boxes to be her only station, but the work of the committee, as it progressed—or did not progress—revealed to her the reason why Mrs. Palmer had assigned her there.

The men of the Columbian commission had overlooked children completely, evidently feeling that children—and also the mothers who might have children in tow—had no business being part of the projected scene. When the women pointed out that mothers who wished to tour the fair might need childcare or a safe place to leave their children, the men said rightly enough that there was no money at such a late date to assign to such a purpose.

In her earnest discussions with Steven, Margaret would tell him of the conflict at the Exposition grounds, of the day-to-day battles therein and of the ways the committee of women to which she was assigned hoped to display items of interest to children, to hold classes in education for the deaf and blind, to have household activities demonstrated, to set up a nursery in which young "nurse girls" could be trained on the spot to use hygenic and pleasant methods in child-care. There would also be, on the premises, children's literature and demonstrations of gymnastics on specially built equipment. The cost of the project was established at forty-thousand dollars.

But the men of the governing commission said no.

Not long after Margaret had confessed this lack of funding to Steven Baxter, there came an unexpected offer from several important businessmen of Chicago to meet the cost of a building for children. The businessmen proposed to underwrite the entire program.

This time Mrs. Palmer said no.

She wanted shares in the endeavor to be offered nationwide as well as throughout the community of Chicago, so that everyone would feel a part of the planning for children, both at the fair and in the future.

"And we need attractive spokeswomen," Mrs. Palmer said. For the benefit of the children's arcade, she opened her own Lake Shore establishment to two hundred intimate friends for a fee for the first in a series of bazaars. Margaret was asked to be one of the hostesses.

Steven brought his mother.

Mrs. Delight Baxter subscribed for a thousand-dollar pledge in the name of childhood. And she thought Miss Marsh quite lovely. A wonderful girl. But not, she said to Steven, *southern.*

"Mrs. Palmer," said Delight to her son, "is southern. She has Kentucky connections. Miss Marsh, I believe, is from Boston, is she not?"

"From Chicago, Mother," Steven said. Steven had nothing against the South, but he preferred Miss Marsh in all things. He patted his mother's hand in gratitude for the thousand dollars and gave another thousand in his own name.

"I hope you and Miss Marsh will become great friends," Steven said to his mother. "She is very intelligent and interested in the vote for women."

"Not for every sort of woman, I should think," said Mama Baxter, blushing. She was looking at Miss Marsh, standing straight and tall and willowy beside the newel post in the entrance hall of Mrs. Palmer's mansion, saying gracious things to all who came near. "Not every woman is as pure of motive as Miss Marsh. The baser sorts might compromise the vote—"

That was as far as Mama Delight wanted to go with her thoughts on women's suffrage. Words like *compromise* could make one blush.

"Well," said Steven, thinking of some men he knew who never failed to vote, "I suppose not, I suppose not—"

He, too, was looking at Margaret and he thought she looked like a delicate flower standing there against the Moorish paneling, wearing a floating dress of deep gold that brought out her green eyes and highlighted her auburn hair. Everywhere in Mrs. Palmer's household were paintings of beautiful women and Steven had been privileged on another occasion to see the gallery of Mrs. Palmer's growing art collection. But none of the beauties displayed could match, in his mind, the live vision at the end of the stairs.

"Arthur will see you home, Mother. I'll wait for Miss Marsh."

"But Steven. I came this afternoon with you. Arthur said he was spending the afternoon downtown."

"I arranged with Artie to meet us here. He'll be along. He just didn't want to listen to Margaret's talk—"

Mrs. Baxter nodded. "No, I can see he wouldn't be interested in programs for children—"

"Oh, no, it's just that we've heard it two or three times. I'll get you some punch."

He introduced his mother to a dowager on her left and abandoned her to wonder how it was that her sons had heard Miss Marsh and the speech on the children's center quite so often.

He had seen Margaret headed toward the punch bowl and he longed suddenly for refreshment.

4

Mrs. W. W. Marsh should have been thrilled that the handsome, intelligent heir to a fortune was courting her intelligent daughter, the educated heiress, but she was not. If any one matter had to be chosen on which to define the difference between Mrs. Marsh and Great Uncle Findley Marsh, this particular matter would have illuminated much. Uncle Findley hailed and approved the romance. Mrs. Marsh, without knowing Findley's opinion, did not.

Mrs. Marsh thought her daughter had been overindulged by Mr.

Marsh during her formative years. From the father, Margaret had learned to argue, debate, to take on adult ways far beyond her age, and as she moved into her adulthood, although she seemed compliant and accommodating on the surface of day-to-day pleasantries between mother and daughter, Mrs. Marsh knew there was a spirit of rebellion and willfulness that could be aroused at any moment. Margaret had never learned that woman's role was obedience. Part of the blame for that Mrs. Marsh took unto herself, but most of it she laid at her husband's door. That Margaret would have trouble establishing a happy marriage, Mrs. Marsh had no doubt. Especially if the husband her daughter chose—or accepted—was not a strong, somewhat overwhelming personality in his own right. Mrs. Marsh could foresee a time when her daughter, married to a man with Margaret's own liberal ideas, went hollow-eyed about the world, doing good and holding meetings, marching here and there for some elusive cause, wearing an out-of-fashion bonnet, throwing her fortune to the winds of chance.

Though Mrs. Marsh had no illusions about foreign titles, she almost wished Margaret might be whisked off to England to make some alliance with a noble house. Certainly the overbearing culture of the husband in such a match would have required that Margaret set aside, for a time, her feminist ideas and once she resumed them, as she would no doubt do, her activities would be in Britain, out of Mrs. Marsh's hearing and sight.

But every time Mrs. Marsh looked up in the coming weeks, she saw Margaret on the arm of the rich, gentle, sensitive Steven Baxter. The looks on their faces told everything even if they had not told each other yet. Mrs. Marsh had as yet received no notice that anything definite was planned.

Although she realized Steven's appearances made her the envy of every mother of daughters in the city, she dismissed the fortune that kept appearing on her doorstep. Instead, she sighed and wished her daughter would bring home a sea captain or a captain of industry, a man used to command. A man like that—

But then she thought of her own husband and for this reason she said nothing to Margaret about the ubiquitous Steven Baxter.

5

On the Fourth of July there was a large party at one of the North Side mansions and Steven and Margaret were invited. The party began in the forenoon with everyone gathering under a striped open tent on the lawn. Hundreds of guests were invited and there was to be a luncheon and then lawn games and singing and a band concert and a light supper, with fireworks to follow immediately after dark.

Late in the afternoon, Margaret and Steven were standing near a played-out snowball bush on the lawn, themselves somewhat spent by the afternoon's activities.

Margaret had taken off her straw hat, which she had to wear in sun to prevent freckles, and she was using this as a fan. The pale blue ribbon that had fastened it under her chin flopped crazily as she fanned.

"Are you tired of this?" Steven asked.

"Yes."

"Shall we go?"

She looked up at him. "There are going to be fireworks—"

"You've seen fireworks before." His voice was quiet. He reached for her hand and they stood there for a moment, looking at each other. "I'll get the carriage," he said.

Margaret went to find her hostess to make her excuses. She had a headache— a little too much sun, she said—and Steven would take her home. He might return to the party. His brother was going to stay.

They made their getaway and, although Margaret's home was south, Steven turned the carriage northward and they rode along under the trees, drinking in the relative quiet. Here and there in the distance, firecrackers sounded, but it was near suppertime. Revelers were conserving their hoards, waiting for dark.

To escape the worst of the crowds, they drove into Lincoln Park and over a small bridge and went east, coming at last to the lakeshore, which was flanked in that spot by a large meadow rimmed with trees planted only a few years before by the park developers. The trees were not mature, but they did provide some shade within view of the lake, so Steven reined in the horse, tied it to one of the trees, and they stepped out to sit in the shade for a time.

Margaret spread out her white skirts on the grass. It seemed cooler here, although it probably wasn't.

Off in the near distance was a party of Germans under a sign that said something about *"heimatstadt."* Perhaps forty people were picnicking and enjoying the day. Children played among them and two small girls, about six or seven, came walking away from the group holding the arms of an infant just learning to walk. The three walked quite a way toward Steven and Margaret. Then the infant pulled loose its arms and got down on its knees, evidently a preferred mode of travel, and made like lightning to the lap of Margaret Marsh.

The child was wearing a dress and could not be established definitely as boy or girl, but the other girls came after, shouting "Lisel, Lisel" and Margaret, seeing the determination on the infant's face, reached out her arms on impulse and the child climbed aboard— home free.

They were all laughing by that time and Steven's look was a grand reward for Margaret. They kept the children there, talking with them about the park and the Fourth of July. Surreptitiously, Margaret and Steven examined the baby. What a marvelous child. The dumpling body, the powerful legs, the tyro's round arms and curly head, the minuteness of everything, the articulation of the parts. Neither Margaret, an only child, nor Steven, the youngest, had been this close to an infant before. Even with his sister's child, Steven had kept as far away as possible. But this baby seemed unusually interesting. The baby used Steven as a climbing pole to stand upright.

Everybody laughed, delighted with one another.

The mother of the infant appeared, speaking in accented English, apologizing for the interruption. Margaret relinquished her new friend and after the family left, she and Steven sat looking at each other. There didn't seem to be much to say anymore. They were not aware that they weren't talking. They held hands and one of them, perhaps Margaret, sighed.

A gift from the lake, a soft breeze, blew across them.

"Are you comfortable?" Steven asked.

"Yes."

Across the grass at the German picnic, the young mother said, *"Liebespaar,"* and the people around her laughed gently.

Margaret and Steven heard the tender laughter, but they didn't know it was for them. They sat under the tree for a long time, till dusk came, and after dark, the horse restive with the sounds and sights and smells of firecrackers all around, they reluctantly left.

After the long ride south, Steven escorted Margaret to the porch on the north side of the house and they stood back against the door in the dark. The servant-girls had the day off. Mrs. Riley had gone to her sister's, taking Henry with her. Mrs. Marsh was at a party. Perhaps Knox, the butler, was at home.

"Will you come in?" she asked Steven.

"No," he said, huskily. "It wouldn't look right."

He came close to her and they leaned against each other. Finally he whispered, "Oh, Margaret—" and gathered her closer and kissed her.

She felt as if she'd never been kissed before. Other young men had kissed her lips. Steven was kissing *her*. He was a novice at kissing, but he did it expertly. She was kissing *him*. She couldn't remember how it had come to this, her arms around him, his around her, as close as two—

"Oh, Margaret—" he said again, putting her from him.

Her voice was low and yielding. "Don't you want to come in for a while—"

He waited for some time before he said, "No. I'd better not," and turned to run down the stairs of the porch. Margaret understood. She felt as if she were on fire.

MYRON

CHAPTER XI

Although he had traveled a great deal with his parents and had lived in New Haven during his years at Yale, Myron Davis considered New York City to be his home. He thought he knew the city as only a native can know it—so well that the changes that periodically overcame the metropolis were like changes to one's own body; difficult to explain to others, but well understood by those who have experienced them.

Yet nothing he'd known about New York previously could compare with the life he had in his native city once he reentered it as the escort of Trudy Jones. *Mrs. G. T. Jones* was the style in which she was registered at that unmarked hotel on lower Fifth Avenue— a hotel that asked no questions, answered no questions, and gave excellent service at any hour of the day or night.

He settled her at the hotel, then went to visit his parents in their thirty-five-room place along the avenue. He told them he was staying at his club.

As a youth Myron had moved about the city and through its societies with freedom. There had never been any attempt to shield him from learning about life. As he became an adult, some of his friends took mistresses. Friends of his father had long-time relationships with paramours. It was a phenomenon unremarked in his social circle; except between the generations. He had suspected, but had never quite known for sure, that his father might have a "special friend" to visit from time to time.

But a taboo existed: Those parents or children who suspected their family members of refined indoor "sport" kept such suspicions to themselves unless the family honor, lineage or fortune might be threatened. Even respectable women winked at such practices among their men. There were, after all, enough strains on society marriage without adding unexpected pregnancy to the travails of the upper-class woman. Her husband could have his "companion" and she could have her opera and her art. It made for a fine balance as long as the financial picture remained rosy and everyone kept to his or her own place and guarded his or her secrets.

In the city of New York, the Athens of the West, Trudy, with the backing of Myron, his money and his social position, was immediately elevated to a social status as lofty as any female resident with the obvious exception of the matrons and respectable virgins of the inner-inner-upper-upper social nub. She had risen far above her own beginnings, bypassed entirely the middle class and become a city notable. Of course, she would never be invited anywhere she might meet Myron's mother. His father, on the other hand, could actually be in attendance somewhere that the delightful Mrs. G. T. Jones might frequent. Father, however, would have had trouble remembering the young woman's name; there were so many women like this, engaged in this life, that it was sometimes difficult to tell them apart. In the main, their circumstances at first were pleasant—more pleasant than those of the average shop girl who only did "it" on the side with stock boys and drummers on Saturday night to make a little extra money for clothes.

In her new life with Myron, Trudy had avoided many pitfalls through luck and chance. She had the advantage of having to please only one genteel lover, almost as if she were married. A relationship grew between Myron and herself not unlike the first year or so of wedded bliss of more conventional unions.

They had entered the city in the spring. The parks were full of the wonder of young leaves lit by electric light. The houses were castles to Trudy; the rich men and women, the marvelous shops, were the occupants of a fairyland. She was enchanted. And she could do anything she wished all the day long, as she said in awe to her Myron. She had only to dress herself and shop for herself and adorn herself and when they went into a group or attended a theatrical or visited a restaurant, she walked beside him with her energetic stride that made her clothing look as if it were the extraneous draperies of a perfectly formed goddess. Their pleasure in each other shone on their faces—and everyone who saw them turned to look again.

He alone knew of her slight imperfections in the boudoir: her chestnut hair was wild and unruly, her bare arms without gloves seemed too long for her body, her wrists were bony and mannish. And her ears did protrude slightly although they were covered by her hair in most instances. Why she should appear beautiful, he did not know, but he had seen it in her that first morning, and since coming to New York, he'd developed the habit of watching the effect she would have on a room as they entered, his soul hungering for the lift he got from her.

There was that matter of her noble walk. And if she walked like a duchess, she sat like a queen. Her eyebrows, dark for her hair and somewhat straight, made her eyes look very golden, when he knew they were only a very light brown. She was somewhat short-waisted, but when she stood up, she was almost as tall as he and this meant that her height and grace were in her legs and hips and about these features, about the marvelous nights between them, about the soft hair tufts and the fruitful look of her, the lush glory of her breasts, he was so besotted he could only sigh and feel smug. She was his. That his luck and taste were superb, that his life was full and full of her marvels, he could read in the envious glances of his fellows.

He spent less time in his father's office than ever before but he made more sales, did more corporate business than ever before. Men wanted to know him. Smiling gentlemen, important and prosperous, crowded up to him in amazing circumstances—at sporting events, at his club, declaring a great need of insurance, especially insurance to be provided by Davis and Son, that up-and-coming small firm which seemed to have the world in hand. His father thought Myron a wizard, but Myron knew otherwise. The word was out that Myron Davis was a man-about-town and men the age of his father, men known for taste and influence, came across thater lobbies to shake his hand. If circumstances were such that Trudy was with him, he could do no less than introduce the handsome Mrs. Jones to this or that gentleman from New York.

They, in turn, seemed to find an introduction to this charmer enough to instill in their hearts great business confidence concerning the Davis firm. Myron's list of clientele blossomed.

And so Myron Davis and Mrs. G. T. Jones became part of the sub rosa life of the city of New York, a life often more public and established than the dutiful marriages of the chaste and homebound. Trudy and Myron, acknowledged lovers, lunched publicly at Delmonico's. They went to plays and sporting events. They rode in an open carriage among other open carriages in the park. They dined early with large parties of friends at notable restaurants. They dined late, tête-à-tête, in their own homey suite at the unnamed hotel where discretion reigned and travelers were not welcome.

Trudy had retained all the tips of Mrs. Asunda and was learning some of her own. She knew how to go about the shops. Salesladies, recognizing a patron who would do justice not only to their finances, but to their clothes, were eager to help instruct her in further modes of dress. Trudy found, however, that their advice must be tempered with her own natural instinct for what looked best and how she would feel wearing a certain frock.

One morning Myron's father called him into his office, a paneled chamber that seemed much too dark to be visited on a sunny day. His father greeted him warmly.

But then he said, "I've been looking for you. What with one thing and another, I haven't seen you for over a week. Your mother's coming home. I don't exactly know when she's leaving Europe, but she will cable from the ship. *She* will want to see you—"

Myron smiled, although his head was thick this morning.

"I'll make more of an effort to be on hand. I feel as if I keep slipping my moorings at the wrong hours. When I come home, you're out at your clubs. When I come back at night, I don't like to disturb you. I've been—I've been—staying at my club—"

Mr. Davis said, "I've been wanting to tell you how we appreciate your work recently. You must be visiting every one of our customers or using some other clever method to bring things along like this. I can't fault your use of time."

Myron nodded, but he could see there was something else and he began to be apprehensive. Mr. Davis settled himself and smoothed at the papers before him.

"I think you should have more money. I wrote to your mother about your success and she thinks so, too. And you've certainly carried the day here. However it was done, you've been bringing in new customers; men I've been after for years in a discreet way. The commissions are rising. Not every father has a son like you, someone who deserves the family name. We know you're looking for a place. A household of your own. You must need funds. I want you to know how your mother and I feel and undoubtedly you can find a place for an increase—"

Myron was overcome. He could buy Trudy a carriage. She was responsible for everything. He would get her a personal maid. Keeping Trudy was damned expensive. The best of a breed always is. Out of respect for corporate gain, he stood up. His father stood also and they shook hands.

Then his father said, "I must remember to drop a note to the dean of your college. I appreciate how your outlook has improved since your education. You've taken on the style of a gentleman and it's made all the difference—"

"Father—"

"My boy—"

They stood, hands clasped, their faces vibrant against the dark walls, the glow of the single desk lamp lighting their pleased expressions; Davis and Son.

2

When Myron told Trudy about the maid, she demurred.

"I don't need a maid. There are maids at the hotel who will dress my hair if I wish."

"A French maid," Myron insisted. He wanted her to be able to say among their acquaintances that he'd provided her with a French maid.

"French," complained Trudy. "You know I speak German and Polish—possibly a few words someone might understand in Russian—but not *French*. How shall we communicate?"

She didn't tell him that she also knew Yiddish and some Hebrew. She had not ever mentioned that. She turned to look at him and a tortoiseshell comb fell out of her hair.

He stooped to pick it up.

"You see," he said. "You need someone to help you."

She stood looking at him, dreaming a little. She was thinking of her mother with the children and the two rooms her family must still live in and the noise of it and the smell of coal oil, if they had it, or the coal, brought home from the railroad tracks, or failing that, the smell of wood burning from a dug-up block from the wooden streets. She was thinking of her mother's hands on her hair as it was braided each morning and of the rough dresses she'd worn to school. A French *maid* for a healthy young girl, to aid her in placing combs properly, to sew buttons and smooth kid gloves and brush dresses and set out lingerie, so that the young miss would not be fatigued for the evening ahead? Trudy almost laughed in Myron's face, but he was so dear. She supposed she would have to do it and then she would have the dreadful uncommunicative person on her hands at all times. The privacy of their nest would be violated.

"But then what will we do with her, when we want to—you know—be alone? When we are in here I suppose you can hear every sound in the next room. Especially the way you—" Now she did laugh. And she blushed. She was trying the best she knew how to change his mind. She *was* witty, as others supposed, but not in the way they supposed.

He was reckless. He was laughing. He thought he was in charge, but the dynamics of their life together had already changed. Yet he said, "I'll get her her own little suite."

Now he'd done it. That would wipe out his increase and he'd not be able to buy the carriage. Well, maybe he could get a French mademoiselle who would be satisfied with a nice room, rather than a suite. But he doubted it. French servants were notoriously temperamental. He could see what the delightful Mrs. Jones meant. Another person in the suite as they played the nights away might disturb the clandestine nature of their bliss.

He changed the subject. "The track is going to open. I have shares in it so we really should go. We could go this afternoon." He anticipated the stir she would cause, the rush of feeling he would get by escorting her into the boxes.

She smiled down at him as he lounged in her bedroom. His collar was open. She admired the pink healthy look of his neck, his blue eyes as he looked up at her, the hint she could see of his whiskers reemerging—

And all she had to do, day or night, was to let him touch her, to encourage him to touch her; to let him make love to her was her sole occupation. It was almost too good to be true. What an easy life.

"Tomorrow," she told him, settling in his lap. "We can't go anywhere today." She gestured toward her overstuffed closets. "I can't be seen anywhere. I have nothing to wear—"

She lay back against him and could feel his response through her clothes, rising against her thigh. She moved provocatively, wiggling as if to settle herself. She loved to do this to him. She could make him do anything she wanted. He thought he was strong, but she knew she could do almost anything and he would follow.

He brought his other arm around her and she let herself melt against him, easing into his arms.

He murmured in her ear: "I wouldn't mind if you didn't wear anything."

And, for the moment, she agreed.

CHAPTER XII

Trudy was surprised to discover that what she missed most during her stay in New York was children. For some reason, lower Fifth Avenue was almost devoid of nannies and perambulators, at least at the hour Mrs. G. T. Jones sailed forth on her various errands. She was not so foolish as to actually *want* a child, but she missed, finally, after these long months, the noise and confusion and sour-sweet smells and the willingness of her infant brothers and sisters to let her hold them and touch them any time she'd had need of solace.

For the first fifteen years of her life, she'd hardly been alone in the physical sense. Often, in the midst of that over-peopled life she had felt very much alone—singular—in fact. But now that she was alone and could be expected to enjoy it, did enjoy it, could luxuriate in aloneness, she would find her body aching to lean on or touch someone who was not a lover. She had put all thought of her mother out of her mind. She could not think of *that* now; that was much too painful to consider.

Besides, Trudy didn't want to go back home. She'd fought hard— against her own nature she sometimes thought—to earn the place she had here with Myron. Yet Myron, though sweet, could be very demanding and he didn't like fuss or discussion. Things must be done *his* way, although sometimes Trudy could see ways she thought might be somewhat better. Sometimes Trudy wished she had a confidante, but there was no one at the hotel or in the crowd they moved among that Trudy felt she would be able to trust. Many of the other girls envied her Myron. And most about her seemed to be too self-centered, too conscious of their own situation. Everyone appeared to be quite old in her eyes, distant and superior in every way. Even as she enjoyed her newly sophisticated existence, Trudy longed for the touch of young skin, the unquestioning love of an infant toward someone who cares and is unfailingly kind. She'd once been "big Gertie." Now she was "Mrs. Jones" and expected to make a "good appearance."

More and more, Trudy's excursions were like appearances. Myron would give her suggestions.

"I think you ought to take up those Spanish cigars. Many women are smoking them. They look very stylish and give the impression of a long, slim arm. I like the way women hold them. Watch and you try it. They even—" here he winked at her"—put a little something on the tip."

Trudy shuddered. "I will never smoke cigars. You know that." They reminded her of the cigar factory and what Myron was suggesting she put on the tip of the cigar was opium or cocaine. Cocaine was very stylish, she'd heard, but she had once had an uncle who was what her mother called "an opium field," who went to places where the signs were in Chinese, and he smoked something in a pipe and when he didn't have enough money for it he would come and sit in their kitchen and act very strange until their mother, his sister, would find whatever pennies she had. Usually it wasn't enough. But her uncle would finally go away, leaving behind a strange odor as of an animal cornered and about to die. Eventually he did die. He ran out into the street in front of the horsecars. Some said he did it on purpose, but that could never be proved. There were many things in Trudy's life like that, things Myron would never learn about, that he would not be able to understand. He thought he knew so much about everything. Well, Trudy was learning that sometimes Myron was more of a baby than she and he was nine years older. Myron had seen nothing. He had never been poor. All he knew about was what was in the vogue. Lately, it made Trudy feel very tired and old.

Myron said about the opium: "They do it to make their complexions white."

"My complexion is white enough."

"It will make you very gay," said Myron, nodding to the bedroom.

"I think," said Trudy, "that I am up to your standards already—" She rarely spoke to Myron like this, but occasionally she resented his treatment of her as a doll to dress and to make walk and talk. She had laughed, removing the edge from what she'd just said.

In Chicago, Mrs. Asunda had told her, "Laughter brings intimacy. Joy is intimacy and vice versa." Trudy did her best to live by that rule, but Myron seemed to invade her being in a way that was more than intimate, that could be as overbearing as her hectic family life had been. The sum of it was, she discovered, that wherever she was, she seemed to be alone.

Today, Myron was restless. "Let's do something," he said. "Let's go to the races."

She was still peevish. "Isn't that in the out-of-doors? In the sunshine?"

"Yes, what of it?"

"First you tell me to put opium on my cigar to make my complexion white and then you want to drag me off to the races where I will be sunburnt like a farmer's wife."

She'd been told her skin was translucent, yet seemed to have a glow behind it, and she didn't want to risk harming it. She felt in a swivet today. She wanted to be mean to someone and the only person she knew well was Myron.

Trudy was changing. She'd come very quickly from one life to another, with hardly a moment to catch her breath, hardly a moment to decide who she was. She'd come on the strength of Myron's good looks and charm, his implied wealth. She didn't regret a moment of what had transpired. But now she had some time to think and no thoughts came; only a feeling of irritability.

"Well," Myron said, tamping out his own cigar, "go buy yourself a parasol. That should improve your disposition."

He was annoyed that she'd put him off again about the track. For two weeks he'd been trying to take her there. She was becoming unreasonable.

Trudy grumped at the mirror. Why did he sit there like that; she could see him in the reflection and he thought she didn't know he was pouting like a child. Why couldn't he be more manly, more in charge?

For some reason she wanted Myron to know things, to be in control. She didn't want to have to think or wonder. If she were his, she wanted him to be the strongest and best. She wanted to be able to ask him questions and trust his answers.

But in New York, she discovered, Myron was just a young man with far to go. Nor was he, she suspected, the most wise of men. One thing she knew: He wouldn't have lasted a day on Maxwell

Street among the street peddlers who had come through three countries and who, every day, made enough to feed their families by overcoming the tough conditions of the street. This realization had shaken Trudy's confidence, had made her peevish. Was there no one anywhere who was strong? Were all rich people so boring and silly?

The nights, of course, were different, she had to admit. She loved him at night, since she'd known no one else. The nights seemed enchanted and she needed nothing to relax her or make her more playful. She could be as tempting as Myron could hope or handle; she had been and would be. He should know that by now. She was terribly annoyed with him this minute. She loved the nights and if that meant she loved Myron and this was a lovers' quarrel, then perhaps that's what was happening, why she felt so cross. Trudy didn't know. She wasn't sure because he wasn't sure. And when he was sure, he was sure about things that were wrong. She threw her hairbrush at the door after Myron left.

That night they went to the roof garden of Madison Square Garden to join a party of Myron's friends. They were a party of six, but their host had them seated at a table for eight. He said his friend, Mr. Graebar, was coming. When Mr. Graebar did arrive, he was escorting Mrs. Asunda.

She and Trudy gave glad exclamations, clutched each other and saluted like two happy French generals. Trudy felt as if a prayer had been answered.

"I met Mr. Graebar in Detroit. On a yachting party. Mr. Graebar loves to yacht," said Mrs. Asunda, and when everyone laughed, Mrs. Asunda winked at Trudy. *Joy,* said Mrs. Asunda's wink. Trudy noticed Mrs. Asunda was wearing a magnificent dog-collar of baroque pearls that Mrs. Asunda hadn't had in Chicago. She winked back and the entire evening took on new zest.

Mrs. Asunda leaned across Myron to whisper to Trudy, "We must have luncheon—"

"How about tomorrow?"

Myron said sharply, "Tomorrow we're going to the races. You promised—"

"Oh, well,' said Trudy to Mrs. Asunda, "why don't you come with us?"

Myron growled when Mrs. Asunda and Mr. Graebar said they'd be delighted to join them to take in the races.

"Call me Beverly," Mrs. Asunda said to Trudy.

"Call me *Mrs.* Jones," Trudy whispered back and both laughed. Myron looked decidedly peeved.

As the evening progressed and the showgirls paraded in their elegant costumes—at least the costumes looked elegant from where Trudy was sitting—a man at their table began to name each of the girls as the performers went past center stage.

And then he named each of the girls' lovers.

"They're all married," the man said.

"The showgirls are married?" asked Trudy. Again everyone at their table laughed.

"No, their lovers are married." The man was supercilious. He loved to impress beautiful women from out of town.

Trudy was suspicious. "How could you know that? Who would tell?"

"Why, it's in all the papers every day," the man said, as if that ended that.

In a flash of intuition, Trudy began to understand why Myron was so anxious that they go to the races. Trudy realized Myron would want her to look her very best tomorrow and it made her rather tired to think of it, as if she were a show-horse or a showgirl, to be paraded center-stage. When they returned to the hotel, she sent him home early.

"After all," she teased him, "we'll be in full sunlight tomorrow. I wouldn't want to have dark circles under my eyes."

He was annoyed, but he left. She was annoyed that she'd seen through his eagerness for the races.

2

She might have made him angrier than she guessed. Mrs Asunda and Mr. Graebar were already on hand and waiting when Trudy received a telephone call from Myron. She didn't like to answer the device. It frightened her. One never learned anything nice from it. But Myron had insisted she have one and that she answer it and she decided she'd been right: He couldn't come just then. And he still seemed out of sorts.

"But we're here waiting for you," she shouted into the mouthpiece as if across a long distance. "We've already ordered the carriage—"

His voice through the instrument sounded distorted and far away. "Why don't you go on without me, then?"

So she did. And Mr. Graebar had the pleasure of escorting the handsome Mrs. Asunda and the beautiful Mrs. Jones to the races. Everyone saw them enter. Everyone who was there, that is. Trudy noticed many people seemed to come late and leave early. There was constant motion in the boxes and in the stands as devotees of the sport of kings went to place their wagers or left after losing. Trudy thought the whole affair was a disappointment. It seemed disorganized and noisy and not at all romantic and she missed Myron, who might have explained who various people were in the other boxes.

The only time the spectators gave full attention to the field was near the end of the race, as the horses tore toward home. Only then did Trudy feel the excitement she had thought racing was supposed to be. And even at those times, not even the wager Mr. Graebar had placed in her name could make the outcome truly thrilling.

What's happening to me? she thought. *A nice afternoon in the outdoors and I'm impatient for it to end.*

But she had worn her best hat and to be with Mrs. Asunda again *was* pleasant. Her cheeks were slightly flushed and she looked smashing. Mrs. Asunda noticed it and mentioned it to Mr. Graebar.

During the third race, Myron arrived. He appeared sulky and he said to her, "I think you might have waited for me—"

"But you said to go ahead."

He didn't answer. He put his binoculars to his eyes, but from the set of his mouth, she gathered that she was supposed to have waited anyway. At that moment one of the hordes of amateur photographers who were beginning to flood New York took their picture. Only Mrs. Jones and Mrs. Asunda were featured. Myron was a faint shadow in the background, the binoculars hiding part of his face. But perhaps his mother would have recognized him.

3

The delay in Myron's day had been his mother. She'd returned from the Continent and her ship had docked that morning. She'd wired ahead and asked—demanded, in the way of telegrams—that Myron meet her, for she had a surprise for him. The surprise was that Mrs. Davis had met an old school friend on board ship and this friend, Mrs. Dubois, had a daughter and Mother was so pleased to have renewed her acquaintance with her friend that she'd invited both ladies—mother and daughter—to join her at the Davis mansion for the next month. And Mrs. Davis made it clear that Myron was not to stay at his club, that he was to be on hand for dinners and other necessary squiring and that Miss Dubois—she was southern—was quite eligible. Myron wasn't interested in her eligibility. He was busy with Trudy, but he couldn't tell his mother that. And Trudy needed looking after. She was becoming independent and willful. He couldn't just leave her to her own amusement for a month. She would escape him. His day at the races was ruined. His night with Trudy was distracted. Myron Davis was not accustomed to being thwarted by the women in his life.

4

Some days later, Mrs. Davis found the picture of her son in a pictorial gazette circulated among the upper social levels of New York. The gazette pictured life on avenues of the city where the sun shone bright enough for casual photography and the chance to make it pay. The stylish always like to see their pictures. And hence subscribe to gazettes. The caption mentioned the names of two women.

"Who is Mrs. Asunda?" Mrs. Davis asked and since Myron had temporarily forgotten, having met Mrs. Asunda only twice, and because he'd been asked to address her as *Beverly*, he said he didn't know.

His mother produced the picture. They were alone in his mother's suite and Myron felt as if he were six and had spilled milk at dinner with the grownups.

"Here is Mrs. Asunda and there is a Mrs. Jones and there you are; I'd know you anywhere," his mother said.

Myron took the picture in hand and blushed very red. He studied it while he framed an answer. "There were other gentlemen in the box. I'm sorry, I didn't catch the lady's name when we were introduced and I didn't like to ask again for so brief an acquaintance. I really don't know Mrs. Asunda at all."

"Whom do you know?" His mother's eyes bored right into him. She had known him too long.

"Oh—" he hedged. "The other gentlemen. A Mr. Graebar. Perhaps he's not in the picture. Has a yacht. Business in Detroit. That sort of thing. Insurance, Mother."

Now his mother was blushing. "And the women? Both of them? I hope they are not the sort that are—" she hesitated, but she was a woman of the world "—available for out-of-town businessmen? I hope our firm does not engage in any such mortifying practices—"

Myron thought an offense might work here better than his defense. "Mother. Really. Do I seem to be that sort?" And he truly was offended. He could not imagine doing such a thing. "And you slander these ladies, whom I barely know. Don't they look respectable? Just because they're attractive—"

In the picture, Trudy looked adorable, her dark hair framing her face against the light color of her small umbrella. She and Mrs. Asunda had leaned together to share a confidence or Myron wouldn't have been visible at all. Damn such luck.

"Well, they look terribly well dressed and *I've* never heard of them. So they can't be society women. They must be of the supper club set and I don't want you to get mixed up in that. That's not for you—"

She wasn't waggling her finger at him, but she might have been. Myron had a distinct urge to blurt out everything he knew about Trudy and their nights together. And about Trudy's relatively innocent, but beneficial, effect on his father's business. His mother, well-cushioned by her own fortune, wasn't interested in business matters per se, but she wanted her husband to be a success, nevertheless. Failure was déclassé.

"Mrs. Jones seems to be well-established. It's a wonder you haven't met her," he finished lamely.

Mrs. Davis knew the location and appearance of every young marriageable female with a fortune in the eastern United States. She'd never heard of *Mrs.* Jones, which could mean any number of things.

She said, "Does your father know her?" This was said offhand and his mother had turned away before she said it, but Myron could see from the position of her shoulders and neck that this answer was the most important one he could give. He could say *no* with a clear conscience, but there might be benefits in giving a less distinct answer.

"I don't know that he does," Myron said thoughtfully. "I don't know just whom Father knows and doesn't know—I don't know just whom Mrs. Jones knows and doesn't know."

"Well," said his mother, waving him away, "it's high time you spent your free hours with respectable girls, known to us, girls who could be a proper wife to you when the time comes—"

Myron, recognizing dismissal, turned to go. But she had one more question. "Myron—"

"Yes?"

"Who is Mrs. Jones' husband?"

"She's a widow, I believe."

"Ah." Grass no doubt, thought Mrs. Davis as her son shut the door.

5

With the specter of Miss Dubois floating about the halls of the Davis mansion and the thought that his mother was scrutinizing the press for his picture, Myron's style was dented. His joy in propelling Trudy into the limelight suffered a setback and because he became less anxious that she make stunning entrances, she relaxed and thereby became more stunning than ever. He was afraid to take her places, where he had loved to escort her before. Her beauty had become even more noticeable.

Trudy and Mrs. Asunda were thick as Gypsy girls. They went about together during the day, although Mrs. Asunda had no evenings available and in any case wouldn't have welcomed Trudy as a third wheel to her evenings with Mr. Graebar. Consequently, Trudy found herself alone even more. She took up needlework. She chatted in French with French Madame. Trudy didn't know French, but she was learning it. And French Madame showed "Young Miss" some lovely stitches in white wool for a large white challis shawl, also in wool, that Trudy was making.

"White on white is so very—so chic," said French Madame.

"I suppose—" sighed Trudy and thought of her mother. The last person who'd shown her how to embroider anything was her mother and many of the intricate designs she was making in white around the edge of the shawl were those her mother had shown her. But to think of her mother led her in turn to think of Myron and she thought maybe she'd better do something else, because she was certainly thinking too much. It was unsettling. The shawl would require a lot of embroidery before it was finished. Trudy put it aside.

She knew where Myron was. He'd had to tell her some of it. And she missed him and she missed their nights together and she wondered about Miss Dubois—

Myron stole time where he could. He came for luncheon, which they ate together in the suite. They went to a workingman's café in the neighborhood; or once in a while they dined in the restaurant of another hotel so that if they were seen, no one would connect them with this one. Myron was doing his best to be discreet.

But trying to hide Trudy was like trying to hide a fire. She was not merely beautiful, she was young and enjoyed what she saw. Her expression was lively and her eyes sparkled. And of course, there was her walk. Wherever she went, she seemed to be full of energy and enthusiasm. Even if she'd been somewhat plain, just this good health and vivacity would have attracted attention.

Next time Myron was called in to see his father. His father had the same gazette his mother had seen on the desk. Mr. Davis tapped the picture with his finger.

"Your mother tells me you know this Mrs. Jones?"

Myron was getting skillful at evasion. "Mrs. who?"

"Jones. Jones. Mother says she is a widow and you know who she is and have been seen with her? Is this correct?"

"Oh, *that* Mrs. Jones. I've met her here and there—" He felt as if he were shrinking in his father's eyes.

"Well, never mind your mother," his father said abruptly. "I—that is—that's not exactly what I mean. What I mean is that someone else—several men—have told me you are off the traces about some filly and that she is stunning, so I assume this is the girl. I've been asked to make introductions, but of course, I could hardly do that. Besides—" his father looked stern "—I don't want you to believe I approve of this sort of thing. But I was impressed at just who it was who approached me—"

Myron risked a square gaze, meeting his father's eyes with curiosity. "Who was it?"

"A friend of Jay Darling's. I had the impression the man was asking because Mr. Darling wanted to know."

"What?"

Davis and Son looked at each other. What Myron Davis saw in his father's eyes was fear. What Mr. Davis saw in his son's eyes was worry.

Myron decided to bluff it out. "And—"

Mr. Davis picked up a letter from his desk. "I have just received a communiqué from the office of Mr. Darling and associates. From the group, as it were. The letter informs me that Darling's corporation has just become affiliated with Stadt and Company and Mr. Darling and his—friends—will be the principals in the Stadt organization. They ask leave to send their representatives to our offices tomorrow—"

"I'm afraid I don't understand."

"For many years, as you may or may not know, I've been placing much of our reinsurance through Stadt and Company." Mr. Davis shook the letter. "I believe this is going to be in the nature of an audit of our position and a review of our reserves—"

"But—but you're not afraid of that? Surely?"

Mr. Davis was silent and then he addressed the wall. "Your mother's style of living is very—demanding. I—would have preferred more time—"

There was a long silence. *Tomorrow.*

"But what has this to do with Tru—with Mrs. Jones?"

"I think you might be able to answer that more easily than I—"

In the dark paneled office where the outside light never shone, the two men sat, each examining the possibilities.

Myron at last spoke the words aloud. "You are saying Jay Darling is so interested in—in Mrs. Jones he would force himself on our company, take it over, make some sort of public fuss about—funds not—not on hand? Why can't I just—" Myron stopped. He wondered what he could do? Was he just supposed to assign Trudy to anyone interested in her? He couldn't do that. He was a gentleman. His father couldn't mean *that?*

Mr. Davis sat in silence for some time. Finally, he turned his chair so that he faced away from Myron. He spoke softly. "I didn't like to bother you. You were doing so well, so quickly. I thought maybe we'd ease out of our cash shortage with the business we were picking up, both here and in Chicago on the Exposition. There have been other moves against us that I've been able to stave off. We're in a classic weak position, ripe for a raid by some firm with a strong, rapacious eye for up-and-coming situations that have some weakness built into them right now. Family firms like ours—with a family name to support—it's not so uncommon, you know, to hit a dry spot—"

The older man was alibiing, explaining. He'd taken on a wheedling, thin tone and Myron didn't like it. He knew his mother's high style and her demands. His father was weak there. He never said no to Mrs. Davis. But that was no reason to put the family business in jeopardy.

Myron cleared his throat and tried to interrupt. "I still don't see what a young lady outside our family, no part of this company, could have to do with it. What could be done to block this move without involving some—passing acquaintance of mine—?"

"They've—made overtures before. I kept pretending I didn't understand. While I tried to put things right here. But everyone is under strain because conditions are bad. Then I had a visit today. A messenger from Darling's office brought that letter with a note to say he would wait while I read it. Then he told me. Darling wants the girl. No introduction. No courtship. Says he has looked into it. She's not what she seems. Just a—" he shrugged, looking at last directly at his son "—a business girl, living with you. As you say, a passing acquaintance?"

Myron cleared his throat again, but finally said nothing.

His father's voice now dropped into a deeper, more intimate register, but with a forced level of joviality to it. "Stick with your old man. Help me work my way through this. I can find you a dozen girls, each as pretty as this one. Why this one?"

Again silence, lengthening. "Why indeed," asked Myron at last.

He stood and without another word went toward the door. Just before he opened it, his father said softly, "It's your mother I'm thinking of. The scandal will kill her—"

Myron went out without an answer.

6

Each night at the dinner table Mrs. Davis and her friend, Mrs. Dubois, put poor Miss Dubois through her paces as if she were a horse performing dressage. Mrs. Davis had, herself, many private discussions with the girl and the only flaw in the picture that appeared seemed to Mrs. Davis to be quite a major one: questionable prospects for inherited fortune.

If Evelyn Dubois came with shaky financial backing, at least those cards should at some time be put on the table. But *Mrs.* Dubois had said not a word. Poor Myron would have to depend on his inheritance from his maternal grandfather, which was substantial, but not overwhelming, and then anything he might in future inherit from his own father's estate. And the bulk of Mr. Davis' holdings resided in his business and that left Myron with the necessity of marrying well. His mother had long ago taken on the task of finding every marriageable rich young woman on the continental United States. That was why she knew about Arthur Baxter. She had mentally crossed Harriet, rich but dreadfully plain, off her list when Harriet's engagement to Arthur was announced.

Mrs. Davis had been prepared to accept even plainness on Harriet's part, as long as the girl was tractable. One of the things Mrs. Davis feared was finding a girl who was rich enough, but one who was so rich she could not be dominated by the elder Davises. Myron, his mother thought, was a good boy, but he needed guidance in the *proper* way to live.

So the question was finding a girl who was *just* right. Rich, not too plain for Myron's sake, and with a pleasant, family-oriented disposition.

Now the Dubois girl—who wasn't the last girl in the world— probably didn't have enough fortune to mingle with New York rich. Mrs. Davis decided to let her visitors' evenings with her family play themselves out. She saw no signs of Myron's enthusiasm being captured by Miss Dubois.

Quite the contrary.

She noticed that Myron appeared pale and listless, but put it down to his having been dragooned into escort service. Myron, as a child, had inclined to be sulky, but he'd grown out of it in the last few years. But tonight, for example, it seemed as if he had no energy.

"Why don't you and Evelyn—Miss Dubois—take a ride in the carriage, dear?" Mrs. Davis asked, and then had second thoughts. "We might drive with you to see the electric lights. We could drive around Washington Square."

Myron didn't know she was there. He looked about him and his expression didn't change. He couldn't hear her and yet he did not ignore her. It was as if there were a wall between them. He sat in his chair and the silence lengthened into an embarrassment.

"Myron!" It was a voice she knew he would hear; not a loud voice, but one he was accustomed to obeying from earliest childhood.

He seemed to blink and start. "Yes—?"

"Whatever is the matter?"

"I—oh—I was thinking about something. I'm very sorry. I'm very rude." He stood up and looked at all of them and bowed and before his mother could say anything, he'd left the room on his way upstairs. But even Mrs. Davis could see he'd not done this in belligerence. He appeared to float through the room and up the stairway without motion, a man reflected in a glass.

"Let him go," said Mr. Davis, standing at the fireplace, warming an uncool back at the picturesque fire. "He has a great deal on his mind." He turned to the Dubois women. "Myron is a great help to me in the business, you know. Indispensable. He seems to be able to attract the very cream of clientele."

Mr. Davis rocked slightly on his heels and then came down on them abruptly. The boy did look pale. Maybe he was sick. They were both somewhat overcome. They'd not counted on Darling. From what Mr. Davis could gather, from what little Myron had told him, the woman—Mrs. Jones—had been under Myron's care for some time. She was a young woman, but under the circumstances, a woman of the world. Surely it would come as no shock to Myron that a woman he could covet would be desirable to others.

Mr. Davis wished he could escape this room and go somewhere to smoke a good cigar. Undoubtedly Myron felt some affection for this Jones person. Mr. Davis didn't like playing with men like Darling. They were way out of his league. Myron surely would not fail to do whatever Mr. Darling demanded of the firm—or of Myron, himself. If they went through the situation, step by step, the matter might be resolved to the best interests of all.

And if the worst had almost happened, if Myron had indeed lost his head over an unsuitable girl, then the sooner that head was retrieved, the better for the house of Davis and Son.

7

Trudy and Myron had been somewhere and she was all dressed up. Or rather, she was dressed simply, exquisitely. She was wearing a white dress of fine material that was rather full and when she walked there was a hint of beautiful lace beneath it. The dress itself was tucked and turned in the most clever way and there was white embroidery at the neckline with just a hint of blue in the thread of it here and there, as if the blue were at the center of delicate white flowers worn round her neck. She smelled of carnations and she was wearing light-blue shoes of the finest kid and her stockings were silk and in her chestnut hair, which had been turned up, there was an ornament of feathers and ribbons in a blue that was almost white.

All evening he'd been conscious of her eyes. Her eyes had never turned on him in such a trusting, golden way. Her feet, for which the blue shoes had been handmade, looked diminutive to him. She was too precious, too tender, to go away from him into another world, another life. How could he allow it?

As they entered the suite, the new French maid came to greet them. This would never do. He didn't want to wait for the maid to brush Trudy's hair or take Trudy's garments, one by one. Damn. He'd had too much champagne for self-control. Each time he looked at Trudy, he felt his manhood rising, straining against cloth, and as he sent the maid away he knew his face was flushed. He could not look at the woman as he rushed her out the door.

He turned back toward Trudy, who had wandered across the room, trailing her white shawl slightly behind her. She was struggling with the clasp of her necklace with the other hand. The delicate necklace was mainly of sapphires with one or two diamonds for added sparkle. He'd bought it after their arrival in New York, at Tiffany's. Before he'd hired the maid. This little romance had proved damned expensive.

He came up behind Trudy and put one arm around her waist. With the other he brushed at her hair. Flowers. The entire room smelled of flowers and Trudy. He found the pins to release the cascade of hair. It was very long now. He liked it long. With his free hand, he brushed it to one side and kissed the nape of her neck.

She laughed and leaned back, letting the curve of her buttocks move tantalizingly against him. He knew she was doing it on purpose. He tightened his grip with a gasp and she giggled slightly, pressing against him with an insistent motion. If she'd been shorter, she would not have been able to do this. In the weeks since he'd known her, in these short months, she'd become a wicked temptress, delighting in his need of her. Seductive. She drove him wild; he sometimes could not enjoy the bed, his need to enter her was so intense from this teasing and foreplay.

He stepped back and away from her in order to control himself and he reached out to unclasp the necklace. It fell forward into the bodice of her dress. He unfastened the dress and reached for the necklace, his hand caressing the warmth of her flesh, his fingers exploring further than necessary. He allowed himself an intimate tour of her, his lips touching the nape of her neck delicately again and again as he did so.

"Ummm," she breathed.

"Ummm?"

He let the dress work forward over her body, took both hands now to do it and as it moved, he urged it down from her arms. It dropped to the floor and she stepped daintily from it. He turned her, in her bodice and shift and silk stockings, toward him. Her breasts rose with her sighs and they were presented to him as beautiful rose-tinted mounds rising above lace. He moved the bodice away from her shoulders and again stepped back from her, his need so great he was afraid the night would be lost. He controlled himself, breathing deeply in strong regular breaths. Impulsively, she raised her arms to his neck and the bodice, already loosened and low, fell away slightly so that the dull violet of her nipples edged over its top. The hell with what the maid would think tomorrow. He ripped at the slip and drawers, tearing the delicate stockings down and away until she stood revealed before him wearing only the ribbon and feathers at her brow. He kicked at the clothes, pushing them aside, stepping over them toward her. She was trembling, helping him, aware of his need and the reason to hurry. She wanted this as much as he did.

His lips were at her, his hands were on her. But with all her strength she pushed back against his shoulders, pushing him away.

"You are—you are—" she breathed.

He would not let her push him from her. But she was quick. Breaking free, she turned, running, her hair streaming behind her, her buttocks creamy in the dim light of the room. She ran from him as if she were wearing her street clothes, without any attempt to hide her body. Just at the door of the bedroom, she turned and laughed. He started to come toward her, but she held out her hand, stopping him.

"No. *No* you *don't*. I'm all ready for something and you—look at you. With all your clothes." She stood there in a broad stance, letting him look at her. He tried to go to her and discovered that she'd somehow, in their embrace, loosened his suspenders and the buttons of his trousers. His pants slipped down to his knees. He stumbled and she giggled at him. She let him struggle; he was breathless in his haste.

At the same time he tried to move toward her, he was loosening and tugging at his own clothes. He tore at his shirt studs. Something dropped and rolled away. He didn't care. He didn't care if he ever saw his clothes again. He was caught, his shoes entangled in his trousers. Somehow he got free of them, only to stumble over his suspenders that, still attached to the rejected garments, tripped him as he went. She had disappeared into the room beyond. He could hear her teasing laugh. He came forward in great staggers and leaps, ripping away his own undergarments. As he reached the doorframe, fell against it, he could see her.

She was in bed, covered up to her nose, her hair blossoming above the bedcovers like a wild dark animal with a life of its own. Naked at last, free of everything that had bound him, he went to the bed and flung back the sheet, laughing with her in a silent way, mock-savage in his own right. He pulled her out of the bed. They were perfectly matched. She was so tall he could take her standing. He began to kiss her, her throat, her breasts; with one arm he held her close and with his other hand, touched her between her thighs, found his way, his fingers searching through the pubic hair, his fingers moving rhythmically. He was moaning. He couldn't help himself. She gasped as he touched her secret places; she threw her arms around him, bringing herself closer still. At these moments she was not coy. Their mouths came together, his tongue tasting what he knew—

With his hand, he spread her legs apart and then moved toward her, presenting himself. He entered her as they stood there, as they were moving backward, toward the waiting bed. It was as if they were flying together through some atmosphere; no, sailing under-water through some sea, and as her back came in contact with the bed, he made the full thrust. They melded then into a taut unit, rising, falling, until they both moved on into that pure moment when everything is left behind and there is only that golden warmth rolling through and through...

8

Trudy woke first, many hours later. She rolled over carefully, so as not to wake him. She liked to watch him sleep, especially when he was lying like this, on his stomach. He was such a unique being, constructed so differently than she in a grand perfect way, different and yet the same. In these separate, quiet moments, she could think about things. Sex, to Myron, was a thing anticipated, a sweet adventure, often discussed, demanded and planned for. He made an art of living for it. Trudy, in her new life with him, had been more amazed at this than at the act itself. The people she now moved among thought more about sex than her parents had thought about making a living. In her parents' lives, money had been coveted; sex had been readily available.

But to Myron and his friends, income was available. The need for riches had been surpassed, in Trudy's opinion, to the point where there was nothing much to do but watch the money grow. To fill their days, the idle rich had turned to idle pleasures. Trudy was smart enough to realize that she and the women she knew represented something to the men who were their patrons. A beautiful woman, beautifully wooed and beautifully kept, was a visible symbol of success.

Mrs. Asunda had explained some of this to Trudy when they first met in Chicago, but it was in New York that Trudy began to understand.

And there were other things she had to think about. She and Myron lay here in a room for two people alone. The luxury of it often overcame her. And the skill of Myron's lovemaking. What she had known of sex before in her old life had been gropings, pressure, a turned-away hand, usually in circumstances in which too many people were present or just near. And in her own family, though they lived so close together, each had known nothing about others' bodies after about seven or eight years of age. At that time, the men went off to the bathhouses to bath. She and her mother and sisters bathed separately at home.

Trudy sighed in content. She was naked now. She didn't know if that was right or not. And Myron wore nothing; she could touch the entire length of him, lie against the length of him with her own full, bare length. She supposed this was the wickedness in her. She liked this. His hair was damp at his neck and curled slightly. It reminded her of the top of a dandelion just before it blows away in the wind.

The hair on his arms was also light and grew most amazingly thick. Now that the passion had been momentarily spent, he seemed like a boy here with her. He always seemed like that in moments after. She wanted to take care of him, to do something for him, protect him, as if the Evil Eye of her childhood, of her parents' life, might reach here into this jewel-box room and touch Myron between his shoulder blades and he would never wake, never turn to her and smile and reach out again. She shivered and snuggled closer, pulling the covers over both of them, even though she could see by his perspiration that he was already warm. Was this what love was like? Had her mother loved her father? By the standards of New York society—perhaps by the standards Trudy had known in Chicago— her parents were not *nice*. They were *the poor*. And that her parents had then proceeded, in their poverty, to bring so many children into the world often made Trudy cringe with dreadful shame. She'd never boasted, as some other children did, about the extent of her family. She wished there were not so many children there. How could her parents flaunt it in such a way?

Even in this warm bed, couched against Myron's back, she could recall her despair when one day, as she and a friend pounded on the door of the flat, her mother had refused to unlock the door or answer her knock.

"I know you're in there," Trudy had shouted. Her friend snickered and said that those same conditions at her flat meant "they don't think we know they're doin' it." Her friend had looked wise and rolled her eyes about and said, "Watch, they'll have another kid nine months from now, see if they don't—" And they had. Oh, the shame. And how could they have done it, taken such a risk? After that, she'd begun to notice things; sounds in the night, a reluctant groan. Oh, terrible, terrible.

But now she saw this terribleness from a different angle. What a terrible thing to be so desirious of each other, to need this delicious closeness and to be separated by poverty and eventually by too many children; and by the lack of knowledge—or acceptance—of Mrs. Asunda's teachings about "protection."

Now she thought her parents might have deserved a time like this, alone in a beautiful room together, behind a closed, locked door. Waking slowly to remember.

His arm was outstretched as he slept, almost touching the headboard of the bed. It made him seem very long and godlike. She knew he was not godlike. Some of the men she'd met had powers that appeared godlike. Trudy had been told of incidents—she had even seen some things, things she would not formerly have believed: winter banquets decorated with plants and flowers that grew only in summer; jewels produced from the toes of bedroom slippers; entire hotels cleared of patrons so that a certain man and his party of revelers could disport as they pleased. Other things had been hinted at: men ruined by other men, all their money gone, all their power stripped away over some little fuss that in other modes of life wasn't worth anything.

Maybe one had to be terribly old before life could be tamed and mastered and Myron would become like that in time.

But she felt she was lucky to be with him now. She was lucky to have found him.

CHAPTER XIII

Mrs. Asunda invited Trudy to come riding in the park in a rented phaeton. Trudy discovered this meant that they would see many people they knew, both men and women, riding in carriages around the paths of Central Park in a sort of social parade. That it was necessary to appear at one's best went without saying. When Mrs. Asunda arrived with her driver—also rented—sitting stoically above, she urged Trudy to step lively.

"Hurry," she said. "We'll be late."

"Where are we going? I thought we were going riding?"

"We are. We are. But there is a time for everything—"

Trudy noticed that their horse—while handsome—was not the swiftest horse on the avenue.

"There is no use in going so quickly past that one can't be recognized," said Mrs. Asunda. She was wearing a very fine hat with a feather that nodded when she moved her head up and down.

As they entered the park they were discussing a current play and whether they wished to see it. A carriage coming from the same direction as their own pulled alongside and the occupants, a Mr. Taylor and a young lady Trudy had never seen before, bowed to Mrs. Asunda and Mrs. Jones. The carriage pulled on past.

Trudy said, "Is that his daughter?"

Mrs. Asunda said, "Heavens no. That's his new friend."

Trudy vividly recalled Mr. Taylor's former friend, a woman of brilliant red hair, about the age of Mrs. Asunda. This girl he escorted today was Trudy's age or slightly older.

Another carriage passed, going the other way, and the man inside tipped his hat.

"Smile," said Mrs. Asunda and Trudy did so. Carriages passed and went on, the sound of the horses' hooves regular against the pavement, punctuating the afternoon with a sense of order and time.

"What happened to Mr. Taylor's other love?" asked Trudy.

"Oh, she probably has a new friend by now," Mrs. Asunda said airily. At the same time she looked at Trudy very sharply. "And these are not love affairs, no matter what anyone tells you—"

Trudy laughed, but to her own surprise, the laughter sounded cold and tinny in the afternoon air.

"I suppose they are not love affairs," she answered.

For some reason, some hint on the wind, this place reminded her of Chicago. Yet if she thought about Chicago realistically, she thought of dirt and papers flying and noise and children. To compare it to this lovely afternoon in the splendid carriage with Mrs. Asunda was not right and within herself, Trudy felt out of sorts, as if her mental accounts did not balance.

And then she realized why. She felt a terrible lack of affection here, as if the color green were missing from a landscape.

She sighed and said, "Does anyone ever love anyone? Truly, I mean?"

Mrs. Asunda was silent. Then she said, "Do *you* know anyone who loves? Do you think it would be a sensible basis for arranging a life? What if the person one loved were foolish or weak? Can a woman afford to give her only life to a weak man?" She laughed. "We are not religious, after all. Making a sacrifice of our life. We must watch out, my dear. We must take care—"

As if this were a new thought, she touched Trudy's arm. "You are taking care, are you not? Are you—are you well?"

Trudy tossed her head. "Oh. Not that. Of course, *that* is all right. I do as you have taught me."

"Fine. Then you'll be able to do as you like."

"But it's not that," Trudy stopped. What did she mean?

Certainly, her mother and father had loved each other. Their passion for each other had made them marry outside their religions. Yet Trudy had never seen a gentle touch pass between them. Whatever love was, it had not survived within the rigors of her parents' marriage. The only surviving glimpse of it, its only monument, was the yearly child that gave the world a hint of their physical need of each other.

Trudy tried to think of someone, anyone, who might have professed love, that their condition might be examined in order that she could identify love. Trudy tried again. "I mean—what I am searching for is a clear view—so you see—well, there must be love—" Her voice was very soft, timed to the hoofbeats of the horse somehow as if to put heart into what she was saying.

"Mmm. Well, there is a side to love that is passionate and silly and I don't want you to get involved in that. That sort of adventure has no reason, no sense to it. An emotional experience of some kind, I suppose, is what you're saying—a woman feels gratitude for that, I suppose."

"It was love I meant," Trudy said.

"Love has nothing to do with it, my dear. Liveliness, a sense of style, a zest for life—that's what we have and in that we have a unique contribution to make. What man can expect such things of his home? And certainly no religion will provide that—to man or woman. And we carry our attitudes right into the bedroom. Not the usual *hausfrau*, who takes her powders and does up her hair in a bun on the top of her head. No, we must remain forever youthful and happy and—above all—willing to try anything our gentlemen propose. I'm not saying it's always easy. And mark you, few lives are easy. So smile and do what you are meant for—"

She nodded this way and that at passing carriages. "And do let's talk of something else. I haven't thought of love for a long time. Sometimes, when I see a wonderful painting or a bit of sculpture in a garden on a spring night, if there should be a fountain and stars, then some feeling comes, a love that is general. But as I've grown more discerning, I no longer ascribe that feeling to an individual gentleman. That would be folly of the worst kind—"

But Trudy burst out again, as if in lament. "Is there no love anywhere?"

Perhaps, she thought, mothers—but then she remembered in what way she'd left home, walking off without a word. Could love survive that? And the long months after? It had been so many months since she'd gone away.

Mrs. Asunda said, "You've been alone too much and you are obviously reading French novels and seeing too many plays. We need to get you out more in the fresh air to clear your head. I think love was invented by poets when they didn't have enough to write about. It's not a trustworthy emotion. And even the best of it seems to fade quickly—like chintz in sunlight. There. That's it—love and chintz—suitable only for country houses. Not for smart living. Don't waste your time with it. It's for silly girls who are rich and not too intelligent. Perhaps they have nothing else to do but moon about. But no, even the rich don't allow that. They're very businesslike about their daughters. They marry them off to the first impoverished earl who'll have them with no thought other than having grandchildren with a bit of the royal in them. Never mind the poor girl or her sensibilities. I must say, I envy their access to those drafty palaces, but not much else. It's exactly the same as our situation, except the girl is expected to perform as a brood cow. You need to learn, Trudy, that our form of recreation and any marriages that emerge from it are commodities, even in the most refined circles, and as a beautiful woman you must plan on making a fine alliance. And be careful you don't lose your head in the wrong direction. Lovers are for after the marriage. When your husband loses interest—"

Trudy was leaning her chin on her hands, which were crossed on the top of her umbrella stick.

"Do sit up," said Mrs. Asunda. "You're a beautiful girl. Don't slouch so—"

Trudy sat up.

"And smile," said Mrs. Asunda. "When you're not smiling, you're inclined to look a wee bit melancholy. Do remember that. Gentlemen like happy young ladies—"

"I was thinking of Mr. Taylor's other friend. What will become of her now? How will she live?"

"Oh, as I said, she's probably found a new gentleman. And there are always jewels to pawn. She'll find someone sooner or later—"

"How is this done? I'd really like to know."

"Well, it's nothing you'll have to worry about for a while—"

Trudy assumed Beverly meant that Myron would be her gentleman friend for several years. That no division in their romance could be foreseen. That they would have time to relax with each other and only when they were both old and tired and uninterested in each other must this question be faced.

But Mrs. Asunda meant that Trudy Jones would have a gentleman friend of one sort or another for many years to come, provided Trudy didn't take to drink or drugs or bonbons. And even then, if she could devise some imaginative sexual technique to restore the failing powers of some older and richer man—the type of man she was eventually certain to attract—she might become legendary within the demimonde.

"It's a delightful afternoon," said Mrs. Asunda, "and we're talking of dreary things like love and marriages. The only way to treat love is like a game of seasons that are always changing. Don't expect it to stay the same. And games are best played by those who are willing to do everything they can to win. Remember, Trudy dear, your style is your fortune—and winners always have the best all-around style, don't you think—"

The carriage rattled on.

When she returned to her hotel, Trudy told French Madame that she would like a bath. There seemed to be a griminess to her clothes and person that she'd not felt since the day she'd descended from the Chicago-to-New York train. That day she'd been so excited, the grittiness had been almost unnoticeable because it had been part of a welcome adventure. Today—in early autumn—the heat and humidity gave her a sense of having put in a hard day's work. Her mouth was dry over her lips from her long-held smile. She wished there was no night of revelry ahead. The day seemed too much to be borne.

"Mr. Davis sent a note," the maid said and set it before Trudy on a silver tray. The maid went on into the bathroom to draw the water and Trudy sat on the chaise to read Myron's note:

> Dinner at eight with a large party of new friends. Would like you to wear your smartest dress. We must make a first-class impression. Friends of my father.
>
> M—

Trudy dropped the letter back onto the tray with irritation. She didn't feel like going out tonight. And the weather was too warm for her smartest dress, which was, she thought, a black and white creation that made her look like a magazine illustration. What she really looked best in, but did not know it, was the simple white dress Myron had whisked from her the other night.

French Madame came from the bathroom and Trudy showed her the note.

"You choose," she told the maid. "Something not too warm. This weather is stifling. Such strange weather for early fall."

French Madame immediately brought out a pale green chiffon.

"That dress is too tight. The last time I wore it, I nearly suffocated after dinner—"

Madame raised her eyebrows. "Young Miss has lost weight. I have noticed—"

Trudy stood up and smoothed her dress over her hips.

"I have?" she asked. Then, "What shall I wear with it? I can't wear sapphires with this."

"The pearls. The one simple strand. It will be wonderful with your hair and eyes. Nothing to distract. Very *élégante*—"

Trudy shrugged. "Oh, well. What does it matter—" and she went in to take her cooling tepid bath.

Some time later, she came back into the bedroom and the maid had withdrawn. The coverlet on the bed was turned down and Trudy slipped naked between the sheets to rest before dressing. Doing nothing all day had begun to be very tiring. She closed her eyes and tried to will sleep. A nap would help. But twenty minutes later she was still tossing and as irritable as ever. She wished in her heart that Myron were here—and she wished just as fervently that he were not. She wanted the comfort of being touched by him, aroused by his body against hers. But she didn't want him with her. She wanted to react to no one, yet have every reaction that a satisfying tryst would bring to her. Her body seemed dead, as if she were under some terrible spell and she must be awakened slowly, tenderly, in order to face the night ahead.

The suite of rooms was entirely quiet. Madame must have retired to her own quarters. Trudy felt both reassured and abandoned by this. Was there no one? She turned on the bed, twisting among the sheets, lost in herself and afraid.

2

After her nap, Trudy came back into the world slowly, not altogether renewed. She decided she must begin to dress. She stood and took up the undergarments the maid had set out. She would not put on her stockings and garters yet. Just everything else: the drawers nearly to her knees, the bodice, the waist-cincher, one of the petticoats— the other petticoat, stiffened to give shape to the skirt of her dress and emphasize her small waist, stood by itself in the corner. The lingerie was of French silk with handmade lace wherever adornment was wanted. The materials were light and cool, but she knew it was going to be a long night.

Half-dressed, she went to the dressing table mirror and turned up the lamp. She peered into the dark glass.

Anyone who observed her would have thought she was enraptured by her own reflection. In fact, she didn't even see herself. She had looked into her own eyes, to be sure, but she'd become lost there and now was traveling somewhere else, not thinking, not even dreaming. Just wandering in a mist of unhappiness that would not reveal its cause. Her outer world, she had now cast from her. That world, apparently orderly and calm, seemed to her more *becalmed*, like a ship lost at sea, caught in circumstances in which there was no chance for motion in any direction. Where was she going? How had she come? There were no words to these questions in her mind, yet the questions were there and understood.

On her mental journey there was only the unmarked passage of internal time. In the past months everything had happened to her very fast and during those events she'd had little time to reflect. But the rush of leaving home, the excitement of meeting Myron, the delights and the dialogue of the bedchamber, the amazing train journey through spring fields, her introduction to New York, were all behind her now. They could never happen for the first time again. She had become, in that swift passage, many different women, none of whom she'd had time to enjoy before being hurried onward into a new facet of herself. Who was she becoming?

She picked up a comb at last and began to run it idly down the length of her hair. But she threw it down and turned again to the bed. She lay across it, her long arms and legs like white slashes across the dark counterpane. Finally she slept again, waiting for Myron to come for her.

3

They arrived at the theater very late and found their places among a party that was occupying three adjacent boxes. Trudy, after all Myron's talk of new friends, knew most of the women present, although there were a few men that were new to her. They looked older than the general crowd Myron traveled with. Mrs. Asunda was there with Mr. Graebar. She was in the third box and bowed to Trudy when she caught her eye.

Myron had arrived at the hotel almost as cross as Trudy felt. He brought her a gift, a bracelet made of delicate ivory and set with odd mottled stones.

"They are carnelian," he told her. "They match your eyes."

But he was nervous about her appearance. He, too, thought she looked best in the smashing black and white creation and suggested she change into it. He told her the air would be cooler in the evening.

"Not in the theater," she told him. "I'll wear this. I haven't worn this frock much at all." She smiled up at him. "After you were kind enough to buy it for me—"

That mollified him and they stood looking at each other, both thinking their own thoughts, both afraid of the future for some reason they would not tell the other.

"I'm not very pleasant tonight, I'm afraid—" began Trudy, who thought she might try to get at the irritation between them, whatever it might be.

"I know just the thing," Myron said and sent the maid for champagne. "We have been together for a long time now. For months and months. We should toast to—to something or other. And then we will be quite gay and have a lovely evening—"

By the end of the disjointed speech, he was pacing; he appeared quite agitated. When the champagne arrived, he took charge of it and in serving, almost spilled it all out.

"It must be the weather," he told her. "We are out of sorts and clumsy because of the humidity in the air."

He and she had toasted the evening. He did not toast to her, Trudy had noticed, but she said nothing.

Usually Trudy didn't like champagne on an empty stomach, and she said as much, but French Madame produced some small cookies—she called them *biscuits*—and they finished most of the bottle before they left the suite. Trudy was very relaxed now, although not tipsy. She found herself smiling and laughing at the least thing and didn't get annoyed as she usually did when the movement of her party friends disrupted the quiet of their box.

Myron's parties were often like this—large groups of men and women, sometimes barely acquainted. Men with their special "friends" meeting to see a play, occupying several boxes—coming and going throughout the performance—sometimes leaving abruptly for no apparent reason, long before the end of the last act.

Tonight there were several men standing in the hallway outside the box. They did this in order to smoke during the performance, although they were warned by management not to do it. They did as they pleased anyway. At one point, Mrs. Asunda joined Trudy and they sat together for a short while, saying very little to each other, Mrs. Asunda, at least, aware of how many heads were turned toward the lovely girl beside her. Mrs. Asunda reached over and touched a gloved hand to Trudy's knee and then pointed to her own box, and indicated she would rejoin Mr. Graebar, who had returned to his seat. Just before she did so, she leaned over and whispered to Trudy, "There are a number of interesting men in this party. Smile for all you are worth—"

Trudy decided she wouldn't do it. She would not sit there simpering for some unknown man when Myron was just a step away.

She turned to watch the play. The actress below was talking about love, was clearly in dire straits over it. She was suffering mightily. Trudy watched to see what the actress would do about it and just when she thought there might be a solution that would make everything all right, Myron came and touched her shoulder and whispered, not very quietly, that they were going to dinner now. Trudy was flushed and distracted by the actress's portrayal of suffering.

"Now?" she whispered and didn't move.

Myron reached out and took her hand. "Come," he said. "It's the end anyway in a few minutes." The entire party in the three boxes, perhaps thirty people, began to move about and talk sotto voce and made their noisy exit, drawing all eyes away from the stage to watch the swells depart on their important round of merrymaking. Oh, to be like that! So elegant. So rich. So unfeeling about the greater good. Wasn't that wonderful?

In the hallway, Myron said, "Mrs. Jones, I would like you to meet Mr. Deel, Mr. Deel is an associate of my father's firm."

Mr. Deel was quite old, Trudy thought, from the vantage point of her sixteenth birthday. And he was stout. And he hadn't much hair. But even Trudy had learned to read the signs given off by wealth. He was wearing a magnificent watch chain in heavy gold and his shirtfront was exquisitely done, with not a hint of starch, only the smooth result of it. His weskit was also snowy white in what looked to be a brocaded material. He bowed to her on their introduction and looked at Trudy with such intensity she felt as if she were a statue.

"My dear," he said. And then, "If I may call you that? Myron has told me so much about you—"

Trudy felt there was something more here than she could see. Here was this man, not of Myron's regular crowd, an associate of Myron's father, he said. Was this an overture of interest from Myron's family? Was she to be made known to them in some way? Or did they already know of her and want to see if she were *nice* enough for Myron?

The gentleman before her was concluding some remarks: "—and I believe I saw you in attendance several times at the race meetings. Are you interested in the turf?"

"I don't know much about it," Trudy confessed. She found this to be generally the best policy. If you don't know, people are always willing to explain, sometimes taking ages and ages in their explanations, which meant she didn't have to talk so much. "Perhaps you could explain a little about the races and I would enjoy them more—"

Myron sputtered and the man, himself, laughed. Mr. Deel was well-known for his interest in horses and had a great stable. He was also an official of the racing commission in another state, an appointed position going to distinguished gentlemen in the sport. Trudy couldn't have said a better thing, but she had only been trying to avoid having to make conversation.

They were now at the door of the theater and were approaching the line-up of special cabs—no one with a private carriage bothered with it for the congested theater district.

"May I?" Mr. Deel said, holding out his elbow to Mrs. Jones, while he looked at Myron. Myron nodded and stepped backward, allowing Mr. Deel to hand Trudy up into a carriage just for two riders. She looked back at Myron but he smiled and nodded and on the way to the hotel for dinner, Trudy was treated to at least a twenty-minute conversation about horses, breeding, jockeys, regulations, betting tips and gossip about the tracks in the New York region.

"I'm going south, soon," Mr. Deel confided. "The horses are already there. We send them down by rail and they train in good weather all winter. Soon enough the tracks down there will open and I'll be on hand. If you are coming south during the winter do let me know. I would be pleased to entertain you and members of your party—"

At the hotel they went to a large private ballroom. There was a fireplace at one end with chairs and couches set before it as if it were a drawing room. Mr. Deel escorted Trudy there and subsequently, Myron rejoined the party but did not approach her.

At the other end of the room there were several tables set for dinner and waiters moved about carrying items on trays. Champagne was being served and tonight there seemed to be an especially large group that was noisy and uninhibited.

A multicourse dinner was to be served shortly. At such feasts, Trudy usually nibbled. Some of the foods presented were off-putting. She did not like to eat birds that still looked like birds nor fish that stared back at one. She preferred anonymous food. Because she'd so seldom eaten meat as a child, her taste for it was slight. Mr. Deel, who had arranged to escort her to the table, noticed she was not eating much.

"Are you in good health?" he asked. "Do you have some dyspepsia?"

Trudy was embarrassed. She didn't think it was *nice* to talk about her health or anyone else's. And if this man were reviewing her for some reason, as he seemed to be, what should she answer? If she said she didn't like to speak of her health, he might be offended. And if she did talk about health, he might be testing her to see if she knew enough not to do so.

She examined the menu at her place as she thought. They had been served oysters and consommé, a fish course, a dish of sweet-breads, pâté de foie gras and now, before her, was some sort of bird in its feathers—or rather trimmed with its former feathers and something to make a beak and eyes. Still to come were lamb chops, sherbet, roast larks, cauliflower polonaise, grapefruit-orange-and-raisin salad of fruit brought in from Florida, assorted cheeses, potatoes—mashed or fried—mushrooms aux fines herbes and a spectacular dessert as yet undefined. With each of these courses she would be served a different wine and she would be expected to dismember and dissect her foods with the daintiness her fellow diners demanded of the female of the species. This particular meal was even more extensive than the usual twelve-course events Myron often took Trudy to.

She said to Mr. Deel, "There is a great amount of this food. It's very difficult to eat an appreciable amount of any one kind, even for those persons in good health—" There. That left all questions unanswered and answered them at the same time.

"What sort of diversions are you interested in, Mrs. Jones? Do you like to go about in the out-of-doors?"

She laughed. "I haven't seen too much of the out-of-doors since coming to New York. There is always so much to do in the evening and getting ready for that takes most of the day—"

Mr. Deel smiled. "My training stables in the South are in the country. Do you like the country?"

"I've never been in the country." She hesitated. What to answer here? Might Myron's family wish to meet her in the country? "Although I've seen it often enough—" she thought this would be an acceptable lie "—from the trains. The farmers in their fields, you know, watching the trains go by. But that's all I know—" If her voice was wistful, it was because she was thinking of Myron—

"Then you do not like the country?"

"I've not had the opportunity to go about in it. Myron—er—Mr. Davis—says he might go to the country sometime, but we have—" She stopped. She didn't know what she should say to Mr. Deel about what Myron had told her. He'd said he would take her south during the winter, if his mother would leave him alone to do as he wished. He said he didn't want to marry the daughter of his mother's friend, that he didn't want to marry for some years yet and that they could spend their winters in the South as well as not. Perhaps Mr. Deel knew something about that, knew Myron's mother and her wishes for her son.

"Yes? You were saying?"

"There may be a party forming for an excursion to see the fall colors along the Hudson," she said. "I might attend that outing—"

"Splendid. Splendid. I know you will enjoy our New York countryside." Mr. Deel addressed himself to the oranges and the raisins.

The dinner continued for more than three hours. Then it was followed by wine and toast-making. Mr. Deel drank to the health of Mrs. Jones.

Trudy blushed.

Myron drank to the health of Mrs. Jones.

The table applauded the popular Mrs. Jones.

"Speech, speech," they cried. But Trudy could not. She smiled merely and raised her glass and this was so graceful, it enhanced her image. She looked demure. She looked like a young lady just presented to society.

4

The next morning Beverly Asunda arrived just as Myron was leaving Trudy's hotel suite. Mrs. Asunda nodded to him and after he left, she sent the maid out for tea and small cakes. The minute they were alone, she said to Trudy, "You see. I told you your style would triumph."

Trudy was still sleepy. She didn't usually drink so much wine. She couldn't remember too much about the evening.

"I suppose so," she said.

"Suppose so. How did you happen to attend that party, anyway?"

"Oh, Myron said we were going. He wrote a note while I was out yesterday. He said these are new friends of his. I didn't know I would be coming when I saw you yesterday—"

"Has anything come for you this morning?"

"Anything?"

"A gift. Some sort of package with a note? Anything?"

"From Myron? No. Not today. He gave me a bracelet last night."

"No. Today. What came today?"

Trudy shrugged. "Nothing. Why do you ask?"

"Where did you meet Mr. Deel?"

"Myron introduced him to me at the party. He's a friend of Myron's father, I think—" At this Trudy blushed. She could feel herself blushing and didn't know just why.

The maid returned with the tea service and the food. They nibbled and while they were eating the desk rang to say it was sending up a package for Mrs. Jones. French Madame took in a florist's box and Mrs. Asunda was much more anxious than Trudy to see who had sent the flowers.

"I imagine it's Myron," Trudy said. She couldn't think of anyone else who might send flowers to her.

The flowers were long-stemmed white roses. The card said "For a lovely flower—regards, A. M. Deel."

"There," said Mrs. Asunda. "There. I just knew it. Something is going on—"

"I know," sighed Trudy. "I think—I think Myron's father wants to meet me. I think Mr. Deel is a friend of his and that's why he stayed with me at dinner—"

Mrs. Asunda was standing now. She was wearing an excellent traveling costume. It was the first time Trudy had noticed the lovely wine-colored suit.

"Are you going somewhere? Are you planning to leave?"

"Mr. Graebar has to take his yacht South. He could send it, but it's a fine time to go, provided the weather doesn't change too quickly. I'm going with him. But you—something is happening for you. You have caught the attention of Mr. Deel—"

"But who is he? I never saw him before."

"He gave the party that you attended last night."

"Did he?"

"And you sat next to him all evening. Everyone saw it. And the toasts to you. And now the roses. Something is definitely going on and I'm going to tell Oscar we must postpone our trip until you're settled."

"What? Settled on what?"

Mrs. Asunda sat down again. "Do you remember Mr. Taylor's previous friend? Do you remember when you asked me yesterday what she would do? Well, if she is very lucky and has not displeased him in any way, she will be taken care of by Mr. Deel."

"Oh," said Trudy. "Mr. Deel will be her new escort."

"No, that's not what I meant. I mean, Mr. Deel often acts as—well—as go-between for a new—ah—arrangement. He knows all the best women in New York. And if one he likes is temporarily without escort, Mr. Deel will arrange everything and things will work out for the best. That way, first-class talent is kept circulating through the city and is not lost to our kind of—society. We do have a society, you know. You're part of it."

Trudy nearly dropped the teapot.

"You mean he's—he's—Mr. Deel is a—" She could not bring herself to say what she thought Mr. Deel was. Somehow, it was as if she had accused Myron's father of being a procurer. She had wrapped the two together in her mind.

"That can't be," she said. "He knows Myron. He knows Myron's father."

"Well, he probably does. He knows all the best people—the men that is. And all the most beautiful—ah—courtesans. He probably has something special in mind for you—"

"Me? Why Myron wouldn't let him. He wouldn't." She felt as if she were shrinking, as if she were going to faint. "Myron's not like that. He doesn't know such people. Why he—why we—"

Mrs. Asunda laughed. "Of course, he is. All men are. And if they have the money for the very best, they go to Mr. Deel. You, my dear, are the very best."

Trudy put her head into her hands. Her long hair, undressed this early in the morning, fell to either side of her face. She was not weeping. She had nothing inside her that would create tears. She felt hollow.

"I think you are about to move on in the world. To become the friend of someone so important, so wealthy, he can allow Mr. Deel to make all the arrangements and he will not even have to appear until you are brought to him by Mr. Deel."

"Brought to him? *I* don't have to do that. I'll stay right here. No-body owns me!" Trudy was standing now. These people were mad with their silly sexual arrangements. Two by two in some perverted game. Not for her. She would stay here. Alone. Myron would never see her again. She'd not have it. The brute. To think he would pass her around like a plate of—of—her mind would provide no simile—like a plate of herring.

She sat down again. Now she wept. Into her hands, she said, "Has he sold me? Is that what's going on? To the highest bidder? Is this some sort of white slavery ring?"

Mrs. Asunda put her arms around Trudy. "Don't be ridiculous. You're a great success. You are outstanding. You have outrun Myron. You will be the star of whatever circumstances you find yourself in for many years to come. You shouldn't let Myron hold you back. He hasn't the resources. If this were Europe, you would be a king's mistress. Don't you understand? Some man—"

Trudy shivered. Some man. Any man.

"—a man as rich and as important as a king, has decided he wants you and he's too important to take time to court you. He has sent his messenger. If Myron is giving you up this easily, don't you see how important this man must be?"

Trudy leaned against Mrs. Asunda and wept even harder. At least I can deal with tears, thought Mrs. Asunda. In spite of the dampness on her new traveling suit, she held Trudy and told her to be very very glad. She was to be a renowned beauty at last.

"I don't want to," sniffled Trudy. "I wouldn't know how."

"You've been training for this for months," Mrs. Asunda said. "You know everything. I've taught you; so has Myron, although he probably didn't think so at the time. Now you're perfect; it's time he let you go. All you have to do is smile by day and be loving by night—"

And, she thought, *and open your lovely legs to him every time he asks.* She, herself had done it so often and what did it matter after all? Mr. Graebar or another? As long as it was with style.

CHAPTER XIV

Myron was irritable.

"I don't see why you want me to be complicit in this," he told Mr. Deel. "I don't want to be accused of—of selling—of having anything to do with it."

"You are entitled to some recompense," said Mr. Deel. In the daylight he did not look quite like the fine gentleman Trudy had taken him for the previous evening. "You've put a lot of money on this little girl's back. I could see it in a minute last night. I think you've done her very well and my client is prepared to—"

"I don't know about your client. I don't want to see him or know his name." Then he contradicted himself. "Is he a gentleman?" he asked desperately in a rushed voice. "Is he kind to his—er—ladies? I wouldn't want to have her harmed. No matter what happens to me, to the firm, I'll not have her go to someone who indulges in—practices—you know—you're aware—?"

"Of course you wouldn't. Just as if she's a good filly you've been bringing right along. You wouldn't want rough handling. I can vouch for that. This is a perfect gentleman. He just wants a bit of ass—"

"What? I beg your pardon." Myron rose and stood there, looking indignant. He would have walked right out, but just the act of standing up reminded him of his father.

"Oh, sit down," said Mr. Deel wearily. "That's what we're all after, however much we trim it up. And if you think anything of this girl,

171

you'll listen to what I have to say. Then you can go and present it to her and that will be it. And she can be delivered to the Waldorf by this evening—"

In spite of himself, at this deadline, Myron had to sit down. So soon he would lose her. So soon. His legs would not support his weight.

Mr. Deel had some papers and there were marks on the papers.

"My client will deposit a sum to her account." He named a bank. "And a sum for yourself to any bank you name. This is in nature of a dowry."

"I don't want anything. Give it to her," Myron said sullenly. He could hardly stand this, but he had to do what his father needed done. For the sake of the family business. A new thought occurred to him. "I'd like a receipt of some sort. About the money and all. To see that it's actually done for her."

At these words he put his head down into his hands. He couldn't help it. The thought of selling a woman, any woman, made him feel as if he were being turned inside out and scraped raw. To sell Trudy, for in his own mind that was what he was doing, was dreadful. He should go to the hotel, take her by the hand and shout, "Run, run," as if she were little Eva crossing the ice only shortly ahead of Simon Legree. He could feel the touch of her on his fingers, taste her skin. He shook his head from side to side and didn't bring it up from his hands.

"Oh, buck up there lad," said Mr. Deel. "Look at it this way. Think of yourself as the proud papa and me as the matchmaker. We're going to make all the difference in this little girl's life, but it's definitely going to be for her benefit. She's going to go through life—a good portion of it now—first class and with her own funds and with furs and jewels and a servant guaranteed—nice places to live—" he shook the papers in front of him at Myron, who couldn't see "—and it's all in these papers and it's better than a marriage. A girl like that's a whale of a lot better off than the average *hausfrau*, I can tell you. And little enough does she have to do for it."

"What?" Myron raised his head.

"Sure enough. Does she have to scrub floors? Does she have to risk herself giving birth to a bunch o' brats? Does she have to sew her own clothes and everybody else's out of some two-fer-a-nickel cloth? Not on yer life."

Mr. Deel's elegant accent was breaking down in his passionate speech. "Fer what she's required to do—which ever' woman has to do if she wants to be kept by a man, no matter what her married state—this little girl is going to get a magic carpet. She's going to see the world and be mighty glad of it. And she'll thank you fer not holdin' her back. She's got the style to be the top and I've seen a lot of 'em. I won't let go of her, that little girl. I'll see her through and if he don't treat her right, she can come to me and I'll set it right. Can a married woman do that? All *she* has on her side is the church and the coffin. She has to wait it out and likely as not she'll fall in her grave afore anyone does anything for her. No magic carpet there, fella. Now—"

Deel shuffled through the papers and said, "I'm going to esk yer some questions and ye'd better answer the truth er we'll have somethin' to say later and my client, as you know, is a very exacting sort—"

"What questions? How can there be any questions? Why should I have to answer questions when the option is on your side? I'm not selling you anything. You're taking what you want—"

"Ah, now, be patient a mite longer, eh? I have to get these down fer my own pertection. Let me ask you this—" he consulted the paper in front of him. "Is she, or has she ever been, a prostitute?"

Myron shook his head. He hoped his face conveyed his feelings of revulsion. He couldn't speak. His throat was full of bile.

"Has she ever to your knowledge had a social disease? Have you ever had one yerself?"

"Now see here—" He was ready to walk out. He had his hat on his head.

"DAVIS!" snapped Deel. And Myron went back to the table at the sound of his family name. He knew what that tone meant.

"No to those questions," he answered sullenly.

"Is she pregnant? We don't want yer bastard on our hands."

"No. Of course not." Why didn't I think of it, he thought. I should have said *yes* and made her pregnant and she wouldn't mind. But then in his heart he knew there was benefit here for Trudy. He would have not come if he hadn't understood that. He'd seen these women, the adored mistresses of the very, very rich. They had everything. They were like princesses. He couldn't deny her that. He supposed that even royalty, making an alliance, asked the questions that were being asked of him today. They had to protect themselves. To be very, very rich and very, very important ironically allowed one to avoid manners and speak as if one were mad—or from the streets.

Mr. Deel was still on the subject of pregnancy. "Does she know what to do if she is? She looks mighty young—which is all right a'course—but we want to know if she's certain of her function. My

CHICAGO GIRLS 174

client isn't looking fer any heirs on the wrong side o' the blanket."

"Get it done and let's not go on with this. I can't stand it. Truthfully." Myron hoped an earnest tone would end the ordeal and Deel's intimate confidences.

"Well, that's on her side then. She seems to make a good amour. Yez liked her the whole time. Does she do tricks?"

"What?" Why had he said that? He didn't want to know.

"Does she hev any specialties—bring 'em back from the dead— queens into kings—that sort? I suppose yez wouldn't know wit' yer age and interest. I don't see yez as a switch-hitter—"

Myron realized he was talking about women who were famous for restoring potency to old men and homosexuals. He sat in deep boiling anger and refused to answer.

"What are her blemishes? Identifying marks? We want to be able to identify her in case she gets ideas—"

Myron thought of Trudy, of her transparent skin, of the lovely veins in her temples.

"None," he answered. "She's perfect. Except—" he stopped. He thought of how her ears stuck out.

"What?"

"Nothing. That was his. He would keep it.

"Don't make a mistake now. Tell all yez know."

"That's all I know."

"Does she run to her family? Is she a whiner? Is she likely to get hysterical?"

"No."

Mr. Deel stood up. He extended his hand, which Myron did not take.

"Then it's done." Mr. Deel said.

"I would like a receipt this afternoon showing the funds deposited to her name," Myron repeated and Mr. Deel said he would do that. He told Myron what time Trudy should be brought or sent to the Waldorf, what room she was to use—

"There'll be a maid there. She should just knock. There will be a new wardrobe of clothes for her and a bit of a present from someplace nice. My client will be along later and the maid will get her ready— I think it best that someone accompany her for her trip across town. I could come if yez like or yez take her there yerself. You'll see to that, won't you, Mr. Davis?" The extended hand had been held out for only a short moment, but Mr. Deel had not overlooked the slight. "And no funny business."

They stood looking at each other.

Myron turned and fled the room. This room, too, was in the Waldorf. Mr. Deel did a lot of business in that new hotel. He had a large suite from which he often began his parties. Myron decided he would always hate the Waldorf. It stank of cigars and elegance and he hated both at this moment. All this reminded him of Deel—and of the mysterious patron who would soon be entitled to paw over Trudy in return for—for everything a girl had ever wanted—

As he went down the hallway toward the exit, there was no question in Myron's mind of Trudy's consent. In a marriage, if the stakes were high enough, there would have been little question of consent either. Marriages between fortunes were arranged with all the pomp and lack of choice of a political alliance. Trudy's style was her fortune. This, too, was a political alliance and Myron felt Trudy must be given this opportunity, whether she completely understood the benefits or not. The only distaste he felt was private and personal.

But for Trudy—well, Trudy had chosen her way of life. Trudy's world was different and she had made it so that day in the restaurant, when she'd let herself step through the door into another place, a world where no man would ever consider her as marriageable—no respectable man, that is. He, Myron, could never marry her. He had heard about—but had never met—eccentrics who married their mistresses and brought them into polite society. He guessed it would never work. Where could the woman find women friends? Not even if she were backed with great wealth could she make her way into society as it was lived by Myron's mother and her circle. There was no way to maneuver a former lover and mistress into a chatelaine. And the man would be brought down with her—and his family as well, if they hadn't already cut him from the family scene. Therefore, how could he stand in the way of her advancement in her chosen profession? He could only try to be certain that she was safe and secure.

Society is so complicated, thought Myron. *We have tricked ourselves up with so many rules—I suppose to protect nice women from the other sort— but Trudy is so—how can anyone think to do her harm? She's no threat—*

And with this noble thought he then began to think of the evening ahead when he would have to bring her here. Myron Davis, as has just been seen, was not a brave young man. He settled his hat on his head more firmly and went to find Mrs. Beverly Asunda.

And so it was that Mrs. Asunda met with Myron and Trudy and held Trudy's hand throughout the painful interview. And so it was that Mrs. Asunda instructed the tearful French Madame to pack Trudy's things. And it was Mrs. Asunda who treated Trudy's red eyes with cold water and astringent so that she would look all right for evening. And it was Mrs. Asunda who let Myron slip out while Trudy wept. And it was Mrs. Asunda who took Trudy in a hansom to the Waldorf and the bedroom of Jay B. Darling.

"And now," Mrs. Asunda made a point to say to Trudy, "now you are truly a woman of the world—"

CHAPTER XV

1

Mrs. Asunda had organized the entire removal to the Waldorf. Myron had escaped out the front door of the previous hotel and Trudy hadn't seen him since. At the new hotel Trudy had withdrawn to the sofa. Mrs. Asunda was directing porters and bellmen and she very soon would have all of Trudy's belongings packed into this suite and then, Trudy had been made to understand, Mrs. Asunda was going south on Mr. Graebar's yacht.

None of the actors before her would look at the new star sitting on the sofa. They avoided her eye. All right. Let them ebb and flow around her, let them evade her troubled glance. She would sit here very still and maybe the wave of their actions would swamp her, wash her out to sea, and she would not have to stand and walk and talk and become—someone else.

No one believed her, no one listened to the way she felt. For some reason, Mrs. Asunda chose not to see that Trudy Jones could not make this awful move to a new lover. Mrs. Asunda made herself very busy and didn't ask Trudy where she wanted things put or how she wanted her goods arranged.

What do *I want,* thought Trudy in despair. *No one asks me, but I wouldn't know anyway.*

She could leave this scene being played out before her—and then what? She had only a small amount of money. That this money was greater by many, many times than the amount she'd once considered large enough to finance her brave departure from home escaped her notice. The sum she had on deposit in her name, any amount she might be able to raise on her jewelry and trinkets, would not be enough, she knew now, to keep her for long in her new style.

Myron had forsaken her and would not help her anymore. He'd left most of the telling of it to Mrs. Asunda—who had constantly interrupted the tale to remind Trudy how lucky she was. Trudy didn't believe any of it. Nothing seemed real to her. But just by deciding to stay still and not run away this minute, she could sense she was changing once again.

There was not only the matter of where she might go. Who would she be if she left?

Wherever she went she would be expected to care for herself or pay in some way for her keep. She could never again work in a loft rolling cigars. And in any circumstances she went to, she would now be expected to play the part of a woman, an adult woman of the world who knew the price of security and comfort. And she might have to do this among persons of less substance than Mr. Darling, men who would expect the same favors Mr. Darling sought from her.

During her time in New York, she'd been aware of girls who held earnest employment—girls her own age and older. She'd often thought of their lack of choices, about how foolish they were to have narrowed their lives and hedged themselves in with rules about behavior and morals—as if it mattered. She'd thought then that it was only necessary to ignore old moralities, to appear happy and carefree, and it was possible to gain the world and rule it with an agreeable smile. Be happy, Mrs. Asunda had said. And Trudy had felt happy once. She'd thought Myron to be, if not her love, her coconspirator. But even now she was honest enough to admit that Myron had never deceived her. He'd told her right from the beginning that he must leave her sometime, that she would always be his mistress only. Well, he'd obviously tired of her too quickly.

She must have been at fault. She had no one to blame but herself.

Against everyone's advice she'd mistaken lust for love. What a foolish thing for a girl to do. She'd never felt so stupid in her life.

With the corner of her very fine lace handkerchief, she wiped her damp eyes. Old eyes now. How could she work in some shop, watch women shopping for clothes she could never again afford? Was this to be the future of her life? Bitterness and blame? Would she become like a discarded shoe, limp and unmatched to any other? No. She knew about and wanted the luxury and maids and feathers in her hair of these last months. She still wanted gifts tucked under her table napkin, just for her delight. If she'd never known such things, perhaps she wouldn't have cared. But she did know and she wanted the ease and comfort of it and Myron as well.

Mrs. Asunda was busily at work. She appeared not to notice the handkerchief or Trudy's tears and Trudy thought it just as well. She was beginning to learn that Mrs. Asunda's advice had its drawbacks. She turned and leaned back against the cushion of the new settee, her face in her hankie. She was breathing rapidly.

The Waldorf turned on its axis. She thought she might faint. She knew at last she was what was considered a sporting woman—

But then her mind rebelled against tears and regret. It said don't let them know. She wiped her eyes and sat up. She sat very straight. She sniffed. "Ah, well," she thought, "why not?"

2

The maid's name was Greta and she was pleased to have the pleasure of caring for Mrs. Jones. She spoke German and the familiar words gave Trudy a wrench in the region of her chest.

There were new gowns in the bedroom and the maid bustled about putting away Trudy's possessions from the other hotel. Trudy wanted to ask her what Mr. Jay B. Darling was like, how he looked, but she didn't dare. She didn't believe her situation was normal or right and she hesitated to reveal it to this maid. What would the maid think? Trudy knew. The maid would think that Mrs. Jones was a kept woman.

Trudy had never before felt so much bought and paid for. She had been given notice of her new wealth and handed an additional small purse of "pin money." She had been afraid to ask Mrs. Asunda— Mrs. Asunda who had told her everything except what she needed most to know—how does a woman go from one man in the morning to another at night, on order? And in her heart she knew the answer. She knew why there were women who took strange tonics and touched their foreign cigars with cocaine and drank to excess. To get them through just one more day, one more night, of those hands reaching out, heavy hands with elaborate rings, searching out women in the night—

These were the thoughts that came to Trudy as the maid chattered. Tonight, in that bed, she would be expected to do as she had done with Myron. Those nights with him had been a spontaneous result of living. This was entirely different and Trudy was shocked at everyone around her for thinking she could do this as if nothing unusual were taking place.

"Smile," Mrs. Asunda had said. "When you're not smiling, your lovely little face looks melancholic and men like happy young ladies."

Perhaps Mr. Darling wouldn't like her and she could be sent back to Myron tomorrow. But she knew that wasn't possible. She'd seen the emptiness of their love nest when she left it. Drawers had been standing open—empty. Myron was as far away from there as he could be. He'd left her to this.

Besides, Mrs. Asunda said Mr. Darling was very, very rich and he'd seen her and wanted her and everyone knew and was very impressed by it. How could the world be like that? That such a thing could be generally known and considered a triumph. She'd felt her interludes with Myron in the midnight hours were their own private business. This new arrangement would be common knowledge. It was already common knowledge among the café society and only Trudy had not known she was being scrutinized and rescheduled. Like a train, diverted to another track.

The world had known all along and had failed to rescue her. Further, any failure in this new arrangement, any lack, would be attributed to her.

For the first time in her life, she wished she took some kind of powders. Or she could get some champagne and drink so much of it she would not be aware. What would she have to do? She'd heard terrible stories from a friend of Mrs. Asunda's about what one poor girl had had to do and that girl had one day gone to a church and made a confession and been taken into the order of nuns and was never seen again.

Mrs. Asunda and her lady friend had talked of it for several weeks. And they both said it was because the girl wasn't well-trained in the art of pleasing that her gentleman friend had asked her to do such a thing in the first place. If she had only satisfied him otherwise, the unnatural act would not have been required.

Trudy wished she could lie down, but she didn't want Mr. Darling to find her prone. She preferred to look as if she expected to go somewhere for the evening. She wanted to delay the consequences of this assignation for as long as possible.

The maid was admiring some of Trudy's dresses and then she suggested that Trudy sit at the dressing table for a neck massage.

"It will relax you for the evening ahead," the maid said and then Trudy realized that Greta knew everything and understood.

Greta's strong fingers felt wonderful. While they were occupied with the massage there came a discreet tap on the door of the suite. Greta left the bedroom to answer. When she returned, she appeared excited.

"Mr. Darling has arrived," she said.

Trudy didn't move. Her head was down, because that was how she was holding it for the massage. She didn't raise it to look at the maid. She couldn't. She was terrified. She would not be able to stand.

The moment lengthened.

"You must come," the maid said softly.

Trudy stood. She could not look at the woman. She dreaded the opening of the door. But she knew she would be brought out of the bedroom one way or another. In her terror, she even supposed the strong hands of the maid were meant to see that she went nowhere before her new master arrived. These and other thoughts, vivid and obscene, washed over her.

Greta took her hand. "Come," she whispered and opened the door.

Greta said, "Mrs. Jones is coming, Mr. Darling."

Trudy stepped out of the bedroom, her back straight, her vision impaired by fright, her hands and knees shaking. Before her, in the center of the chamber, stood a tall man, not portly, yet not thin. He turned a pale face toward her, showing her little expression, neither of favor nor of disfavor. Trudy's thought centered on his face. She knew it was something she would be expected to kiss. She knew it would smell of old cigars. He was not as ugly or as old as she had feared. He looked older than Myron, but he seemed ageless. He seemed to be a pair of watching eyes, eyes almost colorless. His face appeared to float somewhere above her head.

He was in full evening dress. He carried his top hat under one arm and he was leaning on his cane in a dapper way. He seemed to be a cat watching a mouse cross the floor. He had no expression. He did not look human. She would never be able to walk toward him. She was his. She took a step. She was in despair.

And in that one swift movement, he presented his top hat to her.

"Mrs. Jones," he said. "I'm so happy to meet you at last." His eyes didn't smile. "We have both been looking forward to your friendship—"

At first Trudy thought he was referring to the maid, but then she realized he meant something else.

"What?" That wasn't right. "I beg your—"

"My dear," he said, "what is your first name? The name you liked to be called by?"

She looked at him with his unsmiling eyes and his no-expression face. She thought she might die. If she should die tonight in this suite, her mother must never know.

"Pamela," she said. "My first name is Pamela." They would think she was Pamela and her mother would not know.

"Pamela," said Jay B. Darling, "I want you to meet Shu-Shu—"

And from within his hat he produced a Pekinese pup.

3

"We've got to do something with Myron," said his mother. She and her husband were having breakfast in her room. They often met together in this way to plan for coming events, talk over current gossip—for everyone gossips and only narrow-minded fools deny it—and to settle the household matters that needed discussing.

"What's the matter with him?" asked Mr. Davis.

"He doesn't go to his club at all. For a while there, I would have been glad to see him, but now that he is about so much and such a dead weight on the conversation, I don't honestly know what I can talk to him about. He reads no books, attends no parties, seems to have dropped his former friends. I don't understand what's come over him—"

"Perhaps he's in love with Miss Dubois."

"Oh, I hope not—" said Mrs. Davis, wincing at the name of her friend's daughter. School spirit could be carried too far. "Miss Dubois would never do. They live in the South and still they keep only two carriages. They must be poor in earnest—"

"Maybe we don't have to do anything with Myron at all," his father said, ignoring Miss Dubois. "Maybe we should just leave Myron to his own devices. After all, he will soon be twenty-five."

"I know. I even offered to have people in. Celebrate the birthday. He turned me down flat. Was almost angry about it. I've never seen him like this—"

"Hmmm. Possibly he had reverses at the track. I think he backed the wrong horse. Ran into some sort of trouble over a filly—"

Mrs. Davis smiled at her husband. "Like father, like son. I do understand where these old remarks come from, now that I have this travail—" She rubbed her forehead with a daintily scented handkerchief. She rested her elbow on the tea table and her head on her hand. Her hair, not yet put up, fell forward. He liked to see her like this. He liked this part of the day best. She seemed young to him during these morning chats, as if they were newly married again, as if Myron were not yet born and they had all of life ahead of them.

He knew what Myron was going on about. Myron had been farther gone on the stunning Mrs. Jones than he realized, and Myron had been rescued in the nick. Good that his mother has not suspected a thing, thought Mr. Davis.

And Mrs. Davis was thinking, I think Myron has fallen for some hussy and is planning to run away with her. Thank God, his father doesn't suspect.

Mr. Davis said, "There is a great deal of work to be done about the fair in Chicago. We have taken on some risk there and Myron could go back again to look over the exhibits that are being prepared and see what conditions are about the place. It would be very helpful. You know how those places are—"

"Careless," nodded Mrs. Davis. "Shoddy conditions."

"Exactly. It would be the most natural thing in the world if I sent him out to be our man on the scene—"

"—and work never hurt anyone," Mrs. Davis agreed. "He'd be the better for it. I'll do better by him than I did on his last trip. I believe I know one or two people who might be happy to meet our son. He might be well consoled—"

"Consoled?"

"Oh," she waved it away. "Bad choice of word. He'd have a grand time if he got in with the right sort. Our sort of people, you know."

"There you have it," Myron's father said. "A good break in routine with a nice bit of work to do in the bargain." He stood up reluctantly. He would have liked to go back to bed, taking her with him. But she was gathering up her combs and he could hear the maid tapping at the door.

"I'll go now. I'll tell him on the way to the office," he said, leaning to kiss the top of her head.

4

The concierge of the Waldorf—or was he the manager—was surprised by a young man who did not give his name, but who asked to speak to "your most senior employee."

"Do you mean in age, sir? We are a new hotel. None of our employees have been here very long, although all are experienced. I'm certain we can find someone on our staff who can help in any way you wish—"

The young man, with his blue, blue eyes, said he wished to speak to a bellman or a discreet person—

"Fine, fine—"

When the young man and his consultant were alone, sizeable bills changed hands.

"If there is any news concerning this person, please let me know at this address. The letters will be forwarded to me," he told the bellman. He provided a neat stack of envelopes. "I will see to it you are further rewarded for each item of information."

The bellman, who knew the person the young man referred to and had taken her little dog Shu-Shu for a walk that very afternoon, said he would not fail.

"And you must be the soul of discretion," the young man said. "The—er—gentleman—has quite a temper. He is one of the owners of this hotel." That was not true, but the young man was sure the bellman didn't know it.

5

There is the crux of it. Everyone has chosen a path, sometimes without knowing the choice has been made. And once it has been made, no other choices remain, only variations on the theme.

Once the woman has said, "Ah, well, why not?" once she has learned to touch his hand when she speaks to him, once she has run—not away from home but *to* adventure—once she has decided to run away and does—or *does not*—that woman, in or out of love— becomes another and all around her are brought forward into this new design.

After her good neighbor the coppersmith's wife had ladled out the gossip that was known about Gertie throughout the Maxwell Street neighborhood, Tessa had taken her lesson in silence, had given no satisfaction, adding no remark to be made part of the tale in the next telling. After the malicious neighbor woman left her kitchen, Tessa sat in the growing darkness and looked at the wall. Whatever went through her mind then was not revealed by the way she sat at the table, her back straight.

Suddenly she stood. There was something on her mind about a lost child. Vertigo struck her and she grasped the back of a chair for support; she stood there, unaware of what was happening to her, her body feeling as if it were being pushed from side to side by a giant hand. She didn't take a step, but clutched the chair, a feeling of surprise and regret sweeping through her.

In this posture she was found a few moments later by Frank, her second son. Her head was bent forward slightly; she seemed to be staring through the dusk at the stove, concentrating on a kettle she had boiling there.

"Dark in here," muttered Frank and went toward the table to light the lamp. Something, some movement of Tessa's, made him look down.

From beneath his mother's skirts a red-wine stain was spreading across the uneven floor.

"Ma," he shouted. And moved to catch her just in time. She collapsed in his arms. He carried her into the bed, crying out to her.

As he moved her to wrap her in a coverlet, he found the bed beneath already soaked with blood and he, who kept his money and his private life as separate from his family as shared living quarters would allow, bolted from the bedroom, out through the kitchen and into the street to find a doctor. And he paid for the doctor in advance from his own money, a clear measure of his distress.

The doctor moved deliberately, not hurrying. From the boy's description he knew what he'd find. A woman too old to be pregnant, a superstition about the miscarriage—that God or some evil look by a neighbor had caused it—a lack of money, possibly food, many small children about the place and a father who was absent, probably at a local hangout, drinking up his pay.

Tessa's eyes shone out of the dim light of the bedroom. The doctor, she accepted as a matter of course, not questioning where he had come from or who would pay the bill. She lay against the bed, white in the darkness. There were a few hurried breaths from her, a gripped hand; she didn't moan but motioned for water to drink—even when Otto was fetched to her and put his beery face down to brush against her hair, she said no word, cried no tears.

In two hours it was all over. Tessa was cleaned out, the pregnancy gone. The doctor stayed long enough to allow Frank to go for Agnes, his married sister, who came and took the younger children away. Otto and the oldest son, Emil, carried Tessa to Lilly's, the second married sister, Frank stayed behind to clean up the flat.

The departing medic told Lilly, "If she begins to run a fever, call another doctor right away. If she runs a fever it's—" He shrugged. Tessa had been silent even to this last. The doctor didn't like that look on her. The daughter who was taking this woman home should know her mother might die.

During the course of that night, the swift departure of the family to the home of one daughter or another gave the appearance to the neighborhood of flight.

6

At Lilly's, Tessa recovered her strength. If she'd not died of one thing or another in the journey to America, in the move across country or in the previous births—not one lost—then she'd already proved herself stronger than her frail body might suggest. She'd proved herself stronger than most women of her time and place. Tessa's body mended. But still she hardly talked at all.

Perhaps a grief like that, without mourning, can lead only to madness. But even her madness Tessa guarded and edged with her own boundaries. She was never to be accused again of not taking care.

Tessa, although appearing outwardly restored, was never the same. A feeling consumed her without words. She was silent because she was trying to remember—there was a matter of loss, something of value was lost to her. That must have meant she'd not paid attention. She must have been careless somehow.

7

Tessa settled back into the home routine without complaint. She talked to the little children, gave brief greetings to those who came, offered food at mealtime, said prayers. But sometimes her family woke in the morning to find she'd gone out into the streets before anyone was up.

Or she would suddenly turn from a meal she was cooking, untie her apron and fling her black shawl around her like a cloud of woe and go out, not to return for hours.

Otto now slept alone.

The shame of Gertie's leaving, the loss of Tessa's baby, had torn Otto and Tessa apart at last. If she slept at night, she slept on a mat on the floor. As a group, the family would not admit she slept little, but individually they knew it well.

After Otto would make his dreary way homeward, smelling of beer, full of grievances about his day and the condition of his feet and the sores on his hands that would not heal because they were always in the cold and moist air of the meatrooms all day, even after he fell into the bed in an almost unconscious state, Tessa was awake, staring into the dark.

She would let the early evening pass, the settling of the last day-workers into some sort of night accommodation, and then Tessa would rise up from her pallet, going out alone to walk up and down the streets, haunting the places of leftover souls.

As a young girl, Tessa had been instructed in the ways of virtue and purity. From this instruction she'd gathered that sin is always accompanied by poverty and pain. Though the neighborhood gossips had spoken of Gertrude on a grand avenue holding the arm of a "swell gent," heading for a fine hotel, Tessa believed none of that. Maybe that was how sin began—but it ended in the black streets of the poor and that was where she concentrated her search. She could not envision evil dressed in finery, reclining on satin sheets. What she saw before her was real and evil enough that it seemed the place to look for the lost Gertrude.

In Tessa's mind, the sinful hid themselves away and at a certain hour, hours unknown to the virtuous, the wicked come out into the streets. If only she could be there at that uncharted moment, she would find her daughter. So she walked the only ways she knew, watching for a slight shifting of conditions that meant the sinful were off guard and vulnerable. Her frenzied thoughts converted this idea into a driving compulsion to frequent places where people came and went.

The wicked, she thought, were associated with trains. Trains were great black things that moved at night along the rails, seeming to move of their own volition. Evil moved in such a way, coming into one's life without warning, shaking the earth, giving only briefly lighted hints of what lay within for the novitiate. Trains were not far from her home, blocking her way to the city beyond. If she could be at the place the trains yielded up their cargo—there she would find Gertie.

The station she suspected most was the Polk Street Station east of Clark. The dolorous sound of its tower bells, the look of the place, as if it were a castle, spoke to Tessa of wrongful acts. She could imagine the terrible merchants of women there. Even when she stood at one end and surveyed the entire concourse, there was always the feeling that behind some pillar, just out of sight, lurked Gertie's abductor—or the girl herself.

One Saturday night she came out of the Polk Street Station and a policeman stopped her, asking if he could see to it that she was put into a Parmalee cab or some conveyance to get her out of the district. That section around Polk and Clark and Dearborn was a bad area, especially on Saturday night. The city claimed it had ended prostitution in the name of the Exposition and it had stopped horse-betting and dice and card games, but a traveler coming in on almost any train could find all these vices flourishing.

Tessa looked up at the policeman. "I'm looking for my daughter," she said.

"Has she come in on a train?" he asked.

"No. She's—she's run away." Tessa stood looking up at the man in silence, almost challenging him to produce Gertie.

He pointed to the east. "Go down there, Mother," he said. Round the corner. There's a mission there. Perhaps they can help. They often sees the lost and homeless—"

The words choked out of Tessa. "She had a home," she said. "She had a home with me. She didn't need a new one—"

The policeman felt as though struck by a knife. So ancient a cry was this; a daughter lost; a mother grieving; a home left for—for what? For the dangers of the night.

Daughters. The policeman knew there were daughters everywhere in this district. Nightly the streets around this station saw female wrecks in a hopeless parade, making enough money for one personal destruction or another, anything to make the night pass and another night come on.

The policeman looked about in anxiety. He felt as if he must say something, relieve in some way this awful grief that suddenly filled him.

"A daughter," he said, trying to keep his voice light. "A daughter, Mother? Now can't I interest you in a son instead?"

Tessa looked around. There were boys all around them, moving along in perfect safety. Newsboys, messengers, on bicycle or foot. Life and wagons rushed past. Innocent travelers made their way ignoring the boys around them, never looking twice. There was, Tessa could see, a cleverness about these boys. No mother was out in the night, calling to them to return home.

She said, "No. Never our sons. It's our daughters we look for—" She went on, away from the direction he'd shown her, going west away from the mission, watching for a break, a weakness, in the armor of the night.

STEVEN

CHAPTER XVI

1

Steven decided to organize a literary club with the hope that once he and his fortunate friends began to read and discuss, it would lead, as he told Margaret, to "something worthwhile."

The club was a great success, but it wasn't very literary. Billie Shumacher, whose father owned the Middle West's most successful soda cracker factory, said there wasn't enough of summer in Chicago as it was, and he wasn't going to spend it inside reading books. He said they should spend the summer cycling and the winters reading books. Since Billie was a great friend of Arthur's, and Arthur knew all the best places to go on a wheel, the cyclists carried the motion.

Margaret and Steven were together wherever they went. If Margaret had been more of a coquette, there might have been an engagement. But Margaret continued to see herself as a no-nonsense person, and it didn't occur to her that they should announce to their friends the progress of their romance. They were pleased with each other and that was all that mattered to her.

Steven, believing all romances were like his, thought everything was going along well and didn't need to be rushed. Besides, he'd noticed that when Arthur and Harriet had announced their engagement they'd lost all their privacy.

Mrs. Marsh realized that "that Baxter Boy" was more than ever on the scene, but she learned that he and Margaret went bicycling together with a large group of their contemporaries and she thought

191

exercise and good fun in a crowd was a healthy new sign. Margaret, removed from her university life, was becoming less bookish and Mrs. Marsh was pleased. Margaret had said nothing to her mother about romance or Steven Baxter and Mrs. Marsh didn't like to ask directly: She didn't want to pose any questions that might stimulate an answer she didn't want to hear.

Soon, she thought, *we'll go to Boston and then they'll write a few times and that will be the end of it.*

The rest of the household—the servants—had their own view of the courting of Miss Margaret by Steven Baxter. The butler, Knox, could hardly believe that this young man was one of the richer young men of the city, and put down to country manners Steven's polite greetings to Knox himself and to other members of the household staff, Steven's interest in a servant's whereabouts, a warm "hello" to a parlor maid or waitress, a comment to the second man about the difficulty of keeping an entrance clean in rainy weather.

And the gardener had never before met a young man who knew the Latin names of flowers and a bit of poetry—which could be quoted on the spot—about this blossom or that.

Some of the kitchen-girls and the chambermaids, not directly encountering Steven's charm, thought he was not as romantic as might be expected and the girl who dusted the solarium told how she'd come upon the blissful pair in the garden room, reading in separate corners. "What kind of love match is that, I want to know?" Miss Margaret kept dressing in those funny clothes and going off to the fairgrounds or going away on her cycle, a very unladylike and unromantic way to conduct a love affair.

"Why, they must be always out of breath," the maids of the kitchen agreed. "No wonder they don't talk much."

The cycling club adopted the colors blue and gold and went out dressed in a kind of uniform—the men in sackcloth jackets of the club's colors, the girls wearing divided skirts or bloomers in dark blue with small blue and gold hats perched on top of their pinned-up hair.

Their favorite direction was northwest. There were several picnic groves and prairies out that way and, in true Chicago style, they sent their servants ahead to ready their picnics.

Margaret was still spending three mornings a week and one afternoon at the Woman's Building at the fairgrounds, but that left quite a bit of summertime to spend with Steven.

None of the other cycling club members had strong commitments or had to work anywhere and they found the best days for their outings were during the week. The picnic grove they liked best was a commercial one, and on one of their weekly outings they arranged to take over the entire park and its lagoon and its small boats, to the eternal gratitude of the proprietor, who had little business during the week. The park was located in a woodland of oak and hickory, a pleasant spot, though the lagoon was a bit sluggish and cattails and waterlilies choked one side. Even after their energetic ride to the park, the group still had the energy to play catch in an open field next door, displacing a clutch of butterflies. The rowboats were also kept busy.

"It's such a lovely day," Margaret said to Steven, "let's go for a walk in the woods."

The two of them went off alone. "These days are fun," Steven said to his sweetheart, "but they're not exactly what I'd had in mind for this summer. I'd hoped we could do something *worthwhile* with our time. But all we do is play. We ought to realize how fortunate we are and try to bring some of our luck to other people. I'd hoped to introduce this idea gradually to our meetings."

He sighed and Margaret sighed with him. She wished she could demonstrate that she, Margaret Marsh, understood the meaning of *worthwhile*. But all she could do was walk with him and listen to him and look at him. For the moment that seemed enough.

By late summer, the nesting songs of birds are stilled, the wildflowers are gone and woods are green and quiet. It had rained not more than two days before and the wood about them had the heady smell of elemental things—of earth and old leaves, acid, decaying, yet somehow promising secret worlds to be found around the next bend in the path.

"I wish I could find flowers for you," he said, but he was able to show her two different patches of ferns she would not have noticed if she'd been alone. Some instinct told her not to say that she also knew the name of these ferns—but she would *not* have seen them on a solitary ramble and she quieted her conscience with that. Lately she often felt as if she were two women, one the young woman who'd come to Chicago in the spring, full of new ideas about womanhood and independence, and a second woman, yielding, acquiescent, willing to follow where the young man led.

Steven, walking ahead of her, found some mushrooms that had sprung up, probably in a moment after dawn.

"Deadly," he said.

She shuddered, but spread her arms in the still air. Ahead of them something rustled through the undergrowth, but nothing definite could be seen. In the heat, her hair had begun to come unpinned and she found a stump to sit on and began to put it back into order.

He came to her and touched it.

"I wish," he whispered from behind her, "that you would let it fly loose in the air—"

"It's bothersome when I do that," she said, thinking of the night she'd walked on the beach in the storm. But to soften what she'd said, she turned and smiled at him and he kissed her. They stayed that way, holding each other for some time, thinking nothing anyone would have considered *worthwhile*.

Then she reached up and brought his head down to hers again and she kissed him. This was a new, delightful step to both. They finished, flushed and shaken. She stood and took his hand, because their absence had been long enough. They started back, hardly daring to look at one another.

Neither walked on the path itself, because if they had done so, one would have had to lead and the other follow in the way they'd come into the woods earlier. But this time they chose to go along, side by side, each with a hand out to the other with the common way between them.

Arthur, coming along with the water, saw Margaret and Steven emerge from the woods. The expressions on the faces of the two were quite serious. Arthur liked Margaret very much and had admiration for her intelligence and enjoyed her flashes of humor and wit. But he didn't believe she was right for Steven. Why couldn't his gentle brother have found a girl who was a little more merry? Margaret had her social side, but Arthur noticed that when she was with Steven, she often didn't show it. When she was with Steven in public, Margaret took on the characteristics of her mother—whom Arthur admired very much because Mrs. Marsh was so controlled, unlike his own mother. Arthur thought being serene was a good characteristic for a *mother*, but Steven needed an impetuous laughing girl as a wife to lead him into the social milieu.

Arthur had heard stories about W. W. Marsh; there was much gossip about Mr. Marsh and a certain married woman, that the man undoubtedly had been passionate in his style and perhaps foolhardy in his passion; that his death had somehow been caused by an inability to reconcile that passion.

Why couldn't the daughter have a bit more of her father's style? Arthur thought, watching Margaret as the preparation of the lemonade and the spreading of the lunch was organized. What could these two reserved lovers do in their private moments together? He couldn't know that at times Steven had wondered the same thing about Harriet and Arthur, the loving pair who'd hardly been alone or together since their engagement.

That afternoon Steven was quite oblivious to Arthur and his brother's concern for him. Arthur felt somewhat eased when he saw Steven on the other side of the pond, feeding a family of ducks and laughing at the antics of the ducklings with Margaret nowhere near. *Maybe it's not as serious as I thought,* mused Arthur. And when he saw Steven wade out to rescue the hat of another one of the girls when she lost it on the water, a girl known to be almost brainless—hence the lost hat—Arthur decided Steven was still testing the waters in another way.

"Your brother is a living saint," the girl next to Arthur said, "and he has such dreamy poetic eyes."

"I know," Arthur agreed. "That's what worries me. Saints are not known for long life—"

"Hush," said the girl. "To say such a thing's bad luck."

"You're right, I must have been crazy to think it." But Arthur sometimes chafed under remarks—from his mother and others—about Steven's "goodness." Perfection in a younger brother could be hard to live up to.

The older brother went off to see to it that all the cycles were put onto the wagon with the picnic gear. The cyclists were going to go home in a hayride after dark.

They were going to sing old songs all the way.

2

Margaret gave up none of her feminist views, but she found that in Chicago, Mrs. Palmer's conservative thoughts on female advancement were considered outrageous enough, and received as much, if not more, razzing in the press than suffragists. Mrs. Palmer had the power and the purse to make changes; the suffragists did not. More and more, Margaret was swept into Chicago's social climate and there she learned to keep her own counsel about women's rights.

She was welcomed everywhere as a native returned and there was none of the coldness and mysterious atmosphere that had been present during the time of her father's death two years before. Mrs. Marsh still did not fraternize with her husband's business partner, but otherwise, social conditions appeared to Margaret to be cordial.

The silver tray in the hall of the Marsh mansion filled with a shower of white cardboard engraved with the names of Chicago's elite.

Days in Chicago, Margaret Marsh learned, were not at all like days elsewhere. Chicago days were *italicized*. Sunday was not Sunday, but *Sunday*. Monday became *Monday* and each of these and all days between belonged to one matron or another within the social sphere—if that matron was important enough to assume attendance.

For example, Mrs. Henry Featherwaite held *Sundays* sacrosanct: They included not only two sessions of well-preached Presbyterian dogma and a handsome ten-course dinner anchored by roast beef, but also musicales. Thus it went through the week: Mrs. Glessner was allocated her *Tuesdays* and on and on until *Friday*, which had, over the years, become the province of Mrs. Palmer and friends, cherished by those bid to come for an afternoon with the reigning queen of Chicago.

"What am I going to do," exclaimed Margaret. "There will be nothing left of any week. I can't go to every one of these events. With the meetings with the lawyers and other business, there will be no room for my own interests in between. Who will I have become—nothing but a social butterfly, someone who is not worthwhile, full of dreadful opinions about nothing and everything—already there is too much about profit and loss on my mind and now these—"

Several mornings during each month Margaret and her mother found it necessary to meet with attorneys and bankers regarding her father's estate. Matters were being arranged so that Margaret would be able to manage her own wealth from any place she chose to reside. Some assets were being consolidated and it was necessary to pace out sales of large blocks of stock, so that such large divestitures did not affect the total value. The Prairie Avenue house, which they had considered selling, was to be retained—

"—for the time being," Margaret told her advisors.

Her mother looked annoyed, but said nothing.

"We'll be finished with the bankers soon. Then we can scurry off to Boston."

Margaret looked up from the mail in her lap. *Boston.* So soon? She'd planned to stay for a while. Steven expected her to stay. She was twenty-four. When was she to be allowed her own life?

She noticed that her mother was walking about the solarium, touching the edges of a plant here, there adjusting bits of bric-a-brac that didn't need adjusting. Margaret realized something was wrong; her mother usually sat in dignified, queenly repose, while others went to pieces around her. Margaret had a sudden flash of intuition. Her mother was going to speak to her about Steven.

But after a short wait, Mrs. Marsh said in a quiet voice, "I would like to be in Boston by the winter season. I don't mind summer in Chicago, but I don't want to be here in winter." She came and sat on a chaise longue, but didn't put her feet up. She looked steadily at Margaret, as if to meet the challenge she knew would come. That Mrs. Marsh did not mention Steven was apparent to both women.

To answer the question as obliquely as it had been put to her, Margaret riffled through the papers in front of her. "What shall I do about these?" She let the invitations fall on the table.

"I would suggest you attend some of the more important gatherings while we're here, since some are given by neighbors and at least one invitation comes from Mrs. Palmer, who has been quite kind to you." There was a strange overtone in her mother's voice, almost as if she were giving a warning or threat.

"Oh, well," Margaret said, hoping she could avoid answering some quiz her mother might be leading into regarding Steven, "I suppose I could just say I have previous engagements." At the unfortunate choice of word Margaret rushed on. "That's what I say in other places when the invitations don't please me—"

But evidently Mrs. Marsh was on another, undiscernible track. "Margaret, in Chicago you must be very careful that what you say is true and above suspicion. We mustn't offend, you know dear. Chicago matrons can be—unpleasant—to outsiders when they think their institutions are being snubbed. As you found in your own work at the fair. I hesitate to say anything, because I don't want you to be cold and suspicious. But perhaps you've noticed—" here she gave a brittle laugh "—that on certain afternoons one could put a cannon ball down the length of Prairie and strike every important matron in the city. Not only that, but those same matrons have an unrestricted view of our front door. And in addition, there is the inbreeding of the servants to consider. The true state of—" here she took a breath and plunged on "—a woman's private life is hardly a secret anywhere in Chicago."

"What do the servants have to do with it?"

"Haven't you been chattered to as I have? I think they do it everywhere—telling their business and ours to anyone they meet. They haven't been properly trained. Didn't you know that our Molly is the first cousin of Mrs. Field's cook and that both have younger sisters in service on the north side and one is married to the McCormicks' groom and, if not that, they sit about in cloakrooms at the dances and tell all they know—"

"However did you learn that?" asked Margaret.

"There is no peace even in my own quarters if that Irish maid is about. She insisted on telling me as much gossip as she could while she was cleaning my fireplace. Who knows what's repeated about us?"

"Perhaps you'd better come to these various tea parties with me. Then I'll at least have you to talk to—" Margaret's own laugh was rueful. Her mother came to life in the evenings and did not like ladies' teas.

At the suggestion that she spend her afternoons traveling about to gatherings of matrons, Mrs. Marsh looked pained, but when she spoke, Margaret found it was for a different reason. Her mother had been acting oddly ever since they'd come home to Chicago, but still Margaret was startled to see that Mrs. Marsh's eyes were misty and her voice uneven as she said, "The invitations for these afternoon functions are addressed to you. Look at the envelopes—"

Margaret looked down. She picked up one or two. Yes, they were addressed only to *Miss Margaret Marsh*.

"What about those?" she asked her mother. Mrs. Marsh had a separate collection of letters sitting on the fireplace table.

"Those are for evening events—and the opera. From the same people who made arrangements for your work at the fair. From my— expatriate friends, who happened to have returned to town just for the fair—"

3

If Mrs. Marsh was careful in her notice and mention of "that Baxter boy," Uncle Findley was not so chary. If he'd not been so outspoken, Margaret might have run to him to ask him about Mrs. Marsh's revelation concerning her snubbing by Chicago matrons. But because he often pressed her with talk of *Steven, Steven Steven*, she had found herself neglecting the old man unless Steven were with her. Uncle Findley knew enough not to ask leading questions before the swain himself, although Findley had offered himself in the role of "father"— one who might ask the young man his "intentions." Margaret had turned that offer down flat.

Margaret put the snubbing of Mrs. Marsh down to provincialism, some sort of community accord to show that the West was as good as the East and could be just as boorish. She had no other plot she could assign to it and she decided that the way to make her mother more comfortable in Chicago, where Margaret was determined to remain, was to attend every dull ladies' tea she could and earn the right for her mother to be known as "a Chicago woman"—or at least the *mother* of one.

Now and then, she and Steven went to the Tremont and took Uncle Findley with them for a summer outing of one sort or another. Usually, they found he could tell them more than they could tell him. They all three went over to Lake Front Park on the east side of Michigan to see the new building being put up to house the "congresses," discussion groups organized worldwide to run concurrently with the Exposition, to discuss Women's Concerns, World Religions, Peace and War, Government and other topics.

"You know just how it will be," Uncle Findley said. "The powerless of the world will come here and talk and talk and the ones who wield power will stay home and do as they always have done.

"Are you a cynic, sir?" asked Steven.

"About gov'ments and palaver, yes, I am. There's more bad than good around, m'boy. Look around you—"

"Oh, I see a lot of good being done. Look at Hull House. Not that there couldn't be a lot more of that sort of thing. I'd like to see more people work among the poor. Maybe there could be some long-range improvement for their housing, if that might happen." Steven was looking at Margaret when he said this and she knew he was talking about the cycling group.

"How can one person go to another and just say, 'Here I am, I'm better off than you and I want to do good to you'?" Margaret asked. "Isn't that a sort of—paternalism? One could give all one's money away and *still* there would be poor in the world."

"The only way to do it is without any strings," Steven said.

"Or the leg-up method," Uncle Findley said. "Find somebody worthwhile and find out what he or she needs and then provide that very thing. That way no offense could be taken—" Uncle Findley gestured with his cane to a woman crossing in front of their buggy. "Now speaking of offense, have you ever seen anything like that hat?"

Margaret laughed and agreed. "That's what bothers me, I guess, about the poor. You give them a donation from your heart and your hoard and they take it and spend it on stuff and nonsense like that hat. I suppose it's foolish of me, but I really can't forgive the poor their bad taste—"

She happened to look at Steven at that moment and he looked so shocked, she fell silent immediately and said nothing until they reached the Tremont. Steven stayed with the horse and buggy and Margaret walked with Uncle Findley into the hotel.

"I don't think your young man liked our criticism of the poor woman's millinery, Maggie," Uncle Findley said.

"I know, Uncle. I'll apologize to him for what I said." She kissed her uncle goodbye, but he wasn't ready to let her go.

"I hope you're staying around for a while this winter. The winters are the saddest time. I miss—" He didn't finish. "Anyway, you need to tend to your last there, Miss Shoemaker. What does that biology fit you up for in the general way?"

"Well, I thought it was interesting and it underlies everything." She didn't see the trap he was laying for her.

"That's right and you should have a home and children, like biology calls for; that is, if you want me to be able to dandle a batch of red-headed Baxter younguns on my knee. You'll have to start soon, m'girl."

"Oh, Uncle Findley, you've gotten me into enough trouble today. I'll not talk to you about biology or red-headed children." She left him with a quick hug.

On the way to the Marshes', Steven said, "As you unpack the exhibits for the Woman's Building, did you ever think that if the rich female patrons in the smart set would pay better prices for the finery they buy, women who make the goods might be better able to survive? To give a good price might redistribute wealth in the best way—to a worker. I'm thinking of looking into the field of social work when I begin work at the university in the fall. It interests me and I feel so unnecessary in the world of business—"

"I understand. I've been told by Uncle Findley that I should be paid for my work wherever or whatever I do, but I hate to take money from someone who needs it." Margaret hoped to mend her unfortunate gaffe about the hat with this bit of truth.

"That's it. I think I'll just drop my classical studies and take up something in the social sciences. My only worry about it is that I'm—" he hesitated.

"You don't like to impose on others. You just want to help where you can—"

"There. I knew you'd understand, though no one else has. Arthur thinks I ought to set up a foundation and then go off and take up golf. My mother believes business is the highest order of life. And if I don't go into my father's business, into the old firm, she says she will have failed my father—"

Margaret reached over and took his free hand in hers. She didn't know what to say about Steven's mother. She'd heard the woman was eccentric.

4

One afternoon, after a particularly dreadful recital at a neighboring Prairie Avenue home, Margaret came home to find Mrs. Chesterton in the drawing room with her mother.

At the sight of the traveler's handsome carte-de-visite on the hall table, Margaret turned at once toward the stairs, but Knox, passing through the hall with a tea tray on his way to the pantry, said, "Mrs. Marsh asks that you join her, Miss Margaret—"

There was nothing Margaret could do but turn back. As she came into the room she saw Mrs. Chesterton, alone for once, chatting with Mrs. Marsh, who wore a look on her face that Margaret, as a child, had termed *that look.* Her mother was annoyed, but of course showed nothing of her annoyance, her posture and attitude toward her guest impeccable, her complexion appearing so perfect she looked like an alabaster statue.

"Good news," said her mother without any inflection, "Mrs. Chesterton and her daughters have taken a house in the city for the coming months—" The look she gave to Margaret said, Now will you hear me concerning Boston?

"We have sent for our *trunks,*" said Mrs. Chesterton, smiling and nodding at Margaret. "We must be on hand for the coming fair and we want to be here for *all* of it. We don't want to miss one little moment. And as Mr. Chesterton is otherwise engaged at his various businesses, the girls and I thought we'd just come on ahead and make all arrangements."

"Mrs. Chesterton met Mrs. Featherwaite when she visited Mackinac Island last summer. Funny how these island places—" Mrs. Marsh didn't finish.

Mrs. Chesterton did. "—spawn friendships."

There was a certain overbrightness to Mrs. Chesterton's eye as if to say: You see, I'm totally spoken for by Mrs. Featherwaite. You didn't move quickly enough.

Clearly Mrs. Featherwaite would be the Chestertons' sponsor in Chicago society.

Mrs. Chesterton asked, "How are you managing at the fairgrounds? I imagine there are many social activities involved with it in addition to the actual work in progress—"

"No, not really—" answered Margaret vaguely. "There is much hard work though, physical work—" She didn't want to be saddled with escorting the Chesterton girls to the fairgrounds and back again.

"Margaret has just come from an afternoon tea," prompted Mrs. Marsh, who didn't like to hear anything about the fairgrounds if she could help it.

"Oh?" said Mrs. Chesterton provocatively.

Margaret was not to be cornered. "Mrs. Featherwaite would have the best view of afternoon teas," she said firmly, as much to her mother as Mrs. Chesterton. "These teas must be thought of in terms of interests. Mrs. Featherwaite has lived here all her life and I've only been here a short time. She would have the best view of the situation for you and would have the most generous of acquaintances—"

"Yes," Mrs. Chesterton said, "I find Mrs. Featherwaite to be reliable in all matters. I'm pleased with our connection here." Smugness rode on her haughty features. "And may I say—" she leaned forward, smiling "—since we're quite alone—?"

Margaret thought, from a slight movement her mother gave, that Mrs. Marsh was going to object, but then did not.

Mrs. Chesterton lowered her voice, but nevertheless, spoke forcefully and from obvious conviction. "I'm so pleased to learn from Mrs. Featherwaite that you have given up your—ah—notions, my dear," she said to Margaret. "You are to be encouraged to develop your womanly graces. I chose today to mention this to you because my daughters are not present. I was quite shocked on our last visit to hear you mention *biology*, especially in mixed company. I wonder," she turned now to Mrs. Marsh, "that you let your daughter study such dreadful material."

Margaret was quite certain her mother gave a sniff. Her mother had never sniffed in her life that Margaret had heard, not even in the streets of Cairo. Both Marsh women sat speechless as Mrs. Chesterton continued, evidently believing she had their indulgence.

"—young women in Great Neck or Albany or New York City or on our lovely little Sporting Isle do not concern themselves with such subjects. I try to make certain my girls are part of a very genuine society wherever we reside. Gentility does not allow for *biology*—and the best way to avoid it is to know nothing about it, learn nothing about it, never speak of it—"

Mrs. Chesterton finished her speech in a rush. Her face was flushed and she looked as stern as Margaret had ever seen her.

Margaret was trembling with anger—not only at poor stupid Mrs. Chesterton, who was ignorant by choice, but at the entire day she'd just lived through, at the irresponsibility of the women of her class, at her own feelings of uselessness. Margaret rose and stood as tall as only a well-bred, thin, educated red-haired Bostonian can stand when she is dealing with someone from the outer reaches of asininity.

"Mrs. Chesterton—" she began.

"Margaret—" said her mother sharply. Her mother's look said *Remember what I've told you about Chicago.*

"Mrs. Chesterton," Margaret began again, but because of the warning look she moved one notch down the indignation scale. "How can you say—how can Mrs. Featherwaite say—I've set aside my so-called *notions?* How can you say a woman should know nothing about biology? A woman *is* biology. That's where we begin. And each month of our adult lives we're reminded of our function—"

"Margaret!" Mrs. Marsh sounded desperate.

Mrs. Chesterton gasped.

"I'm sorry if I offend you, Mrs. Chesterton. But if more women would inform themselves on matters of biology, there would be fewer unwanted children, there would be fewer deaths at childbirth, there would be fewer ruined maidens and fewer migraines in the boudoirs of the rich. We must know our bodies and take charge of them—"

"Why, why that's just godless. Women have struggled for thousands of years to be the instillers of culture and refinement, the blessed mothers of the next generation. They carry the torch high—"

"Poppycock!" announced Margaret. "Don't you ever look about you when you enter the cities on trains? Don't you see that the world is full of poor, helpless women who live only to reproduce and die? They're lucky to have bread—"

"I don't see such things," Mrs. Chesterton declared. "I pull down the shades on my compartment and I forbid my girls to look. I can't remake every life. I must set the standards for those I can influence—my husband and my daughters. You may not tell me now, after half a lifetime, that what I've been about has anything to do with biology. I regard each of my little girls as unique. They are women, gentle and kind, and as such they must be cared for by some fine husband. I would not have one of my daughters turn into a—a—scientist."

Mrs. Marsh changed her direction. "Mrs. Chesterton!"

But neither would heed her. The young woman and the matron were locked into their argument.

Margaret softened her voice, became almost reasonable. "We are not women only, Mrs. Chesterton. But we have narrowed our lives to only one function. Men marry—but they also build bridges and roads and lead religions and make and steal money—but women refuse to develop anything about themselves except their reproductive function and we have dressed that up to hide it from the world.

We allow ourselves to do nothing but sit on a nest and when that's through, we are through. We have developed nothing except our ability to procreate—"

"My dear!" said Mrs. Marsh, now stepping forward to take her daughter by the hand.

"Such language from a person of your circumstances," said Mrs. Chesterton.

"That's a perfectly respectable word and you've engaged in the activity yourself or you wouldn't have those three interchangeable daughters—"

"Margaret," shouted her mother. "I must ask you to leave the room!"

Margaret Marsh, twenty-four, had never been asked to leave the room before. Not even when she was a child. On the strength of this fact alone, she left.

As she crossed the foyer she heard Mrs. Chesterton say, "Slums, indeed. That's where that thinking originates."

And her mother answered, "She doesn't go into the slums. But she has been to Paris and Naples and Cairo—" The answer was soft and gentle and put the discussion into a slightly different context. Margaret went on up the stairs, annoyed even further.

In her own suite, she lay across the bed, letting her shoes dangle off her feet until they fell with a thud on the carpet. She felt as if she were regressing into childhood—and for no good reason. She'd let her temper rule. There was no earthly good in speaking so to Mrs. Chesterton. That was Margaret's only regret. She had wasted good arguments on a woman who would have none of them and who would make much of the argument itself. There were others, more educated and of Margaret's own milieu, who believed much as Mrs. Chesterton did. Margaret couldn't fault the older woman for her point of view. It was still a current one. Mrs. Chesterton was right about one thing, and that was the change Margaret could feel in her own behavior. She was not living up to the best within her. Her recent activities had not been in the direction she meant to go.

But she didn't know any longer what direction that might be. The room was growing very dim in the fading day. She was exhausted from her anger. She drifted off to sleep and as she did so, she thought of Steven.

Some time later she woke to a dark room and sat up.

In the dark, her mother's voice said, "Margaret?"

"Yes."

"I thought perhaps you are—unwell?" She hurried to correct this remark. "I mean—perhaps you have eaten something that has disagreed with you. These afternoon parties—they have the most dreadful food—should I ring for something now? Are you unsteady—dizzy?"

"No, no, Mother, that's all right. I have no excuse for what I did. It was foolish. Not for what I said, but because—of the person I said it to—"

There was a long silence after this, so Margaret decided her mother agreed and was not going to give comfort on that point. Quite often they talked like this, in a dark room. Somehow, they could say things better to each other when there was no visual confrontation. Margaret's eyes adjusted to the dim light.

She could see her mother sitting quietly in a chair, in her usual way, as if nothing was amiss.

The silence lengthened.

Mrs. Marsh began. "You know, I only want what's best for you. I would like you to have a serene happy life." Again she stopped and said nothing for a long time.

"Yes?" prompted Margaret.

"I thought—Chicago—it's your home. I don't want to frighten you, but you're not a child any longer." She was struggling with some emotion, or could not find the right words. "I tried to explain this once before. Chicago is still a small town in many ways. This portion called society, at any rate. I don't think there is any place that isn't, when it is divided into these cells of wealth. The same people move about in them, and see few others. They carry stories about—"

"Oh, you mean Mrs. Chesterton will gossip—"

"Not exactly. Don't discount her. She's likely to do quite well with an accurate recital of what occurred." Mrs. Marsh spoke with an edge to her voice.

Margaret sat up.

"What do you mean, then? That I should change? Not say what I believe? Become some sort of fainting belle on a divan?" Margaret lay back against her pillow. When she spoke next her own voice broke, "I fear I've done that already—I'm becoming a fool—but I never thought you'd expect that of me—"

"Not that. Never that. But Mrs. Chesterton will now discuss her experience with Mrs. Featherwaite, overheard by two maids serving tea. Mrs. Chesterton's daughters will hear some of it. The truth will be nudged and embroidered to make the story even livelier—"
Silence.

After a while, Margaret said, "I suppose what you want is to run off to Boston right away." She felt sick as she said this. She'd done this to herself, given her mother the ammunition to expect a swift removal to avoid the gossip. *Steven*, thought Margaret in dismay.

"No," her mother said. "No, we must not go for at least a month or two, during which time you must be as circumspect as possible to avoid the appearance of just what you suggest: *Flight*. You did nothing really so terrible except use rather precise language. We must appear—" she hesitated and seemed to be searching for a word, finally settled for her favorite "—serene."

Margaret heard this last with a lightening of heart so abrupt it made her laugh. Across the dark room her mother joined her and they laughed together for some minutes, each feeding on the other's hilarity.

Finally Margaret said, "But you know, Mother, I don't take this too seriously. I suppose I shouldn't say it, but I don't really care what others think or say about me—"

"I know that and that's what I'm warning you about. Others do care and sometime, when you want to do some certain thing—perhaps marry—what is said may affect that. You don't know what direction these strange confrontations will take. I'm trying to guard you against—" here Mrs. Marsh sighed "—against some unknown factor—"

"Why would that be present in Chicago rather than other places?"

"It's in other places, too. But Chicago seems to have more of it. At least, right now. I think it's because—because it is an emerging social scene, not quite up to standard in its own mind in comparison to the East, let's say. It's more open. Many people come here, hoping for greater opportunity. They're not the established sort from their previous homes, or they'd stay where they were. There are, for example, any number of aging bachelors and tired spinsters who have no interests in their own lives and so must feed on the events in others. They've come here because Chicago offers a new chance—a chance at fortune or marriage or some other goal. They have heard things—Mr. McCormick married at fifty or more. Mr. Palmer in his forties. Fortunes have been made here late in life. So these poor unfortunate types come on to the West to visit Aunt Min or Cousin Lou and they haven't any life, you see, so they gossip to make themselves noticed—"

Her mother's voice rose with conviction.

Margaret said, "So you think they will make up some terrible story from what I've said and circulate that?" She could tell her mother seemed to be genuinely worried. "But wouldn't it die down after awhile?"

"I don't know. I don't know. What fuels gossip? Do you know—" here she stopped for one of her long pauses; her voice was fainter as she continued "—there was a story going around once about a woman, married, with a lover and supposedly the firemen were called for a fire one night and the woman and her lover piled out of the woman's home at the same time her husband was carried out on a stretcher, overcome by smoke. That story circulated for years, with a life of its own. It was told about three different women during the time I lived here and no one ever challenged it or said, 'but I heard that about someone else. You're making it fit a circumstance.' You see how vicious rumor and gossip can be? It's a good story so every time a woman was suspected of having an affair, they made it fit. I've heard the same story in New York. Someday, someone will write it down and turn it into the fiction it truly is. But in the meantime, the lives of those three women have been ruined—"

"And it was never true?"

"I didn't say that. Perhaps those women were having affairs. But there was no proof. For if someone—some bachelor gossiping away at the Chicago Club—were asked to *prove* that some woman was having an affair, what could he say? He hadn't been a witness in the bedroom. So he trotted out this old chestnut—"

Again the silence.

For a long time, Margaret waited and then, because it was dark and she couldn't see the expression on Mrs. Marsh's face, the daughter risked one more question. "Was one of those women you, Mother? Were they telling that story about you?"

Silence. "No, Margaret," sadly, "but they did tell that story about one of my best friends. And I—" pause "—I believe my friend may have committed suicide—"

The two women sat on in the dark, each with her own thoughts. Margaret came to no firm conclusion except that she did not want to join a society that could kill with the spoken word. She thought of the various alternatives. If she couldn't handle such small tempests, who could? She had every resource open to her. At the edge of some resolution, her mother spoke and the thought escaped.

"Margaret," Mrs. Marsh said, "I don't want to fill you with fear about others. Live your own life. Don't take on old residue from lives that have gone before you. I'm not as brave as you are, Margaret. You will understand that, won't you? It's because of what I've told you—about my friend. Sometimes, the memory of—that prevents me from facing things as I should—"

After a moment, Mrs. Marsh rose and said goodnight. At the closing of the door, Margaret began to undress for bed. She didn't ring for the maid. She didn't want to see anyone.

In spite of appearances of sophistication, Margaret was a religious young woman in the very best sense. Everything she'd learned in science had only made her more so. The contrast of the minute order and beauty she saw through a microscope set against the order and beauty of sky and stars and natural conditions, reaffirmed her faith each time she considered it. Tonight, she went to the window to look out on the night and think about what had gone before, to gain some perspective on what she knew to be her folly.

She was not pleased with herself at all. Her great error was the sin of pride as had always been the case. She was not proud of beauty, wealth or the way in which she lived. These factors were not of her making.

But she was proud of her mind, her education and the studies she had pursued abroad as she moved through various cultures. Nor did she suffer fools gladly. Caught in foolish situations with people who were banal and tedious, her anger could be swift and cutting. And her remorse great.

The view from her window was of the row of prim Prairie Avenue mansions to the south, looking for all the world like the matrons who inhabited them. Against all advice, she opened her window to the night air and even on this side of the house, she could hear the waves hitting the rocks to the east. The water was far away from the great stone mansions. Which would last longer—water or stone? Would these mansions survive the course of time? They looked now as if they'd stand forever. Young girls with ideas about nature and God would not affect them.

The houses will stand, she thought, and the families in them will live and nothing will be changed, not by me; not by anyone. They are as proud as I.

She sought release from her troubled mind in prayer. Although she was a Presbyterian, she had never fully embraced the idea of predestination. She thought changes might come. In some way, she hoped to change herself, to make herself more acceptable to her Maker through her prayers.

But there was more than that. She wanted to be *worthwhile*.

And there was one thing more. Hidden away under everything, perhaps not fully understood, curtained away because she thought it might be too wonderful to achieve, too powerful for the ordinary, was a hope for a special relationship between woman and man.

Margaret knelt and prayed for each person for whom she wished God's blessing; for those who bore false witness, for those who could not see, for serenity for her mother, for humility for herself and most of all, for the human heart in each. And for the personal connections between them all that those hearts would allow.

As she lay down to sleep, she wondered, is that so much, after all, for a woman to want?

CHAPTER XVII

1

Margaret was out and busy early next morning. The first thing she did on rising was to write a brief note to Mrs. Chesterton apologizing for calling her daughters "interchangeable" and for her own "attitude" of the day before. She mailed the letter at once before she could change her mind.

Then she went over to the Tremont, driving the little buggy herself, and was waiting in the lobby for Uncle Findley when he emerged from the dining room ready for his constitutional.

"Maggie! Is something wrong? You're not going to leave for the East so soon? Or—" He leaned down to examine her expression. "Do you have something exciting to tell me, m'girl?"

"No, not that, Uncle. I want to talk to you about my life."

"Ah, that's a choice subject. Why don't we find a corner?" He led her over to an alcove off the main lobby and asked the desk clerk to send over some tea.

Margaret was not exactly satisfied with this, but it would have to do. After they'd settled down with their tea, she explained a little of what she'd been feeling lately. How her night dreams were full of quarreling voices and the frenzied unpacking of millions of children from a giant sealed box at the fairgrounds.

"Red-headed children?" asked Uncle Findley.

"No, not that. This is something else entirely. It came to me last night. Very late. I've been attempting to change the wrong segment of society, to bring new ideas to persons who are the keepers of the *status quo*. It's like trying to beat a stone into a malleable shape. It will fall apart before it becomes something that one can work with. I want to help women to a better life, but all we're going to do at the Woman's Building is to display what has been—laces, embroidery, bric-a-brac of women's worlds. Glorified and overstated. Made much of in a lovely sort of way. But not for me—"

She was standing, pacing about the little alcove. Uncle Findley was looking at her with concern.

"Why don't you talk to Steven about this?" he asked. "He could probably put some light on—"

"Oh, I have. I have. He said something the other day—that day when I insulted the woman's hat, you remember? He said women should deal fairly with women laborers and then there would be a better distribution of wealth. I'd like to do something like that. But I'm sort of lost. I feel like a salesman who doesn't know his territory. I haven't been in Chicago long enough or often enough to know where to offer my help."

"I still think you ought to consult Steven. I've heard about him here and there and from what people say, he does what he can. That's why I'm so impressed with him and pleased the two of you are getting along."

Margaret, standing, almost stamped her foot. "I know Steven is— almost perfect. I can see that myself." There was a faint touch of irony in her voice. "But I want to do something that is separate and distinct. I want to have something I can point to as my own."

"Whyn't you take up sketching or piano playing, like some girls I know—Thorncastle's daughters. They do things like that and he inflicts them on his acquaintances on a regular basis—"

"Uncle Findley, I have no talent in doing those things—"

"Neither have they."

"Well, then they had an interest. I admire fine paintings, but I know I can't do anything remotely like them. And I have no facility for music. I'm good at mathematics and science. But I want to do something that has a little more heart in it—I envy girls who know just what they're going to do with their lives. Somehow I can't get straight on it. I need a direction—"

Uncle Findley said nothing for a time. Then he said, "Whenever anything in my life looked muddled and unclear, when I couldn't see the way, I found the best thing to do was think of others. Your mother and you have been away so long, pleasing only yourselves on those excursion trains, idling away time for God knows what reasons—" He stopped. He was on dangerous ground and he backtracked. "Why don't I take you a few blocks to the north? There's a church up there where a friend of mine, Mrs. Rose Bright, a young widow-woman, has a little mission—not to the poor as you might expect, but to the middle class. She's been holding classes for the Northside ladies, discussing charitable doings and defining the work that needs doing right here in Chicago, never mind the poor heathens on the other side of the world. She might be able to help you."

"Help me what? That's my problem."

"Mrs. Bright is going to teach that social science or in some way practice it, when the university opens this fall. She's not a silly, idle woman, Maggie. More your sort. You ought to enjoy just knowing her—"

2

While a piano in another room of the church basement thumped away at "Rock of Ages," Mrs. Bright met with Margaret Marsh for two hours concerning collaboration on a future project. Margaret had been vague and questing when she'd talked with Uncle Findley, but it wasn't long into the discussion with Mrs. Bright before it became apparent that an idea had been forming in the back of Margaret's mind that she'd been reluctant to reveal to her uncle.

Margaret wanted to find a sturdy house in a good neighborhood and invite young women of her own age who lived and worked in the overcrowded slums to come and meet with her in the afternoon several times a week. "We can serve refreshments, discuss literature, have a lending library, show them a refined atmosphere—"

Mrs. Bright coughed and said they might approach it a bit differently. "These girls work during the week and wouldn't be able to come during the day. And the place where we meet must be accessible to them without additional carfare on trolleys and horsecars. They need to have a place on weekday evenings, some of them, because their living conditions are overcrowded. They'll be pleased to have somewhere to get away and yet stay off the streets—"

The older woman—not as old as Margaret's mother, yet somehow *motherly*—was not immediately swept up by Margaret's overall plan. She spoke carefully, questioning Margaret about the reasons for interest in such work.

"I would like it to be my own—with your help, of course," Margaret said, "but rather than meet economic needs, which I know are important, I'd like to try cultural needs first. You would receive a salary and lodgings, either in the house itself or whatever you might choose. And also, perhaps you could use some of the observations we'll be able to make in any work you do elsewhere—"

If this young woman had been anyone except the grandniece of Findley Marsh and the daughter of W. W. Marsh, Mrs. Bright would have held back. There was a style now among the rich educated college girls to "go out among the poor," however unqualified they might be to do so. The results, both for those who gave and for those who received, were usually disheartening. Unless the giver were motivated by something other than curiosity and the "look" of being charitable, trouble could lie ahead. And then there were those who wanted to do such work for a few weeks and then flee away into dances and fetes, armed with witty conversation about "the poor" whom they had "helped." Mrs. Bright wanted none of that.

But Margaret Marsh had the right look, intelligent, sure of herself. Mrs. Bright knew the project would be properly funded. Based on the family's previous record of quiet donations to good works, she decided to take a chance. Maybe some good could be done under her guidance. They would move cautiously.

"We must move slowly," Mrs. Bright said. "Find out what the girls' needs are, rather than our own. Some of these girls will not be able to speak English well, let alone read it at a good rate. Perhaps we will have readers, someone to read to groups of women. We must be willing to adapt our goals to conditions that we find—"

Margaret's mind was moving very fast. Mrs. Bright's caution was intruding on the epiphany Margaret felt she'd had the night before. If she couldn't change her peers, she would work with those for whom change was possible. She didn't want to move slowly.

She said, "We'll make friends everywhere. We'll take them on outings. We'll picnic by the lake. We'll go to my house. To the country for fresh air. We'll take them to the opera and the plays. And when it opens, we'll take them to the fair—"

"I think the way to approach this is to let the girls help plan the activities of the—er—club?"

"No, let's not call it a *club*. Let's call it something else. Oh, something like an *exchange*. A women's exchange. Where we learn from them as they learn from us."

Mrs. Bright thought that idea to be more powerful than her new patroness understood, but she smiled and accepted the charge given her. "On the understanding that this be funded for at least a year," she said firmly. "I wouldn't want to enter into any situation that wouldn't continue for at least a year."

"Of course," Margaret said, giving a perfect yet unconscious imitation of her mother's serenity.

3

By the end of the week Margaret's attorneys had arranged a contract of one year's duration with Mrs. Bright and had allocated funds for the purchase of the house. Mrs. Bright had telephoned to report she'd found a place she thought suitable for their project. She arranged with Margaret to meet at the address, a place in the Back-of-the-Yards, next afternoon.

"You'd best bring an escort with you this first time," Mrs. Bright suggested. "You might get lost and this is a difficult area—"

"Are you going there alone?"

"Oh, I go there all the time. But I dress for it. I make myself look very commonplace and no one bothers me. But you, with your lovely red hair, might be very noticeable—" Privately, Mrs. Bright thought Margaret's walk, her air of confidence, her clothing, would shout too clearly that here was a young woman of wealth come down into the slums.

And she'll probably arrive in a carriage with four horses and a driver, thought Mrs. Bright, who was wise in the ways of wealthy young women. Even those that appeared intelligent. Mrs. Bright knew that to go into the slums looking too prosperous was to invite trouble.

Margaret decided to bring Steven with her. She thought it was safe to tell him of her plan, now that it was on its way into reality. She said she'd found a "good woman" to help organize her Exchange, not mentioning the name of her organizer. She and Steven prepared to take the small trap. In front of the groom Steven asked about the neighborhood and mentioned their destination. The stable man was very upset.

"The horse—what are you going to do with the horse while you goes inside?"

She wished she'd not told Steven so much. Her mother was not exactly aware of this new endeavor.

"You can't leave a horse and buggy without a driver in that place," the groom said. "And the horse. Don't let it drink nothing there and keep its hooves out of the worst of the muck. I can't have no sick horses in this stable—begging your pardon, Miss Margaret, but I'm responsible to you for the care of these horses and one gets sick and they'll all get it—"

She'd thought the man exaggerated until they turned into the small lane designated by Mrs. Bright. The street was crowded at midday, when the residents of any respectable working-class neighborhood might be expected to be working. But not here. There were mangy dogs scuttling by, women with baskets trudging down the wooden sidewalks, old men and old women sitting in doorways, children by the hundreds, although it was a school day elsewhere, and many men and women sitting in windows open to the sharp chill in the air.

"Why do they open their windows?" Margaret asked Steven. "Aren't they letting out precious heat?"

"They haven't any heat," Steven said. "Just stoves, which they don't use during the day except for cooking. It's probably warmer in the window than inside where it's dark. These places are hot in summer and dank and cold in winter—"

"What are those great lumps of material they lean on?"

"Featherbeds. They've oftentimes brought them with them from Europe. They consider featherbeds a sign of wealth—at least, of respectability. The beds are used for sleeping, covering, anything useful. Often as not, they have bedbugs in them—" Steven's voice was matter-of-fact, downplaying what to Margaret's mind was strange and unreal.

She'd seen slums before, some close by. In Naples, in Ireland— but they had been part of the exotic scene and she had been passing through. In her own city, she'd not gone about in such places. It was enough that she knew they were there. In that way, she was more advanced than most of her social peers.

"Are they all immigrants?" she asked Steven.

"No. Some are from this country. Not all immigrants are poor. Some come here well able to enter the working class, to have a decent home. But there are others who ran before some evil or who had no chance where they were. They are the kind who live here—"

"How do you know these things?" she asked a bit peevishly. She'd wanted to show him *her* project and he was explaining the need for it to *her*.

"I've been reading up on things. And now and then I do what I can. It's hard to know where to start. But I try to help—"

She was beginning to get a headache. "What," she whispered, because she felt the whole street could hear her, "what is that dreadful smell?"

"Combination of things," he said. "Bad drains. Most of these houses have little or no plumbing. There are outhouses," he murmured, in shyness, "down the alleyways. And the most overwhelming smell comes from the packing houses. What sewers there are receive their waste, overwhelming the river that might be expected to carry it away."

She looked so distressed and worried, he wondered what Margaret really knew of her own city and whether she understood what she was undertaking.

And in her turn, Margaret could tell from his careful speech, his subdued attitude in the face of terrible deprivation, that he was telling her only a small part of the things he understood about the place around them.

"Most of these people have a chance," he said. "Someone in their family is working in the Stockyards or they wouldn't be here. That means money coming in. They live in ways we couldn't begin to imagine, scrimping, looking for a way out, a way up. They're the ones with enough energy to leave Europe, to come all this way. They've survived disease and travel and bad conditions—but we offer them a poor place in their new country—"

"This street looks like an alley."

"I know," he said. "It may have been paved once. But if it had paving it was wood cut off the end of squared logs, oiled and put down. In these poorer sections those without any fuel dig such pavements up to burn them. But the city probably didn't pave this way— or used the burning of the streets somewhere else as a reason not to—"

Margaret spotted Mrs. Bright standing before a wooden cottage just ahead.

Steven also saw her. "I didn't know you knew *Rose* Bright," he said. "Your 'good woman' is Rose Bright!"

He reined up the horse and jumped down from the trap with such pleasure in his face that Margaret, left to tie up the horse, had a slight twinge of jealousy. Steven and Mrs. Bright shook hands and began to talk at once. Then Steven turned to Margaret and said, "The university is really a very small town. Of course, I know Rose Bright— and now I see the two of you are friends."

Both he and Mrs. Bright beamed so happily that Margaret found herself joining their pleasure. She couldn't know, this proud rich miss, that her character soared in Mrs. Bright's eyes as soon as it was learned Margaret Marsh was the good friend of Steven Baxter. Mrs. Bright even spread a small portion of that raised estimation across the project before them. Perhaps this girl wasn't a dilettante after all.

4

Margaret stood on the broken sidewalk and looked at the house where her Women's Exchange was to be held. There was a picket fence, most of it intact, that edged the property at the sidewalk and down the sides. The fence was unpainted and there was no gate. At the back of the property, Margaret could see the fence was higher and was closely constructed of flat boards once painted blue, now old and peeling. A wooden sidewalk led to the front stairs of the one-and-a-half-story cottage. The stairs rose steeply to what looked to be the second floor, but which appeared to be the main floor of the house. Below the stairs was a basement that was on ground level. The yard around the house was dirt. The house, like the fence, was gray with lack of paint. Somehow, Margaret had envisioned something more sturdy, perhaps made of brick. But she didn't want to disappoint Mrs. Bright so she said, "We'll have to fix that walkway," and picking her way down it carefully, went forward to see the house.

"This house was owned by the widow of a plumber," Mrs. Bright said. "She rented out the basement to roomers and it's cut up into small cubicles for sleeping rooms. It's dry and vermin-free—"

Margaret shuddered. She'd not thought of that.

"Are the stairs safe?" asked Steven, moving ahead of them so he could test the way.

"Yes," Mrs. Bright said. "I looked the place over carefully. And you'll see. There's quite a surprise inside—"

On entering, Margaret could not see what the surprise might be. The first room was not more than five feet deep although it spanned the house in width.

"This was once the parlor, although I would use it as a cloakroom," Rose Bright said. "And here is the dining room. I think the old lady ran a sort of boarding table here, with meals for a certain price, and she liked to be able to handle a good crowd. There are so many men in these sections who are living alone while they try to earn enough to bring their families over. There is a good market for a hot meal and a dry sleeping place."

Margaret stood in the middle of the room and tried to envision it filled with young women. Yes, it would do. But just barely. She hated to give up her vision of a sturdy place in a better neighborhood, but Mrs. Bright seemed to know her business.

Rose was walking toward the back of the house, through the dining room door to the hallway. "There is an adequate kitchen," she said, her voice coming back from the empty place in an enthusiastic explanation. "You must come here and see the surprise—"

Margaret and Steven walked through the doorway and saw Mrs. Bright at the corner of the kitchen where there was a small door. She opened the door with a flourish.

"We have here a legacy of the old plumber. A working commode. A real find in this part of the city."

Margaret walked about the kitchen. There was nothing in it except a dark stove and a sink. For want of something to do, she went over and turned on the faucet. Nothing came out.

"We must pay the bill," Mrs. Bright said. "There is an arrears on the property. Then they will give us what city services there are. We'll have to buy a water heater—a small coal oil device."

The rest of the house consisted of three bedrooms on the main floor and an attic room under the eaves.

"This is considered quite a luxurious house in this neighborhood," Mrs. Bright told them.

"Maybe we could have it painted, made more cheerful." Margaret was having a difficult time reducing her vision to this.

"We must move slowly on that," the older woman said. "We'll make it shipshape and clean, but if we put too much money into paint and trimmings in a place where children are hungry—" She shrugged. "We'll be defeated before we start. I think we should mend the fence, put in a gate and rake the yard. That sort of thing. Clean the place well. Let the neighbors see us at work here—" She nodded at Margaret. "Both of us."

Margaret sighed.

Steven wanted to know what they were going to do with the old shed and the basement.

"I thought maybe we could hire a caretaker?" Mrs. Bright aimed the question at Margaret. "We need a handyman, especially in winter when there will be ashes and coal to carry and walks to clean. There will be plenty for someone to do. There is a man in the neighborhood I think I could get to live at the back of the basement. In the front, where all the little rooms are, I would like to clean it up and make a day nursery—something simple, perhaps employing a few of the girls we'll meet in our evenings—but that's much in advance," she finished hurriedly, looking at Margaret.

Margaret had tried to keep the fleeting dismay from showing in her expression. She'd thought of girls her own age, the poor of her own generation. But *children*. The children around this place looked to be the most dirty, ragged urchins she'd seen outside of Naples or Dublin.

Steven was delighted. He'd always thought of Margaret in connection with children. That very first evening when he'd come to
dinner at her house, there had been in his opinion a motherly aura
about Margaret. All these new circumstances—the new friendship
with Rose Bright, the idea of a day nursery in addition to the evening
Exchange—filled him with pride at Margaret, *his* Margaret.

Mrs. Bright looked at the two of them. She wondered if they knew
yet they were in love. Anyone could see it. What a pair they were.
Wealth, intelligence, a social conscience. She was happy things worked
out in such serendipitous fashion for some. The future would be
better for it.

Three people, all believing they knew the other two better than
they really did, left the small house in Back-of-the-Yards that day,
filled with anticipation.

5

Mrs. Marsh was not nearly so pleased as Steven had been about
Margaret's new plans.

Then she brightened. "But perhaps you mean to give up your
work at the fair?"

"No," Margaret said. "I'll keep that for two or three mornings a
week and then, when the bad weather comes and the work out there
is shut down, I'll spend all my time at the Exchange. I don't see how
I'll have too many afternoons for Prairie Avenue," she said with a
certain private relief.

Mrs. Marsh had another thought. "In winter, when there are so
many diseases about—there is often consumption in such places.
And diphtheria. And scarlet fever and that terrible flu. You'll come
down with pox or—oh, Margaret. There is nothing in any of this
that's worth your life!"

But Margaret had made up her mind.

And so Margaret Marsh, who never had handled a broom in her
life, tied a kerchief about her red hair and took over a small house
in Back-of-the-Yards. She and Mrs. Bright and a handyman, plus
Steven now and then and a groom he brought with him, swept and
cleaned and put to rights the yard and fence and house, readying it
for its first critical visitors.

During this operation, they attracted much attention. Children
hung over the fence but were too timid to come into the yard, for
which Margaret was quite grateful. When the sign "Women's Exchange" went up on the front of the house, the new owner had to
take a certain amount of ridicule and baiting from men who passed.

"What do I hev to exchange fer that one?" a voice would call out as two men passed together.

"Hey, Red, how much fer two?"

But these expressions were few and could usually be stopped if Steven came around from the back of the house or the groom came over to the fence and said, "Move along now—"

The work was getting done. They'd been at it for three weeks when Mrs. Bright said, "Have you ever noticed that woman—the one who stands beside the corner of the next building? The one in the dark shawl?"

Margaret said she'd seen no one like that, but two or three days later, when she was standing at the top of the front stairs for a breath of air, she saw a woman that fit Rose's description. Tall, very thin, dark-eyed even from this distance, all clothed in black. Margaret waved, but the woman stared straight ahead.

Turning to the stairs, Margaret went down and came out to the walk. She felt as if she'd kept her eye on the place where the woman stood during the time she'd made her way there, but when she came out the new gate, Margaret discovered there was no one at the corner of the building—not even a shadow.

CHAPTER XVIII

"*Margaret Marsh, will* you tell me what you want?"

Mrs. Marsh was looking at her daughter with annoyance. Margaret, for some odd reason, looked back in confusion. She'd turned brick-red, dropped her toast on the tablecloth, hastened to neaten up the crumbs and in the process had overturned a cup of tea.

Margaret stood, sponging her dark poplin skirt with a napkin, ignoring her mother's original query.

Mrs. Marsh tried again. "Are you quite well?"

Margaret looked up from her tidying. "Of course." Her irritation at this question was plainly visible. Mrs. Marsh knew that Margaret hated the question and as a sensitive mother she would not have asked it, if the signs of some distress were not so evident.

Margaret said, "I'm perfectly well now and probably will be in future. I'm just clumsy this morning. That has nothing to do with health—"

She sat down again and her mother poured her another cup of tea.

"I'm sorry," her mother said, not understanding why she must apologize for the bad humor of her daughter, and then continued with her original thought. "But we must settle some of these—"

The still-remaining flush on Margaret's cheeks deepened to a shade that was almost brown. "I have a great deal to do to get ready for the opening of my Exchange next week. And there is more work on the

221

committee for the Children's Building at the fair. And there's—" she hesitated to say *Steven*, since she sensed her mother was not wholeheartedly in favor of her association with him.

But Mrs. Marsh filled in the blank. "—Steven *Baxter*. Margaret, I can't go off to Boston and leave you unchaperoned with Steven Baxter. Nice as he may be, the family is full of eccentrics. Everyone knows it—"

"I thought you told me not to be swayed by gossip, Mother."

Mrs. Marsh reached out to touch the letters near her plate. She didn't want to be caught in Chicago during the dreadful winter months. They never opened their houses to fresh air; the weather would be terrible and they ate entirely too much beef, in Mrs. Marsh's experience, to be to her taste. Her sigh was like a winged moth let out into the room. It floated between the two women with palpable life.

"I do plan to stay in Chicago, Mother," Margaret said sweetly. "I would be most happy to have you with me."

"But you have done so much. Enough, I think," her mother said. "We could put Mrs. Bright in charge of the Exchange. She's very capable, you say. And buy a few more shares in the Children's Annex. And then we can be off. We could do it all in one day and be gone tomorrow—"

"No, you go ahead. I don't mind. I'll be fine here. There's Mrs. Riley to do for me. And I'm very busy, as I've said."

"It doesn't look right—that you should go your own way quite so completely without—"

The unfilled blank at the end of *her* sentence was left for the words *engagement* or *marriage*, but Mrs. Marsh hesitated to say them. If it had been anybody but the too-gentle Steven Baxter, the son of eccentric parents.

"I cannot go to Boston and leave you here alone," she finished.

"You know perfectly well that I'd be pleased to have you here with me, but if you wish to leave, I don't want to hold you here. If you think that improper—I'll bring in a chaperone."

"Perhaps in New York your attitude and single residence would be considered unremarkable. But here, we must consider—"

"I *will* stay—" said Margaret and she stood and went out of the dining room, going down the hall toward her father's library. Today was Sunday. She was exhausted from her week of hard work at the Exchange and at the fair. She wanted nothing but rest and her mother had visited all these decisions on her. Well, she'd made up her mind. She would not leave now.

She went to the large desk and sat down in her father's chair. There was stationery in a special holder at the corner of the desk. She took several sheets as if she were going to write a letter. Alva Vanderbilt probably should be written to. She stared down at the page, wondering what to write to the East that would not appear as catty and vicious as she felt whenever she tried to describe the Woman's Building and The Exposition and the petty quarrels of her fellow workers. Not every man on the governing commission was engaged in sinister plotting to usurp advantages the women might gain. Not every woman working with Mrs. Palmer for the reality of the Woman's Building or the Children's Arcade had hate or envy in her heart toward women more capable or trained than she might be. But too many did. And to tell such a tale made the teller sound petty and suspicious and went against Margaret's natural inclination.

She would not write at all. Let the easterners come next year to an event undefined by Margaret Marsh. She was tired of the backbiting, the tensions she found at the fairgrounds.

She sighed and looked around. This had been her father's favorite room. It was the most masculine place in the house. The fireplace was faced with intricate mosaics, the walls were lined with books her father had chosen and then had decided to keep here in his own special library. Two large tufted divans of black leather flanked the fireplace. These generous furnishings were each as wide as a single bed and her father had sometimes slept here if he worked late and didn't want to go upstairs.

His desk rose up from the floor like a bluff and was part of the permanent construction of the room. It could not be moved and dust could not slip under it. Silk rugs of deep green imported from Persia were here and there about the floor, adding to the foreign, masculine feeling of the setting.

Over the fireplace was a painting of the sea that Mr. Marsh had chosen because it reminded him of the lake. During windy weather the action of Lake Michigan could be heard even in this Prairie Avenue study and her father had liked to look up at the painting, which had no visible shore, and think about the water. He said it rested him.

Margaret tried the same technique, but when she thought of the lake, for some reason she thought of Steven and was not calmed. She found herself thinking of Steven entirely too much lately.

Margaret reached out and adjusted the green glass shade on the desk lamp. Sometimes her father would wait in this room for clients— special and important persons with matters of law to be discussed—

or he would wait for messengers to bring important papers. There was an outside door to the room for late callers. On such evenings he would wait at this desk, the green-shaded lamp turned high, light shining down against the blotter on papers he had in front of him.

He would look up at Margaret and smile. Yes, this had been his room. She should not come here so much. The emotions of this room were too powerful.

For the last few weeks her mind had been filled with romance, with the thought of a book she'd once seen in this room years ago. Since she'd met Steven she'd spent some time looking for the book itself, a small volume of the Songs of Solomon. She remembered it had been covered in heavy vellum and it was illustrated. When she first saw the book she'd picked it up while chatting with her father, leafed through it and put it down as they continued their talk. The next time she looked for it, she'd not been able to find it. She could look up the passage in the large family Bible, but she wanted the intimate touch of the smaller volume, the exotic look of the illustrative plates. She wanted to show it to Steven.

"—turn away thine eyes from me, for they have overcome me—"

She didn't consciously remember having read the verses, but she could recall small snatches. Of course, such phrases were well-known and often quoted—

"—the time of the singing of birds is come, the voice of the turtle is heard in the land—"

Men in those ancient times had built their lives, not on armies or business or conquests of the field, but on the women of their nation. Courtship had been important. Their lineage was brought forth and went, not to battle, but to love again. And so the world went on—

That morning her mother had said to her, "Margaret Marsh, what do you want?"

What did she want? She wanted it all now. Not just the intellectual exercises of life, but all of it. Her sense of direction had somehow been overcome by the scent of spices, by the drone of bees. She could envision pomegranates and ripening grapes. She knew she was ridiculous.

But she could talk to Steven about anything, tell him her dreams, her goals. He never said to her as other men had done, "Oh, women don't do that. Ladies never do—"

He understood.

And she looked at him and thought, "My love showeth himself to me through the lattice—"

During this past summer when she and Steven had walked and

talked together, she'd often thought of herself as two women, one emerging from within the other, a softness coming to the fore from behind a cool facade. But lately a more intense agitation had come over her. She now sometimes felt as if she were being given the choice of not one or two, but a thousand ways in which to be. There was the tenderness she felt in the moments she and Steven shared—but there was more. She felt a great need for risk, for danger, something she could do to demonstrate . . . she didn't know what.

The painting in front of her reminded her of the night she'd walked along the lake, how she'd felt when the storm struck—not afraid, but eager. Wasn't that feeling supposed to be manifest in love? Shouldn't there be a riskiness in romance, a dare, the offering of everything for which no return was assured?

In this house of her parents, where every conceivable economic question had long ago been answered, she wondered if that risk could ever be there for her, or would her own life involve merely the pleasant merging of two fortunes? She also had discovered, in working with Mrs. Bright, that there was great bravery among women, a bravery she'd not known or realized to any great extent before. She could feel it growing in herself. She believed that any day now, these forces would gather in her, show her the way to some cohesive life: Steven, she believed, could be part of that.

As she thought these things, she was searching the shelves, running her hand over the spines of the books in case the slim volume she sought should hide itself between two heftier neighbors.

Her fingers struck a small book and she stopped, certain she'd found the one she was looking for. She eased the tension on the row and worked out the volume. It was a book of verse, but not the one she'd hoped to find. This was by some poet she'd never heard of and seemed to be a private printing on special hand-rolled papers. She took it with her to the desk. Such things interested her now. And she was always surprised to learn the scope of her father's taste. To look through his books was like continuing her lost conversations with him.

There was an inscription inside the cover: "My Dearest—For everything we have known—"

The hand seemed unfamiliar, but Margaret supposed her mother might have had the book sent from abroad. It seemed to have been printed in England. Maybe that was why the poet was unknown to her.

She leafed through the pages. The poems were celebrations of love—physical love—most of those celebrations amazingly graphic in their content. As she turned the pages, a bit of stationery fell onto the desk blotter. Very fine deckle-edged paper. The letter *L* in script at one corner. Notepaper from a well-run household where attention could be given to such refinements.

The note said, "Darling, don't come tonight. He'll be at home. Save Thursday. I believe I can manage it some way—"

The message was unsigned. No signature was needed. Margaret had seen this paper before, had held such notepaper in her hand and smelled its lingering scent. And the message was quite clear. Mr. Marsh had been going to meet his partner's wife when "he" was not at home.

Her father. And another woman. Margaret looked at the book she held. She wished that she could go back to the moment she'd found it on the shelf and not open it—this Pandora of a book. But her wish was like the lament of virgins. She could not go back. She now knew something that would force her to reconsider things she thought she knew well—the look of certain people on the cold day of her father's funeral; the various divisions of her father's will that had somehow dissatisfied his partner; the look of her own mother as she and Margaret had traveled throughout the world. Traveled so often. So constantly. So serenely had her mother traveled. And then there had been those oblique warnings from her mother in late summer about gossip, the hint at some dreadful fate. The word *suicide*—the book was wicked to her touch. She let it fall onto the desktop. It fell open to a page that had been marked and the corner turned down. She would not look at this poem. But even standing there, with the book on the desk, she could read its beginning.

> Oh, come my Love, with me lie down
> Under the shade of the mushroom
> Where moss grows thick and sweet
> And sunlight children never come to play—
> In this dark tangle of vines and hours
> Let us embrace there in our green language—

Margaret Marsh opened a drawer of the desk, threw the offending book inside and ran from the room.

CHAPTER XIX

1

Margaret turned to her tenement project with all the force of her personality. Agitated and depressed by what she'd found in her father's study, she knew now that she would eventually have to confront her mother for answers to questions no daughter would wish to ask. To divert herself, she became a veritable engine of activity, venting her unhappiness in what she felt would be good works.

Within the packing house district and in adjoining areas, she and Mrs. Bright went from place to place to leave calling cards and notices announcing the opening of Margaret's settlement house, which was now furnished and ready. Mrs. Bright, who'd taken the bedroom on the top floor for herself for the time being, had put in plain furniture in the two remaining bedrooms—iron bedsteads covered with white counterpanes and a commodious chest in each because there were no closets—and the dining room now held a scarred table, which Steven had donated. There were also twenty-two unmatched chairs that Margaret and he had found in various places over on Maxwell Street. From the same sources, they purchased a teakettle, tea cups and the basic goods of a kitchen. The handyman constructed coat racks for the former parlor.

Let the world come to their door!

Rose Bright, a motherly, warm-hearted woman, looked at the tall, highly charged girl and believed she was seeing the Margaret Marsh who'd always been.

"No wonder she was able to do well at her university," Mrs. Bright said to Steven. "Her energy is boundless—"

"She's changed," Steven said. "Just in these last weeks, she seems different than she was. I think she's working too hard or worried about something—maybe the quarrels over at the fairgrounds among the women."

Mrs. Bright thought *Steven* was working too hard. She'd known him off and on for several years. Each time he returned to Chicago he would come to visit her, to see how she was. He'd been a good friend to her husband and during the time of her husband's illness, Steven had been very kind. She knew, too, that he often helped private charities quietly with money and with his influence in Chicago. He had impressed her as being a serious youth. Now she admired his manliness as he approached maturity. She was not surprised to find him part of Margaret's life. Not every girl would suit Steven Baxter. Mrs. Bright was pleased Steven knew enough not to fall for a silly pleasant girl who would make his life miserable with her social demands.

But Steven's face looked thinner than she'd ever seen it and he often looked toward Margaret as if he wanted to gather her up and take her away from her furious attack on the city's slums. He spoke little; neither of them were good at casual talk. Rose Bright wondered if they talked much when they were alone together.

For Steven's part, he knew some change had taken place within Margaret and he didn't know the cause of it. He feared she was harboring some resentment or dislike of him, irritation with something he'd done. Yet he couldn't tear himself away from her side. He sought to please her in all things. During his life with his mother, he'd become sensitive to women's moods and tried to do things that would alleviate unhappiness. But Margaret could not be brought out of her single-minded busyness, her storm of energy turned into work.

Though she appeared less gentle than before, she also seemed fragile. Now and then she laughed, but he could see no humor in her and wondered if she were really laughing at him. Then at other times, she seemed so full of light and fire, her looks almost burned.

Margaret herself could not put her feelings into words. She longed to ask her mother to sit down in frank discussion with her, but her mother had become more elusive than ever, constantly occupied in her own social life. Each time Margaret thought the painful subject might be broached, her mother seemed to gather a hint of what Margaret had in mind and would find an urgent need to be elsewhere.

Because Margaret could not see her own distressed glances, her own air of tremulous intensity, her visible dismay, she couldn't know her mother feared to be alone with her. Intimacy, Mrs. Marsh believed, should be avoided if at all possible. There was only one subject that could have made Margaret look at her like that. They had never had these feelings between them before. Somewhere in Chicago, Margaret had heard something, picked up some strain of gossip.

Whether Margaret's new information was correct or not, whether Mrs. Marsh supposed correctly what was on her daughter's mind, neither knew because each turned her distress inward and feared a direct meeting.

Total frankness might not have been necessary but neither thought of that: Perhaps only kindness to each other, recognition of the dismay of each, forgiveness for the transgressor who was now beyond reform—perhaps that kind of talk between mother and daughter might have solved their difficulty.

But instead they played a kind of genteel hide-and-seek in the grand house on Prairie Avenue, with the effect that if one came home, the other found a reason to be elsewhere.

The impasse came to an end because Uncle Findley became ill. The manager of the Tremont called Miss Marsh to say that Mr. Findley Marsh had been ill for several days and refused to have a doctor and under the circumstances, the hotel did not wish to take full responsibility.

Margaret went at once with Knox and the second man and from the hotel called her own doctor. The doctor said Uncle Findley had a "fall complaint," perhaps *la grippe*, perhaps not, but one that came to many people every year and this year the elderly gentleman seemed to have caught a very bad cold with it. Findley was wheezing and coughing to the extent that his skin appeared blue and transparent to Margaret. Alarmed, she could not bear to leave him alone in the impersonal atmosphere of a hotel. With the doctor's permission and over Uncle Findley's objections, she took him in the closed carriage to Prairie Avenue where she had him put into her father's old bedroom, the largest in the house.

Mrs. Marsh was annoyed and managed to stay at home long enough to convey this to Margaret. "I don't see why you couldn't have sent the second man to stay with him and nurse him at the Tremont. I don't mean you shouldn't care for him, I just believe he'd be more comfortable in his own quarters—a sick man should be among familiar things—"

This had been Uncle Findley's own weak objection and the strange concurrence of her mother and uncle on any subject, especially this one, so annoyed Margaret that she turned on her mother to say, "I think you're just displeased because his room is so close to your own—"

"Well, he does cough almost continuously. It's difficult to rest—"

Did her mother realize how cold she sounded?

Margaret spoke softly so as not to sound as harsh. "As you have often said, Mother, it's my house now. I've often worried about what would happen to Uncle Findley if he should become ill and there was no one to care for him. This is the very thing I've been afraid would happen. I mean to keep him here until he's well. Perhaps afterward, if he'll stay."

Mrs. Marsh had long practiced the habit of letting something unpleasant "blow over." Problems treated thus often solved themselves. She was dressed to go to a luncheon. She turned toward the door. "I'm going out," she said.

Margaret knew something would have to be resolved soon and it would have to include a discussion, however far-reaching, of her father's past. Unless that happened, she was beginning to believe she and her mother might never regain their friendship.

2

Margaret herself returned home that evening from an admirable afternoon with Steven spent down at the Women's Exchange. Steven had been most admiring, complimenting Margaret on finding Mrs. Bright as her "good right arm," and on her sensitive approach to the question of charity. Margaret couldn't know that Steven thought she needed to be handled carefully, that he thought she was too quick and brittle and tentative these last few days. Often, during their afternoon, Steven had repeated the word *worthwhile*. Margaret, as he'd intended, was strengthened by this.

She learned from Knox that her mother was again at home, but Mrs. Marsh was not dining in but going out to dinner and the opening of the opera. Margaret told the butler that she would have soup and tea with Uncle Findley. She went upstairs to say hello to her uncle and found him complaining. Knox would not allow the windows to be opened. Findley missed his walk. He was sitting up, much covered with shawls and backed by pillows. He said he hated it.

"I'm never sick," he said. "I need air. It's stifling in here."

"There's a great deal of fog out there right now, Uncle. It comes in off the lake all of a sudden sometimes. It will only aggravate your condition."

For a while she read to him from the newspapers, there in her father's bedroom, and then, on a whim, excused herself and went through her father's dressing room to her mother's and on into her mother's room without knocking. It was like going from one world into another.

Her father's room was all oak and green plush and deep red turkey carpet and mirrors and cabinetry trimmed out in a masculine way.

But the walls of her mother's bedroom were covered with lavender brocade, Mrs. Marsh's favorite color. The bed, still made up with the smooth counterpane of dove-gray, was turned back for the night, revealing a satin case that held her mother's nightdress. The hangings of the bed matched the coverlet and at the side of the bed was a pair of brocade slippers. On the floor was another Aubusson, nicely faded, which brought together the colors of the room. There was a bright fire in the marble-topped hearth. Her mother was moving about, dressing. The room was full of whispers, the action of silk against silk.

She turned as Margaret entered, startled to see her daughter instead of the chambermaid. Mrs. Marsh was dressed in black faille with a train of the same material pleated at the hem in a graceful way. Diagonally across her bosom there was a mauve sash and on her left shoulder, a great span of orchids. There were black feathers in her elaborately dressed hair. Although these were colors she had worn throughout Margaret's memory of her, Mrs. Marsh looked as if she might be a queen in mourning, interrupted in her ascent to the throne. Her train curled in a formal swath around her feet.

Margaret lowered her voice so they would not be overheard.

"Mother—"

"Margaret?"

"Mother, I must talk to you. There never seems to be time—"

"I know. But must it be now?"

A gold clock on the mantelpiece tinkled out a notice. A large gold fly on the top of the clock tentatively moved its wings and emitted a mechanical buzz.

"I'm late," Mrs. Marsh said. "The Fowlers are always very punctual and I'm not yet dressed—"

"I'm tired of avoiding this. It should have come before—perhaps a lifetime ago. I—"

After her brave start, Margaret didn't know what to say next and so she said, "I'll just sit over here while you continue dressing." She moved to the bed and sat on it, against the rules of her mother's house. She felt beyond those rules now.

"Mother, is there something I should know about—my father?

Things have come up lately. I don't know who to ask except you. I realize this is—painful. But when I sit there in his room, a sense of him alone in this house comes over me. Why did we leave him so much? Why wasn't he with us—there were times I missed him terribly—"

As the fog had occupied the street outside, silence now came to occupy the room. Her mother's back was toward her and she could see that Mrs. Marsh's entire body was trembling in its evening finery. But nevertheless, Mrs. Marsh was drawing on long black gloves.

If I press her too much, if I should stand and stamp my foot and scream as I want to—then she'll bolt. If I'm cautious and quiet, she might answer me, tell me the truth for once. Margaret had never stamped or screamed. It was as much against her own nature as her mother's, yet she wanted to do it.

Instead, she whispered, "Will you please answer me? Whatever happened, whoever was at fault—one or neither or both—I don't care about that. I realize now our whole life must have been some sort of—of fraud. Mother, why did we travel so much, you and I?"

"I thought—" the voice was thin and reedy and her mother was addressing the wall opposite, her back still toward Margaret. "I wanted—to give you a life, some kind of experiences that were away from this—" she waved her hand around the beautiful room "—this swamp on the edge of a frog pond—"

There was a hesitation after this and Margaret filled it by saying briskly, "That's not it. There was much more to it than that. Why did Papa build this house and stay here and you went away? Why didn't he come with us in summers when we went to Vermont? He could have come there—"

"He was very busy. His business was here—"

"No, Mother—" Her voice was very low now, almost indecipherable.

"Margaret, there's no use going into old—things. Your father was a—a good and charming man. He was the kind of man that women—turn to look at on the street. He was kind to everyone. He tried to hurt no one. Sometimes that's misunderstood."

Softer still. "No, Mother—"

At last there was a slight break in the wall. "We—we were very civilized. We all tried to be that. I guess we only succeeded—in our own minds. We tried to keep it—our own unhappiness—not to spread it to others. To you. You needn't have known. I'm sorry Findley has told you." On that last note, Mrs. Marsh's voice was quite harsh.

"It was not Uncle Findley. I don't think he knows what you're talking about. Nor do I, really. Did this have something to do with Papa's death?"

Mrs. Marsh went quickly to her dressing table, a much-draped affair filled with silver-backed brushes, silver containers, small mirrors and large, perfume bottles with silver-tipped stoppers, with the scents she preferred. She appeared calm, but her hand rattled against a bottle, there was a small spill and she righted it with a sound of exasperation. In irritation, she opened a chest so hurriedly its cover fell back against the glass. She took out a bracelet, which she fastened over her glove. She did not answer her daughter or look at her. Finally, fiddling with the clasp of the bracelet, holding in her other hand a clutch of jewels, which Margaret knew to be a matching necklace, her mother turned to take up an opera cloak edged in dark fur and picked up her beaded purse.

"I'm not going to stay here and listen to this. I'm late anyway. I was with you in Boston when your father died. He died peaceably in his own bed. Ask Mrs. Riley. If there had been the slightest bit of irregularity to it, there would have been headlines. There were none. In Chicago, any bad news about Prairie Avenue would be the blackest and boldest headlines in the morning papers, you can depend on it."

Margaret tried to say something, but her mother plunged on.

"Your father died of—a weak heart. He was a passionate man. But he wasted his passion on little things, on matters that should not have won his notice. He—he—squandered love. That's all I'm going to say. You have every right to be proud of him in the ways that are important. Anything else—that's conjecture and gossip and that's the Chicago way of doing things. Now—I'm going out for the evening and I'm determined to put this behind me and enjoy myself—"

She left the room and as she left, she closed the door with a tiny click. Mrs. Marsh would disturb no household by the slamming of a door.

Margaret sat on in her mother's room, feeling horribly cheated—by the two of them. And yet she'd learned something. Her father had loved—deeply. But probably not her mother. And in spite of everything that might have happened, her mother loved him still. Two people, one loving and the other turned elsewhere, secure in their economic world only, lost in the world of feelings—ungrounded in love.

Margaret sighed, turned out the spirit lamp, stood there in the dark for a moment, determined not to be like either of them. Finally she went to her own room, but she did not sleep well that night.

Within the week her mother had fled east, hardly speaking to Margaret before she left except to say that if "—you wish to come later, I will be pleased to see you. Please don't forget to put the silver and plate in at Spauldings before you go—"

Margaret was left alone in the house on Prairie Avenue with her new confidant and chaperone, the ailing Uncle Findley.

3

Among her social peers, Margaret had often heard discussions of what must be done for "the poor." What surprised Margaret was that "the poor" had their own ideas, that "the poor" were not one solid mass of humanity, but a multilayered community with its own standards for behavior, business dealings and life's circumstances. She found also that the veneer of civilization was very thin in such places and came to realize in a few days that her own knowledge of life was meager and subject to reversal should it ever be threatened by the dangers faced by the young women she hoped to reach in her new mission. To be very poor was hard, difficult work and if this population appeared inhuman at times, it could be because poverty was dehumanizing.

Then she met others, proud, hard as steel, grudging the world a glimpse into their own souls. There was no communication with them, but in this Margaret felt communion. She felt kinship to the cold, aspiring ones. She too had things she wished to share with no one.

And there were those who impressed her. Rather than total hopelessness, as she'd expected to find in Back-of-the-Yards, the tenement community teemed with forward-looking activity. There were mission houses staffed by others such as herself, those come from privileged places to give time and money to an ideal. And there were the small businessmen and shopkeepers, the owners of the lofts, the managers of this and that; pocket bankers who kept their businesses in their hats, lawyers who must teach the greenhorn the ways of a new land, doctors and schoolteachers struggling to bring new standards to a population that must be served. As she looked about her and learned, not only from what she saw, but also from Mrs. Bright, Margaret's hopes for her Exchange were not only high—they were flying! Others were succeeding in such plans. Why shouldn't she?

Her Women's Exchange opened the first night with twenty-three girls in attendance, one more than the available chairs, with no chairs for Margaret Marsh or Rose Bright. This dilemma was immediately solved when four girls, on learning there was not to be an exchange of clothing brought in from the Lake Shore crowd, said they would not stay for a meeting. They had been hoping to improve their wardrobes. Margaret thought privately that those four might have been the best of the lot. Those who stayed gave evidence in their slightly challenging stares that they wished to be entertained. They had labored all day and though they'd paid nothing to enter, they wished to get full value for their attendance.

In the room were Margaret and Rose Bright and nineteen girls. At Mrs. Bright's insistence, the meeting was commenced with a prayer that Rose called nondenominational, but which mentioned Christ and Our Savior, even though Margaret knew some of the women present were Jewish. But then, Mrs. Bright was the daughter of a Baptist minister and was associated with the University of Chicago, which was a Baptist school.

Mrs. Bright stood with her dark head bowed, plowing ahead through her treatise, unaware of the shifting and twitching in her audience. Margaret resolved to select the next prayer.

Following the prayer, Mrs. Bright gave a short talk in both English and Polish on citizenship. She was followed by a young woman of the neighborhood who demonstrated several interesting embroidery techniques that she said were used extensively in her home region of Galicia.

But several girls called out that they already knew those stitches and their objections and complaints threw the meeting into a buzz of conversation.

Margaret read from the works of Nathaniel Hawthorne and Mrs. Bright read a poem by Robert Louis Stevenson. This latter rendition the young women with strong English seemed to enjoy. Mrs. Bright asked for comments or discussion and there was a great silence in the house.

Margaret cleared her throat and coughed slightly and this brought forth a chorus of coughing and chair shuffling.

A girl stood and said she thought there were to be refreshments and private conversation, rather than a lecture. She said she didn't like lectures much.

A murmur of agreement went around the room.

On this cue, Margaret and Rose Bright, with the aid of one or two of their guests, served tea and coffee and cakes. Some of the girls asked to have their tea in a glass, which Margaret had never seen done, but she accommodated the request.

At the close of the evening, as the visitors were leaving, they filed past Margaret and Rose with nods and smiles and the two hostesses asked the group to come again on other nights, when special events would be announced.

"We must remain nonjudgmental," Rose whispered to Margaret. "Their ways are so different and yet equally valid—"

"Yes, I suppose so," Margaret murmured and smiled at the departing women.

Out on the porch there was a slight commotion and those women still in the room stopped moving forward through the cloakroom. Everyone waited and Margaret went to the door. On the landing of the porch an older woman in a black shawl and dark clothing was in earnest conversation with one of the departing girls. As Margaret stepped out of the door, the woman looked up the stairway with a frightened look and went down the stairs and quickly out the gate.

"What was it?" asked Margaret. "Who is she? Does anyone know? Can we help her in some way—?"

"She's looking for her daughter," the girl said who'd been talking to the woman. "She lives nearby. She comes out into the streets at night and she asks if we've seen her daughter. But she hardly waits for an answer and she's gone. She goes everywhere like that, dressed in mourning, going out into the streets—"

"Who is her daughter?" Margaret asked. "Is her daughter someone who was here tonight?"

"Who knows?" the girl shrugged. "She has several daughters who come to visit her. I've seen them. But at night she does this—I don't think her family knows. She never seems to want to hear an answer, even if we knew what she really wants—"

After everyone had left and Rose was moving about, gathering up cups and glasses and plates and chattering about the evening, Margaret still stood for a while looking out into the dark, wondering where the woman had gone, wondering what drove her to this form of madness.

4

In the interests of better millinery among the poor, Margaret suggested a class in designing hats and she offered to bring supplies, which she took some trouble to select herself. When she arrived for the evening workshop she found eleven girls there, some with their own materials.

Margaret spread everything out on the table and though she was not a seamstress herself, she had every confidence that she could design a better hat than those she'd seen on her new friends and in the streets of the city. Hadn't she traveled with her mother into the best salons of Paris? She knew what she liked—better yet, she knew what her mother liked—and there would be no problem in creating a master work.

The girls babbled and talked and Margaret tried to explain. She put together a bonnet. Her new friends told her it was "too plain."

She watched in horror what they did with their own creations and tried to give assistance where she could, but she had to suppress her own inclination to stamp her foot and tear off half the cherries and bows the girls had brought from their own hoards.

"Now you see," Margaret said, trying to come up with a reason for what she considered to be her superior taste, a reason that would be so sensible it would offend no one, "you see, the weather here is not dependable. In anticipation of that, it's not such a good idea to put all one's fortune on one's bonnet."

She tried an elegant bird, which she'd had her own eye on ever since she'd found it in the wholesaler's shop, but even she had to admit her hat looked so stiff and unyielding it might bring on a change of weather for the entire city should its owner wear it in the street.

One of the girls, a Russian immigrant, tried to explain something to Margaret about the bird, but Margaret didn't understand; so things were when Mrs. Bright came through the room. She saw a stalemate and suggested Margaret might bring in another lamp from the kitchen to make it easier to work.

While Margaret was in the kitchen, she could hear much chatter and laughing in the dining room at the worktable. When she re-entered with the lamp, there was a swift rush of silence.

The Russian woman was standing, with Margaret's bird creation in her hand. Only now it swooped gaily and there was dash to it. The feathers of the bird matched the rim of ribbon that had somehow been turned to outline the form of the hat. The Russian began talking rapidly and smiling at Margaret, at whom she thrust the hat.

Mrs. Bright said, "Nellie here is offering you a gift. She is one of the designers in a workroom in a downtown shop. Her hats are quite sought-after. She likes to do them and she hopes you will like it—"

Margaret put down the lamp and took the hat with as gracious a smile as she could muster. She saw some of the other girls exchange looks and smiles with one another, which she did not feel were inspired by the generous act of the designer. She could sense a cutting edge that annoyed her, but she thought "it will pass."

She went home and showed the hat to Uncle Findley, who thought it better than any he'd seen anywhere. "I knew you'd do some good in the world, Maggie," he said.

"This wasn't exactly what I had in mind," she said crossly.

Uncle Findley was not recovered, although he was mending. He still complained about his forced confinement and his early bedtimes and his lack of card games. He managed to get a racing sheet delivered when young Henry remembered. Steven, who didn't want to visit the Exchange now that it was in actual operation and full of women and girls, came to see Uncle Findley and play chess with him when Margaret was otherwise occupied. Steven had begun his fall work at school and his own schedule was very busy.

Uncle Findley, on seeing the fancy bonnet, said, "If you and your women down there can make hats that look like that, you ought to open a shop and turn them out by the trainload."

"Oh, Uncle, I didn't mean to start a ladies' ready-to-wear."

"Ought to. Then you'd get some return on your money. Look at Field. Look at Leiter. Look at Potter Palmer. That's how they started. And this is better than theirs—"

Margaret thought about the Russian woman and her talent and wondered if Uncle Findley were right. A smart shop. Margaret Marsh behind it but the name—Madame—what? Not Nellie. Madame Natasha's. Some of the other girls could work there. No. She'd not envisioned another "cottage industry" where women worked at piecework in dark backrooms. That was not what she'd had in mind.

5

There were other problems.

As the weeks went by, the Exchange took its place in the neighborhood. Margaret spent all the time there she could spare from the work at the fairgrounds, but she often felt her vision of the place had gone awry. At first she told herself she could not put her finger on why she felt that way. But then she had to admit she knew. Though there were always girls in the place when she came, not long after she arrived they would find they were expected elsewhere. At the evening meetings she attended she was met with smiles and nods and then groups of young ladies would turn back to their conversations with one another or turn silent. They spoke of people and streets and topics Margaret knew nothing of. And if she asked questions in what she hoped was a friendly way, she was rebuffed by sharp answers or answers that were noncommittal, such as "we were talking about someone you wouldn't know—"

One Sunday morning she came into the kitchen to find Molly, one of the girls, talking earnestly to Mrs. Bright. For once the girl didn't stop when Margaret came in, but began a recital about some trouble with her mother. She wanted to leave her home and come to live in the Exchange.

Margaret looked impatiently at Mrs. Bright. Margaret had brought in several boxes of Mrs. Riley's breads and cakes for that night's general meeting and they were sitting out in the wagon at the mercy of passersby. And besides, Margaret didn't believe Rose should encourage girls to leave their families.

She made a sign at Rose behind Molly's back, but the girl turned and saw and bolted from the room in tears.

"Now what did I do?" Margaret asked and then told Rose about the boxes in the carriage.

"Never mind. We'll bring in the cakes. Don't worry about it. I'll handle it," Rose said.

Margaret, who'd once dreamed of handling things herself, saw the irritation in Rose's manner. She would have to be certain to have a talk with her. Every girl had a disagreement now and then with her mother. Margaret had certainly had her own.

6

"*I don't think* you should worry about it just yet," Mrs. Bright said. She was sitting on a chair, her back to the dining room of the Exchange house, hemming a freshly hung white curtain at a window.

Margaret, who'd hung the curtain for her, was now pacing up and down the length of the study table they used for their neighborhood meetings. As she went up the room, Margaret trailed one hand along the edge of the table and as she came down the length of it, she turned and absentmindedly trailed the other.

"Well, it's not what I thought, in the beginning you know. I thought it would be more—"

Rose Bright's head was bent to her task, but she thought, *I didn't think this would come so soon.* They'd been operating for almost three weeks and already Margaret was dissatisfied.

Margaret didn't realize it, but the talk she'd had with her mother had unsettled her to such a degree she was forcing this issue now, a little too early for good judgment. Only Rose Bright's level approach to life would avoid a quarrel. Anyone else would have risen to the bait.

Rose pinned her needle into the curtain and turned to look at Margaret. "What's missing that you expected to find?"

Margaret made an impatient motion with her head. Even she realized this place was better than she could have made it alone, and was the one place in her daily activities where she could feel some personal success. But something inside her pushed her into a confrontation with Rose.

"I thought it would be more—that they would be more—"

"—grateful," said Rose. Her voice was matter-of-fact.

Margaret started. Her redhead's complexion gave her away. Her face flamed.

Rose came to her and took her by the hand and they sat together at the table. "Tell me again," Rose said. "What did you think was going to happen here?"

Margaret, who was not the type to hang her head, nevertheless had her eyelids lowered and didn't look into Mrs. Bright's face as she said, "I thought it was a personal mission—a way to show—to *help* women of my own age—to lead—"

"You said it so much better that first day I talked with you. You said you wanted to exchange ideas with the young women of the tenements and slums, girls who'd come here from other places in order to better themselves, but who'd hardly had a chance to learn about their new life because they had to work so hard. That seemed clear enough then. But you seem to have some other goal now, that isn't being met—"

"But only ten or twelve girls came the last time. We're losing ground. I don't think they—the girls—like it—like—"

"Like you? Did you expect that they would cluster around you, beg for your wisdom and experience? Did you plan to show them a new world that doesn't exist? Did you want their esteem rather than their friendship? I can't answer these questions for you, Margaret. You have to come to some honest assessment of yourself. It's difficult to be charitable. Sometimes the charity we think should be done is not the one that the recipient believes she needs. We have to take that into account—the only person we can truly know in this exchange is ourselves and we should try to be honest about our own part in this, in order that we not put ourselves in the way of success—"

Margaret's face grew darker still. "I thought," she said, "I could at least talk to them. That they would talk to me. But when I come near, if they're talking with you or one another, they stop and keep silent. And if I ask them questions, they answer with one or two words, as if I were prying—"

There was a long silence and Mrs. Bright reached out to hold Margaret's hand, which came into hers reluctantly.

"You have a lovely face, Margaret," Rose said. "But you should never play cards or games of chance. You can't seem to hide the way you feel. The girls say you frighten them—"

So they had been talking about her!

"—they are afraid of offending you. Molly is very sweet, but in the kitchen the other day, when she was talking about her troubles with her mother, you let your irritation show plainly. Molly stopped talking and went into the other room and she told me later she felt very hurt—Molly's mother is quite troublesome. It's not just Molly's viewpoint, you know. Her mother's a—a drinker." Rose decided she would keep the worst of that tale from Margaret. Molly's mother was an aging prostitute and Molly wanted to get away from her.

Margaret said, "I wasn't irritated with Molly. I was hardly thinking of her. I was thinking of something else—"

Rose patted her hand. "Of course you were. But you were not paying attention to something that was most important for Molly to tell us. It cost her something to confide as she did. And you were irritated and let that irritation be read—I don't want to belabor this. It was just a moment and I was there. Molly's all right. She's coming back—"

Margaret had been thinking of her own relationship with her mother and of her mother's evasiveness. She had been irritated with that. *And*, she had to admit, with the girl who brought it back to mind. Irritation filled her again, annoyance with Rose Bright's smooth assessment of the situation, an assessment that meant another deficit mark for Margaret Marsh.

"Well, it hasn't worked out at all as I thought," she snapped. "They're impolite. They can't speak well and they hardly listen at all. And they—they—wear those dreadful earrings and those dirty ribbons and those velvet hats—"

"And you're above all that? If you were poor you wouldn't be like that at all?" Rose's voice cut through Margaret's anger neatly, right to the center Margaret had thought invisible.

"What do you mean?"

"Your distaste of their trivialities does show. I don't wonder that half the world does not meet your standards, Margaret Marsh. We are all less than perfect. We all need God's hand—"

This was so close to Margaret's own private doubts that she could not continue her assessment of others' deficiencies. The sin of pride. The sin that brought her here. Could she never overcome it?

To Margaret's surprise, Rose Bright smiled.

Rose said, "Oh, Margaret, you're so like the rest of the world—like me—like everyone. You're ordinary in your reactions, only I'm certain you don't want to hear it. But we have your assets and your liabilities, your virtues and your sins as well. Our backgrounds and experiences just force us to sort them out a little differently. Human beings are alike, you know. And I know *the poor* don't please you as you'd once hoped. They're not tasteful nor virtuous nor more clean than circumstances will allow—perhaps we would be the same—or are more than we know. It doesn't matter, my dear. We're not here for that—"

No one had ever seen into Margaret's mind and heart like this, no one had known her so completely, not even the young man she was beginning to love. She bent her head down and began to weep. For the first time in her life, she saw herself. A great shuddering sigh went through her. Someone knew her heart, could read her thoughts, thought of her as less than a perfect being and forgave her for it.

Rose leaned forward and took Margaret in her arms. She was only a few years older than Margaret, yet Rose said, "Oh, my poor child. You don't have to be a model of perfect womanhood all the time—"

GOING PLACES

CHAPTER XX

The New York financiers for whom the phrase "watered stock" was invented were the James Fisks and the Jay Goulds. They knew how to take the bull down to the waterhole and fill up the old beast just before it was weighed in at the yard. True, there was heft there. True, he was entirely one beast on-the-roof, but his belly bulged with weight that would never grace his flanks, and many the poor young orphaned lad and many his widowed mother who were deceived enough to put Pa's insurance money into some shoddy animal trotted out by the New York financiers.

Such were the mentors of Jay B. Darling, who came after.

But the new "gentleman friend" of Pamela Jones (nee Trudy Jones, nee Gertrude Jahn) had added a sexual tone to his management of money. His handling of finances had the element of risk about it, but all the while the poor dupe was fooled into thinking this was the way it was done on the eastern shore, this quickness of hand and wink and nod went with traffic and trade among the sophisticated.

Darling had no more shame than a French cancan dancer. He let the unwary sucker get a brief look at this bit of capital here, a little bit of that capital there and at the last moment the lights went off and the dancer ran off stage—with all the money in hand and the capital still intact—but elsewhere.

No one could prove a thing. In fact, there was nothing to prove.

The wickedness had been all in the eye and mind of the beholder. Jay B. Darling walked out in his silk hat and his silky smile and said nothing, admitted nothing. There was nothing to admit. That those left behind him were much poorer than they had begun, that he had their money as well as his own, was their own damned fault. What could he do in such a foolish world?

Once he'd been heard to say: "It is in the nature of things for the world to want to be controlled."

He had been quoted in various presses to this effect and when a reporter went to him for an elaboration of the remark, perhaps hoping in this way to become as clever and as rich as Jay B. Darling, the reponse had been clinical and nonforthcoming.

Jay Darling had repeated his classic remark and then looked at the reporter and smiled his thin-lipped, closemouthed smile. There was no doubt that he thought of himself as the prime controller and if challenged to prove it, he would simply blink, tip his hat and go on with his day.

He had begun with Pamela as he always did. First, he had been charming. He had brought her the Pekinese. She'd never seen one before. The dog, which cost more, Pamela learned, than her family in Chicago lived on for an entire year, was a marvelous conversation piece, but a bit snappish. Yet it had served, those first few days, as the bridge between Pamela and Darling and had become a marvelous toy to the girl. She lavished all her thwarted affection on it while she learned to live with Jay Darling. Before she realized what had happened, Darling had entered her considerations, if not her affections, through the dog.

Darling himself was a different sort of beast. He soon let her know that she was to count on nothing, be ready for anything and be prepared to travel quickly and with little but her jewelry. When she was accustomed to this, he then would take her on journeys that turned out to be leisurely excursions somewhere within the city or to prolonged sequestered house parties in mansions up along the Hudson, as if there were not and had never been any threat of sudden disaster as he'd led her to believe. In time, after several of these confusing contradictions had been laid out before Pamela, she began to be tense at the sight of him, nervous about what she should wear, about what he would do next and about what she should do next.

His eyes, like Myron's, were blue. But Darling's were the blue of nonexistence. They seemed to have an infinity in them that could catch up and transport one to another place without one being aware.

He never raised his voice. He never spoke carelessly or crossly.

His courtesy was of the patient, oh-so-patient, kind. Would this idiot before him—whoever it might be—never learn such a simple thing as how to please Mr. Darling? Mr. Darling had requested that Pamela wear the blue dress. Didn't Pamela remember he had distinctly said the blue one? But she, alas, had heard green with a further instruction about aigrette feathers.

Yet now he said, "I have always been annoyed by aigrettes on women. They look as if they are molting."

Thoroughly confused and with no one whom she dared blame but herself, Pamela tried harder.

His business interests, he made clear to her—and in this he did not deceive her—lay everywhere. He told her that at any time he might pick up and move to another continent to live and stay in that place indefinitely. Wherever he chose to go, he would have wealth and power. Until he approved of her daily plans, she was to do nothing. He might want to see her. And then again, he might not.

One night, when they were at the theater, he asked, "Where did you get that necklace?" He had leaned over and asked the question during an intense part of the performance when everyone about him had attention riveted on the stage.

Pamela, lost in the performance and without thinking, had answered, "Myron gave it to me."

At once she knew this was a mistake. So she whispered, "I have nothing as neutral as this in color—" and turned back to the play.

The next morning, when she went to put her jewelry away, she could not find either the necklace or the earrings in the set. She knew better than to ask the maid, who was supremely honest. Pamela felt a great, physical twinge, as if Myron had turned from her once again, as if she'd been once more handed into the arms of Jay Darling.

Later that day a messenger came with a package. The messenger was in smart livery and insisted on the signature of Mrs. Pamela Jones, rather than the maid. Brown wrapping paper fell away to an important-looking box, which opened to white satin and diamonds, what Mrs. Asunda had called "the full boat"—tiara, earrings, necklace with detachable clips and a bracelet as well as a ring that looked like chunks of ice. Pamela had never seen anything like it. The maid had seen nothing like it either and she'd been in many other fine ladies' boudoirs. The note inside said, "Diamonds are a neutral stone. Wear these tonight."

Looking at the collection in her lap, Pamela realized she could buy her passage to any country with these. The dog hopped up on the divan and nestled at her side. She gave him a hug. But where in the world could she go?

She sighed and put the ring on her finger. A perfect fit. His attention to detail always amazed her. And she knew she must never forget it.

If only Mrs. Asunda were here. Pamela could show her these jewels and show her the other gifts she'd had from the generous Mr. Darling. She could then have asked Mrs. Asunda what to do when the man on which one was forced to depend was erratic and cold?

By closing her eyes, Pamela could almost see Mrs. Asunda and hear her voice. Mrs. Asunda would say, "And is he cold in the bedchamber as well? Or does he display affection there? If there is passion in him, that is where you will know—"

Pamela reviewed their nights together. She didn't like to think too much about what was required of her. She felt she was a business-woman now and the bedchamber her place of business. The thought was not pleasant or romantic. But, she had to admit, he was a clinically precise lover. He knew women. He knew how to approach her, how to touch her, how to make her bend to his way—as Myron had not. There were no quick, rushed nights any longer. Jay Darling had mastered endurance, had mastered the art of titillation until he could almost make Pamela beg for relief from her desire. But throughout these performances, for that they were, she could recall only one emotion—the murderous delight of a dedicated sportsman who knows he will win every time, but still plays as if each point will be the telling one.

In her mind, Pamela replied to Mrs. Asunda: No, Beverly, in the bedchamber he is not cold. But he is not warm and loving, either. He's just like these stones. He is neutral and reflects light.

That night, for their evening out, Pamela wore gray satin and long white gloves and the tiara, necklace and bracelets from her new collection. Darling seemed pleased with her, but such things were always uncertain. He often took her to odd gatherings of intellectuals, sportsmen, senators and foreign dignitaries. Some of the foreigners might be nobility, or at the edge of royalty, some traveling incognito—a term that was new to Pamela.

Strangely enough, they were quite pleased to know Pamela. On the whole, they treated her with great awe and respect, which she, slightly less than seventeen, found heady and exciting. Her languages impressed them. Pamela discovered that the rudimentary French she'd learned almost inadvertently from French Madame served well enough in the circles in which she now moved. Now and again she used Polish; frequently German. Among their acquaintances there were many actresses and actors, often quite famous, and there were men whose names Pamela had heard while she was still escorted by Myron Davis.

But the women, those who were not the visitors and stars; were always changing. Pamela no longer had friends. The crowd she'd known with Myron seemed to have melted southward for the race meetings. She saw Myron nowhere. The new crowd of men and women came and went without preliminaries. One day they were there, another not. To fill the void of her days, Pamela chatted familiarly with couturiers, with the bellboy, with the German maid, until Jay Darling noticed it and put a stop to it.

"We must be discreet," he said. "There are many people who would like to know my habits, know what I'm going to do next or where we have just been. Please say nothing to anyone. You may jeopardize some situation I've been working toward for some time."

So she was cut off from almost all normal connections. Her function was to dress and act like a duchess, to appear regal and charming, to speak of the weather in New York or the amusing actions of her little dog, Shu-Shu, to discuss the points of a game that was being played. Following this she would be taken home, escorted handsomely by Mr. Darling, where he would proceed to use her as he had every right to.

One afternoon he stopped by the suite to tell her to be ready to sail by evening.

"Where are we going?"

"Important to you, is it? What difference can it possibly make—" He was smiling his eerie half-smile.

"I have to know what kind of clothing to take."

He hedged. "Plan on a warm climate. Bring summer dresses. Something warm to wear at first. You won't be visiting many private households. We're going to have a long sea voyage and then we're going to rough it and be very private."

"Will we be attending the race meetings?"

He seemed annoyed that she would even suggest it. "You know I detest the races," he said. She did not know it and doubted that he did.

"I'll be ready," she said. Anything for a change from the prison New York had become. She would love a long voyage on his yacht.

He left the suite and then came back again.

"On second thought," he said, "I will put some of your more valuable jewelry in safekeeping. Bring me the cases and I'll take them with me."

She went into the boudoir and gathered together her valuables.

She hesitated and then decided to say nothing about the two receipts of deposit she had hidden away amid her dresses. Some of that money had come from Myron. And if some of the rest had been gleaned from her life with Jay Darling, then she'd earned it. Every day she made concessions to him and she felt no guilt in withholding just payment for that.

And to further show her independence—at least to herself—she tucked one or two rings and a full set of garnets into the bottom of her trunk.

She returned to the drawing room of the suite and he opened the various cases, looked through them, took out some items of small value that might be suitable for informal occasions. At the last moment, he smiled at her and tossed her a chamois bag that contained a modest string of pearls that Myron had given her.

"Pearls can be worn at any time," he said, as if he were instructing her in dress, as he often did. He called to the maid to bring a traveling case. He packed up her modest collection—except for the diamonds she believed she had little of unusual value—and he went out the door whistling tunelessly.

2

Several days later a bellboy at the Waldorf inserted a letter, which he'd written himself, into an envelope addressed by a different hand to a Mr. Myron Davis in Chicago. The letter read:

> Dear Mr. Gentleman and Sir: This is the first letter I am having to writ to you. The young lady is gone. She and the mister went off in a boat. The mister gave the little dog to the maid on account of their wasn't going to be more employment. They have vacated the suite and didn't leave no forwarding. All things is put in storage in the mister's name. They left very fast one evening and so I didn't know till next day. I went down to the docks and found out the boat was sailing down to this place somewheres south called the sporting island. They was a party of eight. I trust this will find you well and good enough. I am your respectable correspondent: M. F. Murphy.
>
> P.S. Any farther service I can be to you, I will be most glad to perform it.

3

The yacht itself was a glorious thing—two hundred feet long with a center smokestack. Darling had named it the *Darling Shark* for its sharp-nosed prow. It had crossed and recrossed the ocean many times, usually on some secret business of its owner. Below its decks were many cabins, a large ballroom, two dining rooms—one intimate and one more formal—a wine cellar noted for its variety, a bowling alley and a stable area in which horses were transported for later use on land. Mr. Darling did not like to have to adjust to new horses on his travels.

On the main deck there was a card room, a library and a lounge for bad-weather days. Built into the deck itself was a swimming pool and there were several areas where food service could be received from the galley below for the guests.

The crew was polished; dressed in uniforms of dark blue and white and gold, as if they were a private navy. Everywhere Pamela looked, there were bits of brass sparkling in the sun against fresh white paint.

A red carpet was extended over the gangplank for their boarding.

Except for the carpet, Jay Darling treated this excursion as if it were nothing at all, as if this were no more than the usual weekend trips he'd often shared with his New York crowd. But clearly they were going to be gone for some time. There was that air about the ship.

They were a party of eight when they left the harbor—with the other three women similar to Pamela. She'd seen one or two of them before. They, too, seemed to be under instructions to be discreet, not to be overly friendly with anyone. For the first day or so, they were all quite distant with one another; smiling and nodding as they strolled about the decks or leaned against the rail; cordial during dinner and cards afterwards, much as if they were at a party in New York.

But on the second or third day, Pamela found that a slender blond named Helen had books in her stateroom that she would lend and they became reasonably well-acquainted and spoke less formally after that. But Pamela noticed that although she and Helen were on much the same footing with their escorts and Helen was several years older than she, Helen still deferred to Pamela as if she were the hostess of the voyage, which Pamela did not feel herself to be.

During that day, the yacht stopped at one of the off-islands and took on two more passengers. The man was addressed as *Senator*. The girl he brought with him was Gladys. When she was brought aboard, she looked blowzy and wind-blown, but Pamela thought it was because of the stiff wind that had made docking difficult and required the party to come aboard from a skiff. By the time Gladys reached the deck, much of her clothing seemed askew.

From the time Gladys came aboard, the party changed. The men seemed to come alert and when Gladys was around they teased her and clasped her in mock embraces that bothered the Senator not at all. The Senator liked his cards and his liquor and seemed willing that Gladys do whatever she liked. For the first day or so after their coming aboard the Senator and Jay Darling were quartered in one of the cabins for the better part of each day. Gladys roamed free.

Helen and two other girls were disapproving.

"She's nothing but a tramp, a slut," Helen said primly.

Sherry, a pouty type who didn't seem to like the sea, said, "I don't think she's had all her buttons buttoned since she came aboard. And someone has always got his hands on her—"

"Oh, you're just miffed because Harry likes her," Doris said.

"Yes," said Sherry. "Harry likes her and Billy likes her and Jay likes her and the Senator likes her and so does your Lou—she rolls her eyes at every one of them and I think she'd go down in a minute if anyone gave her a quarter—"

"Hush," Helen whispered. "The men will hear you and then we'll be in for it. You know how they think women are catty—"

Doris laughed and said, "Well, so we are. And I can't think of a better subject—"

That made them all laugh together in a sort of abandoned way and they became friends after that, united against the overlush Gladys.

Jay Darling told the entire party that they were beating the weather change by just a week or two, but they would be able to identify the changes in climate by watching the trees on shore when they were near land.

Some of the days were gray and leaden, but most were sunny and one morning they found that the captain had installed striped awnings of red and white over the upper deck at the rear of the yacht. "Aft," the captain called it. Garden furniture of the most commodious kind was bolted to the deck floor and one enormous settee, easily as wide as a triple bed, covered with the same stripe as the awning, was set up with cushions along its length.

"Cleopatra's barge," said the Senator, expansively. He turned toward Pamela and bowed. "And here comes the beautiful Cleo now—"

Everyone laughed. They were in warmer waters. There were great schools of fish now and then, and when they came close to an island they could see large turtles warming themselves in the sun on beaches.

"We can have turtle soup," shouted Harry.

But the girls made faces at him and waved to the shore, letting their scarves fly loose in the wind.

4

They had begun to take naps in the afternoons, "siestas," as Harry called them, to allow for a more lively air at the evening parties. On one of the afternoons, while Jay Darling still dozed in the main cabin, Pamela took her book and headed for the afterdeck. She planned to get some fresh air and to read quietly under the awning. But as she rounded the corner of the cabin housing, she heard a kind of strangled gurgle and before she mounted the stairs to the little platform she found herself at eye level with the upper deck.

Harry and Gladys were struggling across the generous expanse of the divan, not against each other, but with a unity of nature all too clear. Gladys lay with her head back, her hair a great loose mass behind her, her eyes shut, her mouth releasing rapturous cries. The bodice of her dress was not visible to Pamela, only the free mounds of her breasts, one nipple lost entirely in the eager mouth of Harry, who seemed to be chewing it with his lips, his eyes closed in ecstasy. One of Gladys' bare legs was thrown up against the cushion and the other showed only a white bare knee to the air. Harry's trousers lay beside them and the heavy sounds and groans emitting from both showed they knew their business and would be deterred by nothing, not even the threat of discovery by the rest of the party.

Pamela withdrew immediately, her eyes downcast on her book, her entire body burning with something she couldn't quite name: a kind of shame mixed with precise knowledge of the lust Gladys was clearly enjoying. Pamela was filled with disgust—not so much at Gladys, but at the wash of kinship she felt with the girl and the immediate self-loathing brought on by the realization that she, Pamela, was no better. That she was now the same because each night she did the same thing with Jay Darling without an ounce of feeling for him, only the need to release her own lustful tensions, which Jay could so neatly and skillfully arouse.

She was certain that if she were the right sort of woman, a good woman, she would not be aroused by a man she didn't love. She would be able to withhold herself, would not begin to burn for a certain pressure, a movement, would not cry out just as Gladys was doing. Pamela hurried along and as she turned another corner to go down a ladder, she came face-to-face with one of the sailors who, with an almost invisible presence, made the voyage go smoothly. The man had just come down from somewhere above and Pamela knew, as he looked at her, that he had seen what she had seen and that he had watched her retreat from the open-air seduction and had come to meet her here, just to see her reaction. She looked down at the floor, and felt herself turning a brilliant red from head to toe.

He said nothing either, but he made a motion with his tongue that was obscene. Yet when she looked again, his tongue was not visible. They passed in the small corridor without speaking, much too close for Pamela's comfort.

Back in the cabin, she found Jay awake.

"Where have you been?"

"Oh, just out on the deck for some air."

"Are the others about—"

"No."

He stood up and came to her, began to unfasten her dress at the front. His hands were long and slim and almost bloodless. He slipped a hand beneath her shirtwaist and her upper clothing, letting his fingers touch lightly on her nipple. She felt it rise to his touch and she pulled away, stepping backward, annoyed at her own body, wanting to deny it.

"I've been meaning to talk to you about that," he said.

"What?" She was turned from him. He came up and put his arms around her from the back. He massaged her waist.

"This," he said. "All these clothes. It's getting warmer. It's almost sultry out, yet you are bundled up like Mrs. Grundy. I'm tired of struggling with all these underclothes and stays—"

"Well, the dresses require it," she said. "They won't fit right otherwise."

"In what way?"

"They'll fall off my shoulders. They'll hang too low in front. I would be too much exposed. More than decolletage—"

He was petulant. "I don't care. We're alone on this yacht. I want you looser, more responsive; quicker to my touch. Look at this—" He pulled her skirt up.

Beneath the dress was a silk slip for "show," a flannel slip to keep off the ocean damp, a batiste slip next to her corset, a corset cover over her corset. He tugged at each layer.

"Leave all that off. And what's beneath?"

"Well I have to wear something—"

"What?"

"Pantalettes—"

"Remove them—"

She looked at him straight, having turned toward him while he yanked at her skirts. "I'll have nothing on if I do that. I'll be nude."

"I don't mind."

"What about the others? It would be—unseemly—"

He walked away from her a few steps and leaned against the doorway to the cabin. "I don't mind," he said at last. "I think the others already know what you are—"

He smiled his ice-cold smile and then said, "Come out on deck at dinner as I have told you, or I'll throw your clothes overboard for our after-dinner entertainment—"

Pamela appeared as late as possible before the dinner hour. She was dressed as Jay Darling had suggested, but the dress she had chosen was of thick material, almost a brocade. Even in this dress she was certain anyone looking closely would be able to discern her nipples beneath the cloth. Under the skirt she felt safe enough, but her chest seemed dangerously unbound, as if she might burst out into the air as Gladys had so willingly done on the upper deck. Pamela was wearing no necklace, with the hope that no one's attention would be drawn to her neckline.

The quantity of drinking on board had increased drastically when Gladys and the Senator had become part of their little band. Even before dinner there was enough champagne to put everyone into the giggly stage, and sometimes by the time a full-course dinner had run through the lavish service of wine from Jay Darling's amazing floating cellar, there was little restraint on the behavior of those who'd heavily imbibed.

This evening, the already flushed Senator shouted at the sight of Pamela in the gangway, "Here comes Cleo." He went to meet her, but she evaded him and went to sit beside Jay.

Jay put his arm casually around her waist, felt no stays, let his hand trail intimately along her upper thigh and felt no garters. He smiled and whispered in her ear, "Be nice to the Senator, my dear. Ask him to bring you a glass of champagne."

Feeling a quick rush of disgust she turned toward the Senator and did as Jay asked. When the older man came toward her, Jay rose abruptly as if to offer his seat. As he did this, a small cushion fell off the divan to the deck. Pamela automatically leaned forward to pick it up. The Senator leaned down at the same time and as they came up together, she saw him leer into the amazing spectacle of the half-naked Pamela Jones. To cut short the moment, she smiled coyly at him and turned to look coldly at Jay, who faced the two of them without expression.

Lou, Doris' gentleman, was seated on one of the divans near enough to have had the same view as the Senator. He quickly changed his seat to be closer to Pamela. He sat next to her casually enough, but it was quite close, close enough that his thigh and hers touched from knee to hip and she knew he was exploring just as Jay had. Lou put his arm around her, laughing about warmer weather ahead as he did so. Pamela smiled directly into his face. She decided to ignore the rest of his body. The Senator, who'd chosen to stand beside her and was looking downward, was not ignoring his view.

Pamela could see Gladys at the rail, chatting with Billy. Gladys seemed to have no remorse or regret about her style of life. Pamela wondered how such an existence would be and if she could handle it as smoothly.

The Senator leaned down to whisper in her ear that he would like her to be his dinner partner. Although she agreed, she found in the small dining salon that they were seated across from each other and she was next to Jay. The quarters in this room were cramped for ten diners.

Well into the dinner, well into the wines, Pamela felt a silk-clad foot slip between hers and move up her bare leg with a caressing motion. She turned her torso abruptly, trying to evade the gesture. She was certain it was the Senator. But the confines of the seating would not allow her to turn her body far enough to lose the Senator's groping foot. He seemed oblivious to what was happening. He was engrossed in his wine glass.

By now, Pamela realized, his leg must be horizontal to the floor. He probed. He drove the silk-clad toe home with skill. Pamela jumped. She dropped her fork and gave a sharp cry, moving her torso back against the settee. Did Jay know this game? Was this why she was instructed to wear nothing?

But Jay was talking to Helen at his other side.

Pamela let her fork lie on her plate. She kept her eyes away from the Senator. Was he under the impression that Jay Darling was just going to hand her over to him for the night—or perhaps for good? Or was she expected now to act like Gladys and be ready at any moment to go with one at a time to some waiting cabin? Pamela felt ill. She put her head on Jay's arm and said she needed air quickly—

He helped her out to the deck and as they walked along the rail he asked what had happened. She thought she would trust him. She

would make her feelings known and thereby stave off some unpleasant business later. Could a man object if she didn't want to
leave him?

She began, "I told you it would be the wrong thing to go so—
undressed—the Senator—" Here she stopped. She'd caught a glimpse
of Jay's smile. His triumphant look.

"So the old bastard groped you under the table, did he—"

"No. He—his foot—" she was whispering desperately. "He
touched—I haven't any clothes—"

Jay was laughing, delighted with her. She'd never seen him smile
like that—openly. He gripped her hand and took her along the
gangway to the stairs of the upper deck. He pushed her down on
the divan and with one motion was out of his trousers, revealing,
under the front of his dinner shirt, a magnificent erection.

With amazing swiftness for Jay Darling, he had spread her legs
with his hands and was inside her, crying out in full ecstasy almost
immediately. He was never like this. She hadn't been ready. He was
rough and was hurting her. His lips sought her breasts, her mouth.
He was groaning with pleasure. She'd never known him to be so
excited, unrestrained—tumultuous. Almost as Myron had been.
Darling began his expert moves. She caught his excitement, trying
to hold back against it, but unable to maintain control. Her hips
moved, rising to meet his thrusts. She didn't want to do this. She
wanted to turn from him, to say she wasn't like that—

"Not here; not now—" she gasped. "Someone will see—"

"Let them," he growled. "Let them all watch. You're mine and
this is how it's done."

5

Later, he hustled her along the corridors to the cabin. She was almost
lame from his use of her. He deposited her in their suite and went
back to join the others. He didn't bother her when he came in that
night, but the next day, when she woke, he was waiting. He let her
go to her bath, but when she came from it ready to dress, he caught
her and pulled her down on the wide bunklike bed next to him.

"It's raining today," he said. "I've sent out for some food—" He
gestured toward a desk on which there was a tray covered with a
napkin. "I think we'll just let the others amuse themselves and we
will amuse each other—"

He sat up and from the pocket of the dressing gown he wore, he
slipped a small jar. He opened this and scooped out a dab of some

heavily scented lotion. He opened her wrapper and began to apply it across her body with a sensuous massage. The odor of the cream, released under the heat of his hands, assailed her eyes and nostrils, making her dizzy. As his hands moved on her, he began to talk, quietly, hypnotically.

He told her he'd traveled everywhere, that he'd studied the art of love and learned a great deal in the Orient, where he'd learned the habit of control, which allowed long, elaborate wooing.

His voice was as sure as his hands. "I don't mind telling you these things," he said, "because you will never be able to forget me. You will have other lovers, but none like me. No woman has ever left me—because I satisfy her very being, I am the reason she has been created—and a very good reason, may I say—you see, you see how you like this, how your body responds to me—in the Orient there are books—but these books are a farce—a travesty on art such as mine—there are many, many positions of intercourse described in these books—what a mockery—those books are for the man with one woman—" His hands were at her and she felt herself lifting to his touch.

"—a man with one woman can control her in many ways—by force—through economics—through law by marriage—but a man with a hundred women—a thousand women—he must have the sureness of the universe in his touch—he must know the ways to please a woman in the shortest, quickest way—which is the longest in one sense—but he will be pleased by it as well—I gain pleasure from this and I will enter you soon—in the way that gives women most pleasure—" He was touching her with hypnotic motion and a sigh escaped her. "—I will enter you slowly, penetrating deeply with a fully frontal entrance—the way a woman gains the most sensation—taking care not to damage fragile nerve endings that will be my ally in this—these nerve endings brought to the surface by my touch—alive to me, allow me to enter you to the greatest extent—

"—and then—and then, the ancient movement begins to a rhythm that matches her pulse—her heartbeat—the thread of her life—this is a woman's life—all of it—she should be allowed nothing else—and if a man should please her here—she will wait for him through empty nights while he goes to others—that is the secret of the harem, my dear—oh, you are so lovely—so unsullied—I do not like women who are coarse and overused—you are proof of my wooing—that is the secret—the long wooing—the touch—insistent—mine—the frontal entry—the special rhythm of each woman, meant for her alone—women can never escape this—will never try—I can tell you—tell you anything—it won't matter—you will never want our mating—our beautiful copulation—to end—"

Her head swam with words, she tried to move away from his hands, but something within herself kept her there—brought her body to terrible life with the most urgent sensations she'd ever felt. What was he doing—why did he do this to her?

He was above her now and she was open to him in every way. He whispered words she could not understand at first and then he moved his mouth to her ear and began—

"You are so innocent—I knew that—I could tell when I first saw you—oh, see how I endeavor to please you—" And he began as he touched her to name the parts of the body, to explain various kinds of fornication; he used words she had never allowed herself to say, words that were correct and clinical, street words, foreign words. The words fell from his lips softly, as if he were reciting poetry, telling her about love in its highest form, as if he were a religious devotee reciting the beads.

She tried to speak to him, to ask him to stop. She put up her hands. At least she thought she did, but her hands would hardly move. He grasped them in his, kissing them, as if to stop their movement.

"I don't like—" Her voice was strange, thick and deep.

"Hush, hush," he said. "You do like; you know you do—we're going to have a wonderful, wonderful day. I will teach you everything—you'll be able to service kings—you look so young and innocent—you'll know so much—you will be a famed courtesan—I'll see to it—I—oh—"

And for the balance of the day, off and on, he availed himself of her. He taught her. He took her to the bath, soothed her with creams and lotions, always speaking in his slow, insistent way. The compartment seemed filled with him, with his words. The door was locked. She could not escape. She was horrified that she did not want to escape. The walls of the cabin were the walls of her world.

He showed her every position, but did not use them. He described different seductions learned, he said, from a woman in a harem: how she could restore an air of titillation to a jaded lover, how to present her breasts to him as if they were ripe fruit. He told her about the positions of homosexuals, about oral sex; he showed her everything. Finally, toward the end of the day, he took her harshly, pleasing himself. She began to cry and at last he let her rest.

She woke one or two times during what she thought was night and saw him sitting on the lounge, drinking something from a small glass, watching her. When she woke, he would lean slightly forward, but say nothing. She slept for a longer time and when she woke again, he was gone.

6

Pamela learned that she'd been away from the party for almost thirty-six hours. The hours in the cabin were hard to recapture in her mind—she didn't like to think about what had gone on there. She thought she might have to explain to the others, but no one asked her if she'd been ill or why she'd not been with them.

They ignored her absence and wished only to tell their own news.

The yacht was anchored in the sea, some distance from an island. Sporting Isle, everyone told Pamela. Jay Darling had told them this was their destination, but they could enter the harbor only under cover of darkness for some reason. He'd gone ashore on the steam launch and come back again.

Pamela found that other things had changed, too. For one thing, Gladys was gone.

"They just left her on the sand back there," Doris whispered to Pamela.

"Back where? Why?"

Sherry said, "It was back a ways—they left her on the shore. They took her ashore in the launch. She did some sort of unnatural act with a sailor. And they caught her—"

Pamela's newly educated mind supplied the word *fellatio*. She didn't want to think about it. She half turned away, but Helen said, "They took her and that ratty carpetbag and dropped her off with nothing—no money—nothing, and she has to figure out what to do next in the middle of nowhere—"

To change the subject somewhat and ease the moment, Pamela said, "Well, she can always take the train—"

The other girls hooted. "There's no train where they put her. Just alligators and turtles and snakes and hopping things and swamps to be got through—and it was dark and the next day it rained. And besides, the train don't take you without a ticket. No matter what—"

"Gladys'll do all right. She's probably into some sharecropper's bed this minute—" Doris was almost gleeful.

"What did the Senator say?" asked Pamela.

"He was right there with 'em when they did it. I think he was tired of her."

"What about the sailor?"

"Oh, him—" The woman looked grim. "He's down below. They said they needed *him*. But not Gladys. The women always get it—"

"Where are the men now?" Pamela hadn't seen any of the five all morning.

"They're having some sort o' meetin'. Sir William says—"

"Sir William? Did somebody new come?"

"No," said Helen, "that's just Billy. He's Sir William, but we call him Billy—"

Pamela also discovered that Billy had taken Helen as his new "friend" and Sherry was now with Lou. Doris and Harry now shared the same cabin.

"The men had a meeting the day you—were ill—and they came up here hotter than a pistol and we had a great party on the deck and everybody switched," Sherry said.

"Only you and Jay Darling are the same," Helen said. "Isn't that sweet? He's such a wonderful man—"

Pamela didn't agree. She felt as if everything on this yacht were running out of control. She wanted to put her feet on dry land. She'd heard and learned too much. She'd seen things she would not have believed. In New York, there'd been memories of Myron, a sense of order and time, as if she could at some moment choose to leave. Here, things were entirely different. She went to the rail and looked over toward the wooded Sporting Isle with its white sand beaches shining in the sunlight.

She could just see the dull red roof of a large building distantly visible through the trees. She wanted very much to be there now. She hoped things would be more—normal—there.

The men were coming up on deck from their meeting. They moved among the women. From her stand at the foreward deck rail, Pamela watched them. They were different, as if the ship, resplendent in its paint and polish, had sailed through some invisible barrier that could never be recrossed. These people were now as unreal as she, Pamela, was unreal. She was a creation of herself, not the Gertrude Jahn who had stirred pots in her mother's kitchen.

As the ship rode the waves, she gripped the rail to steady herself. Here, in this unreal place, she could not even call up the vision of that kitchen. In truth, she'd not seen a kitchen since she'd left home. The people she now moved among had no use for such things. Food was brought to them, as if they were gods. They had delegated all human endeavors to servants but one—and that one they had altered, made less than human. Pamela felt diminished. She was no longer on an exciting adventure on the arm of a powerful man. Jay

Darling had power, but he would use it, use her, only as such things pleased himself. And if she were lost in that use, he would think no more of it than if an expensive horse he owned fell lame at the races.

Pamela waved toward Jay Darling. She forced herself to smile. Well, there could be delays in the outcome. She would try for that. That might be within her control.

She walked past the Senator, his white hair blowing in the sharp sea wind, his face turned toward the sunshine. She would avoid her reassignment to him—or to someone like him—as long as possible. She'd heard Jay Darling's words. He was planning that at some future time she would leave him—undoubtedly to his advantage. But by pleasing him, she might delay. She would do everything he demanded of her. She would try to prevent her own further descent into the degrading game of perverted mating she'd witnessed on this mad voyage.

She didn't want to become like Gladys, cast off on an unmarked beach on a dark night, alone...

CHAPTER XXI

Arthur Baxter, on his marriage, would be one of the richest men in America. He had his own fortune, of course, which had almost doubled in value. It would have had a greater increase if Mama Delight Baxter had not been so cautious. Further, Arthur, as the fiancé of Harriet the hatchet-faced New York maiden, would also acquire the enormous fortune her father had wisely hinted would be hers at marriage. While Harriet retained her rights in certain ways to the gilt-edged securities and train stock and actual cash, those rights during the time of her marriage would be considered to be "silent" and Arthur, who had difficulty managing his checkbook, would be "in charge" of the great mass of their combined assets. Fortunately, the amounts concerned were so wonderful that even Arthur's determination to live according to his station would not be able to deplete the hoard in the smallest part. The bucket, in other words, would miraculously refill.

The marriage was scheduled for a year away so that Harriet might have the lingerie and linens properly initialed and handmade. The exact figures of the upcoming merger were, however, whispered accurately about in the right circles and new respect was paid to Arthur on his return to Chicago. His name was proposed for membership in the Chicago Club; not only because of the money, of course, since that would be outré, but also because Arthur had attended Princeton and he was from one of the oldest Chicago families.

1

263

It was true he did not live on Prairie Avenue, but his address could not be faulted and if his mother was eccentric, so much the better, since that often was the way of the odd bunch who had founded these moneyed clans.

Mama Delight said, "Oh, Arthur, must you do this? I would much rather you spent your time in other ways. Your father was not a club man. He detested clubs."

Yes, thought Arthur, *they wouldn't do what he told them to do*. But aloud he said, "Now, Mama, you know that most of these men are members of our church and some of the more influential members have been guests at our dining table."

Mama stitched her lips together in that way she had and gave a little sniff to let him know she would not burden him more than this: "Well, I will say what I must and then I will be silent. Those places, in Pa's opinion, lead to riotous behavior on even the best sort of occasions. I once heard of a young man who gave a disgraceful performance on the very day of his father's funeral."

Arthur knew the young man she meant. The man was older now, nearly as old as Arthur's pa would have been if he'd lived, but he was said to have gone to his club on the funeral day, gotten smashed and shouted, "It's all mine now you bastard, you," at a portrait of his revered forebear hanging in one of the great paneled rooms. Unfortunately there were several people in attendance, well-disguised behind club chairs, who had leaned forward and laughed aloud. The story had been too good to keep. It became the first lecture of every pa to his son about intemperate living. And the first story told at stiff gatherings whenever the hero of it, who was one of the most charitable men in the city, entered the room. But Arthur loved paneled walls and Gothic arches and massive fireplaces and historic collections of art. And he loved billiards and a drink or two and a place to play cards for high stakes; a place he might go to talk about Chicago and business—although he had no business. Only money.

He thought he might acquire a downtown office and collect stamps. He was very interested in stamps and already had an extensive collection from the time he and his family had spent abroad. But he thought he might take up the hobby in earnest, put some muscle into it in the form of money, get himself a reputation as a great philatelist. Steven had his school and his ancient Greek poets. He, Arthur, would take up stamps and that would give him time to do other things, such as attend the race meetings at Washington Park where he was a new member of the clubhouse, and he just might look into the new sport of racing motors about a track.

"Not to drive yourself?" Steven looked worried. They were walking down one of the city streets on their way to an interview with Arthur's club sponsor.

"Oh, I might take that up, but it's possible to sponsor others and I think I'd like to be a part of the sport—there is so much out there. And there is the cycle club—"

Steven laughed. "Are you sure you're sedate enough for these downtown types?" He was half teasing and half annoyed. Arthur had been engaged in this interview business for some time now, and both Arthur's sponsors had been perfectly willing to put up Steven's name as well. But Steven said he had no time for membership now, he was attending classes at the University of Chicago. And escorting Miss Marsh to all those dull converges, thought Arthur. His brother was a trial to him. So earnest. So like their mother in many ways. He could tell that Steven thought this club matter was a waste of time.

Arthur and sponsor were expected to visit the office of each member of the committee. No business was discussed. Only the weather and various social events on the calendar were acceptable topics. No mention of membership crossed their lips. And after a discreet interval the interview ended amicably and the small enclave dispersed. No resolution of any interview was forwarded to Arthur, who was expected to continue his visits without a word of encouragement along the way. He would receive the approval or disapproval of the entire committee through the voice of its chairman, an elderly man who held a pew one row back from Arthur's mother at the Presbyterian church. There was no pew in that church occupied by anyone who was not rich, old-family, old-school. But then, neither the Presbyterian Church nor the Chicago Club had ever been accused of being run like a democracy.

The weather was sharp and blustery. The city had just been christened the "Windy City" by Charles A. Dana, editor of the New York *Sun*, for its overwrought self-praise as it sought to be designated the site of the Columbian Exposition, but those living in the city knew how apt that designation was on another front. The wind of Chicago, augmented by canyons of tall city buildings making deep wind tunnels of the streets, cut tall men down to size and blew small women before it as if they were leaves.

Arthur, who was taller than Steven, took the lead today and they went along, their coats flying. He held his head down and his hat windward. Arthur could hardly see where he was going with the wind tearing his eyes. The two brothers inched along, unable to speak, and nearly toppled a man coming out of the Palmer House.

"I say. So sorry—" began Arthur. Then he said, "But aren't you—you're—give me a minute—"

They were standing near the entrance and they moved into it, to momentarily escape the wind. The young man looking at the two of them held out his hand.

"I know you. You're Baxter—Arthur Baxter. I'm Myron Davis. I believe my mother is acquainted with your family. Or I have met you somewhere? Sorry, I can't recall—"

"Some dance or other, I think. In New York. I've been at Princeton—"

"And I at Yale—maybe it was—oh, well. Obviously, we've met. I know we have. Aren't you engaged to—"

"Yes."

They looked at each other a few minutes, each thinking about poor Harriet, but in different ways. Then Arthur introduced Steven.

Arthur was hearty. "You must come to dinner. My mother would surely like to meet you. Are you in town long? Where can we reach you?"

"I've just come back. And I must say your weather here is a shock. Spent the summer in New York and thought I was coming to the Middle West for fall. But it's hardly the end of September and you've winter already. I'll probably be here several months. Our firm has work at the Exposition. Insurance. That sort of thing. Family firm, you know—"

"Oh, this is just a cold snap. Fall will return. Indian summer is one of our features out here in the West," Steven said, doing a little warming dance and laughing as he did it.

"Are you staying here?" Arthur persisted, indicating the Palmer House.

"Yes. I was expecting mail here but my letter has come and now I want to move somewhere else. I'd like to go into the Lexington. It's closer to the fairgrounds, but just at present it's booked solid. Say, you wouldn't care to have a drink with me, would you?"

Arthur was sincerely sorry. "We have an appointment and we're a little late now." He eyed Steven as a signal they must be moving along.

Myron, who needed a diversion, had hoped these men might provide that. He did nothing except go to oversee his part of the work at the fairgrounds, come back to his dinner at the hotel, eat, sleep and go back to the fair. His father's firm was underwriting some of the individual displays and some of the artwork coming in from other locations. But the temporary nature of the buildings, the odd habits of Chicago construction, worried his principals. The responsibility of choosing sites and situations had fallen on Myron. Why this should so exhaust him, he didn't know, but he was grateful that the work made it possible to fall into bed at the Palmer House without remembering who had been his companion there on his last visit.

The three men parted with the usual words of polite regret required of impromptu meetings. As they walked along, Arthur explained to Steven that Myron was a working man, that his family, although wealthy on the mother's side, only *owned* a business on the father's.

"I suppose he's employed there," Arthur said, dismissing the notion of such busywork with a wave of his hand. "He will probably marry some rich girl and settle down one of these days, but right now, I suppose it's all right to get an understanding—it helps when there's money later, if one has been active, I suppose—but he's in the right set to marry a fortune and I know his mother thought Harriet might be interested. I met him there, actually, but I didn't want to say anything. I didn't want to embarrass the chap. He might have been turned down—" Arthur's voice was smug. He was as handsome as a collar ad and he knew it. Money wasn't everything, his voice said. Some women like a good profile for their dowry.

And Steven, walking beside Arthur, thought maybe Myron was too smart to be drawn into the money game played by mothers of marriageable sons and daughters. Myron looked as if he might have a mind of his own.

"We'll have to invite him for an evening. We can have a fine talk. He probably would like to meet Margaret—"

Arthur laughed. "Oh, you think everyone wants to meet Margaret—that the whole world is just panting after Margaret." He punched his brother on the arm. "Just look in the mirror, old sot. There's the world that's after Margaret—"

2

Mama Delight enjoyed the idea of entertaining some wandering boy from New York. She enjoyed anything that underscored what she saw as the cosmopolitan nature of her family. Other Chicagoans had a tendency to be too insular, to travel in schools wherever they went. She liked to think that in their years abroad they had learned how to meet suitable people, and when she heard who Myron's maternal grandfather was—Mama Delight always asked who each person's people were and Arthur could always supply a resume—well, there was no question that Myron should be invited to dinner.

Steven was careful in his approach to the second part of the plan.

"Perhaps we can ask Miss Marsh to balance the table. And one or two other young ladies," he amended hastily when his mother gave him a sharp look.

Mama Delight thought That Girl was entirely too much on the scene and privately thought she would find several young ladies and a mother or two—

"We might ask Miss Marsh and her mother," Mrs. Baxter suggested.

"Oh, her mother has gone away. She's in the East—Boston, I think—"

Gone away. Leaving an unmarried daughter unchaperoned. "*I* never left Fanny alone," Mrs. Baxter said primly. "What can her mother be thinking of?"

Mrs. Baxter looked again at her favorite son. He looked absent-minded. But then she said, "Perhaps we should have a larger company. After all, this young man you speak of is from New York."

"Miss Marsh is from Boston. That should be adequate." He didn't want to have to suffer through ridiculous galas just because some minor acquaintance of Arthur's came through town. He wanted a chance to talk to Margaret alone. If Myron would keep busy with Arthur and the other young ladies with Mama, then he might have a chance to—he had not yet come to grips with what he wanted to have a chance to do.

Futures, he thought, should just be plunged into. What could he use as a steppingstone to the right approach? There was nothing to hold them back. What possible objection could there be to the union of two intelligent, healthy adults with no cloud on the economic horizons of either? Weren't they as suited to each other as Arthur and Harriet, as Fanny and her husband?

The person Steven most feared was not Margaret. Previously he'd not gone as far as considering what he would say to Margaret. What he'd been worried about over these last few weeks was what he was going to say to his mother. In his haze of euphoria over Margaret he just assumed that—Lord, it was all so complicated. Others seemed only to hint their intentions and they were rushed before the altar to forever pledge their troth.

Steven was happy about one thing. Arthur's friend, Myron, would make a perfect foil. He would probably go on and on like all New Yorkers do about New York and maybe in the meantime Mama Delight would become used to the physical presence of Margaret Marsh at her dinner table and to the idea that Steven Baxter, her darling son, at some point was going to have to be allowed a life of his own.

"Now you see," Arthur was saying to their mother. "Isn't it a good thing we have everything in order? The butler is functioning well and the carpets are laid. Otherwise we could not have such a felicitous evening—" Arthur knew his mother liked to hear such talk. It made her feel that she was the chatelaine of a sophisticated establishment. In her youth, the society in which her family moved had had "felicitous evenings" of "company" that would be termed "brilliant" the next day in some local journal of fashion. Usually the term was applied, not to the conversation, which the uninvited journalist could not have heard, but to the economic barometer of the gathering. Mama, who didn't like the trouble of entertaining, nevertheless missed being noticed in print as the hostess of brilliance.

Steven said, "Please don't use the best china. The summer china will do." The "best" china, in his mother's eyes, was a gift to their father from Napoleon Bonaparte and it was, in Steven's mind, entirely too *French*. Too much gilt and design. He preferred to use the blue and white kitchen dishes, but he knew he'd have no luck with those. "Use those nice plain ones with the green and gold rim. After all, we're not out to impress. That's common—" And with that parting shot he left the table before his mother could argue.

Not everything went as planned. In the first place, his mother insisted on inviting Mrs. Featherwaite and *her* daughter and Mrs. Featherwaite's new protégée, Mrs. Chesterton, and her *three* daughters.

"Mrs. Chesterton is acquainted with Miss Marsh," Mama Delight explained. "Mrs. Featherwaite said she was. And she also said you've met the Chesterton girls. So you see, it's serendipitous. Our soiree will be a grand success—"

Oh, dear, thought Steven. And he was right.

3

Mrs. Baxter suggested to Mrs. Featherwaite that since most of the guests were coming from the South Side, it would be most kind of the Featherwaite party if they could bring Miss Marsh. Mrs. Featherwaite contacted Margaret to invite her to ride north in her carriage with the Chestertons. Since Margaret, invitation in hand, hoped soon to hear from Steven with the thought that he would escort her, she didn't know what to say.

Mrs. Featherwaite again mentioned that Mrs. Baxter had suggested it would be such a convenience for the guests to come together and she, Mrs. Featherwaite, was only too happy to extend the invitation. From this, Margaret assumed that Steven already knew and approved of the suggested arrangements. Besides, she could hardly give a hint of offending the Chestertons again.

Margaret rode north in the Featherwaite carriage, submitting to the Chesterton chatter almost as if it were a penance. Her conversation with Mrs. Bright still hurt, most of all because that conversation connected to an inner truth she recognized. She did feel she was more intelligent, better, than most women she met. It was her greatest flaw and she knew it. She still prayed for guidance on it. But she'd not known it was so visible that even shopgirls guessed her feelings.

She was not angry with Mrs. Bright. Rose Bright was the best woman in the world.

"My, you're quite pensive this evening, Miss Marsh," said Mrs. Chesterton. "I imagine you're quite alone in that big house since your mother left for Boston—"

"Oh, I'm not alone," Margaret answered. "My uncle Findley is with me, but he's ill at the moment." She kept her voice light. She didn't want another quarrel with anyone.

"Are you still at work at the fairgrounds?"

"Yes, until after Dedication Day when the grounds will be shut down during the winter months. With no heat, it's too cold out there for the women to work. But then there'll be holiday parties so everyone will be concentrating on family matters from then on—"

"Do you know," Mrs. Chesterton's voice was casual, "what Mrs. Palmer plans to do in the coming months?"

"She's planning a great bazaar at her home for the Children's Annex," Margaret answered and touched the curtain at the carriage window to look out. How much longer would this journey take?

"Might anyone attend the bazaar? I did so hope to meet her before we leave for the East," Mrs. Chesterton said.

Mrs. Featherwaite reached over to pat her friend's knee. "Don't worry, my dear. We'll have an opportunity to bring you two together before long. And your young ladies—we will attend the dances and the dedication ceremonies. Mr. Featherwaite has been quite generous to the various committees of the fair—Mrs. Palmer's endeavors as well. And since he will be in town again with Mr. Chesterton for the dedication ceremony, we'll make ourselves known everywhere. Your daughters will be on everyone's list; just you see—"

Margaret sat in the carriage and felt like a wet sponge. Already, her head ached. If it weren't for the prospect of attending a party in Steven's own home, a party that he quite obviously felt important, she might have thrown open the door of the carriage and bolted, sin of pride or no. Stupid conversation was stupid conversation, no matter how much goodwill she applied to it. These women were scheming to become ladies-in-waiting in a false court and Margaret could hardly hold her tongue. But by thinking of Mrs. Bright, Margaret was able to gain control over herself and arrived at the Baxter's in a mild state of triumph, which Steven read immediately as he handed her out of the carriage under the porte cochere.

Steven had not been told of Margaret's difficulties at the Exchange.

4

The entire company was surprised to learn that Margaret Marsh had seen Myron Davis, the young man from New York, before. She'd seen him at the Woman's Building, climbing among the burgeoning arrivals of parcels from other countries, his face caught up in study, his mind on the thousand things before him. This evening Margaret and Myron delved into vivacious conversation right away, to Steven's dismay. He'd hoped to have some time alone with her.

The party that night also included Mama Delight's favorite cleric, a visitor in Chicago from St. Louis who was in his seventies and reminded Margaret somewhat of Uncle Findley at first, and a mystic with fuzzy credentials who might have been from India. These three were the Reverend Dr. Oates, Mr. Terrill-Peabody and Mr. Singh.

Mrs. Chesterton was appalled. But then she recalled what Mrs. Featherwaite had said—that one was likely to meet most anyone at the Baxters, not to be alarmed at anything Mrs. Baxter might do and just to remember that Mrs. Baxter was "either the third- or the fourth-richest woman in America."

But in Mrs. Chesterton's opinion the dinner table was horribly out-of-balance, excusable only for a house-party or a country weekend— or perhaps a dinner on Sporting Isle where one did what one could. Here, in the city, to have five young women with three young men was unthinkable and Mrs. Chesterton believed it was a slap in her daughters' faces. That Marsh girl needn't have been invited at all. Enough that Miss Featherwaite was here, a tiny little girl of charming blond curls and blue eyes, who twinkled at every young man she met.

Well, the Chesterton misses were a comfort, their mother thought. Not so diminutive as Miss Featherwaite, nor so wealthy and stunning as Miss Marsh—whose looks were rather exotic, Mrs. Chesterton had to acknowledge—but her girls were comforting in their brunette charm. If they had Miss Marsh's wealth, they'd be married by now. Miss Marsh must be—let's see—older. Old for *no engagement*, certainly. And what can her mother be thinking of, leaving town when her daughter would be left alone and unengaged.

Mrs. Chesterton stole a look at Steven. That other boy was engaged to that hatchet-faced girl from New York—purely a matter of money marrying money. But Steven, if Mrs. Chesterton understood correctly, remained unattached. Mr. Singh was saying something about the weather in Chicago, so unlike his homeland. Mrs. Chesterton nodded, but addressed herself to Steven, across the table.

"My daughters were so pleased to learn we'd meet again, Mr. Baxter," Mrs. Chesterton said.

Steven bowed courteously and answered, "And I also was pleased to learn you are in town for some time—" but instead of turning to a Chesterton daughter seated at either hand, Steven looked diagonally across the table to Miss Marsh, whom his mother had seated between Arthur, as host, and the Reverend Dr. Oates.

Mrs. Baxter addressed Mrs. Chesterton. "Are you planning to stay in Chicago long?"

"I've taken my own house for the fair," said Mrs. Chesterton, who knew that must be done. One could not stay for extended visits in the homes of friends or in hotels. "We thought we'd best find something early and whip it into shape, before everything in the better sections is swept away. But during the worst of the winter we plan to run down to a little island club we frequent. I do love the South, you know—"

As their mother mentioned the island, the Chesterton girls were a study in disgust. One of them said, "Little island—very little, Mother." "Much too little," added another, speaking to Arthur. "There's not much for girls to do there," said the third, "it's all planned for the men—"

"Oh, we women have devised our own amusements," Mrs. Chesterton said, and turning graciously to Margaret she said, "That's where your mother and I met for the first time, my dear," as if that set a special seal on the place.

Mama Delight said, "We used to visit Warm Springs, but since my husband's—" She made her face dreadfully sad and left the sentence unfinished.

After a decent interval of silence for the long-dead Mr. Baxter, Mrs. Chesterton said, "My husband, S. K. Chesterton, is a member of a club—an island club actually. There is really nothing to do there except enjoy the pleasant climate. There is golf for the men, of course. It appears to be a wonderful game. I may even take it up myself."

"Do women usually play?" asked Mrs. Featherwaite. "I've never heard of women putting themselves forward in this way."

"They are beginning to. It's quite sedate. You walk around the course, hitting a little ball. It's quite like croquet except the ball is smaller and instead of wickets, there are small cups sunk in the grass. The walking, of course, is the exercise."

Mrs. Featherwaite said, "I prefer lawn tennis. It's such a graceful sport for girls. My daughter, Glenna, plays beautifully."

Glenna nodded at this and smiled and said nothing. She was totally under her mother's domination, but only when her mother was present.

"What was the name of the club? Is it on the ocean, you say?" Mama Delight wanted to know everything about it, although Steven knew she'd forget about it in a minute.

One of the Chesterton girls said, "It's called Sporting Isle because there is wonderful hunting there and nearby. There are white deer and wild turkeys and some boar on a nearby island. Probably you know people who winter there. Several people from Chicago come down in their cars." She meant railroad cars.

The girl turned to Arthur and began to quiz him on Chicago names. "Do you know—"

And Arthur had to play that dreadful rigamorole new acquaintances inflict on one another. "Do you know—" "She's a cousin to—" "He owns the—" "She married the second son of an earl—" "Were you in school there when—?"

Mryon, who'd been talking to Margaret and Steven, now turned to Mrs. Chesterton. "The Sporting Isle? I've heard of the club there. But I don't know where the island is—"

Mrs. Chesterton was flattered. She'd known immediately who Myron Davis' mother was. She preened. "I didn't know there would be such interest in our little hidden island. It's—do you have a map or globe? I'm not even certain it's charted. I couldn't say this to everyone, but you will understand—it's very exclusive there. Not just anyone can be allowed—"

Steven was annoyed about his evening plans. "We'll look after dinner," he said. Now he would never get a chance to be alone in the library with Margaret. She was looking strained. She'd come with the Chestertons and Featherwaites, and had undoubtedly had to listen to a lot of blather on the drive north. He'd never seen her the way she'd been these last weeks, but he was certain she was overworked, what with the Exchange and her work at the fairgrounds, too.

He caught her eye and they smiled at each other while their Italian ices melted in the dishes before them. Just that look refreshed Steven and he ignored the muted clatter of silver spoons. Margaret was near and she'd smiled at him.

5

Coffee was served in the library. Myron, whose memory had been jarred when he heard the words *sporting island*, had not the nerve to ask Mrs. Chesterton if Jay Darling lived on her winter retreat so instead he asked, "I didn't know there was such a population on Sporting Isle. I rather thought it was secluded and there was some sort of castle or estate or club—"

"Oh, but there are family cottages there as well," Margaret interrupted. "My mother often goes there. My father helped set the organization of the club in motion. I don't know if he—" She stopped suddenly at this thought. Might he have gone there—with someone else? She refused to consider it, but she blushed—mysteriously, Steven thought, who watched her continuously—and then Margaret continued:

"My mother goes there to rest, almost every winter. After the northern season. There is a grand hotel and some sort of athletic place—"

"Yes," Mrs. Chesterton said, "a playhouse belonging to a group of investors who go over there to play cards. My husband is one." If only she'd mentioned Jay Darling, Myron would have been instantly alert, but as it was, he was thinking of something else when she proceeded, "I think—" she looked quickly at Mrs. Baxter, who was busy shouting at the slightly deaf Reverend Oates, and plunged ahead "—I think they have high-stakes games there and drink a little too much and make business deals in spite of their wives' wishes that they take a much-needed holiday from business. It's quite—" she shrugged and blushed almost as well as Margaret Marsh "—innocent I expect."

Mrs. Baxter asked, "Is there good society there? Do the people mingle?"

"Oh, yes," Mrs. Chesterton answered. "Most assuredly. People come and go. And at times there are more women than men about the place—especially during the day. The cottages are of modest size and can be rented now and again. Meals can be taken at the hotel. Why I go there without my butler!"

"Like an enchanted island," said Mama Delight Baxter, glaring at the back of the hated butler Arthur had supplied her with.

"A pirate's lair," said Myron Davis, thinking of Darling.

"Yes," said Mrs. Chesterton, "our Sporting Isle."

6

Margaret Marsh and Rose Bright met in the dining room of the Exchange House. They decided that Rose would continue to live there and she would invite Molly, the girl who needed to live apart from her mother, to live with her. During the week Rose and Molly would operate a free day nursery on the first floor and on the weekends, the same discussion group Margaret had founded—now consisting of about ten neighborhood women—would continue to meet. Margaret would absent herself for now—perhaps for the winter.

The plan was Rose's, but it was made on Margaret's insistence. Margaret gave as an excuse the great demands the rest of her life was now making and pleaded a proposed trip to the East for business reasons. Neither explanation was true. But just because she couldn't bear the rejection she felt at the Exchange House and just because her heart didn't warm to the community there as she'd hoped, that didn't mean the place had to be dismantled. Rose Bright was willing to continue with the work and Margaret decided there would be at least some remnant of her own original dream saved if the little cottage could remain open.

As they made their new plans, the day outside turned sour and dark, as if the light were being stolen away.

Margaret was filled with disappointment, mostly at herself. "I'm sorry," she said as they finished their talk. "I wish I could have stayed longer—that things could have been different."

Rose stood up. She patted Margaret's arm. "Don't worry. You'll be our silent partner. We'll get along fine—"

Fine. Nothing is fine, Margaret thought. She wanted to have the pleasant relationship Molly and Rose shared spontaneously. She wanted to meet with girls in the neighborhood and help them find their place in the New World. Yet here she was, unable to find her own.

She wanted to stamp her foot at Rose and vent her jealousy openly. But as a mature, educated young woman, she couldn't do that. She had to sit there and look as if all were in agreement. Why was she always left unfulfilled, not able to choose a direction, and then unwanted when she did make a choice?

She wanted to belong with the rest of the world. Instead, as she reached out her hand, the world seemed to move away. *There is no place in the world where I fit in, she thought. Steven is busy at the university; my mother has left. Everyone can do as he or she wishes, except me.*

She regretted the loss of her father, and more than that she regretted the alteration in her memory of him. He must have been so different than she'd thought. It was as if she'd been cheated in a way that could never be mended.

Margaret sighed.

Rose went toward the kitchen, saying, "Let me make some tea. That will brighten the day—"

Margaret followed her into the hallway, taking her own hat and cape from a clothes hook there. She called out to Rose, "Never mind the tea. I think I'll go on then. They could probably use some help down at the fairgrounds—"

Rose came back into the hall. "We'll miss you, Margaret. Whenever you come back in town and want to visit us—"

Margaret tried to ignore the irrepressible hurt that welled up inside, a hurt that retorted, *You can wait until I'm ready to see you.* But she felt childish and disliked herself for it. This need to get away, to be done with all this, was as much her own fault as anyone's. She mustn't blame Rose. It wasn't Rose's fault that Margaret Marsh could not accept the facts of poverty as they really were.

Forcing herself to speak pleasantly, she said, "I don't know. I'll write if—when I go East. I have to settle some things with my— family. If you need anything, there's money in the account for the Exchange and if not, the attorneys can arrange it—"

Rose came up and held out her arms and Margaret embraced her briefly. "Goodbye, my dear," Rose said. "We'll work this out. I think the community is used to us now. We'll just make friends where we can and let time do its work—" This was a double-edged remark, but there were tears in Rose's eyes as she said it and Margaret knew it was meant in love.

Margaret went out into the dull day feeling more than unsatisfied with everything, and when she reached home she put on her tramping boots and went out to walk on the lake shore, despite the late September cold.

The following Sunday, after church service, Margaret went to the minister's study and asked to see the marriage records dating from the time of her parents' wedding. With a beneficent smile, the prelate brought the book to her and helped her find the place. Margaret stood looking down at the names, startled by their clarity—as if the ink should be tarnished by what she knew, or as if the lines might have disappeared through evil magic. She shut the book with a snap, thanked the minister and left abruptly.

CHAPTER XXII

The cycling club was going to meet at Margaret's house. She didn't want to leave Uncle Findley for another evening out, but Steven had held the group to their original motion—after the fall set in they would consider *worthwhile* matters. Steven had met a man at the university he wanted his friends to hear speak and short of hiring a hall, the second best was to bring him around to Margaret's house and present him.

"He's well respected around school," Steven told Margaret and Uncle Findley. "Why don't you come down, sir, and hear what he has to say? He's doing some writing and he teaches a few classes. Very deep and original. You don't have to agree with him. Just hear him. You should know that there are people who think as he does—"

"Oh, I'll stick to my chambers here," Uncle Findley said. "That old worm of a doctor won't let me go downstairs—"

"We can carry you, Arthur and I—" Steven was really pleased to be in charge of the evening.

"No. I'm going to read a little and take my medicine and my snooze after dinner. That's what I do until bedtime usually. Sleep and then rouse and climb into the bed. Terrible. You'd think I was an old man—"

"Well, then," Steven said. "We'll invite the servants. This is someone that everyone should hear—"

"There aren't too many servants in the evenings if I'm not having

277

a dinner party. For things like this, Mrs. Riley leaves refreshments on the table and we help ourselves. The girls go home early unless I'm going out and need to dress. Knox and the second man went East to help my mother. The grooms are out in the stables to all hours, but I think they play cards out there and won't want to give that up—"

"Well," said Steven, looking around with eagerness for worlds to conquer, "why don't we call in everyone on Prairie Avenue and let them hear Ned—?"

"The library," said Margaret, who'd not seen Steven alone for some time, "won't hold them all—"

So it was the cycling club that met Ned the Worker. He refused to give another surname and Margaret was glad she'd not rung up Prairie Avenue. The club members took the odd name well enough and accepted him at face value. They'd been warned by Steven that the man's talk would be provocative.

Ned stood beside the large oak desk that had been Margaret's father's. He looked somehow at home there. Margaret had not come back into this room alone since she'd found the book of poems with the terrible inscription and had thrown it into the drawer that was now near Ned's rough hand. Inadvertently, she thought about the book for a minute and so lost the beginning of Ned's remarks.

He was speaking about the fair.

"—I have gone down to walk among the emerging constructions of the fair. And what does it say to me—what does it say to the world? You—the young elite of Chicago had best be watchful because the message is given in your name and it is to your shame.

"What I read is that Chicago has taken on the ways of the Old World. There will now be an aristocracy of idle rich in Chicago. We've not had time for that much. We had the Fire and the rebuilding and that came hard on the heels of our beginnings. Then we had the second fire and the depression and the panic of the '70s. There has always been hard work to be done here—

"But now—but now—look you, the children of the rich—the fancy world laid at the city's doorstep says you are to become dilettantes and idlers concerned only with your own play. All over the grounds of the place they are building pedestals for statues to the glorification of swans and imaginary gods—

"Where is the monument to the common man—to the common woman? All the money collected from private and public donations is poured into facades and fountains, while the worker gives what he has—his back, his hands, his skills, his art—his life—

"And you women here. You *daughters* of the rich; overclothed and overfed. You and your fellows give your hundred dollars and your old clothes to the poor to buy your way to heaven—while every day on the streets of Chicago are thousands and thousands living in a kind of hell who need your time and your attention. In your houses you hire women to tend and mend and will not let them go at night after a sixteen-hour day—they must be on call for the princess of industry—even though they've left their own lives and children and their men to serve you in your vanities—

"You say you have an interest in women's rights and women's work. But you pick and chose your definitions of that work. Not all women are artists. Some women scrub your floors. That woman, too, is a worker. Where is the monument to that? And some women, out of desperate need, walk the streets. Where is the notation anywhere that the greatest number of self-employed women are the madams and whores of Fourth Streets all over the world?

"Most of the women of the world, of this country, of this city— are in want. More of them are poor than are middle class. More of them are middle class than have wealth. Only a small minority— you—the new generation of Chicago wealthy—have most of the wealth of the city. How will you spend your lives?"

Ned stopped talking abruptly and went to sit on the chair of the desk, still facing them. He stared at them and the young people stared back. He let the silence grow.

Outside, thunder sounded somewhere near.

There was a stirring among the group. All of them, if the truth be known, had wondered at times at their luck. They might never have discussed such feelings, but Ned's words tapped some hidden doubt within themselves. Margaret felt as if they were a cruel knife. Why had Steven chosen this night to bring the man here? So soon after her failure at the Exchange, when her doubts about the fair and the role of women in it were so acute?

Steven, who'd brought Ned among them, stood and asked, "But isn't this country the one place where the best chance lies—where the ordinary worker, time and time again, has risen to a position of wealth? Our fathers and grandfathers began as poor men—and began again after the Fire. At least they had no money. So it is with many."

"Yes," Ned said. "And you know that poverty exists. You've come from it—and lately. That's what makes your fathers, especially your fathers, deny it so emphatically today. They believe that by hard work—they now discount luck—anyone can rise. They hate what they've been and so they ignore the truth. You, yourselves, have heard your fathers deny the poor, but the poor will not be done away with—"

Steven said, "But I still say that if a man believes in it, really believes in this system, it can work for him. He can prosper."

"And when he does, he should pay a tax on his prosperity so that some of it may be redistributed to the poor." Ned's voice was very quiet.

"Do you mean," a sausage scion asked in horror, "an *income tax?*"

"Yes," Ned said. "The country needs some means to help the poor—"

On this horrifying note, to the sound of distant thunder, the party broke up.

As she left, one of Margaret's friends said, "Look at him." She pointed toward Ned. "He's awfully grim. How could someone look at life like that? And after all the work we've put into the fair. To have it called elitist when it's just something nice for everyone to enjoy. I don't know. That's a kind of thievery, too. To steal away all good times and fun—"

"I think there must be lives like that—without much humor," Margaret said.

"But even the poor people laugh," the girl said. "Don't they?"

2

Steven, who'd stayed behind to talk to Margaret, went back into the library with her to take advantage of the dying firelight and warmth in the cool autumn chill.

"I'm sorry," he said, "I guess I should have warned people a bit about Ned. But he does make you think—"

"He's provocative." She was standing by the fireplace and turned to look at Steven. *She* looked provocative, her hair highlighted by the fire glowing in the same warm colors as her complexion. "I think," she said, "that you know his name—"

"No. That is, yes, I thought he'd have something new to say and no, I don't know his name. Someone told me he's Stein—Nathan Stein—the oldest son of a very rich Jewish banker. But someone else, equally certain, told me he's French and a direct descendant of a leader in their revolution and has another name entirely. Or perhaps a combination of all that or something else entirely. You know how gossips are—" he laughed. "No one really knows unless the subject reveals all. But Ned wants you to take him at face value, without a family name, without a background. He's an enigma, but he makes us examine ourselves at this moment, right now, for what we as individuals do—not for who we are—or who our families are. If we act responsibly, I think he means, we can make a difference in the world."

"Yes," Margaret said thoughtfully. She turned back to the fire. "Just about the time everything is to end, the fire comes right," she said, with her back to him. She poked it with an iron. She was tired, but keyed-up. She had an urge to tell him about the book she'd found in her father's bookshelves, the book that told too much. But she could not betray her father. Instead she asked Steven, "Is there a lot of gossip do you think—in Chicago? About people like—us?" She didn't mean to go on with it, but without control or voluntary thought she turned and faced him head on. She blurted, "Did you ever hear any kind of gossip about my—about my family? My father, for example—"

Steven was sitting on one of the divans. The room was warm, but he was immediately warmer than he'd been before. Yes, he'd heard something—one of those ubiquitous stories of a man and a woman surprised at night by the fire brigade, the man not in his own home, the woman entertaining him illicitly in the middle of the night. There had been—a quarrel over it between W. W. Marsh and his partner, the cuckolded husband, according to the report. Steven had refused to listen and when the teller of the tale persisted, he'd threatened to knock the youth's block off.

He knew he must say something. She was looking directly at him. "I think gossip usually originates in the mind of the teller. At least, the trimmings of it are applied there—" He hoped she would not pursue this. "Maybe a small incident is blown out of proportion. But usually that's all it is."

She came to sit on the couch next to him. He could see she was not going to drop the subject. "Have you ever heard," she whispered, "anything about my father's death? Anything at all, that it might have been—different?"

"Your father had a heart attack. That's what I heard. Didn't anyone tell you how he died?"

"Yes," she said. "I just—well, I didn't know he had something— anything—wrong with his heart. I didn't know—" her voice broke "—he had anything wrong with him at all—"

She could not tell him about that small accusatory volume: She could talk to Steven about anything—but not that.

She stared at the fire with him beside her. Finally she said thoughtfully, "It must be interesting to live like that—as Ned does, without any need to justify a family name—he doesn't have to live up to it—

or live anything down. He just is. And goes on from there—"

Steven was glad she'd dropped the former subject. "Yes," he said eagerly. "I'm glad you understood. I'm glad you like him—"

"Oh, I think he's got his flaws. I think all of them take advantage of women, just as others do—"

"Who?"

"Orators like Ned. They group women's status in among every other flaw they see in the universe and they don't help us redefine ourselves. We've become something of a catchall for their anger at the world. Women speakers do the same. And when it comes to remedies? I just don't know what I should—suppose I were to say that I wanted to be known as Margaret the—the Worker—or Margaret the Good? You'd tell me to join a nunnery—" She laughed.

"Never," he said. "I would never send you to a nunnery—"

He pulled her back against him and began to nuzzle her ear. She smelled of those small flowers that grow only in spring and this he told her. The kind of flower that has the deepest scent and is found in secret—niches of the garden. He loved her—

But she was still in an argumentative mood, his Margaret. "That wonderful smell is probably something someone gave to me. People give me scents and I wear them—"

"No," he said. "You always have the same air. I'd know you anywhere, Margaret Marsh. I think it's meant for—" he hesitated "—for me."

"'The scent is not for thee, but for the bee,'" she teased, quoting something he didn't recognize. "I suppose I'm only being a fulfilled maiden when I choose it. We must have our choices, you know. You heard Ned—" But she changed the subject back again. "You have a scent, too. Like cinnamon or something. I can't exactly tell. Perhaps it's tarragon—"

Steven didn't want to explain that all Baxter goods smelled of Mama Delight's potpourri ordered up from various places and mixed in with the contents of her trunks and their trunks, until they could almost pick their own goods by the delicate spiciness they exuded.

To change the subject, he put his arms around Margaret and began to nibble at her ear again. Such advancement had the shy Steven come to. He had put aside his dislike of the world and stepped up to this—ear-nibbling—to the warmth generated by two rather than just one. This night seemed to call for it, with the fire, the storm gathering outside, the dim light in the room. His own mood. Her restlessness and strange questions.

Perhaps this was what she'd really planned when they came back into the room—not for time alone with him, but for the sweet hour they would have together to kiss and be kissed, while the fire died out on the hearth and she could allow herself to be soft and yielding just before she went upstairs to sleep.

With a bright flash of lightning and the sound of rain, the storm finally struck. Thunder hit the lake, magnified, unsettling. Steven reached behind him to the desk to turn off the electric light. Strange things happened to electricity during storms.

"Let's watch the storm a minute and then I must go," he said.

"You'll have to wait now," she said. "The horse will be nervous. You might have trouble. I wouldn't want to lose you—" Her voice was low.

He stood up and went to the window to see if she was right. The rain did look as if it might be a heavy shower that would end soon. He came back and sat closer still. He took her in his arms again.

"I know," he said and began to kiss her. "I must go soon," he murmured into her neck, her hair.

"Yes," she said.

These two educated adults, who'd studied the advanced sciences and knew every strategic device in the approach of bee to flower, put themselves into this moment of jeopardy, alone in the pleasant, comfortable room on the commodious divan. And they allowed the ancient ritual to reach for its natural conclusion. The storm was at one moment outside—and the next *they* were raging with it. Everything dropped away. One moment they were in control.

And then they were not.

They were caught, united as they'd never been. No danger was too great to hold them back, no sound could have reached them except their own breath and the exclamations of love. His hands, the hands of a shy, unknowing man, were sure and wise. He touched her; she helped him; he came to her; she guided him. They were alone; they were one single unit in time—

Their united power allowed them to reach into the future, gave them a chance at immortality, although they thought, as they moved closer and closer, nothing of tomorrow, nothing of anything. All acts moved beyond thought. All maneuvers, irrational and unreal, became swift and sensuous. If there was pain, there was more pleasure and they clung to each other finally in their warm scented haven, the new world of the library couch—

Their pasts faded. They were at the center of the tapestry; they were the loving couple of a Chinese needlepoint. They were as old as that and as young and alive as they would ever be.

Afterward they slept.

3

Sometime toward 1:00 A.M., Steven woke and touched Margaret, who woke to his touch, kissed him. His voice was rough, "What have I done? What have I done—"

She put her finger to his lips. "No, no. It's all right. That's all right for us. We wanted that—*both* of us did."

But she glanced toward the ceiling and he knew what she meant. There were others in the house. "You'll have to go," she said, reluctantly. "I wish you could stay here tonight, but you'd best not—"

"We'll get married," he said. "This week. I don't care what anyone says. I can't wait any longer. For you. For this. If you'll have me, I mean. I don't want to go even for tonight. I can't bear to leave you. I want you all the time—"

"Go now," she said. "We'll talk tomorrow."

"When?"

"Come to the fairgrounds. I'll be finished early."

"I don't want to be around other people. I want you alone. I—" he groaned. His body betrayed him. He wanted her again and he could not contain himself. He moved away from her, lest she suspect and think him an animal. But it was as if some great engine had begun to run inside him and already it was so insistent and powerful, it occupied all his sensations. She was a part—more than half—of it. They had become parts in a strange, inhuman invention that turned them from self-willed adults in charge of their lives into involuntary beings of future energy and growth. As Steven fought against this takeover, he knew he would feel this way about no other woman. His hands shook as he reached out to her.

"What have I done? What have I done?" he whispered.

"Tomorrow," she said gently, detaching herself from his arms. "It'll be all right. We must wait until tomorrow."

Of course, she was right. He knew she was right. He went home through the storm, letting rain fall on his face, leaving the horse to the groom at the Baxter stable without apology, tiptoing into the house as if he were a burglar come to steal the silver. He'd not been in bed long when there was a light tap on his door and Mama Delight entered.

"Are you asleep, Steven?" she whispered as if he might be.

He did not sit up. "No," he said.

"I've been so worried. This storm. Are the two of you all right? Are you all right, Steven?"

"Yes," he said. "The two of us are fine—"

CHAPTER XXIII

In the late afternoon Margaret Marsh came out of the Woman's Building at the fairgrounds and a carriage was there for her. Steven was waiting the longest wait he could ever remember.

Many people going by turned to look at the young couple. She was stepping up into the buggy, her hand placed trustingly in his. He was smiling at her, clearly in love, his face like the face of Michelangelo's *David* except—except there was a sensuous ripe look about the eyes and mouth, as if he'd only this moment stopped kissing this fortunate damsel now entering his carriage.

They rode along for a way without speaking. Finally, he had to say something. "How *are* you?" he asked significantly. "Are you— are you quite well?" Then he blushed.

She didn't see him blush. Her expression was bland. She didn't turn to look at him. "I'm fine," she said. "Why should you think otherwise?"

He cleared his throat. He could think of no reason why she should not be fine except the reason that was between them. "I'm glad you're all right," he said.

Again there was silence between them, broken only by the sounds of everything else; by the shouts of workmen, by hammering, by the clip-clop of the horse, and the rattle of the buggy.

"Where would you like to go?" he asked.

"Why don't we go to my house?" she asked. "We can talk there—"

"No!" He cleared his throat again. He knew what would happen if he went home with her. Nothing would be solved by *that*.

"Let's ride along then," she said. "Maybe you can find a park and we can stop along the paths."

He drove down to where the streets and roads ended at the lake. There was no park there, just the edge of the land descending into the water as if it had no other place to go. He stopped the horse. The water was choppy and looked cold. They sat there and said nothing and only the horse moved at all, stomping now and then, moving its head under the harness, but holding the place.

Steven turned in the buggy and put his arm around Margaret, then took it back. "That wouldn't look right," he said, blushing again.

She turned toward him at last. "Don't worry so," she said to him. "I don't care what people think. Why should they think anything? We're two adults. We can do as we wish—"

He looked straight at her. "What is it you wish, then? I want to marry you tomorrow. I would have married you today, if you would have let me. I can't wait through the formalities of it. Let's just go and be married. There now—" He laughed as if he had discovered a joke among scraps and shards and the sand along the beach. "Don't I flaunt convention enough for you? We'll be married tomorrow; no matter what the people say—"

"I don't want to marry you, Steven."

"What?"

"I said," her voice very clear even in the face of the lake wind, "I don't want to marry you."

He began to stammer. "I know I'm not near good enough. That's plain enough after last—after what I did. I don't blame you for that. But you must let me make it right. I'm dreadfully—terribly—" he stopped. He sat without speaking. He turned toward her, forgot the reins and people who might be watching and put his arms, both of them, around her. She didn't move into them and settle against him. She sat stiffly, as if waiting until a child had stopped having a temper.

The silence lengthened. He could think of no argument. She loved him. He knew she did. She had courted him all these months as he had courted her. She had kissed him. She had—his mind went back over the night before—he had *not* forced her. Everything had been acceptable to both. They had blended and melded and swept every consideration aside. What could she be saying now? How could she have changed so completely?

Margaret was afraid to look at Steven. He was so appealing. And she knew he had the strength of the truly powerful. He waited, quietly, until all had had their say and then he would express his thoughts, simply, putting everything into perspective, making so much sense that others went his way as a matter of course. She'd been awake all night, since he left, thinking about what she must do, what she must say to him, and she knew he was stronger. He'd learned that strength with his family and used it so instinctively she didn't believe he actually knew his own power.

She must convince him of her viewpoint. She looked only at the lake, not at him. "I don't think I can ever marry."

"What—"

She stole a look at him. His face was beet-red. She'd not seen that in him before. He'd never shown any anger when she was with him. She hurried on to say, "I want to continue as I am, without ties to a new condition. I know what the present condition is and I like it. Why can't we go on as we are? We can go somewhere—to a country town—take a little house and live there, just the two of us. We don't need to get married—"

He stood up in the buggy. The horse turned around as if to question this act. Steven was so agitated he dropped the reins again. "You mean, live together without marriage—! What are you thinking of—"

"Ned, that's who I'm thinking of. He's right, you know. We have just one chance, one small chance of sixty or seventy years to do anything at all, to set things right around us. We shouldn't let ourselves fall into the old ways. Our—families have put too much emphasis on the wrong things. Laws. Marriage. *Names*. Ownership of one person by another—"

"Ownership? What has ownership got to do with marriage?"

"Ownership. He owns her. He puts his name on her, owns her goods, her children. Why, if they get a divorce and he hates children, they're still his automatically because a man's name must be taken into account. He mustn't lose his *namesakes*—"

What she said was true. Divorced women did lose their children unless the man was clearly insane. Even then, the children might be assigned to paternal grandparents.

"But you *love* me. I know you do. We're not talking about that kind of marriage. We're talking about *ours*." He sat down in the buggy again and the horse stopped moving nervously. Steven played his trump card, "And last night—"

She turned on him. Sweetly; acidly. "What has love got to do with anything? With marriage? Look around you. Whom do you see who has married for love? Men marry for wealth or social position. Or they marry to have children by the 'right sort' of woman while they run off and dally on Fourth Street or in some hideaway with a woman they—" Her voice choked. This was getting too near the crux of it. She made herself calmer by sheer will. "I don't say you're one of these. I say, let's just start out with simplicity and love and not with one of these marriages that have all the habits of a badly run corporation—I just say I've never seen it otherwise. And perhaps if you don't want to love me without marriage, I will go away and recover from love and then love someone else later—"

He looked straight at her, unbelieving. His eyes were wide, troubled. "Margaret! How can you say that? How can a woman talk like that?"

"Do you mean I sound like a man?" Her voice was harsh.

"No. I mean you sound—you seem to be—I know you didn't mean it and you're not like that, but I thought you were willing to—let me—I mean we had something *together*, not as a man doing—something—to a—woman. But together. We were—equals."

"Yes," she said, touching his hand. "We are equals. And I meant to have that—what happened—if I had nothing else. I knew some time ago that I would never marry. But I decided—I wanted to know—how love could be. The best of it without—the other."

"How can you talk like this? You know the consequences of such irresponsibility. I couldn't say this to anyone else as I am saying it to you. You might bring children into the world without—"

"Without the proper label? Children of a love union without the so-called protection of society?" She stopped talking and fumbled in her lap for some time, as if her glove did not fit right. "I think you know me better than that," she said. "I'd never harm a child. There are ways—"

"I don't want to talk to you about this."

She fluttered her hand to one side. "Oh, Steven," she said, anguished. She was crying now. "Don't make it so difficult. We can be lovers. We would not be the first lovers in the world—"

They sat together in the carriage. Nothing changed. He lifted the reins and startled the horse into movement, but then turned to her as if in afterthought.

"Is it something—something so terrible you don't want to tell me? Some *medical* reason? Are you ill? Are you—" he choked but persevered "—are you pregnant by some other man? None of it matters—"

She laughed again. "No, Steven, no. I am not pregnant. I love you. I've just offered you the dream of every sport up and down the town. I'm willing to live with you or sleep with you—as long as we love each other—but once it's over—well, I do not want to be caught in a loveless marriage with you or anyone else—"

This time her laugh was ironic in tone, but at the same time she put her finger to the corner of her eye and he could see she had caught a tear on it, darkening the tip of the glove.

He was so angry he was plum-colored. He knew he was not dreaming this conversation. He knew it was the most real conversation he'd ever have in his life, yet it seemed grotesquely unreal.

He turned the horse and they rode in silence back through the streets to her door. She had removed her gloves in an irritated way, but he saw that she put them on again, as if her hands were too cold without them, too warm with them on. When the carriage stopped in front of her door, she removed them once more. With this opportunity, he reached for her hand.

"Margaret, I don't care what you say. Please, Margaret, do me the honor of—"

With her other hand she reached up to touch his face, to still his words on his lips with her fingers. At this touch they could both feel the current between them. She leaned forward and kissed him regardless of all Prairie Avenue—none of whom was watching—and she said, "No. Don't say it—"

She started to leave the carriage.

He reached out and caught her arm.

"Can't you feel that? You know how it is with me—I think you feel the same. How can we live without each other? What will we do alone—?" His voice was thick and low. Desperate.

She settled back into her seat. Her face was as red as his, her lashes were darker than usual. Her hands were in two knots on her lap. Then she gestured toward the street, toward the grand avenue of mansions.

"You see them there? None of them are happy. I know it. I know for certain about two of them. Can it be different for the others? Nothing lasts fifty years. Oh—some ruin falling into disrepair." She shook her head. "I can't have that. I can't live like that. The weddings are—"

Anything to stop her from saying these painful things. "What weddings do you mean—"

"All weddings. These grand businesses on the avenue. These weddings are so appealing to young women and men. The attention. Everyone there. The parties and the gowns and the furnishing of a life—the household, the trousseau. Everyone comes," she said again, as if this were very important. "Then afterward. What's left? A whole lifetime of nothing else. Do they delight in each other? Or are they destined to have separate lives that touch only in their children, in their public appearances—in the charade they play before others—and then there is nothing left."

She was describing her parents, but he didn't know that. What he saw in his mind's eye was the wedding picture of his own mother and father. What he remembered of their life had been dreadful. His mother, so much younger, had spent at least fifteen years tending her "dear invalid," as she called him, and now knew no other way. She yearned to tend something, someone. And it was too late. There would be no other chance for her. There was some truth to Margaret's argument, but Steven would not allow it.

"No," he shouted, frightening the horse, which began to pull at the reins he held tightly in one hand. "No. I won't let you assign me to some style you think I would take on. I'm not like that."

"You can't make promises for such a long time. No one can. And when the love goes, there is nothing left but that church vow. And an inscription in a ledger that binds people for life. That can't be broken without terrible hurt. Much worse than if it had never been made at all—"

"But Margaret. We're two intelligent people. We can avoid it." He didn't deny what she had described, she noticed. He just said they would avoid it.

"Do you want me to pledge to you—in writing—that I would obtain a divorce if we ever agreed that we felt differently? Is that what you want?"

"No, I—" It wasn't that she didn't know what she wanted, she just couldn't tell him all of it.

What she really wanted was to correct some terrible wrong in her parents' generation with a new rule, a new regulation that would exist in her own. She wanted to be able to reach back, to come to the place on the shelf where the little book was hidden and to pass it by, never knowing the lie her parents had lived. She wanted some unexpressed escape clause in her own life for an escape she never intended to make. She wanted, without knowing it, to give up her life to correcting the maladjustment between two people whom she loved and had once respected.

He saw that she was quiet and listening and he began to lecture, a habit he had. "A long time ago, in the middle ages, people were—even more cruel to each other—to their children. And that's why the church came into it. But you know that. There had been no order. The church brought order into it—"

"And now we have too much. When passion goes, there is only the appearance of order, the sham of it—"

"But for the children—"

"After the children are grown."

"Women might be abandoned then, and not cared for— A man can—" He blushed and would not continue. He loved her. He could not tell her what a man was capable of doing for the major part of his life. "I can only speak for myself," he finished lamely. "The pledge I make to you is true as it can ever be. Even if you wanted, at some time, a divorce and I gave it, I would still love you forever—"

Her head was down. He could not see her eyes as she said, "And I will love you, Steven Baxter, as long as ever I can." She stood. "But I can't marry you at all—"

He waited and watched as she went into the house alone.

CHAPTER XXIV

1

Mama Delight Baxter put marmalade on her toast every morning. The bitter with the sweet—and more than that—the zest was in it.

"Steven," she said to her favorite son, "I'm glad you have been staying home these last few evenings."

Steven had been staring at his cornmeal mush, a perennial on the breakfast table because his late father had insisted and Mama, these many years later, knew no other way.

"What?" he asked. "I'm afraid I didn't hear what you said."

"I said I think Miss Marsh is a lovely girl, but I can't agree with that mother of hers—that's what I said."

"What do you mean? Have you had some sort of disagreement with Mrs. Marsh? How could you have? She's been away for several months."

"That's what I mean. Going away and leaving a young girl like that all alone. And then there's the matter of her education."

"What?"

"The subject matter, dear. It's too unseemly. Not unless she plans to be a doctor. For women, of course. Women can benefit by having a female physician, I think. Not nursing. One never knows about nursing. One might be misunderstood if one were not truly professional. But as a physician a woman could limit her practice to women in confinement, as it were. That would be lovely. Appropriate. But just to take on information, to no purpose except general knowledge,

I don't think is right and I fault her mother for her allowance of it—"

"Margaret's very intelligent, Mama," Steven said, giving defense automatically, since at this moment he, too, was horrified at the ideas she'd come home from college with—the notion of *free love*. It could ruin her life. He *might* have ruined hers. He could not accept what he'd done, and what she had done subsequently. There was intense pain within him, as if he'd been sliced in two parts and the parts were now irreconcilable.

He hadn't talked to Margaret or seen her for a week. He'd called and she was out—undoubtedly working very hard on last-minute business at the fair. The dedication was to be held—when—this week—today? He couldn't remember.

And he didn't know what he was going to say when he did finally reach her. What could he say? Yet every night, when he went to bed, he ached for the warmth of her body against him; to sit here at his mother's breakfast table and argue about Margaret's education was more unreal than his night fantasies. He was living, and had been for almost a week, in his mind.

"And then there's the rest of it—" Mama said. Now that she'd embarked she might as well take the whole journey.

"What rest of it?"

"She's a suffragist. I don't think you know about that. Those women have the must unusual thoughts, Steven, about the feminine gender. And if we do what they say, there will be—well, I should think there will be chaos in the streets—"

Steven laughed.

"I don't see what is funny about this. I am having a serious tête-à-tête and you start to laugh. But then—" she rose to stand as tall as she could "—I'm only a woman, trying to make some sense in the man's world. And you mock me—" Her lower chin quavered and her voice broke.

"Oh, Mama, I'm not mocking you. It's just that I would like you to like Miss Marsh. I think she's a delightful person."

Mama Delight sat down abruptly. "You're not—engaged?" Now her voice was horror-struck.

"No," said Steven crossly, reaching for his coffee cup across the table top. "No, I am not engaged to Miss Marsh."

Mama was coy. "Are you planning to be?"

"No." Steven let the *no* rest for a moment, his face reddening. Then he said, "I am not planning to be, because she will not, at this point, have me."

"Steven!"

"It's true. She turned me down. She says she is never going to marry. She wishes to remain independent for the rest of her life."

Mama was silent for a moment, furious that any woman would refuse her dear—

"Well, it's just as well. She's not near good enough for you. There will be other—romances. You'll see. She just did not love you—enough."

"Oh, but she said she did—"

"Do you mean she loves you and will not marry you, because she wishes to be independent?"

"Yes."

"So you see—I was *right. Those women.* They have such strange notions. She would not be right for you, dear, in any case. You can see that, can't you—?"

Mama was glad Steven had confided in her. She felt very close to him, very intimate. Otherwise she might not have felt comfortable in saying to him, *"Those women* can be very abandoned. If we allow them to have their way, everything will change for us. Women will no longer be protected from the crassness of life. Why I've heard—" here she leaned forward in order that no servant overhear "—I've heard they advocate *free love.* If that should happen, if everything were swept away, there would be no order to life. No one would be able to say which child belonged where. And there *would* be children, mark my words. Society would fall. We would have nothing but a poor woman's word against a man's—" she stopped. She was his mother. She could not really spell things out for him. But he could see, couldn't he? After all, he was an intelligent boy of twenty-four.

Yes, he could see. Steven said, "But isn't that the way it's always been, Mother? Since the beginning of time? The woman's word? What else is there—?"

"Really, Steven. I'm sorry I began this discussion. There *is* the law and there *is* the church—"

"But those were not always there, Mother. And conception is such an earlier event than birth. Nobody really knows what happens except the child's mother and even she might not know—"

"Steven! Even though I am a married woman, some things are inappropriate in mixed company, which is exactly my point—"

"Sex implies mixed company."

"Well, I know about these things and you don't. I have a recorded marriage. A pledge was made before God. I certainly know who your father was. Because I did not engage in, heaven forbid, free love and voting!"

"I don't think free love will be practiced in the voting booth, Mother."

His mother was grim. "Possibly not. But it is all part of the whole. One goes with the other. In the name of your future children, you must take care. And if a woman begins to act as if she is as important and independent as a man, soon we'll be living like savages—like they do in Paris—"

"You are changing the subject, Mother. I still say that even your piece of paper and your pledge leave the rest of the world with only the woman's word that she is chaste and that the man she says is the father is actually the one—"

Mama Delight Baxter was silent. She'd never been so angry. Or so frightened. She stared at him.

"I think," said Steven, "that what you and the rest of the so-called civilized world believe is that without legalities, solemn pledges, altars, no man would acknowledge his child, no woman would truly name her lover in joy, no child would be raised with the love and concern of both parents—that men would vanish into the forest again. You are saying, over and over with your weddings and your maidens and your vows, that without law and church, human beings would never cherish each other—that they would not act human toward each other—"

"I did not say that. My heavens. You get too excited, dear. Don't go on so—" She was pulling back now, retreating into trivialities in the way she had.

But he persisted. "This is important, Mother. Think about it. You're saying there isn't any such thing as love—not without law—"

Having convinced himself thoroughly, Steven Baxter put down his napkin and rose, bowed curtly to his mother and left her staring after him, speechless in the dining room.

His only regret was that Margaret had not been there to hear him.

CHAPTER XXV

A glorious autumn day in Chicago, relatively windless and pleasantly warm.

Steven Baxter left his house on the North Side of the city moving briskly. He went down the walk to the iron gate and let himself out onto the street. He would walk to Margaret's house. It was not enough that he had finally realized what she meant. He must take some action immediately; slay dragons, travel on hands and knees through the swamp, ford the river, climb mountains, to reach his lady love.

There were, of course, no swamps and mountains before him; the mountains had never existed and Chicago had been raised from the swamp by George Pullman. As for the river, Steven crossed it in the usual way, on the Rush Street Bridge.

If he noticed that there were more people than ever before on the streets around him, if he noticed the absence of carriages on the avenue itself, he gave no thought to it. It was early in the morning, not yet nine o'clock. Perhaps all these good, wonderful people were going to work. Were there flags flying from the light-standards, was there bunting hung from windows of buildings when he reached the avenue? Was the pervasiveness of policemen on horseback, the milling of the throng, a clue to him that he had chosen an unusual day for his insight? Or did he just assume that the rest of the world was as happy as he that the question of Margaret had been addressed at breakfast and solved in conversation with his mother? No. He was altogether taken up with the fact that Steven Baxter loved Margaret Marsh more than he respected convention.

Somehow, he did not quite recognize that all the people he moved among that morning appeared to be going the same direction as he. He was more aware that all the women seemed inferior to Margaret. None had her green eyes, her cluster of auburn curls. None were just the right height or had such charming, erect bearing. On a sunny day like this, with his thoughts in the clouds, he got the intense feeling that he was a lucky man, the luckiest alive, because he had noticed and won the person of Margaret Marsh. To this tune in his head, he marched straight down the avenue in a singular parade.

As Steven marched along, here and there having to inch and edge himself through what appeared to be growing crowds of idlers in the sun, he gave no thought to the engraved invitations nestled in his breast pocket which entitled Steven and Arthur Baxter and Mrs. U. V. Baxter to front-row seats in the Manufacturers and Liberal Arts Hall at the hour of 11:00 A.M., October 21, 1892, for the purpose of dedicating the buildings of the World's Columbian Exposition.

New York, slighted in the search for a site for the Exposition, had pressed the inarguable advantage of geography when it came to the opening of the international four-hundred-year anniversary. If visitors from foreign lands were to reach America, much as Columbus had done so long ago, then they would first have to touch foot to the eastern shore and on what better day than October 12, 1892? And in what better place than New York? So the honor of the opening gun had gone to New York City in the final count and Chicago, panting to begin, but not quite ready, had settled for the specious argument that on the "new" Gregorian calendar, October 21 would do very well as a stand-in for the twelfth. Besides, it would take that number of days for the dignitaries to find their way West after the revelry in New York ended.

None of this filtered through to the bemused lover as he strolled amidst the tide of humanity.

Margaret. That was the one other person in the world. He should have known, that day beside the cold lake, that he would be willing to love her for the rest of her life in whatever form of living she chose for them.

Oh, bother these crowds. There seemed to be some sort of human wall settled in around Adams, across from the new conference hall. He cut back to Wabash. He came to Twelfth Street and went east again to Michigan and then zigzagged back toward the lake and Prairie Avenue.

As he turned into the familiar street, he met a wagonload of young men and women who were involved with the fair. He'd had contact with them off and on throughout the summer. The wagon had stopped at Margaret's house, but one of the girls from it was returning from the northside porch alone.

"Where's Margaret?" Steven asked, without formal preliminaries. She ignored his question and asked, "Are you coming with us?"

"Where are you going? Where's Margaret?" he repeated.

"Margaret left early this morning. Aren't you coming with us to the dedication?"

"She's gone? How did she—?"

"You might as well come with us. There aren't many carriages and traps let through. We fixed this up with the committee." And the girl ran down the steps to the wagon.

Steven had no choice but to follow and find a seat on the over-crowded wagon where everyone talked at once and he could not determine exactly where Margaret had gone early in the morning.

As they rode along, singing and waving at everyone who looked their way, he realized Margaret had probably gone ahead to do something in the Woman's Building. The dedication ceremonies were to be held in the largest building—the Manufacturers Hall—but perhaps Margaret had some official part to play.

He'd not heard from Margaret all week. Maybe she'd been busy with all the last-minute details of closing things up for the winter.

He became acutely conscious of the invitations rustling in his pocket and had an irrational thought that he could see Margaret and settle their future and get back to his mother and brother on the North Side in a borrowed carriage before the big event actually began. He guessed it was then about nine-thirty. He would have an hour and a half to accomplish his missions.

But he had reckoned without the officiousness of young guards, some of them wearing authority and badges for the first time in their lives.

The wagon was stopped everywhere. The riders were forced to explain at each place, complicated by the roar of laughter and the singing by part of the group in spite of delay.

Steven, finally impatient, jumped off and began to run.

"Here! Here you! You can't do that."

Steven took his invitations out of his pocket and waved them in the air like the baton of a long-distance runner; at each checkpoint he paused barely long enough to show his ticket and went on. Finally, winded, he came to the north gate and entered the grounds through there, displayed the ticket one more time and went directly to the Woman's Building.

But he found it locked. There was a guard at one entrance.

"I need to talk to someone inside," Steven panted.

"Ain't nobody there," the guard said. "Place is deserted. Everybody's over there—"

He waved southward toward the Court of Honor where Steven could see flags flying over Manufacturers Hall, the building declared to be the largest anywhere under one roof. Crowds were headed toward it. No one had counted on such fine October sunshine in Chicago for the dedication.

Steven plunged through the crowd and approached the shore of the lagoon that established the Court of Honor. When he finally reached the hall, where the greatest congregation stood, he made his way to the entrance.

Margaret! She must be inside here. Somewhere.

But inside, already gathered for the big event to take place several hours hence, was the greatest part of the nearly one hundred thousand who would attend. Each of these supposedly had made a contribution of some kind to the future success of the fair. Perhaps amid this throng, Steven would yet be able to find his Margaret.

He started down an aisle, but was stopped by an usher who demanded his invitation. Steven and his family had reserved seats. Would he come this way?

"No, I—let me look around here, just a minute."

"Nossir. I can't. You can't stand in the aisle or loiter. Vice-President Morton is coming today. We have strict orders. Everyone is to be checked and seated. No one can stand around in the aisles. You'll have to go directly to your seat or leave the hall—"

Steven, exhausted, looked around. At one side there was an enormous choir, dressed in white. A thousand singers. Or was it five thousand? And a large band at the other side. Before him was a platform that looked as if it would hold a regiment.

"Is there a telephone nearby?"

"I don't think so, sir. Not in this building anyway. And if you leave now, you might not make it back in time—"

Steven was up the aisle, headed for outdoors. He would call his mother and Arthur. And then he would call Margaret's house and talk to the maid.

2

Myron Davis looked down on Michigan Avenue from his suite in the Auditorium Hotel. Chicago. Two days or more wasted on these foolish heroics. Pompous sorts strutting around like pigeons. He wanted to get finished and leave—back to New York in case Trudy might reappear there. He could not stand Chicago anymore. It reminded him of her constantly.

He opened a window to look out on the avenue at the federal troops below—he thought maybe the vice-president was in this hotel. He couldn't remember what he'd read about plans for the day. Everything left his mind these last few weeks. He cared about nothing. What did it matter where some politician was staying or that the President had not come because his wife was dying?

He sighed into the wonderful air, looked at the lake, thought its aspect ugly, the trains running along its shoreline dirty and unwise. Everything about this place was a negative and his reports reflected that. No, he would not approve certain private works of art, insured by his company, for early travel to be installed in the Fine Arts Building. No, he did not like the idea that buildings of the fair would be unheated in the winter. No, he did not plan to approve the early shipment of any manufacturing displays insured by his father's firm. Not until the buildings had been certified as sound by himself or another of their company officers or inspectors. The buildings, temporary, but meant to last at least two seasons, had relatively standard structure covered with a mixture of limestone and gypsum. The windows were in place on most of them, but there was no guarantee that these windows would not leak Chicago's winter down on whatever was underneath. No, he would not be swayed by amiable pleas. He was no longer an amiable sort. Why should he risk his company's existence on this fair when he'd not risked it for something more important to himself—for Trudy's life with him?

He longed for Trudy. He'd moved from the Palmer House because of her. He couldn't stand coming down the grand staircase and seeing the lobby that she'd once so admired. The only place he'd been able to get had been this wedding suite at the Auditorium. More modest suites were taken. And so in these passionate chambers he was reminded of her once again.

He slammed the window. A perfectly beastly day. He decided to go downstairs to find something to eat. He knew he would not get room service today. Probably nothing was going to go right for the entire week.

In the lobby of the Auditorium, most of the chairs were empty. Everyone was out on the street. As Myron came out the door to look around, there was a division in the crowd ahead of him and he had a clear view of some men entering a six-man carriage. Soldiers were waiting. The men settled in, the horses began to move; the man on the far right turned his head and removed his hat. Was it—?

Quickly Myron was at the curb.

But the carriage pulled away abruptly. Myron broke through the line of policemen at the curb and began to run after it. Several pairs of arms came out to catch him and hold him back.

"Let me go," he shouted. "I am Mr. Davis. I am a guest here. Let me go."

They put him back on the curb and he ran inside to the desk. A cool-looking clerk was standing, staring out at the lobby. Myron leaned across the counter.

"Tell me," he said. "Is Mr. Jay Darling registered here?"

The man looked at Myron as if he were an insect. "We do not give out the names of our patrons. I have no information concerning the party to whom you refer—"

"I am a guest here," Myron said, as calmly as he could. "I just missed the carriage to take me to the fair. I thought I saw Mr. Darling in it—"

"I wouldn't know, I'm sure," said the clerk, dropping his eyelids in an affected way.

"I am actually looking for a Mrs. Jones. Is there a Mrs. Jones with Mr. Darling's party?"

"Sir, I've told you. I cannot discuss the names of our guests. It's a house rule. If you know the name of the guest and the room number I can ring and announce you—"

"Look. Don't break your damn rule," growled Myron. "Just tell me, yes or no, is there a Mrs. Jones registered here—?"

The man moved away and proceeded to open a drawer and busy himself with something. Myron followed him on his side of the counter and reached across to clutch at the man's tie. He gave it a twist.

"Now tell me. Was that Jay Darling?" The man's face was turning deep purple and he flailed his arms. With pantomime he indicated that he couldn't talk with his tie cutting off his windpipe, so Myron released him.

"HELP! Officer. Security. Arrest this man—" The voice was reedy, but loud enough to make a proper commotion. The second clerk ran toward them.

Myron turned and was across the lobby in quick strides, bolting out the entrance again. He looked back, but no one appeared to follow. He moved to the edge of the walk and caught the eye of the doorman. He removed his wallet from his breast pocket, extracted a bill and his honorary "official" pass, which he handed to the uniformed factotum.

"Here," he said. "I am Mr. Davis. I'm expected at the fairgrounds. I've just missed my carriage. What should I do—?"

As if by magic, hands helped him, moved him toward the street. "*Mr*. Davis has missed his carriage." "*Mr*. Davis is overdue at the fair." "They can't begin without *Mr*. Davis." "Help *Mr*. Davis—"

He knew they were confusing him with George Davis, the director general of the Exposition. Myron let the error stand.

"Hurry," said the soldier standing at the curb. And the carriage they stopped—containing two worthy gentlemen who were only too glad to give a lift to an important citizen—took off with a rush of hooves, headed rapidly toward Jackson Park.

Why was Darling in Chicago? Was Trudy with him? Or had she left Darling? Might she be here, just a few doors away in another suite at the hotel? He must find Darling and follow him. Myron was determined. He would find her if she was in this city. He would do anything—

At each carriage they passed, Myron leaned forward and tried as casually as possible to screen the occupants. Maybe Darling was here to help open the Exposition. But one or two of the wagons ahead turned off into side streets and he realized that even today there were destinations other than the fairgrounds. How was he going to guess which way to go? He moved and twisted and jumped about so constantly along the route that the men with him began to stare and pull back, at the same time nodding at him in the most congenial way, as if soothing the writhings of an idiot.

I must look it, he thought. *I must appear mad. I am mad. To be separated from her has driven me mad. I must calm down. I must figure this out. What would be the most likely thing?*

He realized he had no choice but to continue to the fairgrounds, enter the arena and look about at the important dignitaries assembled. That would eliminate one possibility and he couldn't be in two places at once. As he decided this, he had no idea there would be one hundred thousand in attendance in the great hall. He had not the slightest glimmer of the sea of top hats and dark coats he would have to search among.

Jay Darling, Myron thought. *I could pick him out of any crowd. Haven't I seen his picture often enough? And in my nightmares? And he's just the one to take a prominent spot. I'll smell him out. Sure enough—*

3

"*I'm at the* fairgrounds," shouted Steven into the telephone. "I took your invitations by mistake. I have to leave here now. Why don't you come along and I'll leave the invitations with—with—at the north gate in your name. I'll give the guard something—I'll tip him to see that you get through and get seated."

"Listen," said Arthur, annoyed that he must escort Mama Delight by himself. She would be cross. And now the added hassle of the missing invitations. "I don't think we can get through at all. There are too many roadblocks—"

"Oh, you can do it if anyone can. Just tell them you're U.V. Baxter's son. Nobody knows he's dead. They forget things like that. But they'll remember the name. Take the carriage right down the avenue. Nobody will bother you if you act like you belong there. Not with Mama aboard. And you can lord your way in. You do it often enough. You know you can—"

Arthur had to admit he probably could.

"Where will we meet you?"

"I'm not going to stay for the program. I'm looking for Margaret. I can't find her anywhere. I think I'll just go back to her house and wait there until she comes. She has to come back sometime and that's the safest way to catch her—"

"Isn't she there—?"

"Somewhere. But you've never seen such a crowd. Hurry, or you'll miss the great ode by Miss Monroe—"

"Maybe the luck will be with us, after all," said Arthur with malice. He was going to this event only because Mother would want to speak to the vice-president afterwards. She often had advice for such officials. And she would want to send a personal note to President Harrison about his wife. That was the way Mama was—

4

"*Sir*—"

"I beg your pardon?"

"I'm sorry—I thought you were someone else. I'm looking for someone. You haven't seen a man, slight, about my height or a little taller; light hair—top hat and a dark coat—"

The absurdity of this question was lost in some shout or other from the far end of the hall and Myron turned to look and when he turned back, the man he'd been questioning was gone. The hall was full of thousands of men that fitted Myron's description of Jay Darling. He was overwhelmed. Flashing his badge and his ticket he started down the aisle.

The usher reached out and clutched at his arm. "You can't go down there now. The vice-president is coming. You'll have to take a seat—take any empty seat. No walking around once the program starts—"

Myron pulled loose and began to run.

The usher, having been warned about assassins and foreigners and madmen, came close behind him and because he was slightly younger than Myron, he soon had his quarry wrapped in an armlock.

But Myron, a little heavier, turned in the right way, breaking the hold. He sprinted down the aisle.

"Stop him," shouted the usher, but the band had begun and no one heard. Myron cut across the front just below the stage. His official badge was priceless. He spotted a small row of three empty seats and dived for one, turning to smile at an usher who came up behind him. Nothing happened. In the din, no single voice could be heard. Everyone was cheering. A woman in a dreadful fringed dress had just taken center stage and appeared to be going to sing. He wished desperately for opera glasses. He wanted to look at the men behind the diva.

If Darling was anywhere, that was where he'd be—*prominently* in a back row, behind the scene, yet one who had some hand in it.

Myron turned to the woman next to him. "Pardon me, ma'am," he said as politely as his impatience allowed. "Could I borrow your opera glasses for just one moment?"

"Certainly." The lady smiled.

But Myron didn't smile back. All he could think of was that man on the stage in the fourth row of seats, dead center amid the dignitaries. *Let him turn this way. Let me see him. There.*

I think it might be—no—yes—I think it is *Jay Darling!*

5

"*I know she's* not at home, but I'll wait," Steven said to the maid.

"But, sir." The maid was near tears in her desire not to offend Mr. Steven Baxter, that kind friend of Miss Margaret's they'd all thought she was sweet on. But the earnest girl had to convey to the lost suitor this fact: "Miss Margaret has gone out of town. She didn't say when she'd be back—"

The door was still open. The young servant was still smiling. But Steven couldn't understand the words.

"Out of town? May I ask where? I mean—did she leave an address—?" He took a breath. "Did she say anything to you about me—I'm Steven Baxter?"

"I know who you are, sir. But only Mr. Findley is here and he's asleep. May I suggest you call another day? Miss Margaret went to join her mother. For Christmas later—"

"On the island?"

"Yessir. On the island." The maid was relieved. "I think it's for the winter, Mr. Baxter—do you want me to ask Mrs. Riley?"

Steven was too wounded to face Mrs. Riley. "No. No, that's all right," he said kindly, speaking softly so as not to jar any of this painful message further into his consciousness.

He turned and went carefully down the stairs.

6

Myron felt as if he were made of coiled springs. An usher was standing at the end of their row, which was, after all, the first row and a natural place for an usher to stand. So far, on this program, one man had stood and tendered the half-constructed buildings of the Columbian Exposition to the commission and a man from the commission stood and tendered the buildings to the federal government and the federal government had accepted the buildings and someone had sung something and Myron kept watching the usher. The vice-president said something. There was much cheering.

How can I be first from this section and get into line following those worthies on the stage? thought Myron. *If he is here—could she be here?*

It was like a little song that sang in him. Maybe she was only a few miles from here, maybe they were in the same hotel and he had been unaware. How *could* he have been so unaware, so blind, as not to sense her near him?

A great cheer went up.

Mrs. Palmer, that Chicago woman, had just said, "Even more important than the discovery of Columbus, which we are gathered here to celebrate, is the fact that the general government has just discovered women—"

Following the program, Myron's attempt to exit the great hall at the center of the group of important personages from the stage had been foiled by the formal retreat of the vice-president. All adjournment of the audience at the front rows was held back until a small procession of dignitaries left the area. Somewhere during the line of march, Jay Darling just disappeared.

Panic rose in Myron. The man was a magician. One minute Darling was there and the next he was not. Or maybe it was that the man only looked like Darling from a distance. Myron finally forced the issue with the usher.

"I have to leave," he insisted and the usher, evidently thinking this excitable man needed to find a public facility, let him step out into the line.

Once into the line-up of those exiting, Myron realized he'd made a tactical error. The aisles had solidified into an inching mass of humanity. He'd spent this irritating day on nothing. He saw remembrances of Trudy everywhere else and this had just been another example of it. Oh, how besotted he was. He should never have let her go.

Under the high roof of the thirty-two-acre Manufacturers and Liberal Arts Hall the truth broke out like sunlight. For the past few months he'd been running away from everything. Now he was captive and his mind spoke to him.

He did not care what his parents thought, what they did, what Jay Darling did. He wanted Trudy for his own. How curious that he was the one who'd told her marriage was out of the question. Now he regretted her new status, her more elegant life.

But he loved her. He had hurt her. He must find her and tell her that, if he did nothing else. He would be disinherited. He need not worry about pleasing his mother anymore. He would take things unto himself. He would do his damndest. If Trudy was not in Chicago at the Auditorium Hotel, if this was all a curious figment of his overwrought mind, then he must cure himself.

He would somehow arrange to go to that island and find Trudy and tell her he'd been wrong. He owed that to her—and to himself.

And if she were living as a princess or a queen, in charge of a large establishment, he could still woo her, tell her he could not forget her or live without her. She might not wish to love him in return, but at least he would know she was aware of his feelings. Now that she'd seen true luxury, would he ever be able to win her back?

7

On that important day in Chicago, on Dedication Day, there had been many possibilities in the air.

Margaret might have waited for Steven and learned he would love her any way she chose, live with her in any condition.

Jay Darling might have stepped out from behind a pillar and told Myron Davis where Trudy (Pamela) waited in isolated luxury.

But neither of those things happened.

As Myron came to a corner near the loop where the new construction of the elevated railway encroached on the sky, a woman came toward him, her head lowered. She was a small woman, thin, her body wrapped for the most part in a black shawl. He had almost passed her when a train roared above them, throwing eerie sparks and light into the air. A flash of light illuminated the woman's face.

Myron stopped walking. The woman stopped also and faced him. They looked at each other. Trudy, he thought. And yet—

No. He shook his head. He was going mad today. Every woman he saw looked like Trudy, every man like Jay Darling. Even this poor bedraggled thing, out of some other life, had the look of Trudy Jones. But this old woman was too old—old enough to be Trudy's mother.

The woman stood quietly looking at him, searching his face for some clue, just as he looked at her.

Myron said, "Beg pardon. I thought you were someone else—" He felt as if he'd been saying those words all day.

Because he could think of nothing more to say, he made a motion of dismissal with his hand. They each turned to their separate ways, traveling away from each other.

JAY
JDARLING

CHAPTER XXVI

1

Mrs. Stanley K. Chesterton of Great Neck, New York, didn't like the turn the conversation at her dinner party was taking. She liked the conversations at her parties, especially those given at her cottage on Sporting Isle, to be of refined topics, matters of culture and delicacy, and now the guests at the far end of the table, nearer to Mr. Chesterton, had begun to discuss "the scream."

Bad enough that the dreadful business had occurred, and what might have been its cause no one had yet been able to determine. But to discuss the matter three days later at a mixed dinner party at which the Misses Chesterton were present was in the height of poor taste in Mrs. Chesterton's opinion.

"Imagine," trilled the aging Miss Garner, "what could have caused a woman—for obviously it was a woman—to scream like that at that time of night—or should I say morning? Too late for anything respectable, I'm sure—"

Her remark fell at first to silence and her chin gave a little wobble on the top of her long neck and one knew she was aware she had just embarrassed her hostess and that she knew she had gone too far and could not recall her remark so she was going to bluff it through. Out of courtesy, to rescue her from the stern look of Mrs. Chesterton, everyone began to talk at once about that dreadful night.

Mrs. Chesterton, herself, was not without heart for whatever woman's plight had been expressed in the wee dawn hours three days

311

ago. She had sat up directly in her own bed, had put on her glasses without washing her face and had looked directly into the face of darkness and found nothing. She'd gone immediately to her daughters, swiftly from one to the other, where she found each well and asleep and not roused by the sound she'd heard. She thought then that she might have dreamed the sound, but Cook appeared at the bottom of the stairwell with a lighted lamp and the youngest maid had run up the stairs to inquire. Mr. Chesterton had been roused from his bedroom. He had not been disturbed by the scream itself, but by the commotion in the hallway. He retraveled the same route from bedroom to bedroom. They spoke sotto voce. Mr. Chesterton and the cook's husband went into the garden with lanterns, but they found nothing. They did report seeing lanterns and lamps in the gardens of other cottages, so their own household came to the conclusion that everyone had heard some sound, but nothing of bad news was brought to their door. Perhaps it was a cat in the woods, caught by a wild pig. Surely it was a cat. Mr. and Mrs. Chesterton and their guests—those who had awakened—had returned to their beds. They thought they would learn the answer in the morning.

But they didn't.

The Misses Chesterton were still quite angry about the excitement. They had heard nothing while several of their friends had heard the scream, and the Chesterton girls felt cheated. So little of interest happened on the island. Of course, that was precisely why the Sporting Isle Club had been formed—to allow for tranquil life for three months, or six months, depending on one's need for tranquility—and yet Mr. Chesterton could still have his ticker tape and cronies nearby in the Playhouse of Jay B. Darling.

Mrs. Chesterton looked down the length of the dinner table at her husband, but he seemed to be enjoying the discussion and was giving his opinion in resonant tones.

"I shall speak to the authorities," he said. "They must be letting their locals row over here to the island. True, this is private property, beyond the jurisdiction of local law, but mainland constables have the authority and power to control their own citizens and they should do so."

Mrs. Chesterton had not thought of locals. Who could it have been? And the anguish of that scream. She could think of a time or two she might have wished to cry out into the dark night, but there were, after all, marriage vows. But in the main, Mrs. Chesterton was pleased with the new thought of *locals*. She had been worried about her youngest maid. She feared some involvement with a chauffeur or valet at the hotel. She really wished not to know, but if something were happening she would have to deal with it eventually. That was really the sort of thing that put one off hotels. The servants there could not be controlled as one did the servants of one's own household.

Miss Garner, on the other hand, must be dealt with now. Mrs. Chesterton leaned over and spoke to the maid. "Give Miss Garner another serving of the fruit cup," she said. And she smiled at Miss Garner in a way she knew would still any further prattle.

Miss Garner was silent from then on. She was happy to be a guest at this lugubrious place. Previous to her faux pas she'd had so little to say and had been so ignored by her fellow diners that some inner need to be recognized, to take part, had brought the unfortunate topic to the tip of her tongue. Now she was, had become, the center of attention. There was danger in it, but there was satisfaction as well. She just wished that in her new visibility she was not quite so visible to Mrs. Chesterton. But the talk was well underway now and everyone at table had to tell his or her own version of the incident— no one really said anything different. But there was a point in each story where the recital faltered. No one knew what the scream meant or who had uttered it. And while they were willing to speculate, they could not bring themselves to do so, perhaps out of concern for Mrs. Chesterton's daughters.

The topic waned. Someone mentioned tennis. Mrs. Chesterton was glad to see her girls brighten and begin to take part. And soon it was time to have the light water brought in.

During the Sporting Isle season, wine was not served at the Stanley K. Chestertons'. Mrs. Chesterton had always been a teetotaler herself and she didn't like to serve wine even during winter evenings in New York, but could excuse the practice as stylish and "warming to the blood." But in the South she was adamant. Persons like Miss Garner were a fine example of why wine should not be served in mixed company. After dinner, the men could do what they liked, but the rule of the household was "light water" with the summer china. And in this way, she could also avoid having to bring her butler down from New York, since service of light water did not require the versatility of a butler, while it did take a butler to select, decant and serve wine. Mrs. Chesterton's English butler thought anything outside New York state was the frontier. This location, inaccessible and remote, would have made him so distraught the entire staff would have been constantly at war. No, he could stay behind and manage the New York establishment, while the Chestertons roughed it with the maids and light water.

But let no one say that she had not done right by her guests this evening. The water was shipped in from White Sulphur Springs. She might have used island water—it was pumped to the door of her cottage and was perfectly fine—but she always went the extra mile for her dinners on Sporting Isle. Very often dinner guests on this island were business acquaintances of her husband, men it was important to impress. She beamed at her husband with admiration across the light of the magnificent candelabra. His shirt front gleamed white like snow under the moon. His hair was precisely parted down the middle and his mustache was broad and imposing to match his embonpoint. If she had ever had any complaint about him it was that he was hardly ever with her, what with business and his new penchant for the golf links and his old penchant for cards at Mr. Jay B. Darling's Playhouse. Mrs. Chesterton did not like Jay Darling, but she didn't tell her husband that. She just didn't invite Mr. Darling to dine. Other business acquaintances were welcome. She liked to hear their views of the world.

And the world was the particular bluepoint oyster of Mr. Chesterton and Friends. They owned the railroads and the riverboats, the storage sheds and the steamships; *they* were the holding companies that held the mineral rights, the rights to all things that were over and under the earth—almost as if they had the right to the air the world breathed. These were the men who'd had the vision of Sporting Isle and made it come true.

Mrs. Chesterton could not fault them for that.

But a famous roué from New York, who visited the island during the first season, complained to a friend on his return to the city, "The Clubhouse is all right; respectable types stay there. And the Playhouse is amazing if you can stand the pace. But don't go near the private cottages. They're all owned by rich Presbyterians who live on tea and toast and won't serve a man a good glass of wine or Scotch whiskey."

2

A typical day for wives and daughters at the Sporting Isle Club began with tea and toast served at bedside early in the morning by one of the servants. Coffee could be substituted for the tea, but no other sustenance could be served in the rooms because of the insect problem. No sugar appeared on the tray.

Many of the private cottages did not contain a full kitchen, but householders traveled with their guests and families to the dining

Edith Freund 315

room of the Clubhouse where an elegant English breakfast was served each morning until 11:00 A.M.

After breakfast, the ladies would stroll around the grounds or go for short nature walks, often to the very edge of the wood. Their men had long disappeared in the direction of the golf links—which were raw and moist, since the greens had been cut from the wild underbrush not too many seasons before.

There was no beach bathing as such, but in nice weather members of various parties took the air on the white sands, looking for odd stones or intriguing shells.

After luncheon on cottage terraces and beside the pools, the families would gather their own parties up and the siesta hour would begin. Ladies who didn't care to nap were given novels from the hotel library or smart travel books brought down from New York. Everything was made as pleasant as possible. Everyone rested, waiting for the island night when dinner parties were held everywhere, when the men and women would mingle—often with the very same people with whom they socialized at home.

And after the families had retired and the prim householders had separated—he to his bedroom and she to hers—then the men would gather at Jay B. Darling's for their cigars and their cards and their other amusements.

Only the most sophisticated, most suspicious wife could guess what the Playhouse really held. To be sure, there were rumors. And there had been the scream...

A well-traveled woman of the world, perhaps, might guess at the cleverness of the Playhouse, at the terrible joke it played on the good wives and mothers and daughters of the members of the Sporting Isle Club.

Few of these wise women ever voiced their suspicions, but now and then, as one or two women rode together in a ponytrap around the crushed-shell paths of the island, one woman would say to another—

"What do you suppose Jay Darling is really up to in that place?"

3

On the first days of her menstruation, when Pamela knew she would be alone in the mornings, she would will herself to rise before the sun came in off the ocean on the eastern shore. She would spring quickly from the bed and its hangings and run barefoot, her feet hardly touching the floor, to the bathroom for her morning ritual.

Then she would put on a pair of Persian slippers, much admired and envied by the other girls, and trail in her dressing gown to the raised platform that led to the turret room, just off her bedroom. She loved these mornings alone and even though the walls of the turret were covered with red silk hangings, much like those on the bed, and although the floor was covered in turkey carpets and the cushions and benches that hugged the perimeter of the small space provided hundreds of nooks and crannies along the surrounding windows, she did not fear the turret room as she feared the bed.

She would lounge against the sill, trying to keep out of sight, but anxious not to miss anything in the meadow below.

The first movement could not always be attributed to the deer. Sometimes a rabbit or a late-retiring possum would be first. But the deer could be counted on.

Usually, Pamela leaned far forward as she waited. No one would see her at this hour. She could do as she wished. So she would lounge in the window, her left arm extended toward the breeze, her right elbow propped against the sill, her head resting on her right hand, her wild hair framing her head in a dark halo.

The window toward the sea was large and curved to make the better part of the turret wall. During the day it had to be covered with layers and layers of gauzy white stuff to keep the disastrous sun from the red silk of the walls. But in the mornings she could pull the curtains away and be as free as she liked.

The deer were white. The male would come first, moving across the meadow as if alone, his head dipping slightly with each step, his ears alert, his eyes showing some white, giving the lie to his dun-colored coat, antlers held precariously balanced on his head. He would cross the meadow completely and re-enter the wood at the right, as if taking a shortcut from one dense bramble to another.

Pamela had never seen anything like these animals before coming to the island.

The head of the buck would reappear and he would wait at the edge of the forest, as still as a trophy hung on a wall of Mr. Darling's billiard room, and then, if nothing about the meadow disturbed this watchful male, he would move back into it, coming across about halfway, still with his head high, his eyes watchful.

When the male lowered his head to graze, the female would step from the forest on the left, moving daintily, her head rising to the breeze, sniffing it and reading it. If she continued at a steady pace, then shortly after her would come the fawns, darker buff than their parents, delicate and unreal to Pamela. They would feed for a while on the lush grass below her, lifting their heads occasionally, then dropping their muzzles to the grass. Too quickly, the sun would rim the edge of the ocean. The light would change to gray hung with ground mist, to copper and silver. The ocean would begin to move back from high tide, turning from dull green to blue.

Distracted by the approach of the sun, by the moment when the brightness seemed to threaten to hold back, Pamela might not notice that the deer had left, so easily did they fade into the forest. But on other mornings, they left suddenly, rising as if on wings, flying across the lawn in a family demonstration of swiftness, flashing off into the woods to become invisible.

By these moments, Pamela was left exhausted. She'd been watching so intently, had held herself so still, that she was weak from the exertion of it. She would ease back against the cushions in her Persian den and wait for the sound of a wagon on the shell-paved road below.

Sometimes she dozed, because it was so very early and the nights were often humid and involved such effort on her part that she frequently did not regain her full personality until noon. If she were still awake when Nora came, Pamela would inch herself up to the sill again and look out. She always felt guilty about observing Nora and Ephraim in this way, but she was drawn to spying for some unknown reason. Nora would be talking; Ephraim hardly talked at all. Then they would embrace. Nora would reach out with her arm and Ephraim would move across the seat to be closer and the kiss was not a quick peck on the cheek or the lips, but a full-armed, lip-smacking salute to their parting.

In a short while Nora would burst into the room in all her gentle blackness, laughing and talking and calling *Miss Pamela, Pamela, Pammie, my dear*, and they would go together and examine the bedclothes and turn over the small rugs and shake out the clothes and shoes. Pamela knew Nora had been ordered to do this by Mr. Jay Darling, but the energy and good humor that Nora put into the search and the tenderness with which she always treated Pamela were the best parts of the day.

Could the best part of the day in any other place be considered to be a thorough search for spiders?

4

"See here now, Miss Pammie, this ain't got nothing hung on it—" and Nora would beat at the bed hangings, necessary to keep out flying insects, and would lift the hangings and give them a good shake and

turn them this way and that, over and up, until Pamela was satisfied and they would both go to the back of the bed against the wall and look there. And then they would each go down on their knees on each side of the bed and at the foot and then Nora would take a rug beater that she kept in the room for that purpose and she would vigorously flap away at the top draperies of the bed.

"And how is my little girl this morning, Miss Pammie, have you been up and done yourself? Are you ready yit for a sponge bath? Did you sleep through that whole night long or did you hear that little bitty storm we had round midnight? I slept but I heard it, too, and I almost wisht I was back here wif you looking right at yer, 'cause I know what it does to you to hear those ocean thunders."

Pamela had to admit she'd slept through the storm. She was finally getting used to the island. When she'd first come, she'd been frightened of the lack of light and the silence, but now and then at night the silence had been terribly shattered by storms. This last week she'd learned to sleep through and make it to morning.

Nora attacked the bed itself, tearing away the bedclothes, shaking and patting, talking away about the weather and the other girls. Pamela yawned her way through these searches, but she was ever on the alert to the completeness with which Nora did the room.

"Don't forget the back of the bell-pull, Nora," she cautioned. As Nora eliminated place after place, there was an increased tension in Pamela. If the spiders were not in those other places, then they might be in the next and the likelihood—the odds as her patron would say—about the next location were increased in favor of spiders and other small squirmy things that Pamela could not abide.

Some days ago, when she'd come to the island, perfectly willing for adventure but overwhelmed by the strange voyage on Mr. Jay Darling's yacht, she'd not been afraid of things much. She'd been brought in the night hours from the yacht, together with three other girls, to this brown-shingled mansion known as the Playhouse. As reigning favorite with Mr. Darling, she'd been installed in this turret room, accessible by secret stair from his private apartment on the third floor. She'd expected the large room, the maid, the private bath, but the turret was a delight to her, with its powerful spyglass, its fairy-tale look—and the deer in the meadow below.

But for the first time in her life—and her relationship to Mr. Darling—she was not allowed to go outside for any reason. On some days she was not even allowed to go down to the first floor to the game rooms. For the first time she felt like a *kept woman*, a phrase that had not applied to her relationship with Myron—or even to the arrangement with Mr. Jay Darling, her present benefactor.

Before this, Pamela had always done as she wished, had made her own plans wherever she'd found herself.

Pamela had to admit that complaints about staying indoors might be considered, from some points of view, unjustified. But she had never counted on the outside coming in to her.

The trouble with the spiders had not taken place until a few days after her arrival on the island. On that night, entertainment of the party in the parlor had consisted of ghost stories, told by various members of the assemblage. There had been much laughter and a lot of wine and sherry. Pamela didn't like sherry in this heat—she had not ever thought she would be too warm in winter but there it was—and instead of wine she had taken water imported from White Sulphur Springs. But rather than making her feel healthful and full of ideas for fun, it made her bilious and she had gone to her room to lie down for a short time. She had been escorted to the room by Mr. Darling, whose concern was proprietary. She told him she would be fine and she lit the lamp and moved about the room by herself and then lay against the bed cushions and fell asleep fully dressed. She woke once to find Mr. Darling standing over her, swaying slightly, his shadow moving strangely against the bed draperies, and then he had called for Nora, who was on hand for the party, and he had gone away and Pamela had gone to sleep, dreaming of seafood, which was new to her in such quantities and in the rich sauces she was learning to like.

She had slept till dawn and she guessed that Nora had stayed with her all night, because the Negro woman was still there when Pamela woke before dawn. Nora was sleeping in a chair by the bed and Pamela was so happy to see her that she touched the bed curtain to raise it. As she put her bare foot out to stand, a large, black spider, as large as her hand, ran down from the top of the bed and hung at the edge of the curtain, not six inches from Pamela's hand.

Her scream cut the holy quiet and rolled on and on into the dim light. Pamela screamed and screamed and screamed—

Nora ran to her, flailing at the spider, which she also could see. The bedclothes swung inward toward Pamela and the spider dropped into the blankets. Pamela screamed again and pulled herself to the other side of the bed, but then was afraid to step barefoot onto the floor. She was half-standing, half-crouched at the headboard. The bed shook under her. Nora was leaning into it and searching. Men burst into the room, followed by some of the girls. Everyone was in night dress, everyone running—

"Shut her up. Stop that caterwauling—"

Arms reached for her. A hand went over her mouth. Her feet flailed against her captors. They carried her to the bathroom, which was on the ocean side. Nora came then and took Pamela into her arms and sang to her and coaxed her and she became quietly hysterical instead of noisily so.

Nora, thus occupied, couldn't explain what had happened but the noise, the danger of discovery, had been taken care of. The parties eased back to their own rooms. They would learn in the morning what had happened. Pamela, held by Nora, hiccoughed to sleep in a chair. She didn't trust sleep, but exhaustion overcame her and when she woke in the full light of day, she was surrounded by a conference of "proprietors."

The owners of Sporting Isle could not allow one of their indiscretions to become indiscreet.

They were not even kind about it. The rule about quiet, about not being seen, was the most important rule, they said. Without adherence to that rule, she could not stay here. She must be quiet, no matter what happened. Even if the place should catch on fire, they said.

She tried to explain to them about the spider, but they would only repeat the rule about quiet. Pamela cried and decided she would never tell Jay Darling the truth about anything again. She knew he could stop this lecture she was receiving, just by a nod of his head. He waited until the others had left.

Then Mr. Darling told her that he enjoyed her company more than that of any young woman he had ever known, but he must go along with the majority on this. Pamela knew this was not true. After all, he had once told her he was the sole owner of the Playhouse and held controlling interest in the shares of the club. His rules could be the most important rules of all. If he wanted her to go outside at high noon, she would have been able to do it in spite of the objections of the "others."

Now he was staring at her in that measuring way he had. "Are you with child? Are you pregnant?" he asked.

Pamela was shocked. "Of course not."

"Well, then, you have no reason to be hysterical," he said.

He said he knew she was reasonable in being frightened of the terrible large spider, which he said did not come from the island, but had prospered there, probably having been brought in first with some bananas. But he explained that the people—most of them ladies—who lived in that large hotel that could just be seen through the trees to the west and in the private cottages, did not know there were friends of Mr. Darling and the other men staying at the Playhouse. Those ladies must never know the secret, and that was why on certain days she and the other girls could not go downstairs to the tennis courts or the indoor pool or the billiard room or the shuffleboard or the masseuse. They must stay out of sight because these other ladies did not like all-night parties for men and women.

He did not caress her.

After he left, Nora came back and said she'd been ordered to search the room for spiders each day. Pamela didn't think that would help, but it was Nora who came up with the great idea of removing the floor skirt on the bed and changing the top draperies to gauze curtains that could be seen through. In that way, Pamela could first look before she leaped, even if Nora was not yet in attendance in the mornings.

CHAPTER XXVII

1

Jay B. Darling, who liked to edge as close to danger as he could and then laugh in its face, had imported a woman to decorate the Playhouse when it was first built. He made it quite clear other that he intended to use the upper floors of the building for amusement—that girls would be kept there. He told her this plainly and said the topmost floor would be his own apartment, which should have access to the third floor's most prestigious quarters through some sort of private stairway. And in all other circumstances, the girls themselves were to have the facilities of the most exclusive of private country houses. Beauty and good taste were to be everywhere. He wanted none of the cathouse spittoons and overdone window treatments of more notorious brothels. This would be a special place for the special friends of special men.

"After all," he told the decorator in such a pleasant, frank way that she was charmed, "many of these men have had long-standing relationships that they would not care to set aside for six months while their wives visit the hotel on the island. And we could not have their paramours staying at the hotel, now could we? They might have to dine in the same room with a man's wife—"

So the decorator, who was just beginning to gain important commissions and needed the work, took the assignment in confidence and did the Playhouse in the most elegant of styles. But she confessed to Darling when she'd finished that her favorite room, outside of the turret room that Pamela now occupied, was a large space on the north side of the building on its second floor. The room was almost a porch, with doors that could be folded back to reveal floor-to-ceiling screens. It faced north so that it caught the morning sun, yet lost it soon to sea breezes. Below the windows, the decorator had had gardeners make a clever planting of small trees and dense bushes. Just beyond that was a slough that eventually became a small stream that emptied finally into the sea. These conditions made it impossible to stand under the windows or near the building, so there was no danger that those on the porch above would be seen or overheard.

Yet the loungers would have the expansive distant vista of the blue ocean, the freshness of the air, and they would be able to watch ships coming down from the North to sample the winter climate.

The floor of the porch had been delicately washed with white paint over blue, giving it a pearlescent quality. Around the edge of it, a border of seashells had been painted. Everywhere there were wicker settees, tables, bright cushions and pale chintzes. Scented candles were provided to insure that odor of cigar smoke would not taint the atmosphere for long. Great stands of exotic plants were here and there about the room.

Usually the men were not around when the girls gathered in the northside room for their morning chats. It was like a pleasant club where the girls could speak freely.

A new girl had arrived. Women were always coming and going. Sometimes as many as twelve were in residence, but they might leave when their "gentlemen friends" went elsewhere—or, as sometimes happened, when they were replaced with newer acquisitions. Doris had appointed herself the official greeter and questioner. Doris liked to hear everyone's life history right away, because, she said, that made it just like home. "And besides, we were the first here, the longest here; we should make others feel comfy and welcome."

"Cleveland is a funny name," Doris said to Cleveland.

Cleveland was sitting with Doris and Sherry on one of the settees. Pamela was standing at the screen, looking out the window.

"That's because I came from there," Cleveland said. "That is, I came down here from Cincinnati with Sonny, but I originally came from Cleveland when I was a baby. Then my family moved to—say, that's the most beautiful girl I ever saw. What's her name? I didn't see her last night."

"Oh, that's because she wasn't with us. She's Jay Darling's girl and he's off over to Casino Island. He's there with my Harry and two other men—"

Cleveland leaned forward and asked Doris, "How come he didn't take her with him? They went over on his yacht. There must of been plenty of room. I hear that stuck-up one went with them. Her and four men—"

"Stuck-up?" Doris looked at Sherry and Sherry shrugged. "I guess you mean Helen. They have Helen with them. I hear Darling left Pammie behind because he's losing at the tables. He said she brings him bad luck over there—"

"Too bad," Cleveland said. "I'd take any luck she'd want to make—" She looked at Pamela and then at Doris and Sherry. She seemed to be making up her mind about something. She nodded toward Pamela and whispered, "Does she pet?"

She was using the current slang for lesbian love.

Doris said, "No, and none of us do either. The men would throw us out if they caught us doing that. They dump girls all the time— for hardly anything at all. This is such a swell place—we have to be very careful to do just what they want—"

"Too bad," Cleveland said. She lit a cigar. "Where is everbody? This place is like a tomb."

Sherry didn't want to be left out. "Sir Billy took a big shooting party out to another island—one where they ain't even a house or anything and they're hunting. They left before dawn. I don't see how they do it. Up all night. I'd hate to be anywhere near them guns. It's a wonder they don't shoot themselves in the foot—"

Cleveland nodded. "Sonny went with them. He says they might not be back for days if there's good game—"

"Lots of girls are sleeping yet. That was a great time we had last night—"

"And that girl—that one with the very wavy hair and the big bosom—I thought I'd die when she took off all her clothes and stood on the table like Saint-Gaudens *Diana*. That statue they took down from the building in New York. I never seen such charades as that—"

"Oh, she just wanted to show off her figure 'cause they's so many new men lately. They say—" Sherry leaned forward "—that she's not gettin' much. That guy with her has trouble—y-know—gettin' it up and she's goin' crazy with him. He wants blow jobs all the time—"

"You mean that guy with the beard that talks about it all the time? You'd think he was the raunchiest guy in the place. And he was all over her after that. Just like some back-door place, y'know? I thought this was a high-toned party. He damn near took her on the table. Sonny and me almost left—"

Doris and Sherry laughed. "Jay Darling ain't here. They act more—fawncy—when he's in the place. Besides, there's some that always has to do it almost in public. It gets 'em very hot to make a big show of it. Seems like once they get the go-ahead in private, like it's all right and not too shocking, then they want to move out on stage. I don't think that old man has had it up fer a month, accordin' to that girl. But when them others all saw her naked and applauded and shouted, he was drooling and all set—"

Doris said, "If Darling had been here, they wouldn't have done none of that. He likes everything terribly smooth and high-brow. Look at Pamela. Ain't she sweet? But she *is*. She's nice. It's just that she's a real innocent."

"And Harry told us about Helen—"

"What about Helen?"

"You know how she looks like she come from choir practice? Always holdin' a book? Well, not so. My Harry used to have Helen as a special friend until he couldn't take it anymore and he made some sort of deal with Billy—that's Sir William that's off hunting. Harry made a deal to switch, because Helen is—" She inched her chair forward. "Well, she's cock-crazy, that's what she is—"

"You don't mean it? With all them buttoned-up frocks?"

"Yes," nodded Sherry. "Helen's as prim as a schoolteacher out here and the minute the door is shut she goes crazy fer it. She just wants it all the time and if they don't make it right fer her, she beats on 'em and cries and almost pets 'em until they can start. And she won't do it no other way 'cause she hates to waste it. And—" Sherry was almost drooling herself with her good gossip "—she likes to talk dirty to 'em—"

"No kidding? Without them asking her? I'd never do that—" Cleveland assured them.

"That's why," Doris said, "they need only Helen over there. She can handle all four of 'em without no trouble."

"But still—" Cleveland hesitated. "Some men don't like muddy waters—"

Doris and Sherry nodded. "That's true. And you can bet Darling goes first. But some men—if they're havin' trouble—it turns 'em on. I think Darling's in trouble—"

Cleveland was skeptical. "Now Harry didn't tell you that—"

"No, but look at Pammie. She's mooning around over there like she lost her love. Who knows what goes through a head like that? Maybe she does care for 'im. I don't think she's ever had anoth-er—"

"You mean Jay Darling took her—bought her somewheres as a virgin? True, she don't look very old—"

"She says she's twenty-two," said Sherry, "but I'm twenty-three and she doesn't know some of the things I know about. So I think she's much younger—"

"Like how much—"

"Oh, I think she might be sixteen or seventeen."

"She's better-looking than when we first met her, which was three months ago," Doris said. "She gets better-looking all the time and sort of more mature. So that's why we figure she's still in that time when the face and body change very fast and that has to mean she's about sixteen or so—"

"So—?"

"Well, half the time around here she doesn't get the jokes and she's not dumb. She just doesn't know the language. She's not been around. She's been one place and one place only—"

"Where's that?"

"In a rich man's bed."

"Well, maybe we can get her to tell us."

"I don't think so. She really keeps her mouth shut. Darling probably has her do that—"

Pamela *was* mooning around. Darling had come to her twice during the previous week but had lain beside her only, without touching her. Once, when she'd thought he wanted her to be more seductive, she'd turned toward him, but he moved away; stood up beside the bed and looked at her.

"Don't touch me. You must wait until I'm ready," he'd hissed at her.

The room was dark. He didn't seem to be aroused, but she couldn't see him to tell. He put on his robe and stood above her. He started to say one thing, then stopped and hesitated. Finally, he said, "All these fears of yours. They're changing my luck. You didn't used to be like this—"

He left the room. He'd not been back since, except to tell her he was going to Casino Island for a short stay and he was taking the yacht. She didn't know what he meant exactly by this. Did he mean to go elsewhere and leave her here to fend for herself? Would he just take the yacht and go away for good? Later, she'd learned he'd taken Helen with him.

Pamela's feelings were confused. She sighed deeply. What if he tired of her? What if he told her to go to another bed—demoted her to someone else in the place? It happened to other girls all the time.

She'd seen it. She hoped that if Darling had good luck at the casino, he would not attribute it to Helen. But Pamela feared his reaction if he had bad luck. She dreaded being abandoned. She didn't know where else she could go. Yet she longed to be free to go; just to leave. But she believed that outside this building she would be without any resources whatsoever and that the world outside was fraught with swamps, alligators and the sea. None of these things could she cope with by herself.

"Pammie, come sit with us and talk to Cleveland," Doris called and Pamela joined them.

Cleveland told them that she'd lived in Cincinnati all her life after a short time in Cleveland, and that her mother and father were dead and she'd been with Sonny for about two years.

"Where were you livin' before that?" Sherry asked.

"If I tell you, will you promise not to tell the men?"

Doris and Sherry nodded in complete agreement, although Pamela knew they were the worst gossips in the place. She told them nothing unless she wanted others to know it. And sometimes, even innocuous remarks came back to her with a delicate, nasty twist attached, so that she appeared to have been catty about someone when she was not. But Cleveland appeared to trust them and Pamela felt that was Cleveland's business.

"When I was a very young girl, I had an infection inside. A terrible thing. The doctor told my mother that I could never have children. And my mother was so upset about it, she told too many women in our neighborhood. And that was it fer me—"

"Why was that?" asked Pamela.

"Well, I was still about fourteen or fifteen and no one was in love with me yet and so there was no chance that anyone ever would be. Men wants children, honey," she said. "To carry on their names and all. If a man had been in love with me and something like that had happened, he might have loved me still. But because I was a child and everyone knew—well, I got a terrible reputation from it—

"No, it wasn't my fault. But the women my mother told—they warned their sons not to take up with me. And men that wanted children didn't let themselves come near me. Men that had big families already and that were widowers—now *they* were interested. I was to come and take care of their kids and their houses and their sex. And what was that for me? And then there was the other kind. Wanted to try me out right then. They knew no one would know. They wanted me for a good roll in the hay. An uncle even tried to force me. But I got away from him. I got away from all of them—"

"But how—?" asked Sherry.

"I met a girl named May. May was some older than I was and I was working in the same place she was. She knew everything, May did—" Wonderful admiration crept into Cleveland's voice. She seemed to have become softer-looking all over; she spoke dreamily.

"May showed me what to do in the store and one night I went home with her and then we—" she paused for effect "—we became lovers. It's very nice, you know. Not like men. And I just stayed there with her and we went back and forth to work and we had begun to save money. We had a good amount put away from both of us workin'. We were going to buy a house."

"How could you do that? Houses must cost an awful amount. You'd never have enough," Pamela said.

"Oh, they don't cost all that much if two are working and you save fer it. We almost had enough, in an account in May's name. And then May died—"

They sat in silence. There seemed to be nothing to say.

Finally Sherry asked, "What did you do with the money?"

"I didn't. I couldn't get it. May had it in the bank in her name only. I guess she thought that I might go away and leave her and the money was her way to keep me there. But I never would've left her. Never. I went to the bankers. They wouldn't give it to me. They said I wasn't a relative and there wasn't no will or anything like that—so they got it, I guess. I'll never know. I had to give up the flat we had."

"Where did you go?"

"I got a job as a maid to an old lady. A very old lady. And she liked me and made me her companion. Then one day she said to me 'I'm going to die tomorrow,' and I said, 'You ain't,' and she said 'I am. And I want you to take care of Sonny. He's never been with a woman, you know.' And so that's why I'm here with Sonny—"

"You mean the Sonny that's off shooting?" asked Sherry.

"That's him."

"But he's ever so old. He must be over fifty."

"No. Forty-eight. He gets his inheritance when he's fifty. And then we're going to get married. But his mother fixed it up at the bank and they pay me to be his companion, you know. But they wouldn't like it if we got married. They would hang on to all the money if he don't seem to do things right. According to his father's will—"

Sherry and Doris and Pamela were amazed. Sonny was twice as old as Cleveland, yet she talked of him as if he were a child.

"Is he simple?"

"No, not that, exactly. But he never has had to do anything. He just does what pleases him. He's like a good-natured child that never learned the world won't make way for 'im. He doesn't like reading, so he only knows a few words. The bank handles the money and pays the bills. He knows how to dress in beautiful clothes and he can dance and he knows about opera 'cause he likes the costumes and the music and he knows about horses and dogs and—"

She sighed, almost as sadly as Pamela had sighed. "And now," Cleveland said, "he knows about love. I had to teach him that. He was interested, but not very much. I had to explain to him that it was like the horses and then he knew—but he's real, real sweet to me."

"How did you know about the will and the bank and everything? Did Sonny figure that out?"

"No. His mother told me just what to do. And she said to wait until he's fifty and after we're married he's to make a will leaving everything to me." She yawned. "Someday, I'll be the one that's rich—"

"But what do you do now?" asked Pamela. "How do you live? Doesn't it take a lot of money to be rich?"

Doris and Sherry and Cleveland laughed at her. But then Cleveland explained. "Oh, no. It ain't like that at all. Somebody in that family got rich a long time ago. And they bought three or four houses to live in different places. We go to all of 'em. And the servants are paid by the trust at the bank. And the food is there for us when we need it. It really doesn't take so much money to be rich when somebody else in your family was rich before you. All you have to do is keep it up and not let things slip—or let the damn bankers get it— but I figger I'll get even—with them other bankers—the ones that took May's money—when I marry Sonny right under the nose of this bunch—"

"Goodness," said Sherry.

"Why I never," said Doris.

"Then why are you here?" asked Pamela.

"'Cause it's lonesome in all those houses. I can't meet anyone until we marry and I can't stay alone. And Sonny likes to be with the men in the shooting parties and the casino parties and the card parties—"

"He can play cards?"

"Oh, yes. They love him 'cause he constantly loses. And he says how do you do and it's a lovely evening and you're looking glamorous tonight and the garden is so fine this year and what a beautiful gown. He says to people that he doesn't like to talk business and they believe him. Nobody notices he ain't as swift as some. He's very *presentable*. His mother said that. *She* knew. He gets invited everywhere. He's really very charming in that way, y'see—"

Pamela still was puzzled by something. "How much does a house really cost?" she asked. "I mean a little one? And how were you and May going to pay for everything?"

"We always said we'd have a little shop. May liked to bake and we were going to hire a baker and go into trade. I would run it with her. May was very, very sharp about business—"

"But I'd think it would cost too much for two women—I mean—" Pamela didn't know what anything cost. She knew about the price of elaborate costumes and dresses. But in all other matters, she'd had no experience. She'd been very poor. And then she'd been treated to the cosseted life of the demimondaine. There was no part of her life that *cost* her money. Sometimes she had been given money to use in the Chicago and New York shops where an account would not be advisable. But her clothing and her living quarters, her maid and her food, were all supplied for her. Her entertainment was, while she was in Chicago and New York, at every hand. She'd had no way to learn about the relative prices of various kinds of life. The men among whom she moved during the past eighteen months had required large amounts of money for their lives. Pamela thought everyone required such great sums. Hadn't her mother and father always talked of the lack of money? Wasn't that what made her life so unbearable? She had no notion of the middle class, having hardly been among them.

"We had chosen a very nice house, in a new subdivision just outside the city limits," Cleveland said. "They were very good lots with a tree on each. And an artesian well. May just insisted on that. We looked at a number of houses and we were just about to buy one. I think I may have the brochure in my luggage. I'll bring it to you, if I find it. I think the six-room house with an indoor bath and a fireplace would be one thousand dollars fully paid or one thousand two hundred, if paid in four years. I think May intended—I know she did—to pay all at once. I know the lot was one hundred. We already had the lot—but I had to let that go as well. It was also in May's name—"

"One thousand dollars," said Pamela. "Why that's—"

"What?"

"Nothing."

She was about to say that she had many times that amount in her various hoards. She was certain she did. She still had the $150 she'd left home with. A mere pittance, she knew now, but it had been so hard to come by that a small superstitious knot in her mind had kept it from ever being squandered on some pretty trifle. And there was the money she'd received from Myron from time to time. He would give her money to buy clothes and she did; but he gave her so much and she knew how to shop carefully. She'd been saving little amounts and putting them away, thinking to surprise him with a gift, when he'd turned so terrible about Jay Darling. And then she'd seen why the little knot inside her told her to be careful about money. Such precious money she'd hidden away in the white shawl she'd embroidered, a shawl of wool challis, which she'd made during the time she lived with Myron. She wore the shawl frequently and it always gave her warmth, in more ways than Myron could have known.

Within the embroidery stitches were other hidden stitches that held the money to the garment.

On the back, these were further covered by a white silk lining. And the fringe. Within that shawl was—perhaps—as much as two thousand in rolled bills of large denomination. Then, on an impulse, she'd carefully sewn pearls from a necklace into the design of the embroidery, here and there, so that the average person would not notice there were a great many over all. And no one would know those pearls were real rather than cheap beads. Those pearls, clipped and restrung, would make a very fine necklace, a necklace that might be sold and if it brought half its value, the pearls themselves would buy the kind of house Cleveland was describing.

Pamela discounted the two banknotes that were hidden among her goods. One of those banknotes was Myron's portion for having sold her—she didn't know that, she only knew Mrs. Asunda said Myron sent it—and the other was an amount that came from Mr. Darling through Mr. Deel. Pamela knew nothing of commercial banks. Her ideas of them came from people like Cleveland and friends of her father who railed against banks as well as mill-owners. She thought banks always cheated one of money put by. She thought she'd never be able to get out her savings—if that's what they were—in excess of twenty-five thousand dollars.

Nor did Pamela consider her other jewelry. She'd hidden various items after the incident with Darling and Myron's sapphires, partly because she was sentimental and most of the items had come from Myron. In fact, Pamela Jones, if she had been a small entrepreneur, would have been considered a modest success in any community.

Her success had been achieved on her own initiative, on her own beauty, and she'd been careful of what she'd earned because of her early experience with the Evil Eye. If the Evil Eye could reach into the crowded ghetto, why not into the less crowded confines of yachts and fine avenues? Times could be hard again, something told her. But the increased number of options her hoard gave her had not filtered through to her inner being. She'd squirreled and tucked and sewed and stitched—but never thought to figure what this all might come to. Nor where she might travel with it.

Even though she did not fully grasp it yet, at this moment sitting with Cleveland and Doris and Sherry in the Playhouse lounge, Pamela suddenly gained an insight into her financial position. The cash alone would allow her to make some dignified future for herself, by herself. She would not have to be dependent on anyone else. The thought seemed daring. She felt excitement rise in her. She smiled at Cleveland in such a warm, sparkling way that Cleveland almost gasped.

Amazing that the price of houses could so thrill this lovely girl. Cleveland leaned forward again: "And the cost of houses in the country is much, much less—" she said.

Doris and Sherry, watching this, could not imagine what these two saw in the price of real estate that made them both so pleased with each other, but they were impressed to be a part of what was clearly a blossoming friendship.

2

Later, Pamela wandered off down the hall, thinking. She went into her suite, where Nora was waiting for her.

"See what I have for you? Iced tea—"

"Ice? Oh, how wonderful—"

"I bribed the chef. I told him not to carve it. My lady needs it for her tea, I told him. I just come up the stairs with it."

They went to sit in the turret and Pamela shared her tea with Nora, who sat on the voluptuous bench that circled the room just under its windows. Pamela sat on the floor at her feet and sipped from her glass.

"Tell me a story, Nora," she said, resting her head on the black woman's knee.

Nora brushed Pamela's hair from her forehead. "Which one do you want to hear? The one about the goat in the tree or the one about the time Leonard caught the giant crab or the one about—"

"Tell me the one about how you were married to Ephraim—"

"Waal," said Nora, tilting her own head back, looking at the ceiling with concentration as a born story-teller does, "there I was in the yard of my momma's house. Playing with my brothers and sisters and never thinking I was different from them in any way at all. And down the road comes this great black hulk, tall as a tree, laughin' at somethin', singin', singin' to the wind, comin' at us like he seen us from afar."

"And had he seen you before?" Pamela knew this story and she knew just where to interrupt.

"Of course he had; you know that. He'd been in the meetin' and he heard me sing and he said to hisself I must have that singin' next me for the the rest of my days—"

"But you didn't know about that then—"

"No, I didn't know it and I saw him comin' along the road and I went into the house and I told my momma that a big man was comin' and she laughed and she said 'comin' to git you—'"

"But she didn't know that then—"

"No, she didn't know it atall. But somethin' tole her that he was comin' and why would he come to her po' house—not for the big supper on the table—"

"Nooo."

"Not for the wide crystal stairs—"

"Nooo."

"Not for the rings on her fingers and the bells on her toes and the hoards of gold under her little ol' bed—"

"Nooo."

"So my momma just laughed and say 'He comin' to git you—'"

"And she was right—"

"My momma is always right—"

Silence.

"Nora, start with your house. Tell me the part about your house—"

"Waal. Ephraim—that was his name—he worked down to the big sawmill that's over to the other side of the inlet there, but he come to the island for the meetin' here because it was so good for singin' and he liked for to sing. He was here and my momma tole him, yes, he could court me and take me around but it better be pretty quick 'cause she could see he was a man already, even though he was not more than sixteen or se'teen—like you—"

"I'm twenty-two—"

"Hush. So Ephraim said let's get married tomorrow and not waste time—he'd waited a whole week since last Sunday and he said he was sure enough for two—" And Nora threw back her head to laugh, which always made Pamela laugh and that was why she loved this story. Nora went on, "So my momma took us over to the preacher, ridin' up in her wagon—the same wagon I got now—the same wagon you see when you watch them deer from the woods and you spy on me and Ephraim down below—"

"I didn't think you saw me do that—"

"I know what you do. I know where you be. And we took that wagon to the preacher, me and Ephraim and Momma; and the preacher says to Momma he says—"

"NOOO!" Pamela liked to chime in here.

"That's right. The preacher says, I can't marry this little girl to this growing boy. They's not old enough fer to be wed—"

"And your momma said—"

"And my momma said—she looked that preacher right in the eye and said—if you don't marry 'em the devil will. Cain't yer see the look in that 'er one's eyes—"

"And she pointed right at Ephraim."

"Right."

"So the preacher married you right then."

"Right."

"And there was a big party for you that lasted two days."

"Right."

"And everyone that came—tell me."

"Everyone that came, they took a board or two out o' their houses and brung 'em along to the party. And Ephraim took those boards and made a little shack and that's all we had at first. But it was ours and that was enough. Later, he got more lumber from the mill and made a re'lar cabin in the colored quarter. But nothin' was as beautiful as that little shack. We keep it yit—"

Pamela finished her tea, stretched and stood up. She hugged Nora. And then she went into the bedroom for her siesta. Now she would be able to sleep for a while.

3

After Nora had gone home for the day, Pamela was sitting once again in her turret room when there was a light tap on the door. As Pamela opened it, Cleveland came in. The sound of the nightly party demonstrated that the Playhouse was in full operation. The hunters had returned, bringing nothing but chigger bites. Jay Darling, as far as

Pamela knew, had not come back to Sporting Isle.

Cleveland, already in, said, "Can I visit? Sonny is sleeping. I'm kind of lonesome."

"Yes," Pamela said and turned toward the turret. She'd been hoping that her caller was Darling, although he usually approached by the stair. But she had bathed and perfumed herself and put on an especially pretty peignoir that he liked. She would try to be more accommodating. Maybe she could conquer her fears of the storms and—and everything.

"Oh, this is nice," Cleveland said, crossing the turret and taking a seat in the unlit room. Only backlight from the room and the faint light from the dying day gave any illumination. She settled herself where Nora had been that afternoon.

"I brought the brochure I promised—"

Pamela must have looked puzzled.

"About the house May and I were going to buy. Here, sit here by me. I think you can see enough in this light and get the price off it. I don't want to leave it—" She patted the cushions and Pamela had no choice but to sit down.

By turning the paper toward the light, Pamela could just read.

—CITY FRAME HOUSES OF MODERATE COST FOR FUTURE EXPANSION—

The exterior of this $1,000 cottage will bear few explanations. The bay window is for both parlor and second story and the large, one-light window in the basement makes all the front rooms decidedly inviting. The judicious use of sawed shingles along the front and at the base of the bay serves to relieve the monotony and...

Along the bottom of the illustration text was printed in heavy letters, "Artesian wells on all fully improved city lots."

"Why did you want a big house like this, just for the two of you?" asked Pamela. "There are seven rooms in all and that seems a lot—"

"We thought if we couldn't open the shop, we could at least take in a couple of lady boarders," Cleveland said. "May had everything worked out to a *T*—but she never thought she'd die—"

"What did she die of?"

"Heart. Stroke. She worried just like a man—she was as smart as any one of 'em. Didn't take enough care, I think—"

"Oh, that's terrible."

"But you see—houses aren't so terrible dear as all that. I didn't make it up."

"I didn't think you did."

"Sometimes I think so—" Cleveland's voice was wistful.

They didn't talk for a while. Pamela didn't know quite what to say to this girl, with her strange ideas and her sureness that gave way under any pressure to almost total uncertainty.

"Darling didn't get back yet." Cleveland didn't seem to be asking.

"No."

"They sure have a lot of fun at those parties. Lots of laughing and all—"

"I don't get to go to all the parties. Just some. Sometimes I just read or sew after dinner—"

Cleveland looked around. "Maybe sometimes I could join you after dinner. I like to do that. Read and sew. Both. Maybe we could do it together."

"If Mr. Darling isn't—"

"Yes."

Cleveland smiled as if she'd gained some point. When she was smiling, she was very pretty. Other times, her face had a sharp look. Her chin was somewhat pointed and her eyes slanted in an interesting way. She had similar coloring to Pamela. Cleveland said, "You're a beautiful girl, Pamela. I've never seen anyone I've admired more. Do you know your hair color is the same as mine? I'm not beautiful like you, but we could pass for sisters. We could pretend we were that—sisters."

Pamela smiled. That seemed strange, but acceptable. "I think that would be nice," she said. "I had—" She didn't know whether she should confide in this person, but she plunged ahead "—I had two older sisters."

"There. You see. We were meant for each other. I need a sister and you had sisters before. And we both like to—do other things than go to loud parties."

"Yes."

Cleveland stood up as if she were going to leave but she came over and knelt at Pamela's feet. She looked her in the eye and said, "Pamela, will you do something important for me—?"

"Why—I guess so."

Cleveland lowered her gaze to Pamela's chest. "I want you to open your robe for me. I want to touch your lovely nipples. I want to kiss them. Will you let me? I want you so much. I've never even seen anyone like you—and I think you're like me—alone—lonely—"

"What?"

Cleveland's hand was already on her robe and Pamela's breasts already exposed when her hand flew to the other's. She turned Cleveland's hand away. She looked directly at her guest.

"No," she said. "I don't want to do that. I know what it is—and I don't want to make you angry, but I don't want to do that—"

"It would be nicer than you think. Very sweet. We could take our time. No one would know. We don't have to worry about—rushing—"

"No."

Cleveland sat back on her heels and then she stood up.

"Well, at least you turned me down in a ladylike way. I can say that for you. You have style clear enough. Not just on the surface the way it might seem." She was standing. She reached into her pocket and took out a small folded piece of paper.

"You've been very nice to me, Pamela. It helps to have someone to talk to. I want to give you a little present—"

She held out her hand with a many-folded paper in it.

Pamela took it and started to open it, but Cleveland said, "No, not now. Later. When things just don't seem to be going right and you need to feel better, to feel surer and able to handle things, then open it—but be careful. Don't spill it. It's a powder. A doctor gave it to me, so it's all right. You just put in on the back of your tongue. It makes everything—" she was looking out the windows at the night that was now quite black "—bearable."

"You mean, when—before he—" she stopped.

"Yes. Especially then."

Pamela waited until Cleveland left and then opened the folded paper cautiously and saw the white powder. She wet her finger and touched it to the white grains and put some on her tongue. She knew what it was. She didn't like to think about it. Nothing happened when she tasted it. It had little or no flavor. Just the faint scent of Cleveland's perfume clung to it.

She put it on the table beside her bed and when Darling didn't come that night, she forgot about it.

But later, in the night, when a storm broke flashing in from the east across the ocean, she sat up, terrified, and remembered. She reached out to the table and found the little packet. She tipped it and let the fine dust settle on the back of her tongue.

"Now it will be better," she thought. "I won't be afraid now—" And at last she went back to sleep.

4

In the dream Pamela was having, Cleveland was touching her, touching her nipples with a hard tongue, but when Pamela opened her eyes, the dream altered and she was with Jay Darling and they were alone in the turret room. The wind was whipping the long, white curtains around them, now snapping the cloth over their heads, now wrapping them together as one; when she opened her eyes in the flickering silent flashes of the lightning—and in the thunderstruck moments after the light—she saw his face. His eyes were closed; he was smiling his half-smile and she felt his hands bringing her toward him; her fingers and toes seemed numb—her mouth was numb— her hair had fallen forward and whipped between them, going into the wind—wildness was around her—her whole life was here but only part of her was alive—the part of sensation and feeling—she had accepted him; she would not be able to live without him—she let everything else fade away; let the storm come, she was not afraid, not afraid of anything at all as long as she could move with him— riding out the storm.

CHAPTER XXVIII

"Pammie? Miss Pammie? Little Miss Pamela? Oh, wake up, honey, wake up. It's almost noon now. Why are you sleeping so long? I've been waitin' here and waitin' here. Wake up, baby. Don't sleep no mo'."

Nora was shaking Pamela, shaking the bed; the curtains above Pamela trembled as she opened her eyes. She smiled at Nora.

"Is it morning?" she whispered.

"It's very, very late. The sun is up. The brunch bell is almost rung, honey. Oh, what is the matter with you today? Are you sick? Did you get sick in the night because of the storm? Where was you, Sweet Face? The little deer was there. They was lookin' for you. I was lookin' for you. And I didn't see your little eye peepin' over the sill—

"I said to Ephraim I said, 'Miss Pammie ain't there. She's not lookin' down at us, spyin' on our kisses. Oh, how she likes to see us kiss'—I said that to him. And you didn't even hear it. I thought you would hear it—

"What is wrong, baby? Your eyes hurt? Is they poorly in this light? What happened to the Little Girl? She got a pain in the head—

"Oh, come *on* now, I don't like to see you sleepin' this way all the time when the sun is shinin' and the little deer is lonesome and gone away without their gal cause there wasn't no Little Gal there—"

Pamela sat up groggily and thought: What kind of powder did

Cleveland give me? What a wonderful powder, to make everything so clear to me; to make everything black and white with nothing in-between—

2

The girl was coming along fine. The past week, in fact, had seen the correction of all flaws marring the horizons of Jay Darling. He'd been right to leave New York. The vultures had been circling and when he left, albeit in a poor cash position, he had removed himself as a factor in the rising outcry against "robber barons." That is, with his presence removed, the daily activities of Jay Darling would go unreported and unembroidered; his critics, if not silenced, had lost fuel for their critical juices. So he had taken the leisurely tour south, picked up the Senator—in every sense of that term, and now had him in thrall—and in the vacuum in financial circles caused by his own absence on the Street, he'd recouped his losses. The vultures, circling ever closer and closer to the center, watching for the prey below, for the main chance, had been unaware of watching eyes on them, eyes set to watch by the "robber baron" himself. Did they think he was a fool to leave his back uncovered?

Darling smiled. When everything had seemed so black, when he'd been losing heavily at the Casino, when the girl had turned into a mass of frights, he'd taken himself out of each situation with flair, turned to a new idea, and thereby broken the bank.

At the right time, in New York, he'd let the others expose themselves and he'd sold short. The news of it was everywhere by now and everyone knew who had done it and how he had done it. They just could not see how anyone could have skirted that close to total annihilation and made it out with a thousandfold more than he had going in.

To solve the problem of the girl he'd removed himself to Casino Island via the yacht with poor, unfortunate Helen aboard; Helen, who was so pleased that he'd noticed her, so sure that she was going to steal him away from the nubile Pamela. He'd watched Helen. He'd already known all he'd needed to know about Helen.

One night, as the yacht lay anchored at the Casino's dock, he invited Helen to his cabin. And she came, of course, dressed in her usual style for evening, as proper as a charity matron. He'd heard she liked it that way—to be undressed slowly, to beg for what he was going to give her. But when she arrived, he invited her to play chess. It was a long game, fraught with tension. Hers. He liked to watch her anxiety grow; he luxuriated in it. He did not allow even his hand to touch hers as they moved the pieces across the board.

She was an intelligent woman. He knew she could have beaten him at that game if she'd not been distracted. In the end, he won both contests, holding himself aloof, keeping the tension within him. She had been in tears when he left, so ripe for rutting that he suspected she had gone to the Senator's cabin within the quarter-hour.

But he, Jay Darling, had entered the Casino with renewed energy, and as he swept through, he had scored everywhere.

He was a winner. Helen was not.

Helen, like many losers, wanted the best, but if she could not have it, she would settle too easily for second-best in order to satisfy her overwhelming lust. That was how losers arranged their lives. The wrong priorities. If she'd put the acquisition of Jay Darling ahead of her own lust, if she'd played the game to win, perhaps she would have done so. She might have laughed with him at the end of the game and gone with him to the Casino and won there, taking everything right out from under his practiced hand. That would have given her what she wanted in every sense. He had known when he first saw her and heard about her peculiarities that this information could be useful and used against her to his own advantage.

He knew a winning streak when he felt it wash over him. New York, the Casino—on the basis of these wins, on the hint that a storm was coming in off the ocean, he'd returned to Sporting Isle and Pamela last night. That had been his best move. The girl had been ready.

He'd never seen her like that. She was first-class, unlike Helen. She knew where her duty lay. He'd entered the suite and she wasn't in the bed. He found her standing in the middle of the small turret, naked, trembling, the wind blowing everything about her—

When he walked into the room she turned toward him and smiled a very odd, almost enchanted smile. He thought she said "Dear—" He could barely see her face. Never looking away from her dark form, although he could not discern her features, he'd undressed, feeling her effect on him, beginning to tremble himself. He was glad he'd saved himself for this. He picked her up and put her on the divan under the windows and then, as he had done in recent circumstances, he'd withheld himself, although he could sense she was ready for him—for anyone perhaps—no, for him alone. She was as wanton as he'd ever seen a woman. He didn't question his luck. He never did. He let her happen to him. And she had performed as skillfully and lustily as the most experienced concubine.

Even the memory of it excited him. She was now ready for any-thing, would do anything, to please him—and thus please herself. Her body craved his now. He knew the time had finally come when she could be truly counted as his. She would never leave him and if he sent her away, she would aways dream of him, even in the midst of receiving another man.

More important than that; she seemed to have lost her fears. What man wants to ride a bundle of weeping nerves? Not only would she be no good for his own use, any future plans for her would be aborted. No powerful man wanted to have to soothe his way through a laying. Darling hated to see valuable property go to waste. He was glad she'd come around.

Next morning, he'd gone to her room again. The blackie was comb-ing the girl's hair. He'd watched them.

"I'm going away," he'd blurted. He saw the black's hands hesitate and then move smoothly on, brushing the long, tangled mass of hair.

Pamela had turned to look at him, but said nothing. He was sorry he'd revealed that much. It was uncharacteristic. He liked to keep his moves to himself.

To cover the slip, he said, "I had planned to go to France, but the weather has turned foul early. I may not. But I'll be away; possibly for some time—"

The hairdressing continued. No one spoke. The windows were closed and the room was somewhat stuffy. He waved to the maid to leave them. He wanted to talk to the girl alone.

After the door had shut, he went to her and stood behind her at the mirror. He put his hands on her shoulders. He felt her jump under his hands—anxious to have him, no doubt—and he began a slow massage of her neck, moving his hands over her. She belonged to him and she knew it.

"As long as I'm going away," he whispered, "perhaps you will please me one more time, as you did last night."

In the mirror, he saw her eyes, which had appeared sleepy and sensuous, fly open. Through the medium of the mirror she looked directly at him and then her eyes were hooded again. He turned her and lifted her to her feet, kissed her, moved his body close to the length of her, let her understand his need. He felt her lips soft under his. He caressed her. He moved again, coming to her, letting his flesh press into her clothing. He would have this moment—

THE ISLAND

CHAPTER XXIX

1

They rode in basket phaetons pulled by ponies and in barouches with emblems on the doors and in thin-wheeled traps pulled by fine chestnuts, out into the sunshine along the crushed white-shell paths to the far north end of the island. There, with a view in the distance of men at golf, under the live oak trees hung with Spanish moss, the servants had spread white sailcloth to protect the skirts of the women and to keep the red ants from joining the picnic.

The ladies were wearing hats to protect their complexions, although they were seated in the shade; they were wearing white dresses of soft material with string gloves for their hands, because they were in the South; they sat on small gilt chairs and did not stand or walk about except to show the cut of their dresses and the line of their figures. There were no children with them, although they spoke constantly about their children. There were mothers and daughters but both were adults. Servants moved among them, handing out sandwiches of precise geometric cut, in circles and squares and stars, sandwiches of foodstuffs that had been chopped, diced, mashed and spread, served with dainty cakes, with rich sweetmeats. Tea with ice. Tea with lemon. Lemonade.

The women talked of the weather and about the men on the course at play. They spoke of recipes that they had gathered and that they would not share; places they had traveled where recipes had been obtained. None of them were cooks. They talked of jewelry, of pearls especially, of carnelian, aquamarine and sapphires. All wore diamonds here or there.

They remembered the last time they had seen a certain important woman, the wife of an important man, wear a certain important parure. She had not worn it for some time. Did that mean that her husband had suffered losses? Might he lose his place in the social order? Did that mean her status would be altered as well? Who was she without his importance?

They spoke again of the weather and the ocean and how the ocean sounded at night and of the trees, which were old and large and strange-looking here, and they mentioned how odd nature seemed to be. They spoke often of the marked improvement in the class of servants as one travels to the North.

And the servants moved among them and brought them tea and cakes.

2

Margaret's feet twitched and she stood and walked about, going behind the gilt chairs to walk up and down. They thought she did this to display her figure and her clothing. Her mother was still in the North and wouldn't arrive for almost three weeks, just in time for Christmas. Margaret had been trying in every way to abide the conversation of these women from the hotel, but she'd been too long away from this sort of thing, too long in the company of women who spoke otherwise. Didn't they see this was almost 1893? No woman should count her status through her jewelry, her servants or her husband's place. They spoke of nature and children and servants, but they made it clear from their manner that they were determined to know nothing of these on a practical level.

I suppose I shall be like them directly, she thought, and she walked up and down, up and down.

She would have preferred to stay behind at the hotel, but there was the subtle domination of the staff. She'd been told by the manager that no one stayed at the hotel during these grand outings— unless one was ill.

Margaret toyed with the idea of illness and rejected it as being a fiction she would have to maintain. No, she wanted more vigorous activity, not less.

She should not have come. She paced up and down beneath the moss-hung trees. She should have not come.

The women around her now represented the conventional approach to life, an approach she was trying to circumvent. Yet she loved Steven. She missed him terribly. She would never be entirely happy in the world that didn't have Steven in it. But neither could she be like these women or her mother, taking the smooth course, never disturbing the surface, moving swiftly away. All about her were examples of women's acceptance of the name of marriage without the reality of it. She'd hoped for the opposite in her own life and each day she was horrified anew at the quiet convenience marriage was considered by the members of the Sporting Isle Club.

She reached this assessment without any knowledge of the true nature of Jay Darling's Playhouse.

And in the evenings, when the men joined them for dinner, she saw that men, too, wanted little from marriage except that such marriages exist—that life, through marriage, be "taken care of," that the domestic "business" be out of the way in order that one might "get on" in other aspects of life. Men, she noticed, did not tend their marriages or their wives. Marriage was a thing done, handled, then set aside.

Her father had been the same. He loved someone besides his wife. He had another life that did not cut across the course of his wife's existence—was not expected to—as if that were normal and right.

She wanted one life, one love—for Steven and herself.

But if her father, a good man, had done this awful wrenching thing, didn't every woman who loved a man, who allowed emotion to run deep into her marriage vows, let herself in for just such jeopardy? Wasn't it better then to be open about emotion, to declare love, watch it grow—and if it faltered to walk away?

I've done that and it should be right, but I don't gain anything from it. In order to save the way I feel about him, I've come here to think it all out and all I think about is how I feel about him—

And so she understood at last the most difficult part of it: She had no understanding of herself. She'd been as generous in Chicago as she knew how to be, with her time, her money, and finally, in the case of Steven, with herself. She had given in a charitable way and on every front her most private being had been turned away—rejected.

In the name of charity, the world had been uncharitable. The world would take what she offered, but would not accept her on her own terms. Steven had his own definition of love. Mrs. Bright had her own definition of charitable works and the women of the world were in no way ready for reform or the franchise. The human endeavors of Margaret Marsh had been turned aside.

At the core of it, Margaret was angry, but she was even further angered by her honest realization that she was muddle-headed, she who thought of herself as intelligent and educated and wise, could not divine her own place in the world and had faltered at every opportunity to take a stand. She saw herself as false as her father and as weak-willed as her mother. Hadn't she left without a word?

I should not have come. I should not have come.

In Chicago, the similarity of her own flight to her mother's had not occurred to her as she boarded the train. It had seemed the next logical step to take. But here, faced by the implacable matrons of Sporting Isle, she lost faith in everything, remained silent, couldn't fight on any front, felt she was composed entirely of surfaces. She was being nibbled away by littleness.

She played croquet.

The conversation of the women about her was so superficial, so light, she could let it pass across her mind like drifting mist. She answered direct questions, let the voices become a hum, while she walked up and down under the trees. Even that had earned her the reputation of being the "almost odd" Miss Marsh.

3

On the third week she was rescued. It rained. The rain each day was of short duration, coming first in late mornings, saturating the ground, making it uncomfortable for the excursions planned.

Margaret wandered through the corridors of the hotel and found the library. This room, off the main lobby, was round, a small two-story tower with no separate floors in it, only bookshelves that must be reached by ladder and a special hook. Books lined it part of the way and above that was a fine skylight. Only there were no readers.

No one came to the place except Margaret and the librarian, old Mr. Peabody, who shuffled about from place to place in the room, humming to himself. His job, as far as Margaret could see, seemed to be to deliver light reading to the suites of guests who requested it, and to see that the books were eventually returned before the guests went north again.

Margaret spent several days with Mr. Peabody and in the course of their conversations learned he was a native of the region and had lived in a small house back in the woods for thirty or forty years, long before the Clubhouse and the large private cottages had been dreamed of.

"I'm a squatter," he said, "and I begged them for a job, so this is it—it's not so bad really. I get to read a lot, which I like to do, and they'll order most any book—"

He showed her a special shelf—several of them—in which there were books about nature, about the world and science, much different from the novels and inaccurate travel books that the guests were so fond of reading.

"You might enjoy these," he said, somewhat reluctantly she noticed, and she could tell he loved them and was afraid she might lose them somewhere.

In conversations that spread over several days, she learned from Mr. Peabody that the island was larger than she'd thought. He said there were many interior paths and rough roads, all of them shortcuts to here and there, some of them direct routes to the sea. He said there were many buildings she couldn't see from the outer path that circled the shore—Shoreline Drive—a laundry; a tool house and a mechanic's shop; a garden and brickyard, that electricity was generated on the island itself and there was an artesian well and a tinshop. He went on and on.

"Then it's like a village," she said.

"No, it's more like a large plantation with its various dependencies. There is no independent living here. No villagers are allowed. Everything is done for the Clubhouse—or the Playhouse, which is just beyond the trees. You can't see it from here. The only cottages—officially—are the large homes of members who don't wish to stay at the hotel. But nonmembers may not live on this island. That's the rule, but—"

"But—"

"Oh," he shrugged, "I guess I can tell you. The others must know anyway—" He stopped and began again. "There are others like myself. We have washed up on this shore and we cling here. We're not official, mind you. But we have our places, back in the trees. Nobody notices. Officially, that is. We just sort of appear during the day and the fiction is maintained that we 'disappear' at twilight—"

Her friendship with Mr. Peabody restored her somewhat. She looked forward to other mornings and, unlike other guests, did not complain about the change in the weather.

One day she was helping him rearrange some shelves when they came across a large notebook with many loose pages, musty and falling apart in the damp.

"You might enjoy this," he said, taking it down. "Somebody started it, years ago, I guess, when the Clubhouse was in its first season. And then nothing further was done. I'm too old to tramp through the woods and over the sands—"

He showed her sketches of sea birds, of shells and grasses.

"Someone was making a nature notebook about the island—"

She took the pages and leafed through them. "This reminds me of work I did in college—"

When he realized she was a trained observer, he became excited. "Maybe you'd like to continue this work? You'd have to go out early in the mornings. Wouldn't have time for socializing." He twinkled at her.

And so she was excused from the Sporting Isle female conventions. Her "oddness" was explained. She was a *naturalist*. She could be as different as she wished as long as it was within the framework of some ladylike official role.

Margaret brought out her cycling clothes and her high boots.

Mrs. Chesterton, accompanied by her husband and daughters, met Margaret in the hotel dining room and learned of the new project. She looked Margaret up and down and sent one of the hotel servants to the Chesterton cottage with a note. The servant returned with a pith helmet that Mr. Chesterton had used in Egypt years before.

"You must protect your complexion," Mrs. Chesterton said. "Girls as fair as you can get a nasty burn, even on the cloudiest days. You must protect your face—"

And so the pith helmet was added to the cycling clothes and boots for a grand effect. Mrs. Chesterton returned to her own cottage with an air of having made all the difference and indeed, she believed she had. Foolish young girls, traveling without their mothers, needed tending, even if they were the haughty Miss Marsh.

And to her daughters, Mrs. Chesterton confided, "I saw no sign of engagement and there was not a word said. That means the Baxter boy got away, my dears. I think we can safely restore him to our lists. His fortune is immense. And if one of you should let him catch you—" here she winked "—you could set up your principal residence in New York and not have to see his mother with any regularity—"

One of the men at the hotel presented Margaret with a sharp stick, sharpened at both ends to be used on her rambles.

"I made it for you myself," he said modestly. "If you find an alligator, just put this into his mouth when he yawns and you'll be perfectly safe. He'll not be able to get free of it and so won't be able to eat you—"

Margaret wanted to laugh, but did not. She put the stick in her pack and thanked the gentleman profusely. She did not, she said, want to be eaten alive.

And so next morning she went out, dressed like a traveler to distant places, clutching her goods and her notebook, to head for the shore.

4

"*Nora, did you* see? There was a girl—a woman walking along the road through the meadow. Did you see her? She was on the same path you take through the woods. Did you meet her on the way? Did she see you? Did you talk to her? Was she an ordinary girl, not like—?"

"I seen her, Miss Pammie. She was walking along, just like you, just like a goddess, her head up and a smile and she walked and looked at us pass and she said to us 'Good mawnin'' like that she say, 'Good mawnin'' and went on into the woods and up over the rise toward the sea, walking along, carryin' her hat—pretty lady, hair oh so pretty—color of strawberries—"

"I thought—I thought, well, maybe she wasn't there. That I was seeing things. That she was like the spider—or something in the mist. She went on down the path and then the deer—the deer were here again—they are real, aren't they—I know they are—they must be—"

"Don't worry, Miss Pammie. Nora's here wit' you. I'm here. Everything is all right. Everything is real as daybreak."

"Sometimes I don't know, Nora. Sometimes things seem to float away on the edges. I'm glad I have you, Nora. Then I know everything is all right—"

"Is he still gone away, Miss Pammie?"

"Yes. Yes, he's gone. I think so. He hasn't come—I'm glad the girl is real. I'm glad I really saw her. I'm glad you're here with me— I don't know why I think such odd thoughts when I'm alone. Do you think that girl down there feels alone when she walks along the path—does she have thoughts like mine? No. Nobody does. I suppose she's not like that, is she, Nora?"

CHAPTER XXX

1

Nothing had meaning.

Steven gave up his work at the university. Arthur tried to interest him in the club life, but Steven had settled in and seemed more like his mother every day.

Arthur knew about Margaret's flight. That is, he thought he knew about it to the extent that Steven did. He knew she'd gone off without a word to stay on that island off the eastern coast and he knew that Steven was somehow different than he had been and close to illness. The similarities between Mrs. Baxter and Steven seemed to become sharper and clearer every day even to Arthur's inexpert observations. Arthur sat down at the desk in the library and wrote to Fanny and then wrote a letter to his betrothed, Harriet, who was traveling with her family in Europe for this last year before her marriage. In both letters, he expressed his worry about Steven's attitude, about Steven's new reclusive habits and the way he looked when he turned his head a certain way—like a male version of Mama Delight interrupted during her evening prayer hour.

"One girl and he goes all to pieces," Arthur wrote to Fanny. "Isn't it just like that type—to fall once and hard and then the rest of us can do nothing for them. They just suffer and suffer. What shall I do? I'm going to have two hermits on my hands—"

Two days later Fanny wired back, "Have a party—"

So Arthur planned a party over the objections of both mother and brother. Arthur had no trouble planning. He just told the butler, who told the cook. Arthur ordered the flowers and favors himself. After that he gave the invitation list to Mama Delight and saw to it that she wrote them out in her own hand. He felt this was good medicine for her. She must be brought out of herself as much as Steven should.

Steven protested when he heard the news. He said he would stay in his room.

"No, you won't," Arthur said. "Fanny wants the servants to have lots of experience before she comes to the fair next spring. She wired and told me so—"

The two reluctant partygoers, host and hostess, went through the motions of a happy winter social in Chicago. The party was a great success. Everyone in Chicago society likes to have a place to go in winter.

"Isn't this fine?" asked Arthur, looking over the company.

"Where is Steven?" he asked his mother. She, of course, knew.

"He's in the orangery."

"With a girl?"

"No. He's talking to that Mr. Davis. A very nice young man. He came to us once before. When that Chesterton family was here—"

"Ah," said Arthur and gave an arm each to two young debutantes. He remembered Myron Davis very well and what he remembered was the young man's reputation with the ladies. A man of that sort was just the one to bring Steven out of himself. Arthur escorted the two damsels out to the orangery to his brother and his friend. After introductions all around and a discreet interval, Arthur, the excellent host, faded from the scene.

Some time during the evening, in spite of the light conversation carried on with the young women who'd been left in their care, Myron and Steven managed to learn of their shared interest in the South and one island specifically.

"Do you remember that island we spoke of one night at dinner here?" Myron asked Steven. "I can't seem to find it on any map. Where exactly is Sporting Isle? And is that club totally private or may members of other clubs—"

The next night at dinner, while Arthur and Mama Delight were running through a postmortem on the party, Steven sat silent and brooding. Suddenly he said, "I think I'd like to go off and spend some time in a warmer climate just now. I feel terribly off, you know. You might have noticed it. As if I need sun. I could have the parlor car sent over, and go off to look for a bit of scenery. Or maybe I'll take up golf—"

"You? On the links?" Arthur almost swallowed his tongue.

"Why not? It looks easy enough. You just thwack that little white ball and count to 100. I've watched you—"

"Try 150," said Arthur drily. He was still a duffer himself.

"Winter is such a sad time to spend alone in Chicago," said Mama Delight. She waited for Steven to say he'd forgotten she would have only Arthur for company, but he did not. So she said, "I suppose I could close the house and Artie and I could go."

"You mean dismiss the servants, again?" asked Steven.

"Oh, that doesn't matter. This house is so drafty in winter. And besides, I believe my new maid is Roman Catholic. She doesn't know a thing about chapter and verse when I quote to her. Not even common verses. I suspected—"

"You'd be better off here." Steven's voice was sharp.

Then he began: "Myron says he'd like to try golf, too. We both might take it up. Sounds health-promoting. You get all that fresh air walking on the links. I've been tired lately. Outdoor activities do one the world of good. That's my trouble. I'm inside too much during this bad weather. You're always telling me that, Artie. Maybe I could take up membership in a club or two. Learn the right way. I'll use your equipment. Or I'll buy some—"

Steven seemed to be talking to his water glass as if he could not stop.

"Do you know what I think?" asked his mother. "I think you need a masseuse—" She excused herself and left the room. She was not quite as silly as they thought her. She went right to the telephone and ordered someone to come in tomorrow. Steven had every sign of a lovesick youth, even if he was twenty-five. There was nothing for it but to pummel it out of him and the sooner the better. She was not going to have him go off just when she'd got him home again.

Steven endured the pummeling. Nothing was endurable and so everything became so. He had lost the power to object. His only plans became *to go south.* Soon. Somehow. Whether he would be welcome or not, he did not know. But these last months had been terrible. He was going to have to settle this. He had to see her. Why had she gone? Their breach had not been that terrible. Yes, it had.

"More," he muttered to the masseuse, determined to rid his body of its passions, its evil desire for Margaret's body.

And if I go to her, he thought, *what can I say? I am as aimless as Arthur. I do nothing. I read. I think. I remember her. But I'm almost twenty-*

five years old and I don't know what I want to do with my life. I only know I want to be with Margaret.

"Ohhhh," he groaned.

"Yas," said the handler. "Yaas, dat's right."

After five days of daily massage, two nights of enforced partying with Arthur and a series of prayer sessions with his mother, Steven agreed to put off his trip until some later time. Since that time better dovetailed with Myron's requirements, Steven felt there was a certain reasonableness to everyone's advice.

"Well, I guess I can wait another month," Steven said.

Mama Delight thought, *when the time comes, I'll coax him into waiting until April—*

Myron Davis, working to finish his duties to his family once and for all before he resigned from the family firm, thought: *I hope I'll be able to get everything in order by May—*

And Arthur thought, *If Steven is ever going to get out of here, I'm going to have to arrange everything—*

2

The island, before it was discovered by the millionaires from New York, Cincinnati and Chicago, Louisville, Minneapolis and Des Moines, Toledo, Akron and Detroit, had always existed. First it might have been only rock rising from the sea, but the action of the waves, aeons ago, had brought sand up around the rocks, building land to the north of the outcropping until the land became large enough for habitation by plants and animals, which in their annual seasons, died and formed humus, building up the land mass still further, aeons and aeons ago.

Centuries later it had assumed a leaf shape, pointed at its northern tip, wide at the middle and falling away again where the original ancient rocks trailed out, stemlike, into the sea at the south. On the ocean side were beaches, flat and white; after high tide these beaches were as easy to read as the school slate of a child.

In her search for flora and fauna, Margaret started at the northern end, working methodically day after day. On her return to the hotel she would share her discoveries with Mr. Peabody, the librarian. She learned not to bring in findings, unless they were small shells—and even those she was leery of after a hermit crab inched its way out of a small conch she'd supposed abandoned.

Mr. Peabody didn't want artifacts. He had his books, which were more real to him than reality, and he feared some mold or lichen would migrate in the humid air to his bookshelves. He was content with Margaret's sketches and notes, with chaste samples of pressed wildflowers and written paragraphs and diagrams concerning plants.

Margaret was learning that to observe what she wanted to see she must redevelop a trait that was her least favored. Waiting.

Always she had derided waiting as an assumed trait of women, had seen it as an artificial meekness foisted on the female by men. During the time she and her mother had traveled, they had noticed and often remarked that all over the world there seemed to be women waiting; on verandahs, on terraces, in drawing rooms and ballrooms, in parlors and harems, women sat waiting for men to come to them. Was this a natural condition? Margaret had once thought not. She'd been annoyed that men had a life of their own, separate from their lives with women. Men's time was thought too important; men should not wait. And women—they were called ladies-in-waiting, mothers-to-be, women-in-confinement. Always, Margaret had disliked and decried such terms.

But as she sat in the hidden groves of Sporting Isle and let nature reveal itself, she witnessed in all about her this waiting game. The hen sat on the nest; the male was in the bush or had flown away, searching for food.

Margaret waited, too, learning patience, intent in her watchfulness.

In the silence of her new occupation, Margaret began to hear sounds that she might not have noticed before: the call and answer of various bird pairs, the mysterious rustle of the brush as something moved beyond her sight, the sound of the sea at various tides. Some tide within her answered. A feeling of unknown, ungovernable rhythms rose in her, frightening her. She thought she might be pregnant and then learned almost immediately that she was not. The sight of her menstrual flow one morning filled her with a deep sense of regret. A child would have allowed her a direction, forced her to run back to Steven with the excuse that they must meet the child's needs. She'd not known until that moment how completely she'd been won.

I seem to have either no passion or the wrong one, she thought.

The days by the sea passed slowly. She had enough to do to hold on to her hat and her sketch pad and still retain the fiction that she was part of the landscape. She'd never felt so alone and uncertain in her life.

Margaret Marsh at last recognized who she was—the woman she had always been, no matter how she'd preached against it. She was truly, actually, what she'd dreaded most. She saw that she was the kind of woman Ned the Worker had railed against—by wealth and precept, by culture and association, she was, always, a rich, idle, passive woman, who didn't even have open to her the redeeming skills of a middle-class housewife or a gainfully employed old maid. Her former knowing posture, her prattling on equality, must have looked foolish to the workers of the world; those who *knew*.

Margaret finally turned from her inner struggles to the day-to-day business of the small bit of work she was doing for Mr. Peabody. She'd do the best she could with it. She focused on that, allowing herself to think no longer, living each of the days one at a time. The future was ephemeral. A fiction. She would not think of it anymore.

3

One of the more important things she had to learn, Margaret told Mr. Peabody, laughing, was when to come in out of the rain. The rains on the island were deceiving. They could be as soft as a caress, perfect for the complexion, blissful after heat. But they could turn in a moment, riding on some fierce bit of wind, throwing seawater into her face although she was far from shore. The lightning and thunder were whiter and louder than any she'd experienced before, even more fierce than the Lake Michigan storms. And several times, after she'd been drenched to the skin, she'd been severely chilled. She decided storms on an island were wetter than any others. After her third drenching, Mr. Peabody had shown her the way to his cabin. He called it a hut, deep in a stand of pine.

"Use this in case of rain, or if you're very tired," he said with the same reluctance he'd revealed when showing her the special library books.

The interior was spare—a table, one chair, an old cot covered with a white woven coverlet, tucked in all around. There was an iron stove in the corner, a neat stack of wood and some sort of dried flower on the table in a dark brown vase. There was one dish, one cup, a candle, but no lamp. Clearly, Mr. Peabody did not expect or enjoy visitors.

Margaret was touched.

"It's all right," he said, but she could tell this gesture was difficult for him.

She looked around. It was one way to live. Block out others, take on the hermit's existence. Hold life to yourself and not let anyone else in.

"The door is always unlocked," he said. "Nobody ever comes here. I stay at the hotel when it rains. You'll be perfectly safe."

4

Her mother had arrived at Christmas and promptly brought out all the French lotions and crèmes she customarily traveled with under the tropical sun.

"You look dreadful," she told Margaret cheerfully. She was determined to remain cheerful about her daughter.

Mrs. Marsh produced gloves and a hat that tied on with a large veil. Margaret thanked her, just as she had Mr. Peabody, and put the gloves in her knapsack and left the hat on the bed, preferring Mr. Chesterton's pith helmet.

The work Margaret was doing was not difficult; she was not trying to discover some new species, but only to record what she found in her rambles.

The birds and wildlife could be identified from their types. Mr. Peabody knew, from her sketches, most of those that Margaret didn't. She was excited by her observations of nests.

Shore birds—many of them—seemed too comfortable nesting on sand amid rocks and scrub growth. Evidently they didn't fear predators. Their confidence, Margaret discovered, was misplaced. Birds on the wing stole eggs from the sand, eggs disguised only by being laid among small stones. The flying birds then dropped their catch on the large rocks by the sea and ate the embryos inside. She'd never seen such maneuvers before. It seemed clever and beyond the intelligence of birds. She didn't exactly object to what was happening. This was a natural phenomenon. Such a scene, Margaret thought, was primeval and had been played out long before she'd come upon it.

But one morning very early she was waiting below the rim of a sand dune with the body of sand between her and the sea. On the other side was a wide nesting ground—probably the nest of several birds—and she was waiting to find out which birds claimed it. Suddenly she heard the voices of children. They came over the top of the sand from the southern end of the island. Where Margaret lay hidden, she couldn't be seen by them.

The children, children of color, Margaret noticed, were tapping the eggs, trying them for freshness. The little girl had an old straw hat and the two were loading it with eggs to carry away with them, chattering as they worked.

Margaret stood up, her red hair wild in the wind. She was high above them as she stood on the sand, looking down into the nesting site as if into a large bowl.

"What are you doing?" she called.

"What? What do you say to us, lady," they called back. She could hear them because they were standing with the wind at their backs.

She cupped her hands. "Don't take the eggs," she shouted. "Those will be new little birds—"

"Have to," shouted back the boy of the pair. "Got to eat 'em—"

"Yassum," shouted the girl. "He right. Our granny she say we gotta git eggs today for sure—"

"Where is your granny?" asked Margaret, coming closer to them, shouting still through the trumpet of her hands.

"She at home—"

"Tell her—" the wind "—not to eat those eggs."

"Got to. Ain't no other," shouted the boy and the two went on with their gathering as if she were invisible and silent.

She looked for a way to reach them. The way toward the rocks was wet and dangerous; sea water broke against their base with great force. Over the top of the sand and through the nesting grounds was unthinkable. To the west were trees and bramble, an impassable wood.

The boy seemed to be watching her and at last he ran back the way they'd come, off to the southwest, and suddenly reappeared at Margaret's side as if the trees had presented him to her.

He held out his hand, as if she were the child and he the adult, palm downward. "Come," he said. "You come and we'll all go wit' de eggs to see our granny. She ain't *neber* seen you before—"

Margaret looked at him, a boy about nine or ten, the little girl younger still. Margaret took his hand. She would trust him and maybe she would see a new part of the island.

With the sureness of one who has often taken a certain way, the child led her through the tangle into more open woods and then finally into a meadow not unlike the one near the Playhouse.

Margaret said, "Who are you? Is that your sister? I've never seen anyone during the time I—"

She stopped.

He had thrown a look at her that was difficult to decipher. The boy stopped walking and looked levelly at her. He put his hands on his hips and faced her directly.

"This here's where I lib. I been here and been here. And I neber seen you before either. Where you lib? Not here. Whyn't you say your name. *Den* I say mine—"

"I'm Margaret. I come to watch birds along the shore. I want to learn their names and listen to the sounds they make and see how they nest. But I can't do that if you eat up all their eggs—" Even to her own ears this sounded patronizing and she wished she'd not said it.

"My name is Mars," the boy said. "That's my sister, Tyrah. We can't talk nothing like birds. We eat birds. And aigs. And Granny says it's all right. Birds is put into the air by the Lord for us'ns to eat. We got to do what Granny says. Our maw, she say that—"

"Who is your mother?"

The little girl, Tyrah, came up to them in time to hear the question. "Our mamma Nora. She workin'. Granny has keer o' us."

"Where's your daddy?"

"Workin'. In de mill ober to the big island—"

Margaret decided they must mean the sawmill on the mainland.

The children began to walk across the meadow in a southwesterly direction toward an area Margaret had not explored. When she did not immediately follow them, they turned and waved and shouted to her, "C'mon."

Moving swiftly they came to the outer edge of the grassy stretch in a short time. The edge of the grassland was higher than the beach and rocks below. From this point Margaret could see in many directions. She hesitated. She wanted to gather in this sight.

She and the children were standing where the island reached its southernmost point; where the shoreline began to move north again along the inland side. The land above the beach sloped and then rose again and in the niche of land made by this strange terrain, there was a hollow formed by two small hills. Within the hollow were some trees and she could just see the top of a house—a house like Mr. Peabody's hut—standing among them.

"C'mon," shouted Mars, and taking the eggs from his sister, he ran on ahead. The little girl shyly reached for Margaret's hand and led her, all the while staring with large brown eyes at Margaret.

They walked along hand in hand, smiling at each other, playing a kind of flirtation game, until the beach turned and in a place where it expanded and became wide and flat, Tyrah led Margaret back toward the east. Now the house in the trees was fully visible, but to Margaret's surprise, not just one house, but several stood along a central way. Some of the houses sat in fenced yards and others had only sand right to the door. Each house was sitting high above the ground on brick or stone pilings, just as Mr. Peabody's hut was made. Tyrah brought Margaret into the yard of one hut where a cookfire was burning over some rocks. There was a spit over the fire and an old woman, brown and small and wrinkled, her white hair tied up into a fanciful scarf, was tending a pot hung over the fire.

"See what we found," said Tyrah, producing Margaret with a flourish, as if she were some creature from the forest. Margaret looked around her. Then, seeing Mars standing in the doorway of the shack, she realized why he had run on ahead.

Tyrah said, "That's not fair. Mars done told it all—"

Margaret, feeling something was called for, stepped forward and held out her hand to introduce herself. "I'm Margaret Marsh—"

"And I'm their granny," said the old woman, waving her spoon like a queen's scepter. "And eggs be eggs."

5

Many years later, when she was on the verge of growing old, Margaret Marsh would say that this was the day her true education began. Before that time her mind had been full of facts and opinions. After she met Granny and Mars and Tyrah, and subsequently Nora and Ephraim, all previous knowledge she had acquired spun and tilted and took on new meaning. It was as if she had walked through the earlier part of her life asleep to most of what she saw around her. What she'd learned before was useful and true—it was just not adequate to an understanding of the world.

The first problem she faced on that great day was her acceptability to the community called "Little Village." Little Village was technically not there, since official maps showed only the Clubhouse and the Playhouse and the large private cottages.

But the cabins on this ground had been here much longer than the Sporting Isle Club had been in existence. The residents were "old" residents, the *establishment* of their region. They were people of color who valued themselves and kept apart. They had no need of a red-haired socialite from one of the "big places" coming down to look them over, to play Lady Bountiful or Miss Priss.

The last title was the way Mars phrased it. Margaret had asked him if she could come to church at Little Village on the following Sunday.

"Yas," he answered, a ten-year-old sage, "if you ain't gawn to stan' there and look aroun' lak some Miss Priss—"

"Who called me that?"

He rolled his eyes heavenward. "Oh, they ain't no tellin'."

She didn't press for an answer, but came to the church and stood in the back, singing with the rest. This—and her quiet demeanor—seemed to mollify her unknown critics, whoever they might have been. She spent time with the children and was accepted as their friend, their odd adult "playmate." Only now and then, when she recognized some black face among the workers at the hotel and smiled, was she given that strange fawning treatment that she knew to be false, and that she was not accorded at Little Village.

Oh, she made mistakes. She tried to rush things. She saw at once how poor they were and saw what they most lacked. She had a barrel of sugar delivered to Granny's door. Granny thanked Margaret pleasantly enough, but it wasn't long after that Margaret overheard Granny complaining and explaining away this largess to her neighbors, giving out great donations of it. Margaret privately had hoped Granny would use what she needed for the children.

She said something to Granny, who answered sourly, "Held too long, gets ants."

But Mars and Tyrah explained that the barrel was too big, too important. It made the neighbors "look green." It attracted much too much attention. By giving it away, Granny spread the danger of it to others. There was a danger in having too much in a place like Little Village. It upset the balance of things.

"Besides," Mars said, looking at Margaret with one of his looks, "did ya give it or didn' ya? If ya give it, then we kin, too—"

And just when Margaret had begun to feel at home and part of the place and to look forward to her days there, with the feeling that she was friendly to all, she would make another mistake. There was the time of the big celebration. The shrimp were running and they were going to have a shrimp boil and Margaret was very pleased to be invited. So she insisted on "bringing something" to the feast. They said they would be proud to have her come and she could bring what she wanted.

The dining room at the Clubhouse was known for its breads and pastries. Margaret put in an advance order of ten basketfuls. She told the chef she would need them sent out and she would tell him where on the night of the party. That night, at Little Village, there was great amusement.

The "gift" of the red-haired lady meant that the baker, a woman of the village, had almost missed the beach party because some hotel guest wanted "basketfuls" of rolls and little cakes for a party she was attending somewhere on the island.

The *party* from the hotel—Margaret—sat far back from the fire, but still her face was very red. She'd done it again and she was mortified.

From this she learned that she was among men and women who made things run, who somehow "got by." Never having had to learn to make or "do," Margaret was amazed at the skills and aspirations of people caught, it seemed to her, in a hard and difficult life.

But she didn't fall into the trap of looking at her new friends as "innocents" and "friends of the sea." She learned early and soon that they had their own society, as rigid as the one she came from, with its own standards, which might not be broken. And sometimes those standards seemed to her as foolish as those on the Clubhouse verandah.

Humans, she thought, seem determined to make life difficult for themselves, inventing little paths that must be followed when there is a large expanse of uncharted territory. This seemed to be true enough in physical arrangements and in human relationships.

This was brought home to her in the question of the stones. She'd seen that there was a definite status to having a picket fence around the sand yard that surrounded each house. Those that wanted a fence, but might never have it, yet were anxious to make their mark, made an outline of a fence with white stones culled from the beach.

One day Margaret and Mars were walking toward the woods when another boy ran toward them, jumping over the stone line-up along his family's property. His mother called him back to make him go around "the right way" through the "gate." After Margaret thought a while about it, this seemed no more strange to her than having a butler pour tea for twenty healthy women at the edge of a golf course.

Aided by Tyrah and Mars, Margaret was shown things she'd overlooked in her earlier nature rambles and she learned there were zones or habitats that could be counted on to yield pockets of animals or birds or reptiles. Her notes took on new life.

And because she looked at the island habitat with an analytical eye, she found herself carrying this over to her new experiences in Little Village, becoming aware for the first time in her life what community life truly meant.

In Little Village, she discovered, there was not the luxury of "women's work" or "men's business." Women did what they could and in many cases earned money. Men did what they could—and worked in mills and as waiters or cooks, in addition to making their own gardens and fishing for what the sea would provide. One of their own taught in the school. Margaret, who'd thought to offer the children that, could not even make this contribution.

Nothing cried out for her hand.

But that love ran deep through Little Village could be seen in Granny's touch, in the love Margaret saw expressed between Ephraim and Nora, in the way each of the village tended their own, held to it, because this place and those in it were what made them who they were.

Margaret's mother, who had been the one to suggest the barrel of sugar, could understand her daughter's forays into the village as a "lady doing good." That Margaret did no good there, that she was only watching and learning how to live as one among many, could not be understood by Mrs. Marsh. Margaret, after a few futile attempts to explain what was happening to her mind and heart, did not try to bring too bright a light onto it. Let her mother think that a Marsh was superior and generous if it suited the pattern of behavior that had been familiar and acceptable. Again, as with Mr. Chesterton's pith helmet, Margaret clutched at the style in order to have the freedom to go and come as she pleased.

Margaret discovered in her wanderings that the question of food— even the barrel of sugar—had different social meanings in different places. It wasn't only the "natural" idea of which animal or bird ate what. She'd been amazed at the ferociousness of birds as they attacked embryos from broken eggs.

Sentiment, she decided, must be human and should not be confused with survival or love.

Men and women, she saw, ate almost everything. Stewed, pureed, fried or raw. As long as it was not poisonous, it would turn up in the cooking pot. And the greatest surprise to Margaret was that those most willing to eat things raw seemed to be the wealthy visitors to the Clubhouse, rather than the villagers on the beach, who liked their fish done to a turn in one way or another.

There was no species the villagers could afford to set aside from their diet. They needed everything the land and sea and air provided. But there were not many in the village—less than a hundred—and their impact on the elements and world around them was slight and ran to "seasons."

In her inadvertent study of food, Margaret turned up the fact that, even though Granny never lied, eggs were not really eggs every time. Granny had what she called her "reservations" and sometimes she didn't always "lay those reservations out."

The reservation on eggs was plover eggs. Those Granny set aside to sell.

"Rich folk lik to eat 'em," Granny said, eyeing Margaret.

"I never ate a plover egg in my life," said Margaret, feeling she should defend something, since her great oblique sin was "richness." "And I've never seen them on the Clubhouse menu."

"Not there. That other place. The one by the sea."

"Oh, you mean the Playhouse. But I never see anyone there. I thought it was just tennis courts and a pool. Mr. Jay Darling lives there sometimes. I've never seen anyone else. I think the men go over there late at night to play cards and things—"

Granny rolled her eyes. "Turrible," she said. "Evil doings in that place. Things goes on there—"

"Who told you that? Eating plover's eggs isn't very nice, but it isn't evil, it's just—"

"I don' mean eggs. Nora says—" Granny didn't complete that sentence. "Turrible, turrible. Rich folks can be turrible—"

And she smiled a benediction at Margaret and patted her hand. "I don' mean you, honey. They's *rich* and then they's *rich*. And you the one kind and they the other."

CHAPTER XXXI

Certain personalities, so villainous to others, seem reasonable and appropriate to themselves. Villains rarely try to justify their lives. They see no need for it.

Jay Darling thought of himself as free of personal entanglements and hypocrisy, an honest man, neat in his habits, impeccable in taste, not given to emotional displays, clever in the best sense, too intelligent for most others and loyal to any cause or person he found appealing.

That he sometimes changed his mind quickly about who or what he would champion did not conflict in his mind with his idea of loyalty. When he was loyal, he was loyal. When he changed his mind, from that time on, he was loyal to another. He was not a weak man, shilly-shallying between one decision or another. He believed his life was a straight line toward goals only he had the vision to see.

He knew others envied him, admired his judgment and astuteness in business, his taste in women and horses—and wine. Therefore, he must be a superior man or there would have been no envy. His wealth he believed he had earned and if there was a deity somewhere, then that deity rightly recognized Jay B. Darling as a superior man, deserving of wealth.

But forty is the time that the upward curve of luck can begin to change. Those who have been reaping far beyond their own talents and rights, sometimes find that barrier the magic line: Forty means trouble because they must be quicker than they were. There is no surprise left in what they do. Not to those with whom they deal— and not to the man himself. They are known. The adversary begins to take more care when they are near; their quickest ways to glory are now watched. Forty becomes the time of vulnerability.

Jay Darling had made a terrible mistake.

He knew men, but women he'd chosen for his own short dalliances had been young and inexperienced, women he could easily dominate. They might be witty and bright, but he never chose one with a brooding intelligence. That wouldn't have been his kind of girl.

Except once. He had taken Helen on the yacht to Casino Island. Helen: an intelligent girl who forgot nothing done to her, who did not consummate the transaction she thought she was making with Mr. Jay Darling. He had laughed at her and left her full of lust to go to the gaming tables. Helen had thrown herself steamily into the arms of the Senator and there she had stayed.

The subsequent copulation of the Senator and Helen had been full of fervor. They had found their match in each other. They were a team brought together by a satyr. And Helen had ideas...

The Senator was—limited. Jay Darling could have turned him even if the Senator had been smarter, but the Senator was already corrupt, easy to pluck. Many a knotty problem had been solved by his turning for Jay Darling, not the least of which was advance information on various aspects of political and fiduciary activity in the nation's government.

Helen saw things differently.

She saw her Senator as President with herself at his side. He was a married man, but look at the French kings. And *she* would keep her head. And his as well.

They were in bed, eating pears and cheese. She said he might trim his whiskers another way—something more distinctive, like a man in a cigar ad—a little more presidential.

"I could do that," he said.

Helen was reading a New York paper. She had to do something while they lay in bed. They'd already expended their sexual energy for a time.

Helen shook the paper at him. "The word right now seems to be 'reform.' Look here, it's on this page three or four times. Everyone is looking for some relief from bad times. We need to have good news. The man who provides good news, who 'gets' the trusts and the cabals—that man will appeal to voters and bosses in the big parties—"

She turned and smiled at him. They had been heatedly mating not ten minutes before. He'd been away and she was glad he was here with her and now they had several days for amusement.

"I think," Helen said, "you could be that man—"

"Reform?" asked the Senator. "What do I know about that—?"

Helen whispered, "Jay Darling."

"Oh. Yes," said the Senator, not quite clear on it yet.

"You know a great deal about Jay Darling. You and he have done business together. Why don't you tell me what you know and we can work out some plan—"

But the Senator wasn't putting himself that completely into Helen's grasp. "Why don't you tell me what you have in mind. And then I can chart some course of action—"

"Well, you have influence. Commissions can be appointed. Investigations launched. International inquiries are often enough in themselves—without even the necessity of some resolution. There is always—" her voice became hushed "—*publicity*."

She explained to him exactly what she meant, how he should move slowly, gathering his friends in Congress around him, dropping a hint here and a partial fact there, building the case against Darling in such a way that no finger would point back at the Senator himself. She suggested that he keep his fortune separate from Darling's. "It already is," the Senator told her. "We're more discreet than that." And that dinner parties be held by the Senator's wife, dinner parties to be used to join the faithful together to slaughter their sacrificial lamb, Jay Darling. None of the wives liked him much. Any hint that Darling's world was crumbling would allow the wives of all those important men to begin talking and everyone, Helen said, knew where things led when the wives began talking. There'd be an investigation of Darling in a minute, once the wives of Washington made up *their* minds.

The Senator nodded and schemed with her. He would like to be the head of the country, have his profile on some coin, be able to speak to crowds on his front lawn and see his words emblazoned in the press next day. He thought he was just the sort for it. History books. He smiled and gazed off into the distance and Helen knew the matter was settled.

2

Even through the fog of "magic powders" Pamela could tell she was being watched. And Cleveland was always on hand, helpful, willing to provide Pamela with yet another handful of those precious folded papers. Every time Pamela looked toward Cleveland, Cleveland was looking at her with solemn, gentle eyes.

There was ease in the numbness Pamela was beginning to feel. Parts of her, at times, seemed to disappear. That is, she could see her fingers and toes, but at times she could not feel them.

She had never lived in a place with so much light. The spring was approaching now in the South. She realized that Chicago and New York were dark places compared to this island with its sun and ocean and white sand and night lightning. Everything seemed to reflect light, even the white curtains of her bedroom shone with an unnatural brightness. Morning came early here and the light was cruel to the senses. She felt thirsty. She could never get enough cold water. Perhaps it was the heat.

"Drink wine," Cleveland advised.

"I never liked it," Pamela confessed, "it makes me bilious. I seem always to be bilious lately. Except when I take some powders—"

Cleveland nodded. "They're supposed to be good for everything—"

"Do you take them?"

"Only now and then. They help me get started—"

"Started—?"

"You know—with Sonny. Sometimes I don't feel like—working on him—letting myself in for—that—you know—"

Yes, Pamela knew. The powders did help that. They seemed to make her easy with it, gave her the energy to seem more than willing—excited—eager to do what she had done so many times now, willing sometimes to advance on him and bring him into her for the concentrated sensation she seemed to need. Sometimes she thought that if he did not come to her, did not allow himself to be used to satisfy what had now become her own frenzy, a frenzy that only this act could abate, she thought she might die. She must have release from this inner tension, a tension that built within her over and over again—

It was all so different from what she'd known before. Her life with—with—what *was* his name? She'd forgotten his name. He was blond. His eyes had been very blue. Who had he been, that man she had known—?

One night she sat up in bed and said, "Myron."

Jay Darling, annoyed, woke and said, "What? What?"

"Nothing. I thought I heard a noise—"

There were other things. Jay Darling seemed to be coming and going more and more. He would stay for a few days and then he would be off again, sometimes by train; sometimes Pamela did not know how he left the island or when. And there was at least once, when she'd not seen him for two days, that she learned he was on the island, staying at the Clubhouse hotel. Nothing was the same, yet he seemed to be pleased with her, still seemed to want her exclusively for himself. He came to her at night quite often.

Someone said that the Senator and Jay B. Darling had quarreled. Something about an investigation—or the threat of an investigation—which the Senator would not block. Pamela didn't understand what was happening and besides, the other girls didn't exactly know either.

Helen was not in residence.

But what Pamela gleaned from all this was the guess that Darling would not now reassign her to the Senator on some whim. And there was only one other person she need be concerned about. Billy. Billy, she'd learned, was some sort of royal whatsis, she never could remember exactly what. "Is that near to be a king?" she remembered asking.

And someone had answered, "Yes and he's married to a blueblood type over there. That's why he's here. He likes it ever so much better. American girls know how to have fun, he says."

Fun. Pamela tried to remember the last time she'd had fun. Except sometimes when she talked with Nora, and even that had changed. It all seemed to blur in her mind. She found it hard to wake mornings to look for the deer, to watch for Nora. Had it only been only a few months ago she'd been so frightened of the nights and screamed until Nora had comforted her? Now there was something about Nora, about mornings, that annoyed her. She would think of it in a minute. Sometimes now it took a while for her to hold on to what she wanted to think about. This was no climate for thinking. Too hot.

Just lying on the divan in the turret room was an effort. Iced tea, cold juices. That was what she needed. Some pep. Some coolness. Nora bathed her face, washed her hair and rinsed it with lemon water for the cool scent of it.

"Nora—why does Cleveland watch me all the time?"

"I don't know, Miss Pammie. That Cleveland lady sure does like to come round here—"

Jay Darling noticed, too. He'd come back unexpectedly and found

Cleveland sitting in the turret room with Pamela. All the lights were out. Darling simply stood in the doorway and stared and Cleveland left in haste. But Pamela, who was especially foggy-minded that week, hardly saw it. She was listening to the sound of the sea, which seemed unnaturally loud.

Darling questioned Nora next morning.

"Do you leave your lady alone with Miss Cleveland?"

"Not while I'm here."

"Does Miss Pamela visit Miss Cleveland in her room?"

"Nossir. The other lady come here. They just sit and talk. They sits out there and sometimes they don't even talk. Miss Pammie, she don't like it much. She complain to me sometimes—"

"What does she say?"

"She say Miss Cleveland watch her all the time. Just watch—"

"I see—"

For more than a week after that, Pamela did not see Cleveland. Fortunately, Pamela had a few of the little papers tucked away. She began to ration herself on the supply. Rather than just using the powders as she felt the need for ease, she began to stretch the time between, to count them out and plan when she would take them. She saved them for late evenings on the nights she was certain Darling would come, even though she suffered through some terrible mornings as a result. But that way she could use them to maximum effect. The pain of the mornings, the irrationality of the light, were nothing compared to her need at night.

Her enforced withdrawal from the powders seemed to make her ill. Her hands shook; she perspired even more. Nora often found her weeping at the rising eastern sun.

"I can't sleep, Nora. I just feel all at odds with myself. Everything is so sad. My head hurts. My eyes ache something cruel. I was watching for the deer." She looked accusingly at Nora. "The deer didn't come," she wept.

"Maybe you looked too late. I think the little deers always come there—down there in the meadow—"

Again sadness overwhelmed Pamela. She cried even more. "They do come then," she whispered. "They came and I didn't see them at all. They came and I wasn't there—"

"Oh, Miss Pammie. Don't upset y'sef so. The little deers, they know what to do. They'll be all right wit'out you—"

She was abandoned then. Even the deer had no need of her. She was in despair. She wept into Nora's arms. Nora began to sing to her and eventually Pamela slept.

When she woke later, she felt better. After that she seemed to feel better each day. Some change had taken place that had culminated with that awful morning when she'd felt lost and alone.

"Myron Davis," she said. And saw in her mind his smile.

"What did you say, honey?" asked Nora.

"Nothing. I was just thinking—"

The next morning, Pamela woke very early and went to the window without even checking first for spiders. The deer were there. Nora would be coming soon. Pamela could hear the wheels of Ephraim's wagon on the path.

And from the other direction there came a lovely young woman dressed strangely, walking along carrying a hat in one hand, swinging it along, her auburn hair shining in the low dawn light. Everything about this woman looked sharp and focused and sure. She seemed to know exactly where she was going.

Pamela remembered a dream about this girl. The girl had walked along this way and had stopped and talked to Nora and Ephraim. Was it a dream? Or was it something Pamela had seen? Look there. Nora and Ephraim are there and they are talking to the auburn-haired lady.

"Nora, who was that girl? The one on the path? You talked to her and I heard Ephraim laugh. I never heard him laugh before. Why do you talk to her? Is she like me?"

Nora was laughing now. She was standing in the bedroom looking for Pamela's other slipper, slapping away at the bedclothes hardly paying any attention at all.

"Oh, Miss Pammie, you're not like her. That's Miss Margaret Marsh. She plays wit' my children—wit' Mars and Tyrah—she's writing a book—they go looking through the woods for bits and pieces—she's a smart lady, that Miss Margaret."

"And I'm not like that?"

Nora came and began to fuss over Pamela's hair. "Git y'self in the bath, honey. You'll feel better then—"

"I don't feel bad. I feel fine. Why do you talk to her so much—"

"We's jus' passin' the time o' day. She's a lady what can take care o' herself, gets herself out early. She lak to come out early to watch for things—"

"Like the deer?"

"Yas'm. Now git in here while I draw your bath—"

"She plays with your children? Then she doesn't have to work anywhere? Is she rich?"

"Yas'm. She lives over to the Clubhouse wit' her momma. And she comes down to where my children play and she knows their granny, my momma. Even better'n you and you know all about 'em—"

Pamela went into the bathroom. She ran her fingers through the water and she looked at Nora without speaking.

She said, "I think I'll take my bath myself. I'll wash my hair, too. I don't need you to fuss so, Nora. Go sit somewhere and wait for me—"

When Nora left the room, Pamela shut the door.

Seated in the tub, she sat up very straight, unlike her usual lounging posture in the warm water. Her mind's eye replayed scenes of that red-haired person and Nora and Ephraim, scenes of them laughing together.

Part of her was feeling the same feeling she used to get as a child when her mother favored Agnes or Lilly instead of herself.

What could Nora admire about a red-haired person who wore such funny clothes?

Trudy picked up a large sponge that Nora kept in a dish on the side of the tub and with a feeling of deliberate messiness, dropped it onto the floor outside her sight with a wet splat. Then, using a cloth, she scrubbed and scrubbed her body as if she'd never get clean. Without dawdling or relaxing in the water at all, she stood and stepped out and toweled herself dry. Looking down, she saw the sponge and with a guilty bit of remorse, picked it up and threw it back into the tub.

As she did this, the image returned of that red-haired person, so neat-looking, strong, her back straight as anything, her auburn curls pinned to the top of her head; how sure she looked as she disappeared into the dark wood.

Trudy was standing before a full-length mirror wrapped in a towel. That red-haired person went about as she pleased, looked strong enough to do anything. That was what Trudy envied. To be able to dare anything, to step into a dark wood alone. She was certain that red-haired woman did just what she wanted to do.

Unaccustomed resolve straightened Trudy's own spine.

I'm going to be like that. I'm tired of letting things happen to me. Nobody helps me at all. Not even Nora. So I'll just have to make plans for myself. I can't stand this anymore. Even if I don't have any place to go, I'm going to have to get out of here. There are worse things than being lost like Gladys. This is much worse—

CHAPTER XXXII

Steven Baxter had met Margaret Marsh, had loved her—and could it be true?—had lost her. There had been no further correspondence between them since she'd left. A note, exploratory, questing, sent to Sporting Isle at Christmas, addressed to both *Mrs. and Miss Marsh*, had been answered by Mrs. Marsh alone. He realized he'd wasted his last chance.

In her response, Mrs. Marsh was quite distant. At least that was how Steven read the few lines she'd written. Mrs. Marsh returned his regards and his felicitations and his greetings for the season and asked to be remembered to his mother and said Margaret was occupied with "the life of the islander"—whatever that meant. The letter from Mrs. Marsh, in response to his own note, clearly anticipated no reply. It was a note to a remote acquaintance and put an end to the exchange.

So in spite of Steven's wish to be off at once to the South, he was uncertain of his welcome there, of what he should or could say to Margaret to woo her from the "life of the islander." This life, in Steven's mind, became inexplicably confused with the question of free love. He dreamed at night of illicit practices in subtropical rain forests, of love on the white, hot sands of beaches. Margaret, he feared, was every day becoming more lost to him. He would have taken off at once, gone to her and forced her to listen to him, but he was certain she would be like the note. He would rush to meet her and she would turn from him because he would not know the right thing to say, to persuade her to come away with him and be his love.

He went out to Prairie Avenue several times to visit Uncle Findley, but the old man, much improved in health, could offer no clear explanation of Margaret's abrupt departure and seemed to prefer to talk of other things. Findley had resumed his long walks for a short time in the fall and then bad weather made those impossible and he was restive.

Steven took him to lunch at a downtown club. Uncle Findley was very uncomfortable.

"I wish she'd come home," he said. He didn't have to name "her." "I'd like to go back to the Tremont. Mrs. Riley does for me, beautifully—it's more than I'm used to, to be so waited on—but I miss the boys and my card-games."

"Why don't you take one of the carriages and go over there from time to time?"

"Agh—I feel ridiculous ordering up a carriage just for me. Margaret should come home and tend to her own house and then I can go back to where I came from—"

Steven agreed that Margaret should come home and said again that he wasn't certain why she'd left.

Findley said, "I thought it was—um—a lover's quarrel. She just came into my room one day and said she must go, that everything was falling in on her and she couldn't stay in Chicago another minute. I was—disappointed myself."

Steven felt his face grow hot. He looked at Uncle Findley and saw the older man could guess his discomfort. "Too much wine with lunch," Steven murmured and took a drink of good lake water.

As they parted the old man said, in a querulous voice, "I wish to hell she'd come home—"

Myron Davis, who was to be Steven's traveling companion, was not yet ready to leave the city. He was involved in the Columbian Exposition, which Steven, because of Margaret, could hardly stand to think about. Whenever he thought of the Exposition he thought of the Woman's Building and Margaret as he had found her that first day, at work among the boxes of goods. While Steven waited impatiently and yet patiently for Myron Davis to finish his work—Steven had a great respect for work of any kind, since he had none—the two young men had developed the habit of going out every evening for a walk together in the brisk air. They liked each other's company and each felt there was something about the other, some personal sorrow or quest, that had yet to be expressed. Each hoped by spending quiet time with the other, they would bring forth the tale that needed to be told if the friendship were to move to a more intimate footing. Perhaps each also hoped to have his story coaxed from his lips. Then the true purpose that each had for a southern journey might be revealed. Each of these young men was taking to the streets in forced exercise to ease the sorrow unexpressed by the other. But any revelations would be one for one.

Mama Delight, watching the change in Steven, said to Arthur, "I don't like that Davis person who goes about so much with your brother. He's a worldly young man. I can tell from his eyes. I would not like it if your brother were led into coarse ways—"

"Myron Davis isn't coarse, Mama, he's from New York. He's perfectly fine. He's in insurance."

"There," said Mama Delight. "I've never approved of insurance. It deals entirely too much in disaster and death. Not the sort of thing a fine young man would take up—"

"Oh, Mama," said Arthur and rattled his paper, although he was himself a little jealous of his brother's new friend.

"Mark my words," said Mama Delight, "this is all leading up to something. I tell you, I can read it in Steven's manner and in his new attitude toward me—"

Arthur looked at her. Should he take up the question of Steven's departure now? No, he thought not. Better to wait until the day, the very day, of departure. In the meantime, Steven could have his friend and no hysteria from Mama.

He changed the subject. "There's an article here about a woman inventor. What next?" It was cleverly done. Mama launched into a long recital on the women of the day and Arthur was able to read his paper by giving grumpy nods now and then to her complaints.

2

From various remarks that Myron had made, Steven had guessed Myron's life in New York—perhaps his life on campus—had been a worldly one, and Steven thought he might ask some general questions to aid in the quest of Margaret Marsh. As a sort of research—

One night as they walked quickly along, the doorway of one of the North Side mansions burst open and several young ladies—girls, really, of high-school age—came bursting down the stairs from a lighted hall, laughing as they came, rushing toward a carriage that waited for them at the curb. Another young woman, young enough still for long hair in curls down to her shoulder, stood at the doorway and waved, calling out to first one and then another, "Goodbye, goodbye. Drive carefully. Do send me—"

The words were lost as the two men made their way onward.

"Charming, aren't they?" Steven asked.

"Quite. Quite. Such tender young buds. They need—"

"—to be taken care of," finished Steven when Myron paused as they waited at a curb.

"Absolutely. Young women are so—" Again Myron seemed at a loss to finish.

"—tender," finished Steven again, again uncertainly. He had a vision of Margaret at this age. Had she been like that? Innocent and trusting and waiting to be discovered and taken up and cared for?

"Every woman should have a man to take care of her," said Myron, emphatically, now that he could pick up his full stride again. "That's the way it's meant. It says so in the Bible—"

I think I had this conversation before, thought Steven, *with my mother.* But with a man of the world at his side, Steven pressed onward. "Is every woman meant for that, do you think? Or are there some who would rather not? I mean—be taken care of? Have a traditional life with love and marriage? I sometimes wonder." Here they turned to walk past St. James, where Steven had often attended marriages and baptisms. They were making a great circle in their ramble. He said, "I sometimes wonder if some don't want—ought to have—something more modern? Something with less restrictions?"

"Why? Do you mean a woman should have several husbands? That would never do, old man," said Myron with assurance.

Not wishing Myron to know that was not what he meant and wishing at once not to appear naive, Steven capitalized on the unorthodox jump in reasoning Myron had made. "Well, why not? I suppose there are men in the world—in Egypt and in the desert and jungle tribes—who have many wives. Why not a woman with many husbands? I suppose there are places like that?"

"Yes, I think there are. But it would never do here. We don't exactly have primogeniture, but we do need to know the father's name—"

"What for? If the child is well cared for by the mother?"

Myron was nonplussed by this. He'd never heard of such a thing. Steven was certainly more complicated than might be seen at first glance. "How could that be?" Myron asked. "The economics of the world as we know it, the civilized West, won't allow for that. Women can't afford to take care of their own children. They require the help of the husband economically. We're not fishes, living off the bounty of the sea—"

"Suppose the economics of it are a given, then what?"

They walked along without speaking further, Myron and Steven mutually in awe of Steven's avant garde course of conversation.

Steven couldn't believe what he'd said. He was energized by his topic, totally caught up in his own strange logic and pleased that he'd not revealed his own search for information. He wished Margaret were here to hear him.

They were crossing the Rush Street bridge to the south before Myron answered, "You're talking revolution when you talk like that. And if some foolish woman should attempt to run her life like that, she would soon find herself and her children in the midst of want and deprivation. Yet the entire economy couldn't handle women in the marketplace as equal partners or single providers paid as well as men. The economy would collapse from the burden. And there's another matter, Baxter, that you've not considered. Perhaps I shouldn't say this—"

Myron peered around to see if there was anyone close to them who might overhear. "I don't know how much—uh—experience you've had with women—of the physical—uh—sort?"

"Very little. Hardly any, you might say." Steven hoped this might sound nonchalant; forthright, yet guarded.

"Well, I—" Myron paused, his story bursting on his lips, his heart sealed these many months alone, quivering at the thought of a confidant, leaped within him. "I once, some time ago, had a lovely young woman—as my—well, old man, to be frank about it, she was my mistress—"

"I see," said Steven, impressed with the grand gesture in the way of information, but unable to see its bearing on their overall discussion. He waited.

"How could a woman handle more than one—uh—male at a time? I don't mean at once, but I mean in sequence. Don't you see? Women want to marry. That's their nature. They want to tie a man down, keep him from roaming into other pastures. And what woman," Myron continued with an absolutely straight face, "could stand letting one man after another handle her night after night like that? I don't believe it. She'd have to be ready for a man's attentions almost constantly—"

Steven turned to look at Myron to see if the man were serious. They were only a few miles from the levee, where women so offered themselves every night. Yet Steven took another argument. "Isn't what you say much more possible for her than we allow in our thinking and our literature? Isn't it unspoken? In the nature of women? To be a vessel? To receive? Isn't that why we guard her from her virginal years onward? To guard against being fooled into taking care of another's child?"

They walked on, each thinking, each casting mental arguments they would not venture into the air.

"Love," said Myron softly, at last. "Love is a very different matter. A different sort of arrangement—women do like love—"

"That's really what I meant—back there when I first spoke. I'm thinking of the kind of woman who would let everything go but love. Who would say she didn't even want marriage. Only love. A love-bond for life rather than some heavy legal knot lying against her heart. As you say, a different sort of arrangement for an unusual sort of woman. Not a mistress or a paramour. But an equal partner. A life-long love—"

"Very poetic," said Myron. His face was grim. They had reached Michigan Avenue and turned into the wind as if to purify themselves. "You'll never find a woman to go for it. Not one. If they don't want marriage, then what they want instead is material comfort of the greatest degree. To be taken care of in the finest way. You can't ever do enough for 'em. Buy 'em sapphires, they look at diamonds with wistful eyes. Get 'em a French maid, they would like to have a carriage as well—"

"And do they never think of love at all?"

"Perhaps they do. They may feel passion at a certain moment—do you understand? There are women who enjoy that—who want nothing else but that and who want to be rewarded for this one talent, their enjoyment of passion. But no largess is enough for 'em. They know they're different from their sisters and they want to be highly rewarded for their differences. They want to show their women friends, their social stratum—and they have one—how their special gentlemen friends provide. No doubt they talk of it all the time. I suspect they're the very devil about it, eyeing each other, looking their traps over. And then, when things don't go right for their fellow, they go off with the first and next-richest man who eyes them—"

"Well," said Steven Baxter, "I suppose if a woman is not allowed love, she would have to settle for that—"

Myron was completely silenced. The street sloped imperceptibly downward. There is an honesty in walking in the night air with a friend. Myron was thinking of Trudy, of her eyes, of the way she'd looked at him when she learned about Jay Darling.

They were near Washington Street.

"And was your young—uh—friend like that?" prompted Steven.

Stride matched stride, regular as clockwork. Myron was staring stoically ahead.

"No," he said softly. "She was not at all like the greedy women I have just described to you."

The air filled their lungs. One of these men had just been more honest with the other than he was with himself. They knew they were friends at last.

"What was her name?"

"Her name," Myron said, "was Trudy—Gertrude, I think. I never met her family. She was—is—a very nice girl."

"Where is she now?"

"On Sporting Isle. With another man. An internationally famous financier."

"Good Lord—"

"What? What is it? Is this so shocking to you?"

And so the second story was told. What could be told with regard to the proprieties. The story of Margaret, of her flight, her silence. Of the name of the island where she was now in residence.

"Tell me one thing," Steven said at the end of his own story. "Do you love Trudy? Is that why you want to go south?"

"Yes. It will mean a total break with my family. With everything I've been. But if I could convince her to leave—him—that man..." His voice trailed off. "She's so lovely. You can't know. He can offer her so much more than I will ever be able to now. She has every advantage with him. They have been traveling on his yacht, in overwhelming luxury. But if I could just speak to her—once more at least—"

"Well, at least we've cut out the pretense," Steven said. "Now what will you say to her? What can we say—"

Again Myron was silent for a time. Then he said, "Whatever it is a person talks about when he means love—"

Steven nodded vigorously, eagerly. "And what do you mean then? I'd like to know. What? What can we offer them? I don't know what to say and I'm afraid I will lose my last chance. Tell me what to say. Is it only passion that we feel?"

"Passion, certainly. We're made for that, I'm afraid," Myron said, thinking of those wonderful times in the hotel on Fifth Avenue. But then there was the way he felt now. "And more. A softer, better emotion—"

"Tenderness. We're allowed that. And taking care—"

"They take care of us as well. On both sides. Taking care—"

"Then what can we offer if we don't offer security or passion or any of that—what do we have to overbalance reason?"

"It must be love," Myron said.

"I wish I could get a better fix on it," grumbled Steven, the student, the researcher. "I feel so at sea ever since she's gone."

Myron clapped him on the shoulder. "That's it then. That's my feeling exactly. All of the signposts are gone. She is the signpost. I'm left with nothing but myself. I doubt," he said grimly, "that that is enough."

Steven matched his mood. "Then we'll just have to take the chance, no matter how high the odds, because love between men and women is devoutly to be wished for—"

"Then you have some sort of plan? To make this possible?" Myron sounded hopeful.

"No."

CHAPTER XXXIII

There had been rain for two days. Margaret had been restless, roaming about the hotel. But on the third day when she woke before sunrise, her body aching with the need for exercise, there was a hint of bright light from the east and the fresh crisp scent of the air promised that the storm had passed.

She dressed quickly in her field habit and stole out of the hotel with eagerness, walking down the shell path toward the ocean with the delicious joy of a truant freed from school. As she came near the Playhouse, past the meadow where she often saw deer grazing before dawn, she noticed the light in the grove ahead of her was eerily green as sometimes happens after a rain. Toward the top of the trees she could just catch a line of red-gold, the sun rising from the sea, and this, contrasted with the bottle-green of the woods, made the moment seem enchanted, a moment in the forest of a fairy tale.

As she walked slowly into the center of the woods, breathing in the thick smell of pine mixed with the exotic odors of a tropical forest after a rain, there was movement in front of her and out from between two trees stepped a young woman, the most beautiful young woman in Margaret's memory. The vision was dressed in what looked to be a gown of pale green silk and she was wearing a shawl of white wrapped around her shoulders, clutched to her bosom as if she were afraid to open it and reveal what lay beneath. Her hair was thick and tousled and dark; her eyebrows like wings above lovely eyes.

"Margaret—"

Margaret stopped walking forward. In her mind there was the feeling that she was watching this moment played out on a stage and at the same time, she was the player. She watched herself reach out a hand, heard herself say, "Yes—"

Somewhere in the distance there was a sound, the steady rattle of wooden wagon wheels along the shell path. There was no wagon visible, but Margaret knew what the sound was. Each morning she passed this way, she met Nora and Ephraim near here in their wagon.

The dark-haired woman came closer. She reached out and took Margaret's hand.

"Come," said this wild forest nymph, "I don't want them to know where I am—"

"What—"

"Nora and Ephraim. They'll be here soon. They mustn't see me. Come—"

On the reassuring sound of Nora's name, Margaret allowed herself to be led into the trees, into the darker paths of the wood.

"I want to talk to you," the vision said over her shoulder as she walked ahead. "I must know who you are, what you do when you go out each day—in the country like this—alone—"

Margaret eyed the insubstantial slippers of embroidered red velvet that the apparition wore. The ground was still quite wet. She asked her, "Are you alone? Can you walk here?"

The woman paused, turned and looked back at Margaret, then stopped. She motioned for Margaret to go first. "Maybe you know the way?" She asked the question wistfully. "Maybe you know somewhere—where there is a clearing—a log to sit on—where we could sit together. Just for a short time. There are so many things I need to know—"

"What is your name?" Margaret asked. She was somewhat shaken by the girl's uncanny knowledge of her own.

The girl was still facing Margaret. "Pamela," she said, lowering her eyelids as she said it. Her full lips seemed to form strangely around her name, as if she weren't certain that her name *was* Pamela.

Margaret made up her mind "All right," she said. "I think I know somewhere we might be welcome—" She went ahead and found a small path she was familiar with. It led to the clearing where Mr. Peabody's hut stood.

The light had not reached here. The hut looked gray, unoccupied. Sometimes Mr. Peabody stayed at the hotel during rainstorms. Margaret knocked. There was no answer. She waited, looking meanwhile at Pamela, wondering where she had come from.

The second knock was hollow against the wood of the door.

"I don't think anyone is at home here," said Margaret, trying the door, which opened easily to her touch. She motioned for Pamela to follow her and they stepped inside.

"What place is this?"

"An old man lives here. He lets me come here by myself sometimes."

"I didn't know there was anything like this in these woods. I thought there was nothing but that big hotel and then those private houses. You come from the hotel, don't you?" The girl seemed resentful of this.

"Yes." Margaret motioned for Pamela to sit on the one chair. Margaret took the only other seat available, which was the tautly made-up cot.

"Who *are* you?" Margaret asked again.

"I told you. Pamela." Again the eyelids closed briefly.

"Where did you come from? In those slippers?"

"These—oh, these are my—bedroom slippers. My other shoes all have sharp heels—"

"But where do you live?"

"Over there—"

A sudden thought took Margaret. She remembered what Granny had said. *That evil place. But nobody lives there,* Margaret had answered her.

"Do you live in the Playhouse—?"

"That's not important—"

Margaret guessed that the girl did live there. That it was important. That Granny was probably right; some evil was being done there and this girl had run from it.

"Are you—all right? You're not—hurt or anything?" Margaret felt out of her depth. She didn't know what to do about such matters. She was willing to help, but she could see the girl was skittish, ready to bolt. Margaret understood that any questions from her would have to be carefully handled until this Pamela felt safe enough to say why she had come.

"I'm all right," the girl said. "It's just that—sometimes I see you from the window—almost every day when it isn't raining, and Nora said—"

"Nora—?" Margaret was smiling as she asked this.

"Nora. Nora is my—friend. She comes every day. She comes along the path with Ephraim and I see you talking to them. Nora says you know all about them, that you're very smart."

"I just go out to look at nature."

"Oh. I don't know anything about the country. I've never been one to go about in it much." She paused as if remembering something she wanted to say, as if some voice were echoing in her head. Then she asked, "But you do know about—things? Important things—"

"Only some things. Why don't we go to Nora now? She and Ephraim could come back here with us—" Margaret had broken her own rule about questions. But there was a strange light in the girl's eyes, as if a lantern had been turned to its highest flame. Perhaps her incoherence was madness in a reasonable form. It wasn't sensible to stay alone in the woods with a madwoman—especially when no one else knew where you were.

Yet in Margaret's heart there was a tug, a yielding. Perhaps the girl was mad, but she was only a girl like herself; perhaps not the same age, but nearly so. A beautiful girl who appeared to have lost her way in the forest. A girl seeking something; a path, a word. If Margaret called Nora now, too soon, might this child wander forever?

She is very like me, thought Margaret. *I can almost feel her thoughts inside myself. Almost as though I have been walking this path every day, waiting for her.*

There was no sensible basis for this quick acceptance. The words that had passed between them were sketchy. Yet Margaret could feel herself moving into trust, not a thing she did easily. She started, her body almost taking a physical step into a mist of unarticulated emotion that seemed to bind the two of them instantly, more strongly than Margaret felt bound to any other. No earnest argument could have touched her as much as this.

"Who are you?" asked Margaret for the third time.

As if this were the magic number, the girl began to talk. She sat at the plain table in the spare hut and began to tell Margaret Marsh a story about a girl named Gertrude Jahn who'd been born and once lived in Chicago. Gertrude Jahn grew older, learned things no one knew they were teaching her; saw things from an entirely different view from that of Margaret Marsh, also a Chicago girl. The girl, Gertrude, walked along a street one day. Her name became Trudy— Trudy Jones. She went into a restaurant. The girl, Pamela, wove a tapestry of small moments for Margaret, in such a moving way that Margaret found herself gathering all up in complete understanding. Except—

"Did you love him?" she asked.

"No. I don't think that was it at first. I wanted—"

"What?"

Pamela sat straight for a moment. She assumed an air. "I thought I'd be a woman of the world—"

"A woman of the world?"

"I thought that was better than being—caught in the way my mother—other women—it seemed so then."

"And now?"

"Now," the girl looked down. "Now I seem to have no place at all." Her voice was a whisper.

Margaret whispered, too. She repeated her earlier question. "But did you love him? You must have loved him, to go with him, to trust him. And then he—"

She stopped. Margaret was an honest young woman. She recognized that Trudy Jahn had done what Margaret had proposed to Steven; had gone arm-in-arm into a world of two people ignoring the conventions, taking on a style of their own, depending only on their feelings for each other to bind them over the difficult times. And feelings alone had not been enough, for here was Pamela, abandoned and troubled.

"Something must have happened," Margaret said aloud. "You risked everything. You must have loved him. Why did this happen when there was love—"

She leaned forward from her seat on the cot, curving into the question. Trudy, at the table, also leaned forward, two lovely parentheses, enclosing a sentence about love. Could the question be answered? The silence lay before them, palpable and growing, a third factor in the room.

What is love? the silence asked.

Trudy's eyes were wide open now and she was looking directly into Margaret's own with such intensity that Margaret found she must drop her own gaze.

"I don't know," Trudy whispered. "I don't know what love is. I—" Here she made a movement with her hand, palm up, as if begging. "Do you know? I thought you might know—What is love? Please tell me that. How does it feel?"

While the silence became stronger, Margaret examined her own heart. She believed she was *in love* with Steven. "Do you mean passion?" she asked.

"No. I know that to be different," said Trudy with such a flat, certain tone that Margaret had to trust her answer.

She cast her mind about, rifling her vocabulary. She sensed that too much doubt on her part might throw Trudy into terrible despair. "I think what you mean is a kind of cherishing of the other, as if they are—"

"As if *he* is—" prompted Trudy.

"Yes. He."

Trudy was looking down at her hands, touching what Margaret saw was a very fine pearl and diamond ring. "I want to know more about—" Trudy looked up distraught "—about what it feels like. How do you know? There must be some way to be sure—"

Margaret waited. She had grown adept at waiting lately. But Trudy had no more to say. The question still lay between them.

Finally Margaret said what she'd said before. "But you must know. You risked everything once—"

"I didn't say that. You did. I risked nothing. I had no choice—"

Margaret evidently bridled at this because Trudy said, "I don't mean he forced me to come with him. I mean, there was no other pleasant way for me to go. Anywhere. I think we do what we like if there is a choice between an unpleasant and a pleasant thing. I could have stayed at home, I suppose, and become like my sisters or the girls in the factory. And married some man from there or from one of the dances; someone without any more prospects than my own. I would have thought it was for love. People do that. Say *love* all the time. Whether they know or not. Or when they mean security—"

She straightened again on the chair. "Well, then I thought, 'Why not?' Why not go with a handsome man for the day and then it was longer and he was pleasant and the life was wonderful—"

"Then you came to love him? Why did you leave him?"

"I—he sent me away—"

"Sent you away?" As Margaret said this, she felt Steven's hand on hers, she saw the horse of the carriage shying at their argument, heard her own voice saying, "I love you, but I will not marry you, Steven Baxter."

She said to Trudy, but thought of Steven as she said it, "And you? How did you feel?"

"I thought—well, I minded the going away, but I understood why he did it—"

"Why?"

"Another man—saw me. He arranged that I must go with him. If I had been Myron I would have been afraid, too. No one is brave enough to resist—" She sighed. "I've thought about that, too. The young man said it was best for me, that I would be better off. I think he thought I'd gone with him at first because I would be better off, that that was what I wanted. And I would be best off with this new— man. A famous person who was—is—terribly rich and likes me. I didn't want to go, but others—said it was—the way to be—to get on—I had no choice *there*, you see. There was nothing more for me where I was. Just like at first in Chicago. I thought I was choosing. But there wasn't really any choice about it if I wanted to have—well, comforts. But I lost everything then—"

Margaret stood up. She was filled with—she didn't know what— disgust, horror, revulsion. Not at this girl, who'd been through so much. No. What was inside her closely resembled the odd feelings she'd had when first coming to Sporting Isle, when she'd found the women of the hotel useless and silly in their pleasures. No wonder the smell of the place was of sweet rotten undergrowth, an unclean garden. And here was another example—a young woman who evidently had given herself up to pleasure at first, but had come to live with a rich, famous man at the Playhouse, providing him with earthly and unearthly delights, while she, almost innocent of life, was expected to live with the foolish choice she'd made, was expected to look out at the world and let living pass her by in the satisfaction of one's man lust. Yet was Trudy—or Pamela—so very different from the wives who'd idled away their time on the lawns of the hotel, who'd given up their beings in order to be cared for and cosseted?

Oh, thought Margaret, in terrible pain at her thought, *we are all the same. There are no differences among us or between us. We want what is the least trouble at first and then we are in the most trouble at the last.*

As she had under the trees at the hotel tea parties, Margaret paced up and down in the little cabin. How could life be so dishonest about half its citizens? And she knew. The pain of it was that she knew. The words of J. P. Morgan had been headlined in a New York paper: *I can hire one-half of the working force to kill the other half.* And she'd thought, but the other half is letting the killer come, letting the killer get away. So much for the rights of women. The rights of women are abandoned, lying there: Can men be blamed for absentmindedly picking them up? *Some* call it love. But that can't be love at all.

Trudy was watching her. Margaret could almost see into Trudy's soul through the amber eyes turned toward her. To be presented with the decadence of the Playhouse and asked to solve one of its mysteries—no, life's own mystery—all in one day, overwhelmed the intimacy of the cabin. As she strode up and down, Margaret looked about her, staring at the simplicity of the cabin. Was this the answer? One soul, alone, with no other? Everything spartan and neat and no danger anywhere from love?

Margaret had another thought. She whirled and pointed at Trudy. "Are you pregnant?" She had broken her own rule.

"No, certainly not."

"Who is the man? The man you live with now—"

"It doesn't matter."

Margaret stood thinking. "I can't exactly describe love—in all its differences. I think there is a genuine love that does exist. But it's as I have said—more willing to sacrifice for the other than be concerned with—" here her voice was held very steady lest she say too much "—comforts."

"What can I do then? I'm—I have no way to go—"

Margaret stared at her. "You *have* done something. You have come here—I know nothing more than that. You are here. You must have had some reason. Something you have not revealed to me—"

Trudy put her head down in her hands. Of course, she'd not told Margaret about Cleveland, about the powders, about the fear she had that she enjoyed what Darling could do to her, that she was slipping away into a place where she could never do this, come out into the morning, slip away into the trees—she could not tell Margaret this.

"It doesn't matter," she repeated. "Who he is—or anything like that. I put it behind me when I can—"

The silence softened, wrapped around them. Margaret could see her way now. Trudy still had her head lowered. She looked as if she'd been beaten. She must be given will to resist whatever she needed to resist.

Margaret said softly, "There. All right then. You knew the answer yourself. It *doesn't* matter. You can put it behind you. You *are* yourself, you know. You belong to yourself. The man doesn't matter unless you care for him. He may try to come into it at the end, he may actually be there, the right man, but after all, he doesn't really matter. He is either all right for you or you can just walk away. You know that—"

Trudy lifted her head. There were tears in her eyes.

"I knew the answer," she whispered. "I knew it myself."

"Yes," said Margaret, thoughtfully. "We both did. We just knew it from different directions. To walk away. To be alone. That option is always there, right from the very start. Just as we have the option to stay—"

Steven had said, "I love you, Margaret." But she'd chosen to run away. She'd forgotten he was a different man from her father. He'd made a pledge to her. And she had chosen to run from that because of what was inside herself. She'd thought there was no choice.

Margaret spoke in a whisper. "We always have options about that—to go or to stay. Unless we are wearing chains, our choice is our own—we both knew it all the time. That's what was troubling us—"

2

Events in the Baxter mansion were moving toward their inexorable conclusion. Even Mama Delight Baxter could sense it. Further, into her mind emerged the definite idea that Steven, once he left her household, would no longer be her *boy*. No one had said so, not in so many words, but the removal of Steven from the North Side mansion would be the commencement of his maturity. Mama Delight had also sensed that Steven was going to go wandering through the South in search of *that* Miss Marsh. And once he found her, no matter how many times he returned to his former home, nothing would be the same again if that *girl* was on his arm. In his mother's mind, Steven's success in finding Miss Marsh and rewooing her was a foregone conclusion.

But not in Steven's mind. He hedged and delayed. He took on any excuse to avoid the final break. He cited the business of Myron Davis, his erstwhile traveling companion. He cited the weather, his own lack of organization—everything was mentioned except his one true fear.

Arthur took in the situation. He noticed that Mama had managed to get the already disorganized Steven into just as much of a disorganized state as she. Each time Steven set out a firm date on the calendar, Mama found yet another reason he must not leave at just "this time of year."

At the present time, Mama and Steven were rummaging through trunks in the old schoolroom. They were both at it, supposedly looking for some old cycling gear of Steven's.

"I know it's here somewhere," Mama said. "And you should have it. It would save you so much expense—"

Hang the expense, thought Arthur and went out to do his duty. Arthur was *best man* without peer at all the society weddings. He had the kind of intelligence that is best displayed at such moments of social crisis.

He went quietly to consult with Myron to learn when a hard and fast date could be made. Once that was established, Arthur arranged for everything else: for the train car to be put on the right track for the South, for the goods to be loaded, for the letters of credit that

Steven would need, for the cash on hand—even to purchasing a
ring, which he did not show Steven. Arthur was too smart for that.
He put a note about the ring into Steven's luggage in a place he
knew his brother would uncover once "on the road." Arthur knew
true love when he saw it and planned accordingly.

But no matter how discreet Arthur tried to be about the removal
of Steven's goods from the household—he had arranged that Steven
take their mother for a drive during the big event—Mama Delight
knew in an instant on her return that the deed had been accomplished. She came to Arthur's room.

"I just want you to know," she said, still dressed in her dull gray
bonnet—the lightest color she would wear—and her traveling cape,
"I just want you to know that I know what this is all about and I
don't thank you for it, Arthur Baxter."

Arthur came toward her and tried to lead her to a chair. She was
crying, sniffling into a bit of black lace and linen.

"Now Mama, don't let *him* see you cry. He needs confidence—"

"I won't. You know I won't cry in front of him. But he's so young.
And she's—well, Arthur, I shouldn't say this—but I think that girl
has bewitched him—with her talk about independence and all. He
doesn't know what he's getting into. I'm certain she's not a practicing
Christian. How could she be—with those heathen notions put into
her in that eastern school? Oh, it's terrible, Arthur. Girls are so
changed. Remember the old days? Oh, what would your father say?
In the old days we were so happy—"

"Oh, Mama, when was that? I don't remember anything but
this—" He waved his hand toward her gown of mourning, her tears.
"Steven deserves a chance to be happy. He's grown now. You have
to let him go—"

At this his mother began to sob in great gulps into her bit of lace
and cloth. Arthur doubted that the flimsy bit would be able to handle
the torrent. She was swaying as if she would faint but when he went
to her and put his arm around her, she pushed him away.

"Now, now—" he began.

She stopped the tears and looked up at him with an obvious mean-
ness of spirit. "No," she said. "Not now. *Never.* I'd never meant to
let him go—"

This shocking statement silenced both of them. Mama Delight had
revealed the total truth. She wanted a lifetime escort. She'd often
seen it done. Kind and generous sons, waiting on their mothers for
the balance of the mother's life. And now it was being snatched
away. Arthur had done this.

"As usual," she said when she could speak, "I see your high hand—"

Arthur was still reeling from his mother's moment of candor. So he and Fanny had been right all these years. His mother had been playing a selfish game with Steven.

"He belongs to himself, Mama. Not you—"

She sniffed. "Until that girl gets her hands on him—"

Arthur stood up and let his mother stand for herself.

"Unless you give Steven's—um—life and—um—arrangements the respect you would give a stranger, then I don't want to know you and Fanny won't either, if I tell her. If you want to see your grandchildren—both hers and the ones I'll have—then you're going to have to act better. Mothers don't own their children," said Arthur, the newly wrought head of the household. "You need to go on and find some life of your own to lead—"

"Oh, Artie," she wailed, still truthful, as if under some spell to be especially so, "I know I haven't a life of my own. I never, ever did—and now I'll never have another—"

3

The same scene in New York had a different outcome. The break was more severe, but circumstances altered the case.

Myron had written his letter carefully—in thirty-three separate drafts. He finally settled on one that he knew to be inadequate but he knew himself well enough to know that if he went in person to New York, he would never leave for the South. He didn't fear his parents' strength so much as the lack of his own. And they would not have scolded or nagged or railed. They would have been understanding and terribly hurt. Myron knew he loved Trudy, but there were old ways, old ties, in New York, even though he knew he must forgo them now.

He decided the letter must go first to his father at the business address—Myron was resigning from the firm, so to speak, as well as his family. His father could then carry the story to his mother. Myron regretted the scene he knew would follow. He genuinely loved his parents. Hadn't he sacrificed Trudy for them?

In his letter, he didn't speak much of the past. He said only that, "I believe that, some months ago, I made a terrible mistake. The mistake was my own and I have to live with myself for it. I want to change now and go forward as my own man. The kind of life I will lead is still unknown to me, but I think I will remain in the West—

perhaps go further West from Chicago after a trip to the South. I might try some simple occupation that has an element of social worth to it—perhaps I'll become a teacher—or a town grocer—"

Even after many drafts of the letter, Myron didn't sense the inadvertent humor of his plans for a vocation. He could think only of Trudy and the steps he must go through to regain her.

"—I mean to give up the kind of society I've known in the past. I would like to marry someday and perhaps I will, but I plan to find a girl of humble origins, someone who will work with me toward whatever life we can find for ourselves and our own. I will try to contact you once a year to let you know how I am. Don't worry about me. I have to take this step or I will be worth nothing—to you or to myself. Please help me by accepting what I am going to do—your affectionate son, Myron Davis."

Mr. Davis put the letter on the table beside his wife. He blamed himself for what had happened. He knew Myron was going to go in search of the girl Darling had stolen from him. Mr. Davis knew that in his soul. But he didn't believe he could explain that to his wife. So he said nothing.

"I knew it," his wife said. "I knew Myron lost his head over someone before he went to Chicago. Someone entirely unsuitable—"

"No," his father said. "Not unsuitable. We've cut ourselves out of his life with that sort of talk. We can reverse that—undo it—if we learn to control our—our—"

"Snobbishness? Are you accusing me of snobbery?"

He said nothing, but began to walk around their bedroom, his hands behind his back. His heart was full. He turned to look at her. As he looked, her face changed. She looked as the passenger of a liner, unable to swim, might look if it was announced that the ship beneath her feet were sinking.

With a desperate cry she threw herself into the great watery depths, "I'd take him back any time—with anyone. He's all we have. I'm not as bad as that, am I—?" Now she was crying. She, too, had one of those dainty handkerchiefs of lace and linen that were ridiculously inadequate.

He came to her and held her. "No. No, but you have your moments. We just got off the track somehow. Derailed. We were together once. We had him, didn't we—?" His laugh was rueful, coaxing. "We can do something for each other again. We can—" he stopped and held her to him.

"We can be friends," she said, muffled into his chest.

"If luck is with us, it'll only be a year—"

"A year?"

"He says he'll get in touch in a year. To let us know. I know he'll do it the first time. Maybe not afterward. We need to be ready—that first year—willing—"

"We can do it," she said. "If he understands—"

"—that we have each other. That we let him go—those are the things that matter."

CHAPTER XXXIV

1

Against Margaret's advice, Trudy had insisted on returning to the Playhouse.

"If I don't go back, Nora will be in trouble when they find me missing. Even my note wouldn't help then. No, it's all right. I've got to face up to this."

"Come with me," Margaret said. "You can stay at the hotel—"

Trudy turned even whiter than her previous pallor.

"No," she said. "All the men from the Playhouse—they stay at the hotel sometimes. They'd see me—"

"The mainland," suggested Margaret. "I will find you a place there—"

"Yes," Trudy said. "That's where I'll go. When the time comes. I have to go back now—" She went on toward the path. She called back over her shoulder. "I'll send you a message. Soon."

2

The entire company had returned. This was the last week of March, the last week for the season at Sporting Isle. After this week of festivities and reunions and parties day and night, everyone would divide and fade away, turning back to places in the North where they spent their summers.

At the Playhouse, the crew was gathering. Cleveland had come, much subdued, on Sonny's arm.

Someone, looking through the glass out toward the sea, said, "The *Shark* is lying out there. Darling will be here tonight."

Trudy overheard the announcement. She was glad she'd come back to the Playhouse. They—someone—would make it hard on Nora if Trudy Jones just disappeared. She expected some minion to come and fetch her to the ship. For some reason she couldn't define, she thought Darling would not come himself. But it would be even more difficult to explain to a hireling if Pamela Jones was not in residence, or in residence but not willing to sail when her master insisted that she join him on the ship. Her head ached from trying to plan without appearing to plan anything. She would take very little with her and be ready to leave quickly at any moment. She would escape this place. She wouldn't have much to carry. There was the shawl and her banknotes—and some securities that a friend of Darling's had given her once. She'd had them for a while before she understood what they were.

Helen came up behind Trudy.

"Mr. Darling hasn't been around much lately, has he? Are you going away with him, dear? Or will the two of you stay on at Sporting Isle for the summer after we all leave? I hear it's so dreary and hot in this place in summer that no one can lift a finger. Too bad he's worn out his welcome in so many of the finer places—"

Trudy looked Helen over. She was holding a book, her finger marking the place, much as Trudy had first seen her. Helen clutched the book to her breast and said, "We're going to the Continent. To Frawnz—" she drawled it out impressively "—to Cairo. I'll be so pleased to see the pyramids in the act-chew-ality. The Senator and I—" she paused for effect "—will be traveling extensively during the congressional recess. But he must return to Washington in the fall. There is much to do—"

"Isn't—I thought—isn't the Senator a married man?"

"Oh, yes," Helen dismissed the Senator's wife and four children with a wave of her hand. "But I'm going to be his aide, y'know. I'll be his private sec'try, travel with him cawnstantly. One never knows when one might need a sec'try—"

"Well, that sounds nice, Helen—"

"I intend to enjoy myself. I have every intention of succeeding where others have failed—"

Trudy could not decipher whatever Helen's message might be and she excused herself and went on into the hallway where she almost ran into Cleveland. "Oh," she said.

"I'm back," Cleveland announced. "He tried to keep me away, but Sonny brought me back anyway—"

"Who tried?"

"Darling."

"Oh, I didn't know. I only knew you'd gone."

Cleveland looked at Trudy as if anything Darling might do was under Trudy's direction. She said carefully, "Your gentleman, Miss Jones. He's—he's a terrible man, I'm not—I can't get free of him. He has some power over—he told Sonny what to do and Sonny did it. I'm afraid of Darling, Pamela, and so should you be—"

"How is it you came back here?"

"I don't think Sonny believed Darling would be back. Because of the—you know—all the trouble."

"All what trouble?"

"You mean you don't know? The government. They're trying to arrest him—take him into custody. Isn't that unbelievable? There's some investigation. They've seized his assets—except for the yacht and whatever has not yet been found. They've taken over everything he has in this country—"

"But the government can't come here," Trudy said. "The men talk about that all the time. It's their island. The men would have to want someone arrested—"

Cleveland stepped closer and whispered. "I think somebody does. I think it's someone here. Sonny thinks so, too. Those investigators— they know an awful lot that nobody else knows—"

"Do you think he'll come here? That he'll leave the ship—?"

"I don't know," Cleveland said. "I don't think so. He'd be mad to do it. I wonder why he's here at all. He had to leave New York, but this is the first place they'd look. Why would he—?" She shrugged. "How can anyone predict what Jay Darling will do—"

3

Margaret Marsh said to her mother, "I met an interesting girl today—"

Mrs. Marsh busy with a game of Concentration, did not look up. She said, "Someone new at the hotel? This late in the season? Everyone is leaving tomorrow—"

Margaret didn't answer.

"Will I meet her?" Mrs. Marsh asked, placing a red queen carefully on a black king.

Cautious, thought Margaret. Careful play. The winning hand.

"No," she said. "I don't know if you'd like her or not. She's from the mainland. I think she's just passing through—"

"I see."

No, you don't see, Margaret realized. *There are no great leaps in your game. You inch carefully around the edge of everything, keeping your hand to yourself, never letting go. Being alone is not the answer. Not forever, anyway. There will be no other chance for life than this. After a while, being alone—*

She didn't finish the thought. She resolved to talk this over with Trudy.

Her mother was vigorously using a fan with her free hand. "My, it's become very warm here lately," she said. "I'll be glad to go North again—"

"Yes, it's become warmer," Margaret answered and renewed her determination not to leave the area. *I'll tell her tonight,* she decided. *Right after the banquet.*

4

The ladies of the Clubhouse hotel thought their banquets were splendid, their chef divine, the decor delightful and original, the company distinguished. They should have witnessed the wonderful banquets held at the Playhouse—with their own distinguished husbands in attendance.

Oh, the chef at the Clubhouse was recherché. The *Chef* at the Playhouse was world-renowned. The decorations at the Clubhouse might be stunning—black or white or some sophisticated scheme. But tonight at the Playhouse there would be an enclosed pool of blue water, running the length of the table. In the center of this lagoon would be an island in miniature, complete with miniature vegetation and dolls dressed as native girls. Small boats would be used as place-card holders. These same little ships would be used as amusements to carry messages around the table between courses, to stimulate conversation and conviviality. At each girl's place there would be a gold brooch in the design of a sailing ship with diamonds on each mast.

The corners of the room would be filled with tall palms and there would be lanterns everywhere and blackamoors in costume waving feather fans. Enormous cushions and brass jugs had been set around the dining room and birds set out in cages.

It was not dyspepsia that kept the husbands of the ladies at the Clubhouse from fully partaking of the twelve-course spread at the respectable club. No, it was the thought of the midnight supper to come at the wicked Playhouse on the other side of the island. The oasis was theirs for one more night.

Trudy learned the men were taking bets on whether Jay Darling would appear.

Nora was dressing Trudy's hair. "The odds is on you, honey," Nora said. "Them gentlemen say Mr. Darling is comin' back for you—"

Trudy could see in the mirror that her face was white as paper. *I must relax*, she thought. But she *felt* paper thin—a doll being dressed for an imaginary ball.

As darkness fell and the music began in the ballroom, Trudy stayed in her own quarters, dressed and waiting, wishing she could just leave. But instead she found herself looking out to sea from the turret room. She could see lights on the ship. He probably would not come. It would be too dangerous. Regardless of whether he came tonight, she planned to leave in the morning. She would warn Nora to stay away and then—regardless of Jay Darling—she would steal away herself.

As she sat in the half-darkened turret, she wondered if the island could actually be invaded—was that the right word for a place so near the United States?

Her hands and feet felt like ice, even in the warm tropical night.

In this way, Darling found her, rubbing her hands together as if she were distraught with worry for him. It was not displeasing to him.

"Worried?" he asked, stepping through the doorway of the turret. He was smiling that smile of his.

"I—no. I wasn't worried."

"Then you knew I'd come?"

She said nothing.

"You're worth the risk," he said flatly, quietly. He walked closer, came up to her and put one arm out and brought her to him, pressing her pelvis against his own.

"I've missed you," he said, bringing her even closer. He put his mouth to her ear and kissed her there, traveling down her neck with his kisses. He held her for a moment, moving slightly against her and at first Trudy thought he meant they were not going to step out into the party, that his risk was only this much, that he had other ideas. But he released her and turned away. He was wearing evening clothes—except for his coat. He reached inside his cummerbund and took out a small velvet box. He handed this to her.

"You see. I think only of you."

Involuntarily, she took the tiny box. Then she stood with it in her hand. She didn't want to accept any more gifts from him. She wanted to blurt out to him that she was leaving soon, but she knew this was not the right moment.

"Open it," he ordered.

She did so. Nestled in the box in a great knot was a fistful of emeralds. He lifted them out for her and she could see they were a necklace and bracelet, for some reason wadded into this too-small container, as if someone had been traveling with them and didn't want them found.

He insisted she wear these jewels for the evening's revelries and she stepped to the mirror to put them on. As she was fastening them, she glanced into the glass and saw Darling behind her. Caught unaware, he looked wan, unsmiling, almost frightened. He was looking toward her, but as if he saw nothing. He seemed to be studying the edge of her dressing table.

She turned. She would carry this off. She must. It was the last evening like this she would have to go through—

"Come," she said. "Shall we go?" She reached out her hand to him.

At this friendly sign he came forward and offered his arm. She took it and they went out to meet the company, to make their entrance. Since they were somewhat late, this was a small sensation, especially since several of the girls commented on Pamela's new necklace. Even the men seemed to stare at the jewels, as if waiting for them to turn to glass.

Darling ostentatiously adjusted the clasp on Pamela's bracelet, which he said was twisted. She hadn't noticed it and realized he was actually calling attention to his gift, as if to reassure those present that he was still in possession of his wealth. She didn't know for a fact that he wasn't. Only Cleveland had said Darling's assets had been seized. But Cleveland and Sonny had undoubtedly told others the same rumor. Yet here was Pamela Jones with a clutch of emeralds about her neck and wrist to give the lie to the rumor.

For the balance of the evening, Darling was at his most insufferable, leading various members of the party into charming exchanges, and as they relaxed into easy banter with him, turning on them, slicing them up with his vicious tongue. Pamela and the rest of the party squirmed for those so "honored." Finally, he suggested to Sonny that he buy Cleveland a pillow with "Mother" embroidered on it.

When Sonny objected strongly to such a remark, Darling said, "Of course, I forgot. With you as her lover, Cleveland will never become a mother—"

This thrust would have meant nothing in any other gathering, but everyone in the place knew of Sonny's lack of interest in sex and Cleveland's interest in Pamela. Darling had seen to that.

Sonny, well in his cups, stood to deliver an ultimatum.

"You take that back, y'bastard, or I'll—I'll—" Sonny was swaying. Everyone could see it. Darling stood, walked over to Sonny as if he were going to soothe him down. But when he was in front of him, he held Sonny with one hand and hit him from the opposite side with a sharp uppercut.

Sonny fell with a loud crash—to the loud protestations of the rest of the party. Darling had gone too far. After the uproar of the moment, there was finally silence. Hands reached out to lift Sonny up to carry him to his bedroom. Couples retired quickly, leaving Jay Darling and his woman standing alone in the ballroom of the Playhouse.

Darling held out his hand to her. She put hers into it because she didn't know what else to do.

"M'dear," he said. "Go to your room. I want you to undress, put on your robe, wait for me there. I have an errand to do. This night isn't over yet—"

He turned and went into the hall. She watched as he knocked on Cleveland's door. Well, she thought, at least he's going to apologize.

She went quickly to her room, did as he had instructed. He could be gracious if he chose, she knew. She hoped he would smooth things over, end things right, for tonight was clearly an ending.

She took the pins from her hair, let it fall down her back. She put the jewels she wore carefully into their tiny case. She'd heard emeralds were fragile and shouldn't be handled roughly. The room was unlit. There was a bright moon outside and she moved surely in the familiar surroundings. She didn't need light.

He didn't come for some time. She'd hoped to avoid having to go to bed. She'd hoped to be able to talk to him before he required any further act from her. Perhaps he wasn't coming back until morning. She was wearing her robe, loosely knotted around her waist. She brushed her hair, humming nervously, sitting on the bed, her back to the door.

For some reason, she sensed some presence in the dark corners of the room—as if the moonlight itself had become alive. Her heart fluttering in the worst kind of fear, she said, "Jay?"

He moved out of the shadows of the room from the place near the secret stair. He must have come down some time ago and said nothing, waited there until she sensed and acknowledged him; waited there, watching her.

He came into the portion of the bedroom touched by moonlight and sat on a chair near the bed. He still said nothing. Quite often, he was silent like this. But he'd never before watched her from a corner like some animal waiting to strike.

She must say something, break this terrible silence. So she began, "Is it very dangerous for you to be here?"

"Very dangerous. Of course."

There came a light tap against the door. Even in the moonlight she could see him tense, but he rose and went to answer it.

To her surprise, Cleveland was outside. At Darling's nod, Cleveland entered. Was something wrong with Sonny? Cleveland came toward the center of the room. Darling stepped around her, came up to the bed and reached out to take Pamela's hand. He led her to Cleveland, who was also dressed in her nightrobe.

Darling stepped behind Pamela. She could feel his warm breath on her neck as he reached around her to open and remove her robe in one swift motion.

"My dear," he said, "this woman has been employed to give you a massage—lie down on the bed and she will begin—"

Even in the dark, Pamela could feel Cleveland's eyes devouring her. Pamela also knew that Jay, behind her, had the same view of Cleveland's greedy, uncontrollable gaze. He moved closer to her back and she could feel his erection against her. He kissed her bare shoulder.

"Perhaps we should step out there," he said, gesturing toward the turret room. "Where the moonlight will give us all so much more—enjoyment—"

Though he pressed close behind her, moving her forward, Pamela managed to dig in her heels and hold her ground. She put her hands in front of her to ward off Cleveland's impending touch.

"No," said Trudy Jones. "No, I won't do that. I will not do any such thing."

Darling gripped at her shoulders, attempting to force her to move forward, but Trudy twisted and pushed him away, quicker than he could recover. She retrieved her robe from the floor as she ran. She couldn't sort the garment into recognizable parts but she wrapped it around herself and moved backwards, away from him, away from Cleveland, toward the secret stair.

"Don't touch me," she ordered. "You are obscene—"

Silence. But he came toward her. Cleveland had moved backward.

Trudy could hear Cleveland's muffled sobs somewhere, but dared not take her eyes off Darling as he was advancing. As he crossed an open place on the floor where the moonlight shone, the light fell across him and Trudy saw that he had removed his own garment, that he was naked, aroused, coming toward her grimly. She backed up until she felt a table at her back. As he stepped into the dark again, her hand touched a solid object. She didn't know what it was—or care. As he came closer, reaching, she swung out blindly, thinking to hit him in the face.

With luck, she struck him just right. In one swift crash, Jay Darling was brought to earth. Illogically, Trudy noticed she'd hit him with a rare Chinese vase. Its shards lay scattered about him.

He lay very still there at their feet. The two women were crying. They did not move to embrace or touch each other. Trudy put on her robe and then took it off again and began to dress. Her hands shook.

"I'm leaving," she said to Cleveland. "I'm not going to stay in this place any longer. I don't care what happens to me. Nothing could be worse than this. Everything could be worse and still not be this bad—" She wasn't making sense.

She put on her most practical clothes, practical shoes, not looking to see what Cleveland was doing. When she did look, Cleveland was still standing over Darling as if she were hypnotized by his prone form.

Trudy took out her white shawl and threw into it everything of value she could think of. At the last moment, with malice, she put the emeralds into the packet. She tied everything up with ribbons, the only thing she had to use. She hoisted the makeshift sack over her shoulder, discovered she couldn't walk that way and carried it instead as if it were a pail of water.

She went to Cleveland. "Goodbye," she said. "And don't worry— tell them not to come after me."

Cleveland didn't answer. Trudy stepped closer. She could see that Cleveland was shaking as if she had a fever; her eyes appeared to be glazed.

"Can you hear me?" Trudy asked.

Cleveland didn't answer. Although Trudy was almost afraid to do it, she nudged Darling's hand with her toe. His fingers twitched. He was alive, but out cold. She realized that Cleveland was frightened, that she believed Darling was dead.

"He's all right," Trudy said to her. "Don't worry. Go back to Sonny—"

Trudy set her bundle down, wrapped Cleveland in her robe and in a blanket, opened the hall door and peered out. No one was there. "Can you find Sonny?" she asked Cleveland.

Cleveland, partially restored by the warmth of the blanket, nodded and ran down the hall toward her own room. Trudy shut the door again, and taking up her bundle ran for the stairway, dragging the heavily laden shawl behind her down the secret stairs.

For that reason, she was not among those seized when the federal marshals raided the Playhouse sometime after 3:00 A.M. Of all those who attended the grand dinner, only Trudy and two other people—Helen and the Senator—were not arrested with Jay B. Darling.

CHAPTER XXXV

1

When she emerged from the secret stairway, Trudy didn't hesitate. The woods to the east were dark, but the path to the west—toward the Clubhouse hotel—was lit by the reflection of the moon on crushed shell. A few weeks ago she might have been afraid, but tonight, she didn't fear anything except what was behind her at the Playhouse. She ran as quickly as she could, choosing to enter the kitchen of the hotel, because she thought there might be someone there and it would be the quickest way to reach Margaret Marsh.

After Trudy had roused a sleeping housekeeper—the woman was there to watch the great ovens to see that the banked fires did not die—and had sent in a note, she was ushered to the third floor and Margaret's private suite.

They embraced like long-lost sisters.

"I'm glad you've come," Margaret said. She dismissed the house-keeper, whose look clearly said Miss Marsh might do anything.

"I must leave the island as soon as possible," Trudy told her. "And I'm afraid for Nora. We have to warn her."

"We'll do both things at once. We'll go to their house in the village and we'll get Ephraim to row you and Nora to the mainland. It's the best way."

"But we'd have to go back through the woods—past the Play-house. They might be looking for me."

"Never mind. There's a faster way. It's along the west beach and the tide is in, but if we're careful we can go that way, and we'll get there much more quickly."

She looked at Trudy's clothes. "I think I'd better get you something warmer to wear. We're about the same size, even though our builds are slightly different. I think you could wear one of my traveling suits. And I'll give you a suitcase. You'll need to register at a hotel."

As Margaret talked she was opening drawers, bringing out clothing. The two women began to dress hurriedly in the dark, serviceable garments.

"Go to the Grand Hotel on the mainland," Margaret instructed her. "You'll have to register under an assumed name, something I'll recognize when I can come. I think I should stay here for today. It might be suspicious if I'm not here and there are inquiries. Tomorrow everyone else is going to leave anyway and I can join you—"

"I'll use my own name, Gertrude Jahn. He—nobody knows that. I've never told it—at least to him."

"Does anyone at all know it? You might have forgotten?"

"Only—well, never mind. It doesn't matter. No one on this island would know that name. Except you."

Trudy was packing the items from the shawl into the valise Margaret had brought out. Margaret caught a glimpse of the securities.

"What's this?"

"I'm not sure. I think they're worth something. At least they were given to me as if they were—"

Margaret examined them briefly. "You're very right. They're extremely valuable. Pay to bearer. As good as cash—"

Even in the dim light, Margaret could see Trudy blush.

Trudy said, "I haven't much cash. At least, I have cash in very large bills. I think those might be suspicious also—"

Margaret stopped her. "I'll put some money into a purse for you. You have to have a purse. You'll need a comb. Other things. You must appear respectable—"

Trudy turned abruptly away. But Margaret put out her hand in apology. "I'm sorry. I don't mean it that way. I mean you must appear ordinary. Not so exotic and—lovely—and lost. Oh, my dear," she said and hugged Trudy. "I wouldn't hurt you for the world. I feel as if what happens to you happens to myself. I'm so happy you're safe—"

And she meant it. She'd had that sensation once more, the same one she'd had in the small cabin, as if this girl were closer to her than anyone else in the world.

Margaret looked around the room. It was still quite dark outside. She sat down on the bed.

"It's all right. We're still ahead of things. Rest here a minute. We should review our plans—"

Trudy sat in the chair by the writing desk, the small satchel in her lap.

"I think," Margaret said, "that we might plan on a house—a cottage or something larger—that we could live in together for a short time. They'd never look for *two* women—"

Trudy looked down at her gloves. These were Margaret's gloves. She said, "No, I've thought about it. If it wouldn't put you out any, I think I do want to live by myself. Maybe with Nora with me for a while, to help me, you know? But I need to—" She waved her hand vaguely in front of her face. "There are things I must get straight in my mind—"

"I understand," Margaret said immediately. "It's all right. I was just worried that you might be frightened alone—"

Trudy looked up. Her look was clear-eyed. "I will be all right now. Everything is much better." She stood up.

That's good, thought Margaret. She wants to recapture herself. The two of them wrapped up warmly against the ocean chill and went out into the hallway, moving cautiously and quietly down the stairs and out the main entrance. They saw no one. There was supposed to be a night clerk, but he appeared to be away from the desk. Anyway, no one ever appeared at Sporting Isle this late in the season. Certainly no one came in the middle of the night unless they were expected.

Once outside, they hurried to the west and down, stealing along the thin line of beach like the conspirators they were. As they hurried on, Trudy whispered. "What are you going to do? Are you leaving here tomorrow with everyone else?"

"No. I had planned to stay on. After everyone leaves I'll come to where you are. We can pretend we don't know each other and pass notes in the hall like schoolgirls," Margaret answered, trying to lighten the mood.

Trudy nodded absently. "Listen," she hissed. "Do you hear anything?"

Far off in the distance, to the northeast of the hotel, Margaret thought she recognized the sound of dogs. "Just dogs barking," Margaret said aloud, as if they had nothing to fear.

Trudy was moving very fast now, not running, but not walking either. *She's like a fine little watch,* thought Margaret, *heading only one way, intent on her task, wound up and ready to break away from this island.*

Margaret didn't want to admit that she did hear noises somewhere in the distance. It could be a hunting party leaving for another island for one last day of sport before the end of the season. Or maybe it was a large party taking a steam launch to a private yacht. There were several ships out at sea, waiting for their owners' travel orders.

Trudy seemed distracted and Margaret was almost afraid to look behind them. But Trudy burst out, "I've thought sometimes about— you know—if I feel everything is all right I might look for—" She stopped talking and switched hands for the valise.

"Do you want me to carry that?"

"No, it's not so heavy. Everything in it is light. Just my shawl— and other things. I left most everything except two pairs of shoes." Now she stopped walking. She turned to Margaret. "Suppose I wanted to find somebody I once knew. Would that be very difficult?"

"Are you afraid they might manage to find you?"

"No. I mean *I* might want to find someone. After a while, I mean. After I've rested. If I feel like it; how—"

"Oh."

They resumed their quick pace.

Finally Trudy said, "I know what you're thinking. You're thinking he wasn't so nice to me. That he sent me away. But it wasn't really that at all. He—somebody told him that it would be better for me if I went. That I could be—better off that way. So Myron—"

"Myron?"

"That was his name. He—was really nicer than I can say."

"But you're in this terrible place—"

"He doesn't know that. He thinks I went to France—or the Waldorf—"

In spite of the circumstances, Margaret laughed. "They are not the same place—"

"Oh, you know what I mean—"

They were coming up on the village; the villagers were already stirring. Candles were lit in some of the houses, although it was not yet morning. But Margaret didn't feel any alarm. These were the workers who must be ready when others woke.

Margaret and Trudy went to Nora's house and after confused greetings, explained some of what had happened. When Margaret had finished, Trudy said, "It's worse than that, Nora." She glanced at Margaret and plunged on. "*He* came back. I hit him with a vase. He was unconscious—on the floor—when I left. He'll be angry. We have to get away. You shouldn't go back there. He might do something—I don't know what. We have to get away—you and I—"

Margaret stared. She'd thought of the Playhouse as an evil place, as Granny had said, but the short crisp way Trudy and Nora dealt casually with awful facts brought the decadence of the life there into sharp focus.

"There, there, honey," Nora said, and she nodded at Ephraim over Trudy's head.

He said to Margaret, "We jes' had word. Somethin' happenin' over there. Lawmen. Some men with guns and badges and papers. They took away—" Again he stopped. The men that were taken away were powerful men who might come back. "Took away Miss Pamela's fren' and everybody there. All gone. Not an hour before now. Maids and such came home cryin'. Place all bust' up and searched—"

Margaret said, "That must have been what we heard when we came along the beach. Where did they take everyone?"

"To jail, honey, to jail," Nora said. She patted Trudy, who was still leaning against her. She said, "And I thought you was one o' 'em. I wuz so glad to see you at my door—"

Margaret was worried. "Might the police—or federal marshals— whoever searched that place—might they come here?"

"Naw. They let all the black folks go. Jus' white folks went with the lawmen. They say we jus' workin' there. Jus' workin', you know. Anyways we kin."

Granny nodded. "Wages of sin—" she said, sealing the bad place off from her family.

Trudy and Nora made plans to go to the mainland. Ephraim, who worked there anyway, would go with them and stay.

"But what about the children?" Margaret asked. "Shouldn't they go with you—?"

"No," said Ephraim.

Nora explained. "It ain't nice there fer black children."

Granny said, "Over there, where the white folks live, eggs is eggs, but black children ain't children. Don't want none o' mine livin' there—"

2

When all the arrangements had been made and goodbyes had been said, Margaret went alone to the hotel on the island, walking slowly along the sand, thinking Trudy was no longer as helpless as she'd appeared at their first meeting. Margaret admired the way the girl had dealt with the terrible circumstances of her existence at the Play-

house, how she'd found the inner strength to run from it into uncertainty, depending for the most part on her own resources to find
renewal.

I wish I had the definite vision she seems to have found, Margaret thought.

She looked across the estuary toward the mainland, where Trudy
was already headed in Ephraim's boat. The grasses moved in the
wind, as if they, not the water, were the sea. Margaret was in no
hurry to return to the hotel.

She walked on slowly.

The tide was receding on the beach and it had left debris on the
sand; dark seaweed, bits of this and that, which were unidentifiable.
She turned a small shell over and a crab scrambled away. *Like that,*
she thought, *that's how I am. Borrowing. An echo of everything, not the
true sound of anything. Telling others how to live when I haven't learned
myself.*

She looked again toward the west. The expanse of sand was wid-
ening. There was no sign of another human for miles in any direction.
She made an imprint with her toe, moving the sand to one side. In
her excavations, she discovered a sand-dollar. She picked it up for
luck and went on, turning now and then to see her solitary footprints
following her on the empty beach.

After about a mile—the mile she and Trudy had covered so quickly
in the dark—she came around the edge of the jetty and went up
toward the hotel, toward the manicured paths and lawns of the
formal approach to the Clubhouse.

The sun had begun to brighten in the east and the glare from it
and the roots in the path made her look down.

A voice, coming from somewhere, said, "Margaret?"

She raised her head. Steven was standing there.

Margaret Marsh held out both her hands.

"LET US ALL MAKE IT PERFECTLY WHITE"
—Daniel Burnham

CHAPTER XXXVI

On the day Steven Baxter and Myron Davis arrived on the southern mainland opposite Sporting Isle, there were three or four plans in existence among the two men and two women.

Margaret planned to stay for a short time on the island and then join Trudy for a visit on the mainland before proceeding north for Opening Day of Chicago's Exposition. Trudy planned to stay on in the South in a small house she would rent, chaperoned and aided by Nora and Ephraim.

Steven planned to find Margaret and tell her whatever it is a lover tells the woman he wants to spend the rest of his life with. In fact, he planned to say it just that way: he would spend the rest of his life with her if she'd let him.

Myron suggested Steven go to the island alone, that he would wait behind for some word that Trudy Jones was indeed there and then he would come and try to get an appointment with her to plead his case. Myron was very nervous, Steven could see, and because of this, Steven agreed to Myron's first plan.

But as with most plans, all were altered in the living of them.

Margaret met Steven on the beach. They held hands. They walked back to the Clubhouse hotel together, speaking cautiously, both testing the air. They found an unoccupied parlor and talked. In Victorian novels a veil was drawn over such scenes, letting the lovers have privacy in which to make their way through matters of little interest once the dialogue of agreement had been reached. The coos and prattle of ordinary love are not the stuff of which stories are made. But there was one thing the young woman of 1893, so definite-minded, managed to say that might be recorded—

"I went away, but I didn't recover from love. I know now that I will never love someone else. Only you."

Steven, who had tried to put behind him the memory of that terrible day in the carriage on Prairie Avenue, said he could *agree* with that.

But in reciting to each other—or beginning to—their recent history, Steven got no further than saying he'd come down from the North with Myron Davis, who was searching for a young woman named Gertrude Jones—Trudy Jones.

Suddenly various bits fell into place in Margaret's consciousness. Trudy had said the name *Myron.*

Margaret knew only an edited portion of Trudy's life with the mysterious, powerful man, but still Margaret blushed for the evil done to her friend, for the evil men of the Playhouse and the apparently casual acceptance of Myron Davis, not only by tender-hearted Steven, but by what appeared to be every level of *polite* society. Yet Trudy Jones, whose story could not be articulated in that parlor, would have been banned by everyone that Margaret knew anywhere—except possibly Mrs. Bright.

"Yes, I know Trudy Jones," Margaret said sadly.

Steven took notice of her blushes and her straight posture and the shade of displeasure that had just passed over Margaret's face and misread her meaning.

"You mustn't misjudge her," he said. He didn't know what more to say, because he knew nothing at all of Trudy except the little Myron had told him.

Margaret, sitting erect, looking straight ahead, began to cry silently. She made no attempt to wipe the tears away, but wept steadily, letting him see them. She'd just had a second level of insight. If Myron Davis had come all this way for Trudy because he loved her, and if he knew nothing of her recent life—

Margaret cried for those who could not recognize love when it came to them and so let it go and let it change into something else.

What Gertrude Jahn had known back in Chicago when she realized her mother was once more pregnant, Margaret Marsh suddenly understood: Love does not conquer all. Not even half the trouble love makes can it overcome.

"Steven," she said and turned and put her head on his shoulder. She began to tell him what she could bring herself to say about Gertrude Jahn and Myron Davis.

Following this, Margaret and Steven parted temporarily and Steven went back to the mainland to relate to Myron what Margaret had told him. Since Margaret's understanding of those events was a mild version of what Trudy had lived through, Myron's informant could not reveal everything. Myron, on the other hand, knew something that neither of the others knew—he knew the name of Trudy's "important man."

He started up, not saying the name. And then Myron, strong, resourceful male that he was, his face crimson, unable to accept the limited facts he'd been told, fainted.

2

When Myron recovered consciousness, he was extremely weak, and Steven summoned a doctor. For two days, Myron stayed in bed with Steven nearby most of the time. The doctor came again. He told Steven that his friend might be suffering an "adjustment to the heat," or he might be having a mild heart seizure. It couldn't be diagnosed without more definite symptoms and it was just as well not to have those symptoms to insure a correct diagnosis.

"Bed rest," said the doctor. "And perhaps, when he's able, he should go north again, to a cooler climate."

"What about—about emotional events?" asked Steven, not caring to be more precise than that.

"A wedding? A funeral?"

"A reunion—"

"Ummm. Cautious approach if the event is necessary. If not, I'd forgo it—"

"Ummm," said Steven in his turn.

After several days, Myron was able to stand and capable of walking, but he was still overcome with vertigo each time he turned his head quickly and he tired in minutes. His heart raced. His head seemed to be full of squirrels running in circles day and night. He couldn't sleep, yet he felt immensely tired. He'd given up everything, risked all, to court Trudy once again, only to find that it might have been made impossible by a risk not taken long before. Yet his risk was nothing compared to her own. He was overwhelmed by his own guilt.

He refused to let her know he was there. The mention of her name seemed to aggravate his condition and only on the tenth day did he ask about Margaret. As a small test, he suggested, he might meet Margaret to see if his heart, which had never given him trouble until now, could stand the strain—he confessed to Steven that he was embarrassed to meet Margaret. But if all went well, he wondered if he might plan a brief meeting with Trudy by the end of the week.

Margaret, in her secret heart, wondered how Myron could have been so cruel as to tempt Trudy into a life that could never be more than a mockery of love. She consented to visit only after discovering that Myron's greatest anguish was because of his own culpability.

"He sincerely loves her," Steven told Margaret. "But he doesn't know if he can ever face her again. Imagine how that would be—"

They looked at each other in grateful silence and Margaret went to meet Myron. There was only personal discomfort for both, no recurrence of Myron's illness.

But Trudy, when given the news that Myron Davis was at the hotel and ill, also went faint with apprehension.

"I can't," she told Margaret. "How can I just come to him now? If I tell him the truth in his condition, he might die. And if I say nothing, he might imagine even worse things—I can't bear to think of it, to talk of it. Oh, why did this happen so quickly? I'm not ready yet. I'd thought—I'd hoped—to take some time, to keep myself apart. I'm—" She put her head in her hands, not weeping, but distraught and frightened at the way life always seemed to move ahead to the next step before she was ready.

Margaret, sitting in the bedroom of the small house Nora had found for Trudy, didn't know what to say. Instead, she went to the girl and put her arms around her and the two of them cried at love's inscrutable nature.

Margaret could understand Trudy's need for a time alone and apart, a cleansing of the spirit, a renewal of her independent self. She could understand why Trudy would not present herself to Myron, who was himself a frightened, uncertain knight at this moment, without that renewal having taken place.

"It's all right," Margaret told her. "We'll work out another plan— for another day—may I tell him you care for him and wish him well?"

Trudy looked up at Margaret with poignant eyes. "Tell him," she said, "that I forgive him—"

Steven had hired the doctor to be Myron's personal physician. Myron progressed to being able to sit in the shade on the porch of the hotel, well-attended by a nurse who came in during the day. Because Myron seemed well on the mend, Margaret and Steven put a plan of their own into operation.

The two lovers were not seen for almost a week. When they returned to the hotel, they announced they were married. Margaret wore a new gold wedding ring—the very ring supplied by Arthur Baxter in his brother's luggage. Steven reregistered them at the hotel as *Mr. and Mrs. Steven Baxter* and they took the bridal suite.

That night Myron had a relapse.

Try as he might to be happy for his friends, his mind was taken up with envy and his heart yearned for what they had. This translated itself into a more severe attack than the one previous and the doctor sent for Steven and took him aside.

The doctor, in the past few weeks, had gleaned some bit of information about the ailment his patient might have, an ailment common in that era of emotional restraint. He said to Steven, "If there is someone with whom he wishes to be reunited, perhaps now is the time—"

Within the hour, Margaret had brought Trudy to the hotel. The young girl had come hurriedly, wearing a blue poplin dress, covering her head with an embroidered white shawl, her eyes enhanced by the anguish that was in her face.

The doctor noticed that the girl seemed very young, but she was quite self-possessed.

"Where is he?" she asked and they took her into the bedroom where Myron was lying, no longer red-faced and overwarm, but white and shivering in the heat. A cloth was on his forehead. He'd not been told she'd been sent for. His eyes were closed. There was only a dim light on in the room.

Trudy went over to the bed and touched the cloth on Myron's head. She felt as if she'd never been away from him. The cloth was cold. She took it away. She bent her head forward and laid her forehead against his. Her loose hair fell forward, touching his.

He opened his eyes.

"Trudy? I was dreaming of you—"

"I'm here."

"I'm glad you're here. I wanted to say—I wanted to say—" He tried to sit up.

"Don't, dear."

He lay back, but he kept trying to talk. "I wanted to say—it wasn't right—what I did. I should never have let you go. I've ruined—your life. It wasn't right—"

"It's all right. I'm all right now—"

"I wanted to say—I've been trying to say—I love you, Trudy."

She was silent, but she patted his hand. She didn't say she loved him, too. She just patted his hand. Then she began to caress his forehead, smoothing across it with her two thumbs, bringing some ease to him.

She saw he was crying. She remained silent.

The doctor came in then and said it would be better, if she didn't mind, for this first visit to be short. That she might come back in an hour or so.

She bent forward and kissed Myron lightly on the cheek where the tears had fallen.

"Don't go away," he said. "I'd rather you'd stay—"

"It's all right," she told him, "I'll just be outside."

She went out into the sitting room where Margaret and Steven were waiting. She sat with them without a word, her dark hair loose and tumbled, the shawl now over her knees.

Steven had never seen her before. He could understand why both Myron and Margaret loved her. She looked to be a wild sprite, an essence so ephemeral that she was almost unreal in this light, yet someone capable of great love and refinement. Her dress was modest and plain, her manner quiet.

Margaret introduced Steven and they talked for a while about the weather and the heat and the fact that it might rain yet that night.

Then Steven asked, "How is he? Did he speak to you?"

"Yes," Trudy said.

They were all three silent, since Trudy didn't seem to want to say more. They waited there for more than an hour, not talking much. The doctor and nurse came in and out.

"Nothing has changed," the doctor finally said. "I think that's a good sign—"

They waited again.

Shortly before dawn, Trudy began to talk. "I think it's a terrible, terrible thing—"

"What is?" asked Margaret.

"Love. The way we're told of it. We're expected to plan our lives by it. And no one can say what it is. I might be right beside it and not know for certain. And when you've come away, it's easy enough to think love was there when perhaps it wasn't. Perhaps the only love a person might know is something that didn't actually happen, a memory of love that didn't ever exist." She sighed. "And we're supposed to run to it, take the greatest chances and move toward it, give up all reserve and then—we don't know—ever—once we're there—we don't know—"

Margaret was crying, Steven noticed, and he stood and went to her.

The doctor came and suggested Trudy come in again, the patient was awake. She went inside. The doctor left the door open.

Steven and Margaret could see Trudy approach the bed. They heard Myron's voice.

"Don't leave me again," he said.

"It's all right," Trudy answered.

There was silence from the inner room. The doctor came out and closed the door.

"I can't really promise anything," he said. "But I think he'll be all right. He's faced the worst of it now—"

After the doctor went out, Steven turned to Margaret and kissed her. She said, "Love—" She could not go on.

"—a terrible and irrational passion," he said.

Margaret nodded.

3

After several days, Myron was sent North in Steven Baxter's private railroad car with the doctor in attendance—not that the doctor offered much insurance against the kind of illness Myron had been suffering, but Steven would not take chances.

Trudy Jones, bidding a tearful farewell to Nora, followed on another train with Margaret and Steven in a separate compartment.

Margaret and Steven had wired ahead to their various connections in Chicago. What a disappointment the Baxter–Marsh marriage was going to be to Mrs. Chesterton. "That Marsh woman" had carried the day. In future years, Mama Delight Baxter would often report the details of the wedding to Fanny—that Steven and his Margaret had been married in a Methodist Episcopal church by a fully ordained minister of the faith—but neither Steven nor Margaret ever told anyone that. When asked by new acquaintances where they'd married, each would answer "In the South" and turn toward the other to smile with such an obvious exchange of the human heart that no one ever had any doubt of the effectiveness of that wedding, or whether it took place at all.

They were met at the station—a new Illinois Central station at Twelfth Street—by a gleeful Uncle Findley Marsh, who was burdened with flowers for the bride and willing to embrace the groom.

"I knew you'd do it, m'boy. I knew you'd find the girl and make it legal—" Uncle Findley hadn't the least idea of the finer shades of meaning Margaret and Steven applied to that remark.

In Chicago, Trudy refused to join the newlyweds at the Prairie

Avenue mansion and Mrs. Rose Bright welcomed her into the little house down near the Back-of-the-Yards. Trudy was happy to learn she could help Molly and Mrs. Bright in the day nursery there. Mrs. Bright told Margaret that Trudy was "like an angel" with the children. Trudy, for her part, found the location, the children, Mrs. Bright and the familiar ground of Chicago aroused much emotion in her heart.

Myron Davis was settled into the Baxter mansion on the North Side with Mamma Delight as one of his nurses. There were some nights when she padded up and down the hall tending to her new charge that she almost felt as if Steven were home again.

Chicago newspapers were much taken up with news of the Exposition, but they found room for a headline article about Jay B. Darling, financier, also known as Jason Bradwell Darlin, according to his indictment papers, who had been charged with defrauding widows and orphans of monies deposited in his firm's fiduciary accounts. Shortly after this article appeared—which said Darlin was under house arrest in New York City and his yacht and other assets had been seized—a second article appeared. Darling had been mortally wounded in the neck in the middle of the night by a mysterious woman who demanded admittance from Darling's butler by presenting a sealed note to be taken to his employer. She was closeted alone with the financier for only a matter of minutes when the shot rang out and she ran from the house. The butler, prying the note from his master's hand, discovered it said, "I know where the money is kept." Darling's last words, according to the butler, were, "I'm not surprised."

The family of Tessa Jahn attempted to keep her from learning about the great Exposition being held down in Jackson Park, but she heard of it somehow and became agitated anew, resuming her night wanderings in the neighborhood where she lived with Otto.

If anyone stopped her or tried to offer assistance she would ask them, "Have you seen a young girl, dark hair and eyes, my daughter—have you seen my little girl?"

EPILOGUE

In the summer of 1893, they went to the fair!

They went, not on one day or the next, but on many, different days and different nights, together and separately, in large groups and small; anyone who could manage it went to the fair even if they had to sell the cow to do it.

The first day—May 1—was spectacular, a spectacle of men in hats and women in bigger hats and seas of hats moving through the half-finished byways of the grounds. For, of course, the critics' suspicions had been correct. The buildings were completed—mostly—but the grounds were not, and only the splendor of the company disguised the fact that on Opening Day, many of the major exhibits were not in place. But the Infanta Eulalia of Spain was there. And the Duke of Veragua was there. Half a gaggle of English nobility was there. Royals in the democratic garden! But to offset this danger, the President of the United States of America was on scene, and to ease everyone's mind, the queen of Chicago, Mrs. Potter Palmer, was prominently in view. More was to come.

During May, which was rainy and good for planting but not for attendance, sending shivers of more than cold down the collective backs of the Chicago Company, the last of the landscaping was put in place so the fine vistas of the architects would actually look as the much-heralded and much-doubted drawings had promised.

421

Margaret and Steven bought a barouche and agreed to let young Henry drive, to the great dismay of their stableman. He would drive Baxters and guests to the Exposition grounds and return at some later time to pick them up again. The first excursion with Henry at the reins was the night the lights went on.

Margaret and Steven took Trudy Jones and Rose Bright and Molly with them. Mrs. Marsh was still in the East, Myron was convalescing and Arthur had gone to New York to collect Fanny and her children. Uncle Findley was playing cards at the Tremont with some well-heeled out-of-town sports ripe for plucking.

Steven said, "They're going to be sorry to miss this—" and in some ways he was right. Nights would never be the same. Yet in another way he was wrong. Everyone, in future, was going to see the lights. It was the stars they might be missing.

But Steven was so convinced the moment was historic, he helped Henry situate the horses and the carriage in a stable nearby and brought Henry into the grounds with the rest of the party.

There had been lights in Paris the year before—but only the nabobs got to Paris. But right here, right on this very prairie, beside this grand lake, into the encompassing dark, the mysterious machines of George Westinghouse were going to send, for the first time, ladies and gentlemen, *alternating current* into those magical lamps and these, in turn, would illuminate the whitewashed buildings, buildings so large as to be gigantic, buildings so ornamented as to seem spun of fairy stuff.

Henry could hardly stand it.

But it was done and from that summer forward summers at fairgrounds would never be the same. Always, at night at summer fairs, there would be those wonderful *safe electric lights*—and off in the distance on the *midway* of any fair, the cries of hawkers outside the hootchy-kootchy shows would punctuate the music of tinny, ragtime pianos and the sobs of the calliopes. And everywhere, fairgoers would line up to take rides on the *Ferris wheel*, although there'd never be another that could carry thirty-six riders in each plush cab to see the view from the very top.

Oh, the Grand Basin was as promised—lights reflected in fountains and in the delicately rippled water. But more easily spotted across the vistas at night was the oversized Administration Building with its lighted, golden dome, and the lights around the edges of rooflines, the whiteness of everything, the titillating reflection of everything in something else.

Trudy Jones looked around her. As far as she could see there were people and as far as she could see none of them were poor. *This is the way the rich live,* she thought, *always in the midst of wonderful sights, always at their ease.*

The ducks floated on the smooth pond near her, confused by the lights they had never seen before.

During that summer the Woman's Building was a revelation—not to Margaret, who felt a little let down by its precious exhibits, but to Trudy, who discovered herself there. Women, turning out their own work, talking to the world as if the world might listen.

Trudy admired it all—the paintings of Woman, Past and Present, by Mary Cassat and Mary MacMonnies, installed at either end of the great center hall. Margaret thought them hung too high to see. Trudy was overwhelmed by the library on the second floor—a room of books written by women only. Margaret thought they were a bit light on the sciences. Trudy was amazed at the state exhibits in each of the rooms, at the sculpture, the fountain, the building itself, the jewels, the tools, the style of it all, the generosity of one woman to another. Margaret refused to comment. She found Mrs. Palmer to congratulate her. Margaret decided she could be no less generous than that.

It was not Margaret who attended conferences during the summer on women's rights and women's clothing and women's work and women's needs held in conjunction with the Exposition. It was Trudy Jones—Gertrude Jahn—dressed in summer white with a small straw hat over her dark hair, who ran up the steps of the conference hall. Trudy, seventeen that summer, drank in the idea of *woman* and became inspired. And she'd known right where the conference hall was, the building that was to be the new Art Institute, because she'd seen it being built that very first day she'd walked with Myron Davis down Michigan Avenue.

The Woman's Building, surprising to everyone except those who'd worked within it, became the hit of the fair. It was situated at the end of the Midway and many women found it a pleasant respite on a hot summer day, especially after the restaurant was installed in its roof garden—near the angels on the roof. Oh, there was a fine view of the Exposition *from* the Woman's Building.

Margaret, for her part, fell in love with the Children's Annex. She brought Rose Bright back again and again. The children's nursery, where babies were "checked in" by mothers, fair goers all, who were lucky enough to get one of the new berths available where "nurse-girls" provided "ideal care" so mothers could enjoy their day at the Exposition. In this room were demonstrated practical and healthful approaches to infant care.

There was also an exercise room with swings and ladders and

ropes to be used by older children and a library for those children who could read.

"You see," Margaret explained to Rose Bright, who listened in amazement, "I think we should do something like this down at the Exchange. Something scientific for children—"

Uncle Findley came out to the Exposition at last and was finally charmed by progress. He stood in the Manufacturers Hall, tapping his cane thoughtfully, and understood none of what he saw in all its thirty-two acres. He went to the Electrical Building and felt the roar of the machines enter into his blood and he marched back to the Tremont and ordered up a telephone to be put in his rooms.

"That's progress," he told Margaret. "And any day now you're going to want to get a hold of me fast—to tell me of the first of those little red-headed children I'll get to bounce on my knee—"

Myron Davis was brought to the fair and wheeled around in a rolling wicker chair by Steven Baxter. Myron and Trudy had seen each other off and on, but Myron was under the mothering care of Mama Delight for the moment and although Mama had been intro-duced—several times—to Trudy Jones, the situation was uncertain. Mama kept asking "who Mrs. Jones' people are." Steven was glad Arthur had gone to New York, because if Arthur had not been able to make a satisfactory answer, Mama might have become more sus-picious than she usually was.

Myron wanted to see the Fine Arts Palace—that was what he and a lot of other people that summer called the Fine Arts Building. Among the paintings there were many his father's firm was insuring. He was familiar with these works of art and when he was taken to the building, he insisted on walking about on his own.

After he came out again into the sunshine, he said, "It's like a visit home—"

Trudy, off that day to a meeting on women's suffrage, didn't hear him.

In the meantime, the low attendance in May and the ever-growing rumbles of economic distress in the city itself—the panic of 1893 had finally come to Chicago—caused a bank on the fairgrounds to fail. This bank held the deposits of many foreign exhibitors and Chicago men of wealth were pressed into duty to underwrite those foreign deposits. The Chicago Company demanded the right to Sunday openings to offset their losses and every religious zealot from Chicago to Boston and points west again went quickly into the pulpit to protest. That there was to be no tent-meeting on the grounds further excited the divines.

Mama Delight Baxter offered to buy a large lot on the South Side to raise a religious tent for meetings outside the fair, but the city officials refused a permit. Steven reminded her that sand flies could be vicious near the beach at night and she'd best wait for the indoor conference scheduled for the Art Institute, which was to have world-wide representation. Mama thought she might, since she was certain there would be a better chance at that meeting to convert more international heathens to Jesus and the Presbyterian way of the Old Synod. Mama Delight said she'd prayed for it and knew in her heart it would be so.

Sunday openings were accomplished after several false starts through the courts, who ruled finally that capital must be served. The Sunday opening was only mildly accepted by the public, however, for the populace of the prairies was still religious and it rested on the seventh day, even from happy entertainment.

A World Conference on Labor, planned as part of the World Congresses in tandem with the Exposition conferences—separate but equal those conferences were—attracted Steven.

"You'd better not go with me," he told Margaret. "There could be trouble."

The labor conference *was* allowed to meet on the downtown lakefront and Mama Delight took note. But the outdoor conference had been allowed on the lakefront to keep dissenters away from the grounds itself. Conditions in the city could be ignited by one wrong word from the wrong kind of labor leader, in the opinion of the city council, some of whom remembered the Haymarket Riot. At the conference, Samuel Gompers and Clarence Darrow and others were going to be allowed to speak to an impoverished city population about the evils of the super-rich.

Moving through the crowd, Steven met Ned the Worker.

"Stay with me," Ned told Steven. "There won't be any trouble for you where I am—"

There was no trouble at all. Speakers at the conference were cautious. They, too, remembered the Haymarket Riot and the bad name it had given to Labor.

But the Labor Conference created no jobs.

In the course of the summer, Uncle Findley went to one of the World Congresses—the one on government. He pronounced it "Poppycock" and went to the races the next day instead.

Fanny and her husband and children finally arrived for the balance of the summer, distracting Mama Delight. Fanny met Trudy Jones and thought her charming. She invited Trudy to come to Europe with her the following summer as her companion. Fanny had come to understand the young person needed "a good chance."

Trudy smiled in the modest way they were all coming to love and said she'd think it over, that she'd heard Europe was a fine place.

Arthur, on returning from New York, was very nervous. Harriet and her parents were coming from Europe at last. Intermittent reports of this event continued for some time with cablegrams back and forth and much delay until the great arrival was rescheduled for nearly the last day of the fair.

Throughout the duration of the Exposition, Mama Delight had had her eye on some of the laces exhibited in the Woman's Building, some of them made by royals. She had nothing quite like them in her collection and she'd learned that in the closing days of the fair, bids would be taken on them. Unfortunately, when Harriet and her family finally arrived, she too saw them, and her indulgent father outbid Mama Delight for his plain daughter. He thought her beautiful and wanted the laces for her wedding.

In the closing moments of the Exposition, Chicago was saddened by the news that Mayor Carter Harrison, the joyful host, had been shot in his home by a disgruntled office-seeker. There had already been a sense of sadness in the air, even before that, but the assassination added a bitter note that seemed to hang about the closed grounds.

One day, after everything had closed down, Steven and Margaret, Trudy and Myron, with Uncle Findley, rode out in the carriage to look over the grounds again. It was one of those false Chicago days in November when the weather appears to promise that winter will not come, although sleet is just around the corner.

They rode through the sunshine right into the grounds, entering once again from the Midway, past the Administration Building and down to the Grand Basin.

When they came to the Transportation Building, Myron said he'd like to get out and walk and when Trudy started up as if to follow him, he smiled at her and said no, he'd like to walk about by himself for a moment.

The others stayed in the carriage and watched him, in the meantime talking of Louis Sullivan's design.

"The rest of the stuff is old hat," Steven said, waving at the other buildings. "You can see them all over Europe. But look at those entrances to Transpoation, at the intricate carvings on those arches—"

"Leaves and natural things," Margaret said. "Makes it look enchanted. Like an entrance to an enchanted land. Makes me want to go there—"

Uncle Findley laughed. "You would have made a grand pioneer woman, Maggie. Your goods on your back, bringing the family out to the new world, moving West—you were born too late for that—"

Trudy was facing eastward. "Do you think," she said, "I should go to Europe with Fanny next spring—?" She looked off toward the place where Myron was walking. He looked stronger now, not so pale. He seemed to have recovered himself. She sighed.

Myron was looking at the Transportation Building as if searching for an open door.

"I wonder," Trudy said, "what will happen to us all."

EDITH FREUND, a former journalist, began to write fiction in the mid-1970s and since then has published short stories and poetry in various literary and commercial publications in the United States, England and Australia. Her work will appear in the forthcoming *The Woman Poet in the Midwest.*

She is a native of Illinois where she's lived in various settings—a small town of a few hundred inhabitants near the Spoon River, the suburbs of Chicago, and the city itself. She and her husband presently live in Highland Park, Illinois.